A CHRISTMAS KISS

"Need any help?" Erik's face was expressionless, but she could see the laughter in his eyes.

"You think it's funny, don't you?" She was sitting on the floor, in front of the tree, and she was surrounded by yards of green electrical wire and miniature lightbulbs. Behind her there were three stacks of boxes, all containing glass ornaments. Two boxes of silver tinsel were on the chair. Blue bows and the Christmas hearts Erik and she had made were scattered by the couch. A brown box that a friend of Erik's had mailed from Norway was on the other chair. The box was filled with delicate handmade straw ornaments, bent and sewn into different configurations, and tiny Norwegian flags.

Erik gently put down the star that was to go on top of the tree, leaned over, and kissed her. "No, I think you're beautiful."

Sydney smiled against his mouth. "Sweet talker." She pushed the lights off her lap. "Do you know what is missing?"

"What?"

"Mistletoe." She wrapped her arms around his neck and nibbled on his lower lip. "I think we should get some . . ."

Books by Marcia Evanick

CATCH OF THE DAY

CHRISTMAS ON CONRAD STREET

Published by Zebra Books

CHRISTMAS ON CONRAD STREET

Marcia Evanick

ZEBRA BOOKS
KENSINGTON PUBLISHING CORP.
http://www.kensingtonbooks.com

ZEBRA BOOKS are published by

Kensington Publishing Corp.
850 Third Avenue
New York, NY 10022

First Printing: October 2002
10 9 8 7 6 5 4 3 2 1

Printed in the United States of America

To the woman who taught me that dreams aren't just handed to you. They are earned.
This one is for you, Mom.
Love,
Marci

Prologue

Sydney Fletcher parked her car in her allotted space and wearily turned off the ignition. It was only ten o'clock at night, and she was so exhausted that she could barely see straight, let alone stand. Logic told her she should have crashed at the hospital, like she had told Richard she was going to do. But her little patient had made a remarkable turnaround, and she felt confident enough to head for her own bed for the night. If luck held with her, she might even manage to catch six hours of sleep before heading back to the hospital.

She reached over and gathered up her purse and assorted papers that she needed to take into the office tomorrow morning, after she checked on her patient. Who would have thought being a doctor would require so much paperwork? If she had wanted paperwork, she would have been an accountant, or even a lawyer like her sister Jocelyn. But she had known about the long hours and the mountain of paperwork that accompanied it, long before she had made up her mind to become a pediatrician. Her mother was a doctor, so was one of her grandfathers. Even though he was retired from practicing medicine, Grandpop Michaels still sat on the board of the largest hospital in Baltimore. After all the years of schooling and hard work, she couldn't bitch about it all now.

Besides, she wouldn't want to be anything else. Doctoring was in her blood.

She headed for the elevator and chalked up her miserable mood to lack of sleep and P.M.S. Her P.M.S. not only came with the same symptoms that just about every other woman in the world had, but it came with one more. She was due to get her period in the next day or so, and that meant she wasn't pregnant. Over the past year or so the desire to have a baby of her own had grown stronger. She had always loved children and had known she wanted a whole houseful to love and spoil. When her next birthday rolled around, she would be hitting the big three-o, and she wasn't even engaged. Her biological clock ticked one more tock with every box of tampons she bought.

Dr. Richard Wainbright, her significant other and the man she had been living with for over four years now, didn't seem to be in any hurry to "pop" the question. Richard didn't seem to be in a hurry about anything concerning their relationship. Lately, she had been noticing a lot about Richard that left her cold and dissatisfied. Especially in their king-size bed.

Was passion supposed to die so quickly? Where was the desire? The love? How in the hell could she even think about getting pregnant when she couldn't remember the last time Richard and she had made love?

Sydney opened the door to their condo and quietly dropped everything onto the couch. The lights were off, so Richard must have made an early night of it. Great, she had hurried home for nothing. She listened to a low murmur of voices coming from the master bedroom down the hallway. Richard must be watching television. A small smile tugged at her mouth as she kicked off her shoes and started to unbutton her blouse while she headed quietly down the hallway. Maybe tonight would be her lucky night after all.

The top three buttons of her silk blouse were undone as she stepped into the bedroom and froze. The curtains across the balcony doors were pulled open, and moonlight poured into the room and across the bed. A moonbeam highlighted the naked blonde who was riding Richard and muttering something that sounded suspiciously like "giddy-up."

The couple were so engrossed in their game of Dale Evans and Trigger that neither noticed her standing in the doorway in shock.

Richard grunted something low and crude and then issued a command, "Faster." His hand came up and smacked the blonde's bouncing ass.

It was the sound of that slap that snapped Sydney from her shock into a blinding rage. In one fluid motion she picked up the nearest object, a crystal vase filled with silk pink roses, and threw it across the room. "You son of a bitch!" Her aim was off, and she chalked it up to the haze of a red, blinding rage that was obscuring her vision. She missed the fornicating couple by at least two yards. The vase shattered against the wall with a loud explosion.

The blonde either rolled off Richard and the bed to huddle on the floor, or Richard had tossed her in that direction. Sydney really didn't care which. It was pitiful how the woman reached for a pillow and tried to cover herself with it. As if *now* she was embarrassed. There was something familiar about the blonde, but Sydney barely paid her any attention. She was too busy reaching for the next item to throw.

A silver-backed brush went straight for Richard's head, but he managed to duck in time. The brush bounced harmlessly off the wall, which increased her fury. Her breath was coming fast and furious, and her hands were trembling as she reached for one more projectile.

"Sydney!" shouted Richard as he tried to untangle himself from the sheets. "Knock that off."

Sydney took aim and fired off a bottle of perfume as if she were in the World Series and Richard's head was the strike zone. It missed Richard by mere inches. Her aim was improving, and the room was beginning to reek of designer perfume. "I'll knock it off, after I knock your head off, you cheating son of a bitch!" The next bottle of perfume struck the headboard and shattered. The dresser she was standing in front of was clearing off fast. She tossed an eight-by-ten glossy in a silver frame like a Frisbee. She aimed for Richard but managed to knock over the lamp on the nightstand.

Why in the hell couldn't she have inherited the athletic gene like her younger sister Jocelyn? Jocelyn could have knocked Richard's fancy crowns out from his cheating mouth from across the room with any one of those items.

"You're acting like an immature child, Sydney!" Richard finally managed to untangle himself. He stood next to the bed, yanked the sheet off the bed, and wrapped it around his waist.

She rolled her eyes at his display of modesty. Like she hadn't seen it all before. "And you were acting like a *wild stallion* with bimbo the bareback rider doing her best Dale Evans impersonation!" The matching silver comb and mirrored tray went winging their way across the room.

The comb found its mark and bounced off his chest. Richard tripped over the sheet as he dodged the tray and landed hard on his knees. "Damn it, Sydney, stop that. I can explain."

Sydney frowned at the empty dresser top. The only things left were a tube of poppy red lipstick and some pocket change. Two nickels and half a dozen pennies. Not even enough to call someone who might give a damn that her life had just fallen apart before her very eyes. Richard didn't love her. There wasn't going to be any big church wedding or white picket fence. No babies to cuddle or rock to sleep. No houseful of laughing children. Every dream inside her died the moment she had stepped into the bedroom and seen Richard with another woman.

She looked into the mirror and stared at the trembling blonde with huge frightened eyes and huge breasts that the king-size pillow was having a difficult time covering. Sydney finally placed her; she was one of the ER nurses at the hospital where both she and Richard worked. By tomorrow morning, this lovely scene would be all over the hospital.

Life just got better and better.

Sydney turned and faced the woman. Richard was cursing the sheets and trying to get back on his feet, but she didn't give him another glance. "Enjoy him, he's all yours." She walked out of the bedroom with her head held high. She picked up her purse and paperwork, walked out of their condo, and had the buttons of her blouse rebuttoned before stepping into the elevator.

Somewhere behind her she could hear Richard shouting her name and a string of curses, but she never turned around. As the doors to the elevator closed, she glanced down at her nylon-clad feet and started to laugh so hard that tears rolled down her cheeks. She had forgotten her shoes. Before the elevator door reopened at the garage level, her laughter had turned into sobs.

Chapter One

"When I pull on this, does it hurt?"

A deep, masculine negative mumble was the only response.

"How about when I push on this?" Dr. Sydney Fletcher took Bob Newman's wrist, twisted it to one side, and gently pushed.

"Nope." Bob Newman gave her such a big smile that Sydney could see two of his molars were capped in silver. With his free hand he reached for his shirt lying next to him on the examination table. "Have you seen a picture of my tuna boat? I named her *Madison*, after the mermaid from that movie *Splash.*" Bob pulled the same photo she had seen on three occasions from his pocket.

Sydney forced herself not to roll her eyes or sigh. Bob's wrist looked perfectly fine to her. "Yes, Bob, I've seen your boat. It's a lovely boat, and no, I don't have time to go out on it with you." This was the second time in the two weeks since she opened up her office that Bob Newman, a local fisherman, had pulled this number. "Are you sure your wrist is still hurting? It's not swollen, and I don't even see a red mark or anything."

Last week it had been Bob's ankle and another invitation to tour the harbor on his tuna boat. Whoever wanted to sail around the coast of Maine in November just for the fun of it had to have something wrong with him. And it hadn't been his ankle. Sydney hadn't found one thing wrong with Bob's ankle, but he had cheerfully paid his bill and then walked out the door without a limp.

"Wrenched it horribly this morning." Bob replaced the picture and then pushed back a lock of his deep brown hair that had been falling over his forehead.

Sydney studied her patient. Bob was in his mid-forties, had never been married, and obviously had taken great care with his appearance this morning. His aftershave smelled so strong it could be considered a biohazard. Bob didn't seem like a bad man, just a lonely one. Loneliness she understood all too well. "What were you doing when you wrenched it?"

"Reaching for a frying pan that was in the back of the cabinet." Bob gave her what she was sure he considered his charming smile. "I was cooking breakfast. I can cook, you know."

Was it her imagination, or did her patient just puff out his chest? She didn't want to think about breakfast. She had missed hers because she had overslept this morning. As soon as Bob left her office, she was heading for her sister's restaurant and getting something in her stomach besides three cups of coffee and a candy bar she had found in her desk drawer. Peanuts might be a good source of protein, but not when they were covered with artificial flavorings and milk chocolate. But first she had to have a doctor-to-patient talk with Bob before they canceled his medical insurance.

"Cooking is good." She gently released Bob's wrist and sat in the chair across the room from him. "Bob, I don't think seeking medical attention is the best way to get a woman to notice you." She could see the slight flush sweeping up Bob's cheeks. He almost looked cute if a person was into large, lumbering men who embraced the salty seas and usually smelled like a cat treat. She preferred smart-dressed, professional men who smelled like designer cologne. Or at least she used to. Currently, she wasn't intersted in men or relationships. Richard's betrayal had not only soured her on men in general, but had caused her to start doubting herself as a woman. Something she had thought would never happen.

"I'm sure there are plenty of women who would love to spend some time with you." She gave him a small smile to soften her words. She didn't want to embarrass Bob or hurt his feelings. Treading around a man's ego was like tap-dancing with nitroglycerin in your pocket.

"If there are," laughed Bob good-naturedly, "their husbands will be mighty upset to hear about that."

At Bob's laugh, Sydney relaxed into the chair. "I wouldn't recommend looking in that direction." She tried to think where single women would hang out in a small fishing village, but drew a complete blank.

Since moving to Misty Harbor, Maine, last month, she would have to have been living in a cave not to notice the lack of available women. When one did show up, the town's bachelors descended like a swarm of bees to a honeycomb. Her pheromones must be working overtime, because just about every single male within a thirty-mile radius had called, stopped by her cottage or the office, or had sent her flowers, candy, or an impressive assortment of cod. She had to take Gwen's word that the cod had been impressive. After opening the Styrofoam cooler and finding a dozen freshly iced-packed fish, complete with shiny eyeballs, she had slammed the lid back on and delivered the cooler to Gwen's restaurant. She didn't want any more flowers, candy, or beady-eyed fish. But trying to discourage the men of Misty Harbor was like trying to hold back the wind.

A seemingly impossible task.

She was too tired to handle another task right now, especially an impossible one. Between moving and getting the office in shape, she was exhausted. Added to that, her career had taken a left turn at the fork in the road instead of the right.

Three months ago she had been a pediatrician practicing in Baltimore, Maryland, where her oldest patient had been an obnoxious twelve-year-old with asthma. Two weeks ago she opened up her own office on the coast of Maine as a general practitioner, and her oldest patient to date had been eighty-three-year-old George Martin, who had wanted to renew his prescription of Viagra. George's blushing bride of ten months had thanked her profusely and handed her a plate of freshly baked chocolate chip cookies. Sydney had taken the cookies, but she had actually felt a small spike of jealousy at what the older couple shared.

Misty Harbor didn't need a pediatrician; it needed a family doctor. An all-around, handle-anything-that-came-your-way doctor. The nearest hospital was an hour away. The people of Misty Harbor needed her, and she was determined to do her best for them.

As changes in one's life went, she was happy with this one. It was a good change. A challenging change.

"I'm not going to charge you for this visit, Bob. But, I want you to swear not to make up any more aches and pains." She held up a hand when Bob opened his mouth to say something. "Someone else could really be hurting and in need of my attention. You wouldn't want to see someone suffer needlessly, would you?"

"No." Bob jumped off the table and put his shirt back on. "I really did twist my wrist the wrong way this morning."

"It wasn't bad enough to see a doctor, though, was it?" Sydney stood up and made a note on Bob's chart.

Bob looked sheepish as he buttoned his shirt. "No, it's okay now."

She gave him a smile and opened the examining room door. "Glad to hear it."

Bob followed her down the short hallway to the empty reception room. Visions of a bowl of steaming chili and a roast beef sandwich made her stomach growl. Lunch was just a short walk away. Her next appointment wasn't due for another hour.

"I was wondering if you would like to have dinner with me some night this week?" asked Bob as he pulled his coat from the hanger and tugged it on.

"That's very sweet of you, Bob, but I'm afraid the answer is still the same as the last time you asked." She felt like a worm turning him down again, but it was better than giving Bob a sense of false hope. She wasn't interested in starting a relationship, only getting on with her life.

Bob was saved from responding to her by the door opening and letting in a gust of cold November air along with a six-foot-two Viking.

"Erik?" Erik Olsen, who normally looked as healthy as a horse and was probably able to carry one across his massive shoulders, looked a little pale around the edges.

"You can tell which one is which?" asked Bob. "How did you know he's Erik and not his twin brother, Gunnar?"

"His ponytail." It was a lie, but a harmless one. Gunnar Olsen could have walked into her office with his hair pulled back into a ponytail, and she still would have known he wasn't his identical twin brother, Erik. Only Erik made her heart slam against her ribs and her breathing go all funny. "Erik, what's wrong?"

"I think I need a stitch or two."

"You better need more than a Band-Aid, Olsen." Bob zipped his coat and headed for the door. "Dr. Fletcher needs to keep her schedule clear for patients who really do need her services."

Erik gave Bob a funny look as the older fisherman disappeared out the door. "What's his problem?"

"Nothing," Sydney replied as Erik's deep, rumbling voice sent a shiver of desire skirting through her body. She ignored the reaction as her gaze zeroed in on his left arm. He was holding it funny under the coat he had draped across his shoulder. She pulled the coat to the side and looked at his arm. The sleeve of his shirt was torn and bloody, but his forearm was wrapped in a towel, a blood-soaked towel. He was definitely going to need more than a Band-Aid. For the first time since med school, she felt a trifle faint at the sight of blood. Erik's blood.

Sydney took a deep breath and tossed Erik's coat onto a nearby chair. "What happened?" Sydney started to hustle him toward the examination room.

"Caught it on the hatch opening." Erik headed for the chair, but Sydney steered him to the long, cushioned examination bench.

She ripped off the white, crinkly paper Bob had been sitting on and rolled out a new length. "Sit." She positioned a sterile sheet across his lap and gently lowered his still-wrapped arm onto it. "How bad is it?" It seemed like a stupid question for a doctor to be asking the patient, but one thing she had learned in the past two weeks was that residents of Misty Harbor and the surrounding area had very strong opinions. Especially when it came to their health. If Erik told her it was bad, it was going to be bad.

"Just a stitch or two will close it. It's not a deep cut, just a long one."

"Okay, let's have a look." Sydney was surprised that her fingers weren't trembling as she gently opened the towel. It felt as though her entire insides were shaking, but she couldn't tell if that was because of the blood or being so close to Erik. The two times previously that she had met Erik, he had had an unsettling effect on her. It was the main reason she had purposely avoided him since moving to Maine. Her life didn't need any more unsettling effects.

She examined the cut with a practiced eye and felt the pressure squeezing her heart relax. The cut wasn't that bad, and most of the bleeding had slowed if not stopped. "You're half right."

"About?" Erik seemed to be studying her face and not his arm.

"It's not too deep, but you are going to need more than a stitch or two to close it up." She glanced up and encountered Erik's intense gaze. Light blue eyes, surrounded by the most ridiculously long and dark lashes, stared back at her from less than a foot away. She couldn't detect any pain in his gaze, but there were other emotions swirling around in the depths of his eyes.

She immediately dropped her gaze back down to his arm. "Does it hurt?" She slowly pulled the torn edges of his flannel shirt away from the wound. Underneath the blue plaid shirt, Erik had on a long-sleeve thermal top. Both shirts had been torn, cut, and totally ruined.

"Only when I laugh." Erik's Norwegian accent was noticeable with every word he spoke.

"Then, I guess tickling is out." Sydney realized what she had said the moment the words came tumbling out of her mouth. Her gaze shot back up to his, only to encounter the amusement dancing in Erik's eyes. "Sorry, I'm used to dealing with much younger patients." She could feel the flush sweeping up her cheeks just thinking about finding Erik Olsen's ticklish spot.

"Does that mean I won't get a sucker if I'm a good boy?" asked Erik.

"Pardon?" *Sucker? What is he talking about, and why is my mind putting the most inappropriate meaning behind his request?*

"Sucker. You know, the candy on the stick?" Erik raised his uninjured hand and gave a very good imitation of licking a pop.

"Oh, you mean lollipop?"

"I especially like the orange ones." Erik's body tensed as she gently pulled the dark blue thermal away from the cut.

"I'll remember that." Sydney backed away from Erik's legs and frowned. "I'm afraid you ruined both of your shirts."

"They can be replaced."

"They also have to come off." Sydney turned toward the door. "I'll be right back. Don't move. I need to get a suture kit." She also needed to get a hold of herself. She was a doctor, for God's sake, and Erik was her patient. Her injured patient.

By the time she wheeled a cart containing the suture kit back into the examination room, she had herself under control. Or at least she did until she spotted Erik trying unsuccessfully to remove his thermal top with one hand. He had it halfway up his one side and was trying to work his injured arm out of it.

"Stop!" Fresh blood was beginning to flow again from the cut. "The shirt is already ruined; I'll cut it off." Somehow Erik had managed to get the flannel shirt off, and it was now balled up and lying on his lap, along with his injured arm and bloody towel. "I thought I told you not to move." *Men, honestly, they're worse than some of the young patients I've treated.*

Erik seemed to find her exasperation amusing. "You said the shirts had to come off."

"Yes, I did, and then I told you not to move." She grabbed a pair of scissors from the counter and walked behind the table. "This time don't move a muscle, because these scissors are sharp." She reached for the blue thermal top and pulled it from his jeans. She cut straight up the back of the shirt and refused to dwell on the fresh, sea-brisk scent that seemed to cling to Erik. He didn't smell like a can of cat food or rotting seaweed like most fishermen did, especially when they came right off their boats. Erik had a scent of ocean breezes, crisp fall winds, and soap. Fresh, clean soap.

She moved the end of his golden ponytail out of her way and snipped through the neck binding on the shirt. Erik always pulled his shoulder-length hair back into a rubberband. She didn't understand his desire for long hair, especially if he always wore it pulled back. As far as she knew, there were only two kinds of men who wore ponytails. Men who wore black leather and drove big-ass motorcycles, or gray-hair college professors who taught poetry, philosophy, or were into the "arts." Erik didn't fit into either category.

Erik and his identical twin brother, Gunnar, fit into the Viking category. Both men were in their late twenties, an impressive six-foot-two, and weighed close to two hundred pounds each. Most of those pounds seemed to be centered on their shoulders or chest. Long, dark blond hair, crystal-clear light blue eyes, and finely sculptured faces bespoke of their Norwegian heritage. Gwen had told her that both brothers had come to America three years ago looking for their grandfather, found him, liked the coast of Maine, and had decided to stay. It was a sweet story.

A sweet Viking was definitely an oxymoron. One she better stop thinking about as a man and start concentrating on as a patient. Before he bled to death in her office.

Sydney put the scissors back on the counter and walked around to face Erik. The cut on his forearm was barely bleeding, but still in need of a few stitches. "Let's get that shirt off, so I can clean and close you up."

She quickly pulled the shirt away from his shoulder and over his good arm. She refused to think about how she was undressing Erik in her office, or the way her heart was pounding. For cripes sake, she had sponge bathed gorgeous men and never so much as gotten an extra heartbeat. Erik was even still wearing a T-shirt. A blinding white, extremely tight T-shirt that clung to his chest and outlined every impressive muscle and bulge.

They didn't show bodies like Erik's in any med school text book she had had to read.

She refused to meet his gaze as she slowly and carefully worked the other sleeve over his injured arm and hand. She took both shirts and dropped them into the trash. "I need you to lie down now."

"I'll sit." Erik looked at the wheeled cart and the sterile tray she was getting ready to open.

"Afraid not," Sydney said with a touch of amusement. "I've seen bigger men than you hit the deck at the sight of a needle. I won't be able to catch you if you faint, so it's down you go now."

"I promise not to faint."

"Lie down, Erik, or no lollipop, and I'm positive there's an orange one in the bowl at the reception desk." Sydney carefully held his arm and gently pushed at his good shoulder.

Erik went down without a fuss. Sydney positioned the wheeled cart at the side of the examination bench and carefully laid Erik's arm across it.

"Can I watch?"

"Sure, if you want to." Sydney washed her hands and then snapped on a fresh pair of gloves. "I won't think less of you if you don't. Not many people can stand the sight of getting sutured, especially when it's their own skin." She busied herself getting everything ready and within easy reach before pulling over a stool and sitting down.

She looked at the wound one last time before picking up a needle. "This will burn for about ten seconds, and then you won't feel a thing."

"Novocaine?" Erik asked as she injected the cut.

"Lidocaine. Basically the same thing." Sydney placed the needle on the tray. "We'll give it a moment before I start cleaning it up. Do you know when your last tetanus shot was?"

"Four years ago." Erik crossed his ankles and watched as she tore open sterile wipes and started to clean up the blood smeared across his arm and hand. "What did Bob Newman mean about me needing more than a Band-Aid?"

"Oh, nothing." Sydney tested the edge of the five-inch gash with a fresh wipe. "Does this hurt?"

"No." Erik watched dispassionately as Sydney cleaned the cut and then smeared an iodine solution all around it. "So, Dr. Fletcher, are you bored with our little village yet?"

Sydney glanced up just as she was ready to put in the first suture. "Bored?" She couldn't read the expression on Erik's face, so she went back to work. "I've been too busy to be bored."

Erik glanced around the light blue room. "I see that you've been busy. This doesn't look like Dr. Jeffreys' old exam room." A frown pulled at his mouth as he stared across the room. "You not only painted and put up new curtains; you put in new cabinets and a sink."

"Daniel Creighton did most of the work." Sydney concentrated on putting the stitches close together so the scarring would be minimal. "It's nice having a brother-in-law who knows his way around building and plumbing." Most of the improvements she had done were cosmetic and hadn't cost her her life savings. Currently, she was living on a shoestring, but she had the beginning of a plan forming in the back of her mind. An expensive plan. Misty Harbor and the surrounding area needed more than one doctor's ill-equipped office. It needed its own medical facility.

"Gwen and Daniel seem very happy." Erik's voice seemed to hold a wishful element.

"They've only been married a few months. They better still be happy." Sydney had always thought, since she was the oldest, she would be the one to marry first. *Just goes to show you what happens when you think.*

Sydney carefully put in the last suture and studied her handiwork. Not bad. "There, all done."

Erik glanced at his forearm and tried to count the little black threads sticking out. "How many stitches?"

"Eleven very nice and tiny ones if I do say so myself." Sydney squeezed some antibiotic across the stitches and taped a large, clean gauze on the wound. "You are going to have to keep this clean and dry. Change the bandage every day and apply antibiotic ointment."

"How am I supposed to shower?" Erik sat up and glared at his arm and the huge white bandage.

Sydney gathered up the soiled wipes and the protective sheet and tossed them into the biohazard bin, along with her gloves. She washed her hands and refused to think about Erik in the shower. She reached under the sink and pulled out a dozen clear, small garbage bags. "Here, put one of these on your arm and seal it shut with a couple of rubberbands. Just remember, as soon as you are out of the shower, take it off so it doesn't cut off your circulation."

Erik took the bags. "Thanks."

"I'll get you some extra large gauze pads to take with you, and we need to make an appointment for you to come back in seven to ten days so I can take the stitches out."

"Anything else?"

"Call me if it starts really bothering you, or if you start running a fever, or if it appears to be getting infected."

Erik Olsen stared at the woman standing across the room from him and had the insane impulse to kiss her. It was the same impulse he got every time he was within fifty feet of the doctor. Any time he got closer than three feet, his desire was a little more primitive.

He almost sighed out loud when she turned around and bent over a drawer looking for the gauze. The long, white lab coat did nothing to hide the attractive shape of her bottom. His fingers started to itch, and he wondered if the lidocaine was starting to wear off. That might explain the itch in his left hand, but not his right.

This morning when he sliced open his forearm, he

had cursed not only the stinging pain, but the fact he was going to be a lot closer than three feet to the lovely doctor. He had held Sydney in his arms once before, during a dance at her sister Gwen's engagement party back in April. Once was all that was needed to know that Sydney Fletcher fit perfectly into his arms.

The sad truth was, Sydney was entirely the wrong woman for him. He knew it in his mind, yet his body refused to listen to reason. At Gwen's June wedding reception, he had danced with every woman there, except Sydney. He had danced with Sydney's mom, and even her youngest sister, Jocelyn, three different times, but never Sydney. He had stood on the sidelines and watched as she was escorted around the dance floor by every man in the room, including his own brother, Gunnar.

He had still gone home and dreamed of the standoffish, yet sexy doctor. It hadn't mattered one bit that Sydney had been living with some big-shot doctor back in Baltimore. He had to wonder what the doctor thought about Sydney moving to Maine last month? It didn't seem to bode well with their relationship, and Sydney's current "single" status was the talk of the village. He didn't want to think about Sydney being available.

What he needed was distance. A lot of distance. He took the bandages from Sydney. "Thanks."

"The local will be wearing off soon, so it's going to start to hurt. Take a couple of Tylenol if it bothers you." Sydney led the way out of the room and back into the reception area. She glanced at the appointment book lying open on the desk and flipped the page. "How's next Tuesday?"

"Fine."

"Afternoon or early evening?" Sydney picked up a pencil and waited.

"Early evening would be better."

"Six-thirty?"

"Fine." He watched as Sydney wrote in the book and

then filled in the time on a small business card. He didn't want to think about seeing Sydney again. He knew it was going to be impossible to avoid her now that she was living and working in Misty Harbor, but he was giving it his best shot. There was no use tempting himself with something he couldn't have.

Sydney handed him the card. "Remember to call me immediately if anything feels or looks wrong."

That was the problem. Nothing felt or looked wrong when he was near Sydney. Everything seemed so damn perfect, from her sparkling green eyes to her luscious mouth. Sydney was five feet five inches of pure perfection.

Sydney reached into a bowl sitting on the desk and picked out an orange sucker in the shape of a pumpkin, complete with a jack-o'-lantern smile, and handed it to him. "This is for being good."

He grinned as he put down the trash bags and gauze and opened the sucker. "That's me, good." He popped the pop into his mouth and figured he deserved more than an orange sucker for keeping his hands and mouth off the lovely doctor. He deserved a medal. He wrapped his lips around the pumpkin head and stared into the most gorgeous green eyes ever to grace an angel's face.

Sydney's gaze seemed to be fastened to his mouth. He was trying to determine what emotion was flaring in those green depths when the front door was thrust open.

This time the chilly November wind blew in Sydney's one o'clock appointment. Carol Ann Burton and her three kids, including Devin, the human sound track of a crying baby.

Right behind Carol Ann was Daniel Creighton, Sydney's brother-in-law. Daniel was carrying a Styrofoam container and a can of soda. "Delivery man," Daniel said as he put what obviously was Sydney's lunch on the desk. "Gwen was worried when you didn't show up for lunch."

Erik held up his arm with its sparkling white bandage. "That would be my fault."

Daniel raised his brow. "Bad?"

"Eleven stitches and he didn't even flinch," said Sydney as she eagerly peeked into the Styrofoam container. "Roast beef."

He wasn't positive, but he thought she licked her lips in anticipation. Now he felt like a big slug for lusting after a doctor who had not only sewn up his arm, but had been starving while doing it. Sydney had missed her lunch because of him.

Carol Ann was trying to get Devin out of his coat and hat while he screamed at the top of his lungs. Her other two children threw their coats in the direction of the coat rack and made a beeline for the pile of toys in the far corner.

Daniel cringed at Devin's volume. "I'm out of here. I'm due back at the job site."

Erik picked up his coat and eased his now bandaged arm into the sleeve. "Thanks again, Doc."

Sydney nodded as she rushed across the room to pick up Devin. "You're welcome. Remember, dry and clean."

Erik followed Daniel to the door, but turned around once more to look at Sydney. She was standing in the middle of the room cuddling Devin, who amazingly quieted down. A wondrous smile tilted up the corners of her mouth as Devin reached up and grabbed her nose.

Sydney loved babies. No one who didn't love babies would have reached out for the screaming Devin. It was either maternal instincts or she was crazy. He knew there was nothing wrong with Sydney's mind.

Erik turned around and closed the door behind him on the soft and natural picture of Sydney with a baby in her arms. He really didn't need that vision following him home.

Chapter Two

Sydney piled the rest of her packages into the rear of her S.U.V. and closed the back hatch. One of the first things she had done after making her decision to move to Maine was to take her brother-in-law's advice, and buy a four-wheel drive S.U.V. It had been expert advice, and she loved her new car. Since she had left all the furniture at Richard's, she had managed the move in one easy trip and with no moving vans. Everything that she owned had fit in the S.U.V.

Gwen's furniture and most of the household goods were still in the rental cottage, except for the dining room set. She guessed Gwen had liked the set, because it was the only thing she had taken to Daniel's. Gwen had loaned her an extra table and some chairs from the restaurant until she could decide what kind of furniture she wanted in the dining room.

This afternoon's shopping spree hadn't been about dining room sets; it had been about winter clothing. Lots of warm clothing. The sweaters, slacks, and coats she had packed in Baltimore weren't going to handle winter in Maine. The back of the S.U.V. was now filled with wool pants, thermal socks, flannel pajamas, and a queen-size electric blanket. A down-filled parka had set her back a pretty penny, but she had made up for it by finding a shoe store with every pair of boots on sale. Three pairs of boots, two afghans, and a set of snowmen coffee mugs had completed her shopping spree and put a hurting on her Visa card.

It was time to head on back to Misty Harbor, unload the car, and nuke up her usual dinner of cardboard turkey and shriveled peas. She hated cooking and the time-consuming hours it took just to make one meal. She had better things to do with her time than grate, chop, squeeze, and saute things in fancy pots and pans. Besides, no matter how hard she tried, she could never compete with her sister Gwen in the kitchen.

Thinking of her sister's cooking, she decided that dinner at Gwen's restaurant sounded a whole lot better than microwave food requiring her to poke holes in the plastic before pushing some buttons.

She drove the nearly hour-long trip listening to the newest Enya CD. It was amazing that she had moved to a place where the nearest mall was fifty-some minutes away. Then again, with inner-city traffic and stop-and-go red lights, it had often taken her longer to get from one end of Baltimore to the other. One thing she did know, the view in Maine was better. She had enjoyed driving to the mall after closing her office at noon. Now that darkness had fallen, she couldn't see very much, but she still enjoyed the ride. No bumper-to-bumper traffic and no gridlock.

She carefully found the road that would wind its way into Misty Harbor and smiled when distant lights appeared. She was home. She coasted to a stop as she crested a hill, and the small harbor town was spread out below her like some travel brochure picture. Every house had lights on, and she could pick out the park with its gazebo trimmed in white miniature lights. The harbor, with its docks and bobbing boats, was enchanting, and she could even pick out the lights from her sister's restaurant.

She was smiling and thinking about the lobster she would be eating shortly as she started down the hill. One minute she was singing along with Enya and thinking about what she was going to order for dessert, and the next she was slamming on the brakes to avoid hitting the old man standing in the middle of the road. She could hear the packages in the back tip over and slide. Daniel was right. The S.U.V. had brakes that could stop on a dime. It was a good thing, too, because the old man just stood there looking at her. He hadn't even bothered to try and get out of the way.

Sydney put the car in park, but left it running. The headlights outlined the coatless man and the fact that he was shivering beneath his flannel shirt. If she had still been living in Baltimore, she would have locked her doors and called the police on her cell phone. Since Misty Harbor was a far cry from a thriving metropolis, she got out of the car and slowly made her way to the man.

"Hello, are you hurt?" Sydney glanced around the area, but besides a few distant houses, there wasn't anyone else out and about. In the distance she could hear a dog bark, but that was about it.

The old man just stood there and looked at her in confusion.

"I'm Sydney Fletcher, Dr. Fletcher." She could see the anxiety etched into the man's face. He appeared to be in his early seventies, maybe late sixties. She didn't remember seeing him about town.

"Doktor?"

"Yes, doctor." Sydney moved a step closer and slowly held out her hand. "Who might you be? I don't believe we have met." Her gaze was quicky assessing him to see if he had suffered any kind of injury or trauma. The man appeared to be in good shape. His mental health was a whole different ball game.

"Hans." Hans looked at her hand but didn't take it. His fearful gaze was looking around them as though trying to figure out where they were. Or how he had gotten there.

"Hans what?" *Swedish, possibly.*

"Hans Bergesen."

"Are you Swedish?" She couldn't remember if Gwen had mentioned any Swedish families in town.

"Norwegian." Hans rubbed his arms and looked down the road.

"Are you Erik Olsen's grandfather?" How many Norwegians could one small town have? Especially if they were the size of Erik and Gunnar. Erik and his brother had come to America to find their grandfather. Hans had to be that grandfather.

Hans's face brightened with recognition. "You know Erik?"

"Yes, I'm the doctor who sewed up his arm two days ago." She frowned at Hans and wondered how he had gotten to this part of town. She knew Erik lived about a mile or two away, on the outskirts of town. She had no idea where Hans lived. "Did Erik show you his injury?"

"Ya, you did a fine job." Hans held out his hand. "Thank you."

Sydney grasped his outstretched hand. "You're welcome." Hans's fingers felt like ice. "Do you need a ride? I can drop you off at Erik's."

"I came out for a walk."

"It's a perfect evening for a walk." She gave Hans a smile and prayed she wouldn't frighten him off. Dragging a scared, confused seventy-year-old man into her car was the last thing she wanted to do. "Erik's house is pretty far from here. How about if I drop you off? I'm going right past it anyway."

"It won't be out of your way?"

"It's no problem at all." She walked to the passenger side and opened up the door. "How's Gunnar doing? I haven't seen him in a while." The safest thing she could think of to do was to talk about his family. Problem was, she had just run out of subject matter.

Hans got into the passenger seat and seemed to relax at the mention of his other grandson's name. "You know Gunnar, too?"

Sydney hurried around the car, hopped in, and quickly closed the door. "Sure do. Gunnar likes to catch lobsters while Erik goes after fish." She reached over and turned the heat on high.

"Boys look so much alike, but they are so different." Hans leaned back into the seat and rubbed his hands together. "They both have their own boats."

What is it with men and their boats? Sydney drove toward Erik's house and tried to keep the conversation with Hans going. He was explaining something about fishing, but she wasn't really paying any attention. She was too busy concentrating on driving and thinking about how she had found Hans standing in the middle of the road, totally lost and confused.

Erik's file had listed his address on Sunset Cove Road. She knew where the road was, but she had no idea which house was Erik's or if he lived with anyone, like Gunnar or even Hans.

The road was bumpy, so she had to slow down to a crawl. She was trying to read the mailboxes and praying for a name when Hans pointed off to his left.

"Look," Hans said, "they left the lights on for me."

Sydney glanced at the modest-size home and smiled. Every light in and out of the house was blazing. She slowly turned onto the driveway and parked behind a red pickup truck. "How about I walk you up to the door." Hans looked ready to object, so she quickly added, "I really would love to say hello to Erik."

Hans chuckled as he opened his door and stepped back out into the night. "Erik's a good man."

Great, the last thing she needed was for Hans to get any wrong ideas into his head, but she couldn't just drop Hans off and then drive home. "Who happens to like orange lollipops."

Hans laughed as he strolled up the walkway with her. "I see you do know my grandson very well. Erik has a sweet tooth, just like his mother."

They were about two feet away from the door when it was violently flung open. *"Bestefar!"* shouted Erik.

Sydney took a quick step back and would have fallen off the stoop and into a bush if Hans hadn't tightened his grip on her elbow. Having a Viking shout at her from less than two feet away was a frightful experience. No wonder the poor folks from the villages his ancestors had raided and pillaged had thought they were berserkers. Erik appeared to be on the very edge of sanity.

"Why are you shouting, Erik?" asked Hans. "Can't you see we have a guest?" Hans gave her arm a reassuring pat. "A very special guest who wanted to come in and say hello to you."

She rolled her eyes and gave Erik a small smile. At least now he appeared semisane. His grandfather's appearance must have calmed him down. "Hello, Erik." She allowed Hans to lead her into the house. "It was such a nice night that when I offered your grandfather a ride home, I just had to stop in to see how you are doing."

Erik was glancing between his grandfather and Sydney. Erik appeared smart enough to know something was wrong, but this wasn't the time to discuss it. "I'm doing great, and yourself?"

"Gee, it's no wonder you aren't married with a baby on each knee and another growing fat beneath your wife's apron." Hans shook his head at his grandson. "Take her coat, boy, and offer her something warm to drink. It's the cold side of dawn out there." Hans made his way across the living room and stood in front of the fireplace where a nice low fire was burning.

Erik moved behind her to help remove her coat. His voice was barely a whisper, "Where did you find him?"

"Standing in the middle of the road," she whispered back. She smiled at Hans as he turned to frown at them standing in the foyer whispering. "This is a lovely house." She glanced around in curiosity and appreciation. The rich golden glow of wood was everywhere. A large green couch and two chairs dominated the masculine living room. Patio doors opened onto a deck with a beautiful view of the cove beyond. Moonlight glittered off the calm waters.

"Thank you." Hans stepped closer to the fire and did a pretty good show of not being frozen solid. "Where's Gunnar?"

Erik hung Sydney's coat on one of the pegs by the front door. "He's out taking a drive. I'm sure he'll be back in another minute or two."

"A drive at this time of night?" Hans rubbed his hands together and turned his back to the fire.

"He said he needed some fresh air." Erik led Sydney into the living room.

She sat on the couch and tried to pretend this was a casual visit, while keeping an eye on Hans. The old man's shivering had stopped, but he still appeared a little pale. Whatever confusion he had been suffering from out on the street had disappeared. Her medical instincts wanted to give Hans a complete physical, or at least check his head to see if he had bumped it recently. Logic told her that Hans wouldn't submit to a physical, either here or at her office.

"When's dinner?" asked Hans. "I'm starving."

"Gunnar brought home lobsters." Erik stood by one of the chairs, but didn't sit. "Do you want me to start getting dinner ready?"

"Ya." Hans glanced meaningfully at her. "Of course, our guest might be hungry, too."

Sydney could feel her stomach rumble and prayed it wasn't too noticeable. It was the same reaction she had every time someone mentioned the word "lobster." Since moving to Maine, she had been averaging eating lobster three times a week. If she wasn't careful, she would be growing antennas and claws soon.

Erik gave her a very long look before reluctantly asking, "Would you care to stay for dinner?"

Normally, she would have politely refused. Gwen's restaurant had been doing a wonderful job at feeding her lobster addiction, and it was only five minutes away. Erik didn't seem too thrilled with the prospect of sharing his dinner table with her. Well, tough for Erik. She was staying for one reason and one reason only. She smiled at Hans as she answered Erik's question. "I would love to."

Erik seemed surprised by her response, but Hans nodded his approval. "Good," Hans said as he finally left the fire to come sit next to her. "Erik is very skilled in the kitchen."

She would imagine Erik was very skilled in a lot of rooms of the house. "I'm sure he is." She managed a smile for Erik. "What can I do to help?" Usually, if she helped Gwen in the kitchen, it was slicing or dicing something. Gwen always said that since she was a doctor, she better be good with a knife. She had tried to explain to Gwen that she was a pediatrician, not a surgeon. Her sister didn't see the difference. Most people didn't.

"I'll handle dinner," Erik said. "Why don't you sit here and entertain Hans."

"I would love to," she said while studying Hans's expression. The confusion and anxiety were gone, replaced with a loving parental look toward Erik.

The front door opened with a bang, and Gunnar and the cold November night came blowing into the house. "Is Grandfather home?" was shouted as he charged into the room.

Erik grabbed Gunnar's arm and brought him to a halt. "Grandfather is fine and well."

Hans frowned at his two grandsons. "Of course I'm fine and well. Have you ever known me to be sick a day?"

Erik started to drag Gunnar toward the kitchen. "You can help me get dinner ready."

Gunnar glanced at her sitting next to his grandfather. "Dr. Sydney?"

"Just Sydney. I'm not here on official business." She gave Gunnar a wink while casually tilting her head in Hans's direction.

"Erik invited her to dinner." Hans favored Erik with a beaming smile. "It's going to be nice having someone pretty to look at during dinner for a change."

Gunnar gave Erik a strange, considering look. "Yeah, a person can grow mighty tired of looking at Erik's face."

Sydney chuckled, considering Erik and Gunnar were identical twins. They were even tanned the same rich color of men who spent too many hours out in the sun without wearing a hat. She made a mental note to talk to them both about sun screen.

Erik grunted a reply and dragged Gunnar out of the room.

Two hours later, dinner, dessert, and the cleaning of the kitchen were complete. Fresh coffee was slowly dripping its way into a pot. Erik had to admit it was nice having someone different to share their meal with, and the conversation had ranged from his home country of Norway to crabbing in the Chesapeake Bay. Hans wanted to try his hand at crabbing, and even he had to admit it sounded fun and delicious. The one thing he wouldn't admit was he liked the idea of Sydney being in his home. Technically, this wasn't his house, it was Hans's, but he and his brother had been living there for three years now.

"Well, Sydney, this old man needs his pretty sleep." Hans gave her cheek a light kiss. "Thank you for the ride and for the wonderful company during dinner."

"You're welcome, Hans." Sydney's smile lit up the kitchen. "It was my pleasure."

At Sydney's smile, a painful tug gripped low in Erik's gut. Sydney looked so different than what she had looked like the other day. Gone was the white coat and the professional air that seemed to have clung to her. Tonight she was relaxed, yet watchful of his grandfather. Something had happened when Sydney had found Hans, but he didn't know what. Hans never went out walking this late in the evening, nor had he ever forgotten his coat before. There was something wrong with his grandfather, and Sydney knew what that something was.

Hans chuckled as he started to walk out of the room. "No, I believe it was Erik's and Gunnar's pleasure." He turned and glared at his grandsons, but his gaze finally rested on Erik. "Don't let this one get away."

His brother's laugh filled the room, and for the first time in a long time, Erik felt like decking him. He could feel the flush sweeping up his cheeks, but he refused to meet Sydney's gaze. The door to Hans's room closed behind him, and Erik gave a heavy sigh and with a sense of dread asked, "How about we take our coffee into the living room?" It was time for Sydney to answer some questions.

Gunnar started to pour the coffee while Sydney hung up the dish towel she had been using to dry the dishes. Erik paced the length of the room twice before picking up his cup and leading the way into the living room. He was scared, and he didn't like that feeling one bit.

Sydney took a seat on the couch, and his brother sat next to her, giving him a superior smile. He ignored his brother and paced in front of the fireplace. Gunnar had rebuilt the fire while he and Sydney had been doing the dishes. "Okay, what is going on?"

"I'm not sure." Sydney took a sip of her coffee. "When did Hans leave the house?"

"We don't know," Gunnar said as he frowned at his

cup. "I got home around five, and Hans wasn't here." Gunnar rubbed the side of his jaw. "I didn't think anything of it. I thought he probably went with Erik somewhere."

"I got home around five-thirty." Erik lowered himself into a chair. "Needless to say, I didn't have him with me. We started to worry, but didn't panic until we noticed his coat still hanging on the peg by the door." Erik rubbed his jaw. "Gunnar went out looking for him while I stayed here waiting for some word. You pulled up front around six."

Sydney nodded. "I was coming back from doing some shopping, and I almost hit him. Hans was standing in the middle of the road, looking confused and afraid."

He flinched at that mental picture. Gunnar softly cursed. "Thank you for not hitting him."

"Thank good brakes." Sydney crossed her arms and slowly rubbed them. "I got out of the car to make sure he was all right. I didn't see any injuries, but he appeared not to even know how he had gotten there. When he told me his name, and with his accent, I thought he was Swedish at first, but then he corrected me and told me he was Norwegian. I put two and two together and came up with you and Gunnar."

"So you brought him home."

"I offered him a ride, and he took it."

"What would you have done if he had refused to get into the car?" he asked.

"Well, I figured I had two choices. One was drag him into it, which I have to tell you didn't excite me. Your grandfather might be a good forty years older than I, but let me tell you, he's still a big man."

Gunnar chuckled.

Erik glared at his brother before directing his attention back to Sydney. "You're just small."

"I am not!" Sydney glared at him. "My second option was to use my cell phone and call Gwen at the restaurant.

I didn't know your phone number, but I figured Gwen would be able to reach you somehow."

"Not only small," Gunnar said with a smile, "but smart, too."

"I remembered which road you lived on from your chart the other day, but I didn't know which house. Hans pointed it out to me, so here we are."

He nodded slowly, trying to think. "I don't understand why my grandfather would leave the house without his coat. Especially since it's the middle of November."

"He's getting forgetful sometimes, but he's never done anything like this before," added Gunnar.

"What kind of things does he forget?" Sydney asked. Her professional air was back. All that was missing was the white coat.

"Little things, like what he had for dinner last night. Last week I dropped him off to do some food shopping, and he only bought bananas. He claimed he couldn't remember what else we needed." Erik tried to think of some other examples. "Just little things. Nothing serious."

"He's retired, right?"

"Ya," answered Gunnar. "He retired before we even came over to find him."

"Has he taken any falls or bumped his head lately, that you might know of?"

"No." Erik shook his head slowly and tried to read Sydney's face. He couldn't. Either she hid her concerns very well, or it could have been the fact that every time his gaze landed on her face, it slid to her tempting mouth and stayed there.

"Not that I can recall." Gunnar finished his coffee and put the empty cup onto the side table. "He's seventy-three; surely he's entitled to forget a thing or two."

"Everyone forgets things, Gunnar, but your grandfather not only forgot his coat. I believe he had no idea how he had gotten to Eagle's Nest Road."

"Eagle's Nest Road?" Erik groaned, and tried not to

think about how his grandfather had managed to be a good two and a half miles away from home, in the dark and with no coat. It hadn't hit the freezing mark outside, but it was darn close.

"What should we do?" asked Gunnar.

"What's wrong with him?" Erik asked as he stood back up to pace some more.

"I can't answer that tonight." Sydney gave both him and his brother a sympathetic look. "I need to give Hans a complete physical. The sooner the better."

"I can bring him in tomorrow." He didn't care about working or catching any fish. His first concern was his grandfather. His family.

"I could do it," offered Gunnar.

"Thanks, but I'll do it." He appreciated Gunnar's offer, but he wanted to be there with Hans when Sydney examined him. He didn't remember Hans ever going to old Doc Jeffreys. Hans had never been ill a day in his life.

"Around three?" Sydney stood up and carried her cup back into the kitchen.

"Three is fine." He followed Sydney and Gunnar into the foyer.

Gunnar helped Sydney with her coat. "Thank you, Sydney, for being there for him."

Erik frowned at the spike of jealousy that clinched his gut when Sydney smiled up at Gunnar. She never smiled at him like that. "Come on, Doc, I'll walk you out." He ignored Gunnar's knowing look as he opened the door and hustled Sydney away from his brother.

He matched his steps to hers as they walked to her car in silence. Sydney's brand-new, top-of-the-line foreign sport-utility vehicle looked out of place behind his pickup and Gunnar's old Jeep. The shiny silver S.U.V. cost more than he made in a year. The doctor was definitely used to the finer things in life and totally out of his reach.

"Thanks again for bringing our grandfather home."

He felt awkward and somewhat intimidated as Sydney opened the driver's door and he saw the interior of her car. It looked like the cockpit of a 747 airplane. "Nice car."

"Thanks, and you're welcome." Sydney slid into the car. "I'll see you and Hans tomorrow at three, right?"

"Right." He glanced at the empty rear leather seat and then into the storage area beyond. Shopping bags with fancy names and colorful tissue papers were scattered all over the place. Boxes, clothes, and blankets filled the area. Under the harsh glare of the dome light, he could see that a lacy light blue bra had slid out of a Victoria's Secret bag. Something black and silky was under it. He had to clear his throat before saying, "I see when you shop, you really shop."

"I needed to pick up a few things." Sydney glanced over the seat, but she couldn't see the packages.

"A *few* things?" He had seen entire families with less stuff. He glanced at the enticing bra once more before forcing himself to look away. There was something entirely too provocative about looking at Sydney's underwear.

"I'm not used to the winters up here. I needed some warmer clothes." Sydney gave him a funny look as she defended her shopping spree.

He snorted in disbelief. *Warmer clothes!* Yeah, like that bra was going to keep her warm. Then again, if she wore just that in front of him, he would guarantee that she would not only be warm, she would be downright hot. "Good night, Doc. Pleasant dreams." He closed the car door and stood there in the cold evening air watching as Sydney drove away.

Sydney might have pleasant dreams, but he sure as hell wouldn't. He would be dreaming about Sydney wearing a lacy blue bra and a smile. It was promising to be a very long and frustrating night.

Chapter Three

Sydney studied her three o'clock patient and immediately knew that Hans Bergesen wasn't a happy camper. Hans didn't want to be there, and the only reason he was, was standing out in the waiting room pacing. Erik had been anything but thrilled when his grandfather refused to allow him to accompany him into the examination room. She could sympathize with Hans not wanting to be treated like a five-year-old.

She also understood Erik's anxiety. It was going to be a delicate balance keeping both men contented. But Hans was her patient, and he had to be her main concern. Last night, after leaving Erik's, she had spent hours on the Internet looking up the latest research and treatments on memory problems of the aging. This afternoon she felt better informed, but she would still rather see chicken pox sweep through Misty Harbor.

"That boy don't know his place," grumbled Hans as he took off his long-sleeve shirt and sat on the exam bench. "I tell him I no sick, and he still makes me come." Hans gave her a speculative look. "Maybe my grandson just wants a reason to see the pretty doktor again?"

She refused to blush or think how ruggedly handsome Erik had looked a moment ago when he had ushered Hans into the office. "Maybe your grandson is just concerned about you, Hans." She wrapped the blood pressure cuff around his arm. In his younger days, Hans must have been a heartbreaker. Even at seventy-three, he was still a handsome man. "I checked your chart, and you haven't been seen by Dr. Jeffreys in over three years."

"That's because I'm as healthy as a horse and haven't been sick." Hans gave a slight *humph* as he glared at the tightening blood pressure cuff. "There's nothing wrong with me, Dok."

"Then, let's put your grandsons' minds at ease and do a few tests." She couldn't argue with him about being healthy. From his chart, Hans appeared to be one very healthy seventy-three-year-old. His blood sugar and cholesterol three years ago had all been in the acceptable range. He had a few extra pounds, but nothing serious. A touch of arthritis in his hands had been his most serious medical problem. A sprained ankle once, the flu a couple of times over the years, and once, about fifteen years ago, a mild case of pneumonia. All in all, an amazingly uneventful medical history.

"Why would I need tests if I'm not sick?"

"Preventive medicine." She marked down his blood pressure, which was slightly elevated, but nothing that caused her concern. Hans had been extremely aggravated when he had been marched into her office. "Think of it as preventive maintenance that you would perform on a boat. You wouldn't just keep running the engine without doing anything to it, until it blew up, would you? Occasionally, you would have to add oil and do other stuff, right?" She placed the end of the stethoscope on his T-shirt-covered back and listened. "Take a deep breath."

"So now I'm a boat?" Hans took a deep breath and slowly released it.

"If you want to look at it that way, then yes. Your heart is the engine, and your mind is the captain." She moved the stethoscope over a couple of inches. "Again."

Hans breathed deeply and grumbled, "Erik and Gunnar are acting as if this old boat is rudderless."

She hid her smile. "I think they are acting like a bunch of loving grandsons who don't want to see anything bad happen to you."

"They worry like old ladies." Hans gave her a considering look and then grudgingly asked, "What kind of tests?"

"We'll start with some simple blood work." She checked out his ears. "How have you been sleeping lately?"

"Seems the older I get, the more I wake up throughout the night."

"How many times a night do you wake up?"

"Two, sometimes three."

"Can you go right back to sleep, or are you up for a while?"

"Both," answered Hans. "Most mornings I'm up before daylight to put the coffee on. The boys built me a room at the back of the house that faces the cove. There's a set of patio doors that open up onto a deck. I like to watch the day begin from either the deck or from the chair the boys bought me for Christmas the other year."

She thought it was cute the way he referred to Erik and Gunnar as "the boys." By no stretch of the imagination could either man be considered a boy. Both men were forty-six years younger and topped Hans by at least four inches and forty pounds. "Sounds to me as if your grandsons are taking real good care of you."

"Don't need anyone to take care of me." Hans

opened his mouth and allowed her to examine his throat. "I should be taking care of them."

She laughed and then checked out his nasal passages. "In case you haven't noticed, Hans, your grandsons are all grown up."

"They are still my grandsons." Hans gave a heavy sigh. "I missed so much of their lives."

So far she hadn't found one thing physically wrong with Hans. His nose was a little runny, but that could be from his walk last evening without a coat. There was nothing to explain the state of confusion she had found him in last night, and that had her worried. The dreaded "A" word kept popping into her mind. Alzheimer's. Of course, there could be countless other reasons for Hans's disorientation, starting with depression and ending with tumors. Her job would be to rule out all other known causes, because there was no single diagnostic test for Alzheimer's disease.

The depth of sadness in Hans's voice caught her attention. "Why did you miss so much? Was it because you were in America and they were in Norway?"

"It was because I was a fool. A stubborn old fool."

She pulled a stool closer to the table and sat. Hans's mental health was just as important, if not more so, as his physical health. "Why do you think you were a fool?"

Hans looked at her for a long moment before slowly shaking his head. There was heartbreak in his faded blue eyes when he finally said, "Family secrets. Family shame."

"You want to talk about it?"

"No." Hans looked anxiously at the closed door. "Can I go now?"

Something was upsetting Hans, and it wasn't merely because Erik had forced him to come see her this afternoon. Depression couldn't be ruled out, but she couldn't force him to talk about his secrets. "Not yet, Hans." She tried to look less like a doctor and more like a friend. "How about you tell me how you got to Eagle's Nest Road last night?"

"I walked." Hans didn't sound too sure of himself.

"Do you remember walking there?"

"Of course," Hans snapped defensively. "I'm not an idiot."

"No one ever said, or even thought, you were." She silently studied Hans as he put on and started to rebutton his flannel shirt. She had aggravated her patient. It was the last thing she wanted to do. She needed Hans's trust, not his anger. The best thing she could do right now was to back off on the questions and concentrate on the physical. "There's a medical lab over in Sullivan. Do you think one of your grandsons can get you there one morning this week so they can get a blood sample?"

"Does it have to be done in the morning?"

"Yes. I'm afraid you have to fast for at least eight hours before they draw the blood."

Hans stood and tucked the tails of his shirt into his pants. "Erik and Gunnar are very busy. They work hard for a living. They don't need to be carting me all over the place."

"Hans, they're family." She had seen families where there had been no love, no concern, and sometimes not even simple dignity. Hans's family wasn't like that. "Let Erik and Gunnar be there for you."

Hans gave her a funny look, and she was positive there was a gleam of moisture in his eyes. "Why? I wasn't there for them when they needed me." Hans opened the door to the exam room and walked out.

Sydney picked up his chart and followed him out into the waiting area. Erik had stopped his pacing in the middle of the room and was now glancing between Hans's closed expression and her. The Viking looked ready to erupt.

"Well," growled Erik, "is someone going to tell me what's wrong?"

"There's nothing wrong," Hans said. "The doktor didn't find one thing wrong with me."

Erik followed her over to the desk. "Is this true?"

"It's true. I didn't find anything wrong today." Why was it that most people expected doctors to not only find the problem within two minutes, but to give them a magic pill to make it all better? If only it was that simple. "I would like Hans to get some blood work this week, though."

"I'm an old man. I need all my blood." Hans mumbled something else under his breath as he headed for the coat rack and his heavy coat.

"I'll take him," Erik assured her as he gazed at her mouth. "When?"

The heat from Erik's gaze made her mouth go dry, and she nervously licked her lips. A low groan rumbling in Erik's chest made her turn away and reach for a pen. "First thing in the morning would be best. Hans needs to fast for eight hours before the test." She ignored the hot flash incinerating her body and assured herself it had nothing to do with menopause. In a week she would be turning thirty, entirely too young to be going through the change. She filled out the lab diagnostic sheet.

"Erik's too busy in the mornings to run me all the way into Sullivan." Hans looked ready to make a run for it out the door.

"I have to pick up some supplies at Bob's Marine Supply." Erik smiled at his grandfather. "I'll treat you to breakfast if you help me load the truck."

"Deal."

Sydney hid her smile as she glanced through the appointment book and fanned herself with the lab work sheet. Erik had handled his grandfather like a pro. "I need to see you again next week, Hans."

"Why?"

"By then I will have the results from the blood work, and we can discuss them." She flipped the page to the following week and wondered if the thermostat in her office was broken. "How about next Tuesday at four?"

"No," Hans said.

"It's good," Erik answered at the same time.

Hans stormed out of the office without another word. So much for Erik handling his grandfather. Erik snatched the lab paper and the appointment card from her fingers and hurried after his grandfather.

She stood in the silent reception area and felt the cold November breeze that had pushed its way in around Erik as he had left. For the first time the freezing air didn't cause her to shiver. Erik Olsen had that kind of effect on her. The man stood two feet away from her and her temperature spiked like a dangerous fever.

The Department of Energy could market Erik as an alternative fuel source. Think of all the natural resources he could save.

Sydney reached into the bowl of lollipops, picked out a red one, ripped off the plastic, and stuck it into her mouth. She needed something sweet right now, and she was all out of chocolate.

The front door opened with another gust of wind, and Erik hurriedly closed it behind him. Erik crossed the room and snatched up two pops from the bowl. "I forgot my sucker." One was orange, the other green. He stopped directly in front of her and reached up and slowly pulled the pop out of her mouth. He frowned at the glistening red sucker. "I misjudged you, Dr. Sydney."

"How?" She took her lollipop back and wrapped her lips around the sweet treat.

Erik's light blue eyes darkened as he stared at her mouth. "I figured you to be a chocolate kind of woman."

"I am." His deduction wasn't that amazing. Most women loved chocolate. "I ate my last candy bar before lunch."

His smile made her knees feel like two Hershey bars

under a July sun. "Do you always eat dessert before the meal?"

"Every chance I get."

Erik's rich, deep laughter rolled across the room as he headed back to the door. "Hans is waiting for me in the truck. I'll be in touch real soon." Then he was gone.

Sydney lowered herself into one of the waiting room chairs to finish her pop. She slowly sucked on the sweet as she thought about orange lollipops, eating dessert first, and a certain gorgeous Viking.

Gunnar Olsen turned on the windshield wipers of his Jeep as the gentle flurries that had been falling all afternoon turned into a snow shower. The weather station had predicted only a "dusting" by morning. By the thick amount of snowflakes being illuminated by his headlights, he wouldn't put money on only a dusting. Seven o'clock at night and it was pitch dark outside. The stars and the moon were obscured by the clouds causing the snow.

Tonight it had been his turn to do the weekly food shopping. Usually his grandfather joined either Erik or him, depending on whose turn it was. Hans had refused to come along with him. His grandfather was still upset by his afternoon visit to the doctor and the fact that Erik was making him get the blood work. He had stood by his twin brother's decision and told his grandfather he would be getting that blood work, even if he had to tie him down to do it. Immediately after dinner, Hans had accused them both of ganging up on an old man and had stormed into his bedroom without even asking what was for dessert.

Fear twisted in Gunnar's gut. Something was wrong with his grandfather, he just knew it. His grandfather had never backed away from an argument. Hans also had never acted like a spoiled child before. Erik had told him that Sydney hadn't found anything wrong this afternoon, but she needed to see Hans's blood work results. That didn't sound good to him.

All the little memory glitches that his grandfather had been having lately didn't seem so innocent now. Three weeks ago Hans had asked him how Merete was. Merete had been Hans's youngest daughter and Gunnar's mother. She also had been dead for over three years now. Erik and he had chalked it up to "a senior moment." Last night's episode of Hans walking around the town alone and confused, and without any coat on, hadn't been so innocent.

What were Erik and he going to do if something serious was wrong with their grandfather? Hans was the only family they had left, besides each other. Their father, Rolf Olsen, had been an only child, and his family line ended with his twin sons. His mother, Merete, had two older sisters who were living in Minnesota. Erik and he had met his aunts when they had first come to America looking for their grandfather. Both women and their families had had nothing good to say about Merete or their own father. Neither family had welcomed them, and within a day they had left Minnesota with a crumbled piece of paper with Hans Bergesen's last known address, Misty Harbor, Maine.

Thankfully, Hans had opened not only his home to his grandsons, but his heart as well. Erik and he hadn't planned on staying in America, only visiting their grandfather and as gently as possible breaking the news that his youngest daughter was now gone. Hans had taken the news of his daughter's death harder than he or Erik had thought the old man would. Hans and Merete hadn't been in communication with each other for over twenty-five years, since her marriage to Rolf Olsen. As far as he and Erik had known, their grandfather hadn't even known of their existence.

They had been wrong. Hans had known Merete had twin sons and even had a couple of old photographs of them as small boys, which one of the local villagers back in Norway had sent him. By the time their visit was up, not only had their hearts accepted their grandfather, but they had both fallen in love with the rocky coast of Maine and the small harbor town that Hans had called home for over twenty years. There had been nothing in Norway to call them back home.

Not a day had gone by that he had regretted that decision. He was pretty sure Erik felt the same way.

Gunnar slowed down further as the road before him curved out of sight. The thick trees that were on both sides of the deserted road were casting eerie shadows. The shortcut back home was sparingly traveled in good weather. Tonight it appeared he had the whole road to himself. Just him, his troubled thoughts, and a million swirling snowflakes.

The glint of red tail lights and the gleam of metal were the first sign of trouble up ahead. He slowed down to nearly a crawl as a stopped car came into view. It was parked half on the road, half off. Between the swarming snowflakes he could barely see a hooded figure crouched by the rear wheel struggling with the tire iron. A propped-up flashlight was sending out a feeble beam of light at the tire. Someone had truly picked a rotten night to break down. The snow was now coming thick and furious, and the wind had picked up. Snow seemed to be falling in every direction, including upward.

He slowly pulled in behind the disabled car and turned on his emergency flashers. The figure by the rear tire stood up, put a hand in front of its eyes to block the glare of his headlights, and stared at his Jeep. Gunnar silently cursed when he realized the figure was that of a woman, or more probable due to her size, a teenage girl. What in the world was a girl doing out on a night like this? Some parent was more than likely in the process of getting a few gray hairs. He didn't recognize the car.

Gunnar pulled on the pair of gloves that had been

sitting on the passenger seat and cursed the fact that he hadn't thought to bring a hat with him on his simple shopping trip. He tugged the collar of his coat up as high as it would go and stepped out into the blustery night. His long hair stung as it whipped across his face. "Hi," he yelled over the wind and tried to tuck his hair into the collar of his coat. "Need a hand?"

"Thanks, Gunnar." The wind whipped the feminine voice away into the darkness.

He frowned as he stepped in front of the girl. He knew that voice, and it didn't belong to the strange car parked halfway onto the road. Maggie Pierce drove an old green Chevy, not a crimson Ford. "Maggie?"

"Yeah." Margaret Franklin Pierce lowered her hand, now that Gunnar's big body was blocking the blinding light.

Gunnar stared down into the face that had plagued his dreams and could practically count each and every freckle standing out against Maggie's pale skin. A few strands of her red hair were blowing across her cheek, and her normally emerald green eyes appeared dark and worried. She looked half frozen, and he wanted nothing more than to pull her into his arms and surround her with his warmth. He knew better. Maggie wasn't interested in him. In the seven months since she had moved back to Misty Harbor, he had asked her out four different times. She had politely, but firmly, rejected his every advance.

The only thing that had kept his hope alive was the fact she hadn't accepted anyone else's invitations either. In a town the size of Misty Harbor, if a single, unattached female so much as smiled at a certain man, everyone would know. Dating seemed to be a community event.

Margaret Franklin Pierce, with her adorable freckles and fiery red hair, had frustrated him like no other woman. She was the one woman he seemed to have spent his life looking for, and amazingly she didn't come alone. Maggie, who was recently divorced, had a delightful four-year-old daughter. Katie, who was the spitting image of her mother, had stolen his heart the first time he met her along the docks last spring.

"What are you doing out here in the middle of nowhere?" He glanced up and down the deserted road. The nearest house was half a mile away. "Where's your car?" He glanced at the red Ford, but didn't see anyone inside it. "Where's Katie?" His glance slid to her trembling fingers, and his voice rose with each word, "And where in the hell are your gloves?" Didn't the woman have one ounce of brains in that beautiful head of hers?

Gunnar knew he had raised his voice, but he couldn't help himself. The thought of Maggie out here in the middle of the woods with a disabled car in a snowstorm was enough to turn his hair gray. Didn't she realize all the things that could happen to her?

"Are you going to help me, or lecture me?" Maggie jammed her hands into her coat pockets.

"Both." Gunnar stormed over to the red car and frowned at the tire. "It's flat."

Maggie rolled her eyes and muttered something that sounded like "Only on the bottom."

He bit the inside of his cheek to prevent a smile. "Did you say something?"

"I said you're very observant."

"Don't you know how to fix a flat?" The trunk was open, and the spare and jack were already out and lying on the ground. Obviously she knew something about it, so why wasn't it done?

"My father taught me years ago." Maggie reached down and picked up the tire iron and handed it to him.

He could feel the cold of the metal bar through his gloves. The black metal must have felt like ice to Maggie's bare hands. "So why didn't you change this one?" By the amount of snow accumulating on the spare tire, he would guess that Maggie had been broken down for at least fifteen to twenty minutes. Plenty of time to change a flat.

"Because of men and their obsession with power tools."

He squatted down in front of the tire and started to loosen the first lug nut. "Explain that one to me." The second nut came loose after he actually put some muscle behind it. He frowned at the wheel as he strained to loosen the third nut.

"I can hear you grunting, Gunnar." Maggie jammed her hands into her coat pockets and rocked back on her heels. "If you are having that hard of a time, imagine me trying to unloosen those lug nuts. I was straining things no lady should be straining."

The tire iron slipped off the lug nut, and he whacked his knuckle against the rim. "Are you all right? You aren't hurt, are you?" He didn't want to think about what she might have been straining. Just the thought of Maggie sweating and grunting was enough to make him rock hard.

"I'm fine. Whoever put those lug nuts on my mother's car that tight is the one who isn't going to be fine." Maggie kicked at the spare tire lying on the ground. "Half the cars on the road are driven by women, and then some moron in a mechanics' suit tightens down lug nuts so damn snug that it takes a massive six-foot, four-inch Viking grunting and groaning to loosen the suckers." Maggie gave the tire another whack.

"I'm only six-foot-two." Gunnar clamped his back teeth together as he strained against the last nut. He would be damned before he allowed Maggie to see him struggling with something as simple as changing a flat. Masculine pride was one hell of a thing. "Who put these tires on your mother's car?" He would personally see that whoever it was got an earful.

"I don't know, but my father will." Maggie hunched her shoulders against the wind. "I'm sure he'll have a few choice words to say to the idiot."

"Why are you driving your mom's car?"

"Mine wouldn't start, and I needed to get to the university's library to do some research on a paper that is due soon."

"Where are your gloves?"

"Lost them this afternoon someplace. It's the second pair I lost, and it's only November."

Gunnar glanced over his shoulder at Maggie as the last nut came loose. If she hunched any farther into her coat, she would disappear. There was no sense in both of them freezing their butts off. "Go sit in the Jeep where it's warm."

Maggie shifted her weight. "I can finish changing the tire now that all the nuts are loose." She picked up the jack. "Thanks."

Gunnar stood up and took the jack right out of her hands. There was no way he was allowing Maggie, or any other woman, to change a tire while he stood by and watched. "Get in the Jeep, Maggie."

"I really think I should . . ."

He gently took her elbow and marched her to the driver's side of his Jeep and opened the door. "In case you haven't noticed, Maggie, it's damn cold out here. The longer I have to argue with you, the colder I'm becoming." He reached in and turned the heater on high. "Now get in."

Maggie stiffened, but didn't get into the warm vehicle. "I can at least help you."

"Changing a flat doesn't require two people." He gave her a gentle nudge. "Stop being so darn independent and allow me to do a good deed. I need them."

"Good deeds? Are you trying for a Boy Scout badge or something?"

"Nope, trying to impress Santa Claus this year so he'll bring me what I want."

Maggie slid into the warmth of the Jeep. "Must be one whopper of a present."

He grinned. "Oh, it is." He wondered what she would

say if he told her that his list consisted of only one item: Maggie Pierce. Be it a date, or a kiss under the mistletoe, or an evening locked in each other's arms. He wanted Maggie, and he wasn't above asking some fat little man in a red suit, who played with elves, for her. He had tried everything else. He closed the door, ducked his head against the wind, and made his way back to her flat tire.

Four and half minutes later, he slammed the trunk closed and made his way to the Jeep. His ears felt frozen, but his blood was still running thick and hot. Maggie stepped out of the Jeep. Even wrapped from head to mid calf in a wool coat, she still had the power to heat his blood.

"How can I thank you, Gunnar?"

Lord, what a dangerous question that was. He felt a melted snowflake slide down his neck and shivered. "By making sure you don't get another flat again. Do you have any idea of how many different things could have gone wrong out here tonight? Why don't you have a cell phone?"

"Lord, you sound worse than my father and brother put together." Maggie shook her head.

"Someone's got to look out for you!" One good browsing trip through a bookstore and anyone would realize that the entire country was overrun by serial killers and psychopaths.

"I can take care of myself, Olsen." Maggie's chin went up about an inch, and her hands were clenched into fists.

"Oh, yeah, you didn't seem to be doing too good a job at it when I showed up." In the harsh glare of his headlights, she looked fighting mad and entirely too kissable. "What would you have done if I hadn't come along?"

"I would have walked to the Miller place and asked to use the phone."

"What if they weren't home?" Why couldn't she see how dangerous it truly was?

"Then I would have tried the Carsons' and then the Blacks'. You forget, Gunnar, that I was born and raised here. I know just about everyone in this town. Besides, I know how to change a flat. The reason I couldn't this time was because of some testosterone-driven male who overcompensated with his air wrench."

He couldn't argue that point. "That may be true, Maggie, but you were the one who had to pay the consequences for his lack of judgment. It could have been a lot worse than a pair of cold hands."

She glanced nervously down the deserted road and wrapped her arms around her waist and buried her hands beneath her arms. "Why are you trying to scare me?"

"I'm not." He didn't want to see fear in those gorgeous green eyes. Only caution. "I just don't want to see anything bad happen to you."

"It won't." Maggie stood there a moment longer staring at him. "Thank you for stopping and helping me out, Gunnar. Me and my frozen hands greatly appreciate it." She gave him a warm smile before turning and opening the car door.

"You're welcome." It was on the tip of his tongue to ask her out to dinner or even a movie, but he clamped his teeth together and kept silent. He didn't want Maggie to feel obliged to go out with him just because he had changed her flat.

Maggie slid behind the wheel of her mother's car, started the engine, and smiled at him. "I hope Santa brings you whatever it is you're wishing for, Gunnar."

He grinned. He had talked with Maggie more tonight than the past seven months combined. She had even called him Gunnar, instead of Olsen. Things were looking up. "He just might, Maggie. He just might."

Chapter Four

Erik parked his pickup behind Sydney's fancy S.U.V. and stared at her cottage. Smoke from her chimney curled invitingly into the night sky to mix with the few remaining snowflakes still falling. It seemed that every light within the small dwelling was burning. At eight o'clock at night, most of the houses on Conrad Street had a light or two lit, but Sydney's was the only one lit up as if she owned stock in the electric company. Maybe she did. Sydney Fletcher, M.D., came from a background where stock options, 401Ks, and portfolios were probably discussed over cocktails at the nearest country club. Hell, she probably cut her baby teeth on mutual funds and knowing the difference between a bull and bear market. His knowledge of such things came from thirty-second commercials that made him feel totally inadequate because he hadn't a clue as to what they were talking about, let alone selling.

It didn't matter to him that the town's doctor had a few more coins in the bank than most of Misty Harbor's residents. What did matter was how good of a doctor she was. Something was wrong with his grandfather, and not only was she the closest doctor, but Hans seemed to like her. Getting his grandfather to her this afternoon had been a major battle. Getting Hans to see a doctor he didn't know or like would have been impossible.

This afternoon he had told her he would be in touch with her soon, but she probably hadn't been expecting him to come knocking on her door four hours later. He would have been here earlier, but Gunnar had gotten tied up at the food store. There was no way he was leaving his grandfather alone in the house, so he had vacuumed the living room and done two loads of laundry while waiting for his brother to return.

As soon as he had helped Gunnar unload the groceries from the Jeep, he had driven straight to Conrad Street. The inch or two of snow on the ground wasn't worth worrying about. His grandfather's health consumed all his thoughts. He got out of the truck and headed up the walkway to Sydney's little white cottage with its colonial blue front door. He refused to dwell on the fact that his heart had kicked in an extra beat or two in anticipation of seeing the beautiful doctor again.

Erik gave a small chuckle as he sidestepped a group of pumpkins sitting on the stoop and rang the doorbell. So what if all his thoughts weren't entirely of his grandfather? The only thing that proved was that he was human. There wasn't a man alive who could look at Sydney and not appreciate the view. The male DNA wasn't made up that way.

The front door opened, and his heart nearly slammed out of his chest. Sydney in a white lab coat and with her hair pulled back in a clip was beautiful and professional. Sydney dressed in a backless gown with her hair piled on top of her head at her sister's wedding had been gorgeous and sophisticated. The Sydney standing before him was adorable and cuddly, and looked as if she had just crawled out from under a quilt. He was in trouble. Big trouble. He never should have come to her cottage.

This was the Sydney that could tempt his soul and destroy his reasoning.

"Erik?"

He had to swallow twice before he could find his voice. "How is it that you always know which one of us is which?" Tonight after his shower, he hadn't bothered to pull his hair back into its usual ponytail. He had left it loose, just like Gunnar's. Yet Sydney had known it was he, and she hadn't cheated by glancing at the driveway to see which vehicle was parked there. He had been watching her eyes.

"Lucky guess." Sydney opened the door wider and stood back, silently inviting him in. "Is something wrong with Hans? He hasn't taken any more walks, has he?"

"No, my grandfather is fine. Mad at his grandsons, but fine. Gunnar is home with him now."

Sydney closed the door against the cold night air and the few remaining snowflakes still falling. "What brings you out on a night like this?"

"I needed to talk to you about my grandfather." Erik glanced around the living room and tried not to smile. The doctor wasn't actually a slob, but she wasn't exactly neat either. The coffee table in front of a powder blue couch was overflowing with a laptop computer, books, a stack of magazines with an empty frozen-dinner plastic dish perched on top, and a week's worth of newspapers. A half-filled coffee cup sat near the computer, which was displaying a bunch of words he couldn't read from that distance. Two afghans were rumpled on the couch, and a television was in the far corner. Two matching plaid chairs were in front of the huge bay window that faced the street. One was empty with a pile of books stacked by its feet. The other one held a two-foot-high stuffed animal. It was a big, fat, fluffy puffin.

The smile that had been threatening to emerge almost came at the sight of the puffin. The display of three bouquets of flowers killed it instantly. The men of Misty Harbor were wasting no time trying to court the lovely doctor. A dozen wilting white roses sat in a crystal vase by the couch. Daisies, long past their prime, were on the mantel, and a fall arrangement sat on the small table between the two chairs.

"I see the men of Misty Harbor have been calling." He tried to keep his voice even and not allow the doctor to see how the sight of all those flowers had gotten to him.

"They are persistent, I'll give them that." Sydney frowned at the roses.

He knew he should keep his mouth shut, but he couldn't help but ask the question, "Meet anyone interesting yet?" He was curious as to which man might have captured the lovely doctor's attention. Misty Harbor wasn't known for its sophisticated business district or high-powered executives.

"I'm not interested in a relationship." Sydney stepped farther into the room and purposely changed the subject. "Hans is my patient, Erik, not you. There's such a thing as patient confidentiality."

"I agree. Under normal circumstances I wouldn't dream of butting my nose into my grandfather's business." He stared down at his work-roughened hands. "You have to agree, these aren't normal circumstances."

Sydney gave a sigh. "You're right." With a glance down at her attire, she said, "I'm not exactly dressed for company."

He smiled at the baggy plaid flannel pants and the oversized long-sleeve thermal top with a strange-looking cartoon tiger on it. The tiger seemed to be bouncing on its tail. Thick, heavy socks, with honey pots printed all over them, covered her feet. Sydney was covered from her neck to the soles of her feet. Seductive, she wasn't. Warm and cuddly, definitely. He had to wonder if she actually slept in all those clothes. "You wore less clothes to your sister's wedding." The backless rose-colored gown had raised more than his blood pressure.

He had ended up sitting quite a lot during the reception. "If you want to change into something less revealing, like a spacesuit, I will wait, or I could stop by the office tomorrow if you prefer?"

Sydney gave her attire one last fleeting glance, grimaced, and then pushed her still damp hair behind her ears. "I just made a fresh pot of coffee. Would you care for a cup?"

"I don't want to put you to any trouble."

"If it was trouble, I wouldn't have asked." Sydney started for the kitchen. "What do you take in it?"

"Nothing, I take it black." He knew from last night at his house that Sydney took hers with cream, no sugar. He glanced at the smoldering log in the fireplace. "Who taught you to make a fire?"

"No one, why?" Sydney reached into a cabinet and grabbed a cup.

From his position in the living room, he could see part of the kitchen. It wasn't much better than the living room. There were books and magazines on the counter, along with two boxes of candy and another vase filled with flowers. Pink flowers this time. "If you are trying for a smoldering fire that gives off plenty of smoke and aroma, you did a great job. But, if you are trying for heat, you have it all wrong." Thankfully, most of the smoke was going up the flue and not into the room.

Sydney walked back into the room and handed him his coffee as she frowned at the fireplace. "I wanted heat. It took me nearly an hour to get just the smoke. I've been waiting for it to burst into flames any minute now."

He took a sip of coffee and tried not to grimace. He was sure he had tasted worse, but right now he couldn't remember when. Sydney obviously didn't possess the same "cooking gene" that her sister Gwen had inherited. Gwen's restaurant was the toast of the coast. He carefully set the mug down on top of a magazine and glanced at the stack of firewood placed so neatly in the brass log holder with a fancy blue bow tied on top. "Where's your kindling?"

"Right there." Sydney's hand waved in the direction of the thick logs.

There was a wooden box off to the side designed to hold old newspapers. Maybe Sydney had stored the kindling there. He opened the lid and frowned at the few pieces of crumbled-up newspaper. Not so much as a toothpick was in the box. "Do you know what kindling is?"

"Sure." Sydney picked up her half-finished coffee. "Firewood."

"You're half right. It's small pieces of firewood used to start the fire; then you put on the logs once you get the fire going."

"I knew that." Sydney glared at the smoldering log on the iron grate behind the fire screen. "Newspaper seemed to work just fine."

"Where's your wood pile?"

"On the side porch." She led the way into the kitchen where the side door was. "Why?"

"I'll be right in." Erik stepped out onto the small porch as Sydney flipped a light switch and gave him light. A small pile of dry wood was stacked neatly against the house and away from the elements. Farther in the yard he could see a much larger pile of chopped wood. Thankfully, he spotted an axe next to the dry pile. He picked up a couple pieces of wood and the axe and made his way into the yard where a chopping block stood. In a matter of minutes he had enough kindling to last Sydney for a while.

He placed the kindling on the porch and kicked off his now snow-covered boots. He carried the kindling into the living room and dumped most of it into the fancy carved wooden box. "That should last you a couple of fires."

"You didn't have to do that, Erik. Thank you." Sydney moved closer to the fireplace. "I never was a Girl Scout.

I was too busy patching up my dolls to learn how to make a good fire."

He would lay money on the fact that Sydney had never made a fire in her life before moving to Maine. "It's easy, I'll show you." He removed the fire screen and pushed the smoldering log to the rear of the grate. "First you start with crumpled newspaper and the smallest pieces of kindling." He put a combination of both onto the grate and lit the paper. By the time the newspaper had burned to ashes, the small pieces of wood were flaming. "Once you get to this part, you add some bigger pieces." He carefully placed a couple large pieces of the kindling he had just chopped onto the fire.

"What about the big pieces?" Sydney watched as flames licked upward.

"You wait until the bigger pieces of kindling catch, and then you add the actual firewood." Erik sat back on his heels and took off his coat as the heat started to pour from the fireplace. "You had it right, except you were missing the kindling part. An easy mistake."

"I never had a real fireplace before. In our parents' house there was one, but my mom had it changed over to one of those propane gas things. All you had to do was flip a switch and instant fire."

"It's not the same, is it?"

"No, it's not." Sydney smiled. "I much prefer this."

He grinned. Maybe there was just a touch of country in the big city doctor after all. "You can add your firewood now."

Sydney picked up a log. "Right on top?"

"Be careful not to burn your hands."

"I already figured that one out for myself." Sydney placed two fat pieces of wood onto the flames and then repositioned the screen. "That looks much better, Erik. Thank you, again."

"You're welcome." Sydney was entirely too close. He could smell her shampoo from her damp hair. She smelled like exotic flowers from some tropical island

and wood smoke. An enticing combination. This was how he had always pictured himself with his future wife. Sitting in front of a roaring fire on a cold winter night. Of course, he had always pictured his future wife with a lot less clothes on. "Can we talk about my grandfather now that I got your fire blazing?"

Sydney stood up and dusted her hands off. "Of course." She glanced at his coffee cup. "Would you like me to warm that up for you?"

"No, it's fine the way it is." He didn't think heat would improve the taste. He sat in the wing-back chair that didn't hold the puffin. "What's wrong with my grandfather?"

"That I can't answer, Erik." Sydney sat on the couch and tucked her feet up under her. "I need to run a lot more tests before I can pinpoint any one thing."

"What do you think is wrong with him?" Sydney was hedging. He could read it in her eyes. Feel it in his heart. "You must have an idea."

"Right now I'm just trying to gather up the symptoms. Hans isn't the most cooperative patient I've ever had."

"What kind of symptoms?" He forced himself to drink some of the coffee before setting it back down again. "Tell me what you are looking for."

"Anything, and everything." She picked up a notepad that had been hiding in the stack of newspaper and turned to a blank page. "Tell me everything you have noticed about your grandfather, and don't leave anything out."

"He's stubborn, opinionated, and has a heart the size of Maine."

Sydney smiled. "Let's start with his eating habits."

"If it has fins or can breathe under water, Hans will eat it." Erik shuddered at the memory of some of the things Hans had eaten over the years. Things that he or Gunnar wouldn't touch on a bet. "He doesn't drink. On the rare occasion, only a beer or two. He thinks breakfast is the most important meal of the day and insists on whipping up mountains of pancakes or plates filled with bacon and eggs. About six months ago he got on this orange juice kick and forces Gunnar and me to drink a big glass of it every morning."

"So Hans cooks breakfast every morning?"

"Every morning for the past three years. We all fend for ourselves for lunch, and Gunnar and I take turns cooking dinner."

"How's his appetite?"

"Great in the morning, but I've been noticing it slacking off somewhat at dinner."

"Is he tired more?"

"He's going to bed earlier than he used to, but I hear him prowling the house at night sometimes. He falls asleep in the recliner a lot, but he will insist that he's only resting his eyes."

"What about his memory? Does he seem confused sometimes? Forgetful?"

"Yeah, but he's seventy-three years old. Isn't it normal to be a bit forgetful?" He sat forward and impatiently ran his fingers through his long hair. "Hell, even I forget things occasionally."

"We all do that." Sydney toyed with the pen for a moment. "What kind of things does he forget?"

"He forgets words sometimes. At first we thought it was the English translation that was giving him problems, but then we realized he was having trouble thinking of the word even in Norwegian." He gave a heavy sigh and told Sydney his biggest fear. "The other week he was talking about Merete, my mother, as if she were still alive. It was like he expected her to walk in the front door at any moment."

Sydney's beautiful green eyes held sympathy. "How long ago did your mother die?"

"Three years. She was killed when the car she was driving went off a cliff and into the sea a couple of months before Gunnar and I came to America." He finished the story and allowed Sydney to make of it what she would. "Two weeks before that a sudden storm blew up off the coast. My father and two other fishermen were lost to the sea that fateful day."

"Was your mother Hans's only child?"

He could read the questions in her eyes, but she didn't ask the one he had feared the most. *Did your mother purposely drive off that cliff? Had your mother been that distraught at the death of her husband?* Merete Olsen might not have been suicidal, but she had definitely been drunk. His mother had been swimming in a bottle for as far back as he could remember.

"My mother had two older sisters. Both have families of their own and live in Minnesota. When Hans came to America, that was where he had first gone. What happened to him there the first couple of years, I don't know. I can only gather there are some hard feelings, because neither one of my aunts had anything nice to say about Hans or my mother. When Hans left Minnesota, he moved here to Misty Harbor, got himself a boat, and made his living from the sea."

"Why didn't he go back to Norway to be with your mother?"

"That I can't answer." He wearily sat back in the chair and tried to sift through the pieces of his family history. "I do know that my grandfather and mother had a parting of the ways when she turned eighteen and, against his wishes, married my father. Less than a year later, he left Norway. My mother always claimed it was because she married a 'lowly' fisherman."

"She must have loved your father very much to go against her father's wishes."

"If she did, I never saw it." He didn't want to air his family's dirty laundry, but if it could help his grandfather, he would spill his guts on the evening news. "My father was a fisherman who spent sunup to sundown out on the sea and barely kept a roof above our heads and food in our bellies. He was a big man who wanted a large family and wasn't afraid of hard work. From what I heard, Hans was an extremely wealthy man who thought my father wanted my mother for the wealth she could bring him."

"Let me guess," sighed Sydney as she hugged an afghan to her chest. "Hans cut off your mother, figuring that would be the end of their romance. Instead, as soon as your mother turned eighteen, she married your father."

"How do you say? Bingo?"

"Yeah, bingo." Sydney shook her head sadly. "What happened next?"

"Hans left Norway and moved to America to be with his other two daughters." He shrugged. "Ten months later, Gunnar and I made our appearance."

"So your mother and Hans never got a chance to bridge that gap." Sydney glanced down at the notebook. "I'm sure that must play heavily on Hans's mind. Does he talk about his other daughters or their families?"

"Only in terms that are unrepeatable in front of a lady. I don't know what happened out there in Minnesota, but whatever it was, it must not have been pretty."

"Do you think your grandfather is depressed?"

"Depressed how? Are you talking sad, melancholy, or suicidal?"

"Any of those or all of them."

"He's not suicidal. I wouldn't class him as sad; but sometimes I see him look through old photographs, and he seems melancholy. Especially if they are the pictures of my grandmother. Even after thirty years, I think he still misses her."

Sydney softly smiled. "How did Hans seem when you and Gunnar showed up on his doorstep one day out of the blue?"

"Better than what we were expecting. After meeting our aunts, we weren't too sure what kind of reception to expect. Hans was thrilled to see us. He recognized us right away."

"How?"

"Turns out he had kept in contact with a local villager all those years. He knew Merete had twin sons. The villager had sent him pictures of us throughout the years and the occasional update. He had known that Gunnar had fallen out of a tree when he had been six and ended up with eight stitches in a very, let's say, tender place. He also knew that I had my appendix out when I was twelve. The pictures and updates stopped when we were about thirteen or so. The villager had died."

"But he immediately recognized you both?"

"While we were standing on his doorstep trying to figure out what to call him, Hans Bergesen or *Bestefar.*" He chuckled at the memory. "The only thing he couldn't figure out was which one was which. We confused him so often that I started to tie back my hair so he would know the difference."

"That explains it." Sydney looked at his hair. "Why isn't it back tonight?"

"My grandfather is pretty good at telling the difference nowadays." There was no way he was going to admit he had been testing her.

"The Hans you are describing doesn't match up with the Hans I met. What happened to the man who disowned his daughter for falling in love with a common fisherman?"

"I can't answer that either. But I can tell you my grandfather took the news of my mother's death a lot harder than Gunnar or I thought he would, considering the circumstances."

"Regrets. No closure." Sydney buried her feet under the afghan and stared across the room at him. "With Merete gone, Hans could no longer fix what was wrong between them. Time had run out. Whatever was in the past would now follow him into the future."

"That all makes sense, but it doesn't explain why he was standing confused and seemingly lost in the middle of Eagle's Nest Road last night without his coat." He glanced over at the fireplace and saw the flames dancing and giving off plenty of heat. The fire was roaring now, and it had to be at least seventy degrees in the room. He was starting to sweat, and Sydney was now buried under the afghan. The good doctor was never going to survive her first winter in Maine.

"True, but now I have some background information to work with."

"The family's dirty laundry will help you figure out what's wrong with my grandfather?"

"Your family's laundry isn't dirty." Sydney chuckled. "You should hear some of the laundry I could tell you about. It would take more than bleach to get some of those families' stains out."

"So what's your diagnosis?"

"It would be totally incompetent of me to offer up a diagnosis at this early stage, Erik."

"Okay, that's fair. But give me a hint or something. Hans is the only family Gunnar and I have left, and we are worried sick about him."

"I can't, Erik." She slowly shook her head.

He captured her gaze and said the word that he and Gunnar had been dreading. The word they had whispered in the dark, afraid that if they said it in the light of day, it would come true. "Alzheimer's."

Sydney went still, and her eyes widened slightly. "What makes you think that?" Her green-eyed gaze went to her computer screen before shooting back to his.

Erik felt the lump in his throat grow. Sydney had been thinking Alzheimer's, too. "Isn't that the disease that makes people, especially older people, forget things?"

"Yes, but there is no way I can link your grandfather to Alzheimer's after a twenty-minute office visit." Sydney slowly closed the lid on the laptop. "There are a lot of different other disease processes that can mimic early Alzheimer's. They have to be ruled out."

"What kind of diseases?"

"Depression, thyroid imbalances, vitamin B12 deficiency, and tumors."

"Why can't you just test for Alzheimer's?"

"Because there is no single diagnostic test for the disease. First we rule out everything that can be ruled out. If there's no physical abnormalities, then Hans should have a psychiatric and neurological examination."

"Hans will never agree to that, Sydney." Erik felt his world shift a little. It just got darker. He had been praying that Sydney would laugh when he had said Alzheimer's. "I barely got him into your office this afternoon. I'll never get him up to Bangor to see a specialist."

"Maybe you won't have to, Erik." Sydney's long, slender fingers toyed with the fringe on the afghan. "It could be something simple."

"Alzheimer's is fatal, isn't it?" He wanted to know the worst case scenario.

"The course of the disease varies from person to person, Erik. Some people have it for the last five years of their lives, while others may have it for as many as twenty years."

A spark of hope lightened his heart. "Twenty years is good."

"Twenty years is great, but I think you are getting ahead of yourself. No one said Hans has Alzheimer's."

He nodded his head at her laptop. "What were you looking up?"

A soft pink blush swept up Sydney's cheeks. "Memory problems in the aging. Disorientation. Things like that. I'll be perfectly honest with you, Erik. My specialty in Baltimore was pediatrics."

"You were a baby doctor?" That explained why she had looked so natural holding Carol Ann Burton's screaming baby the other day in the office.

"Yes, but I was trained just like every other doctor. I'm just more comfortable with colicky babies and ear infections than I am with memory loss."

"In Misty Harbor I'm afraid you'll have more opportunity to treat high cholesterol and bladder control problems than you will immunizing babies. In case you haven't noticed, our town isn't overflowing with children."

"I noticed, and I think it's a shame. This seems to be a wonderful place to raise a family."

Just the way she had said it made him think that Sydney wouldn't be opposed to raising a family. There had been something wishful in her voice. *Dangerous thoughts, Olsen! Sydney and a family don't even belong in the same thought, let alone the same brain.* He forced himself to look away from Sydney's concerned green eyes and concentrate on the fire. The woman didn't even know how to light a proper fire for land's sake. But she definitely knew how to shop for underwear. Dreams of her and a certain lacy blue bra had plagued his sleep all night long. He had awakened this morning more tired than when he had gone to bed. Frustration had been a burning ache, all centered in one very noticeable place.

"Say it is Alzheimer's, is there anything that can be done for Hans?"

"Yes. Medicine has come a long way in the past several years. There's no cure for the disease yet. But each day they are discovering and understand more and more. For mild or moderate cases there are drugs that on rare occasions can make the symptoms get slightly better, some stay the same or the progress of the disease is actually slowed. Therapy is used regularly."

"You mean lie on the couch and tell me all about your mother therapy?"

"No." Sydney lightly laughed. "I'm talking about art and music therapy. Does Hans have any hobbies?"

"Not really. I wouldn't class fishing as a hobby with Hans."

"Then, maybe it's time he started one. He could keep

his mind active by taking up an instrument or even learning how to watercolor."

He shook his head. "Are we talking about the same man here? My grandfather would never take up the flute or go around painting pictures of flowers."

"Then, I suggest you and Gunnar get busy and try to find him a hobby. One that he can do at home, and that's safe. I wouldn't put him into a garage filled with power tools, though. Even if Alzheimer's never enters the picture, Hans should be doing something with his days besides just making you and your brother a big breakfast. Even I would be depressed if all I had to do all day was cook two Vikings pancakes."

"You're right. In the summer Hans is always taking out the rowboat and fishing in the cove. With winter just settling in for the long haul, he will need to keep busy." He stood up and stretched. For the first time in days he felt good about the future. Talking with Sydney had lightened his concern about his grandfather. He didn't know how Gunnar or he would be getting him to all those doctors' visits yet to come, but they would. Hans's health was very important to them.

Now they at least had a plan. Sydney would handle the diagnosis, while Gunnar and he figured out what kind of hobby Hans might enjoy. He finally had something to do. A plan of action.

"Thanks for taking the time and talking with me tonight, Sydney."

"You're welcome." Sydney stood up. "I don't want you thinking too far ahead, Erik. It won't help or solve anything. We'll take this one step at a time. Okay?"

"Sounds like a plan to me." He picked up his coat and carried the half-filled coffee cup into the kitchen. He poured the black liquid down the drain and glanced around the rest of the room and the dining room. Someone should seriously build Sydney some bookshelves. A square table that he recognized from Gwen's restaurant was sitting in the middle of the dining room. Four restaurant chairs surrounded it. Three of the chairs held books or magazines. A vase of wilted red roses sat on the table, along with more books. A few scattered cardboard boxes took up the corners of the room. Homey, it wasn't. Even libraries held more personality. "It looks like you were cramming for an exam."

"Just keeping abreast of things." Sydney wrapped the afghan around her shoulders. "Reading is my hobby."

He glanced at some of the titles of the books on the counter. *Forensic Art and Illustration, Dead Reckoning, Forensic Pathology,* and a stack of other books by such authors as Jonathan Kellerman, James Patterson, and Karin Slaughter. He never would have guessed that Sydney's reading pleasure went to books about death and murder. "Nice light reading, I see." He didn't know if he should run for his life or be impressed that she could read such books and actually sleep at night. He got squeamish at the sight of blood.

"Fascinating subject."

He looked at her and still couldn't picture this petite woman, who wore Disney pajamas, cuddled up in bed with a blood-and-guts book. "If you say so."

"To a doctor it is." Sydney grinned. "What do you find fascinating to read, *Moby Dick?*"

"Never did like that book." He walked to the door that led to the side porch, where he had left his boots. "When I get the chance, which isn't too often, I prefer history. The American Revolution, in particular, fascinates me." He smiled at the shocked look on Sydney's face that she was trying so hard to hide. "What were you expecting, *Playboy?*"

"Of course not," denied Sydney, but the fiery blush sweeping up her cheeks revealed her lie. "I just wasn't expecting American history, that's all."

He pulled on his coat and opened the door. "Admit it, Sydney. You misjudged this lowly fisherman."

"I did not!" Sydney's cheeks flared hotter.

"Okay, I'll admit to picking up an issue of *Playboy*

once or twice in my youth." He skimmed his fingertips down her heated smooth cheek. "But I only got them to read the articles." With a flirtatious wink he stepped out onto the porch. "I'll see you next week when I bring my grandfather in for the blood test results." He closed the door as her lips curved up into a smile.

Temptation wore that same smile, and he had just discovered he was a very weak man.

He wanted Sydney Fletcher more than he wanted his next breath. His fingers trembled as he dragged his hand down his face and then jammed his sock-covered feet into his boots. It had been a close call a minute ago. Standing in the doorway, he had almost kissed her. Instead, he had run his fingertips down the satiny smoothness of her heated cheek. He had told himself one touch wouldn't harm anything, but it had. That simple touch had started the crumbling around his resolve.

Dr. Sydney Fletcher was definitely not the right woman for him. She came from class and money, big money. He came from hard work and the sea. She was sophistication and beauty. He was calluses, blisters, and fourteen-hour work days come the summer months. He could never give her the material possessions that she was used to. It would be his mother and father all over again.

There was no way he was going down that destructive path.

Chapter Five

Gunnar slammed the hood closed on Maggie's car and glanced at her daughter, Katie. The little sprite was trying to make a snowman from about an inch worth of melting snow still covering the ground. So far the snowman stood about a foot high and seemed to have two heads. Maggie's mom, Connie, had dressed the little girl in so much snow gear, the poor kid could barely move her arms. "So, Katie, do you need any help there?" He had just spent the last hour getting Maggie's car to start and giving it a proper going over. All in all, it was in good shape for being eight years old. A clogged fuel line had been the culprit. A quick run to the nearest auto parts store had solved that problem.

"There's not enough snow to build a big one." Katie kneeled on the white-speckled grass and frowned up at him.

Katie had rolled snowballs across the front lawn, gathering every bit of snow she could. It still hadn't been enough. "It's only the beginning of November, give it time. By March you'll be sick of snow and looking forward to spring."

Katie giggled. "That's what my mommy said this morning before she went to school."

"Your mother sounds like a smart woman to me." He had quite a few opinions on Maggie Franklin Pierce, and most weren't suitable for her daughter's tender ears.

Katie stood up and brushed at a few specks of snow clinging to her pink snowsuit. "You have a white-and-green boat, don't you?"

"You know I do. You saw me on it this summer." Katie was a constant visitor to the docks. Thankfully, her mother usually was tagging along when she wasn't working or attending classes at the nearest college.

"You look like your brother, the one who catches fish instead of lobsters."

"We're twins." He wiped his hands on a rag and gathered up his tools. "Do you know what twins are?"

"Yep. I had twins in the school I went to before we moved here. But they didn't look alike."

"Some twins do and some twins don't."

"Gunnar, I brought you some hot cocoa and cookies that Katie and I baked yesterday." Connie Franklin, Maggie's mother, hurried down the driveway with a heavy tray. Her coat wasn't buttoned, and her yellow boots were unlatched and flopping against her shins.

"I told you, you didn't have to go through all that trouble, Mrs. Franklin." She had invited him inside, but he had politely refused. Maggie was going to be a pure spitfire when she found out he had stopped by and fixed her car. He didn't want to add socializing with her mother to the crime.

"After everything you did for my Maggie last night, a simple cup of cocoa and a few cookies is the least I can do." Connie looked around for a place to set the tray and ended up setting it on the hood of Gunnar's Jeep. "I get chills when I think of all the things that could have happened to her last night broken down like that."

Connie handed him and Katie both a cup of cocoa. His had steam wafting from the hot liquid. Katie's appeared much cooler. "And then you show up here this morning to fix her car." Connie gave him a discerning look before adding, "It's just so neighborly and friendly of you."

He could read the speculation in Connie's gaze, but he didn't rise to the bait. Connie was wondering what his relationship was with her daughter. Wouldn't she be surprised. "Where did you get the tires put on your car?" He still had a bone to pick with some overzealous mechanic.

Connie chuckled. "My husband was taking care of that first thing this morning. He went out of here like a bear who had been denied his winter hibernation." Connie held up the plate of iced cookies. "Help yourself, please."

Katie, who now sported a cocoa mustache, proudly said, "I decorated the Christmas tree ones all by myself."

"You did? They look beautiful." He picked up a cookie he was pretty sure was supposed to be a Christmas tree. The other cookies were either stars or candy canes.

"I made them blue and yellow because they are my favorite colors." Katie chose a blue tree, with red sugar sprinkled all over it. "Grandmom says we need to practice baking because Christmas will be here before you know it."

He noticed that Maggie's daughter liked to mimic adults. Katie was the spitting image of her mother, right down to the horde of freckles, fiery red hair, and the most amazing green eyes. Maggie would have looked like Katie twenty-one years ago. Amazing. "I bet you can't wait for Christmas to come, can you, sprite?"

"Mom says first we have to get through Thanksgiving. Then we can talk about Santa."

He laughed as Connie rolled her eyes. "I bet you already know what you want from Santa, don't you?"

"Yep." Katie gave him a beautiful smile, one that was

guaranteed to break more than one man's heart in the future. "I want a baby brother. A nice, quiet baby brother. Not like my best friend Elizabeth Claire's baby brother, Devin." Katie finished off her cocoa and handed the empty cup back to her grandmother.

He bit the inside of his cheek so he wouldn't laugh at Connie's shocked expression. Maggie's mom was staring at Katie as if she had never seen the child before. "What does your mom say about that?"

Katie pouted for a moment and kicked at a small pile of gray, slushy snow. "She told me to ask for a bike."

This time there was no holding back his laughter. It filled the morning skies and brought a smile to Katie's face. Connie seemed to relax. "I'm going to go pack you up some cookies to take home to your grandfather and brother, Gunnar. I'm sure you men haven't gotten around to any baking yet."

"Can't rightly say that we have." He barely managed to get dinner on the table every other night. Cooking wasn't one of his best qualities. If the men at the Olsen house wanted something sweet, they hit the bakery department at Barley's Food Store.

"Katherine Leigh Pierce, can I trust you not to say anything embarrassing while I'm gone?"

Katie slowly nodded as she bit off the top of her tree.

Connie turned to him, "I'll be right back," and then hurried back up the driveway.

Gunnar stared down at the top of Katie's head. A yellow knit hat, with a bear's head perched on top, met his gaze.

Katie glanced up at him and shyly asked, "What's embarrassing mean?"

This time his laughter startled a couple birds resting in a nearby pine tree. "I bet your mother loves you to pieces."

Katie shook her head, thought about it for a moment, and said, "Sometimes she hugs me real tight, but I haven't broken yet."

Gunnar squatted, so she didn't have to look so far up when they talked. "Can you do me a favor?"

"Okay."

"I need you to give something to your mommy, okay?"

"What?"

Gunnar stood back up and headed for his Jeep. He grabbed the bag sitting on the passenger seat and handed it to Katie. "Give her this, and tell her not to lose them." On the way back from the auto supply store, he had stopped into Krup's General Store and bought Maggie three different pairs of gloves. Technically, two pairs were gloves, and one pair was fat, thick, blue mittens with white snowflakes. Last night he had had a nightmare concerning flat tires and Maggie's frozen fingers.

"What is it?" Katie shook the bag, but didn't open it.

"It's a surprise." Gunnar gave the pom-pom bear head a gentle pat. "If you help me out on this favor, maybe when the weather warms up I can take you and your mother out on my boat. Deal?" Warmer weather was six months away. He should be able to convince Maggie to go on a boat ride with him in six months. But he didn't know how. After seven months, it had taken five stubborn lug nuts to get her to talk to him.

"A boat ride!" Katie clutched the bag against her chest and grinned. "Deal!"

Connie hurried back down the drive. This time she was holding a plate piled with cookies and covered in Saran Wrap. "Here you go, Gunnar." She handed him the plate. "Thank you for stopping and helping Maggie last night, and for coming over here this morning and fixing her car. Bob just didn't know when he would get to it, and Gary, her brother, has been busy, too."

"As I told you before, it's no problem. Glad to help her out." He carefully placed the plate of cookies on the passenger seat. "Thanks for the cookies; they look great."

"It's the least I could do." Connie picked up the tray and put her other hand on Katie's shoulder and moved them both away from the Jeep. "I'm sure Maggie will want to thank you personally later for fixing her car."

He wasn't looking forward to that conversation. He gave Connie a weak smile and waved to Katie as he pulled away. Maggie was too darn independent and prickly. She probably would disconnect the fuel line and beat him over the head with it for butting into her business. Then again, he was beginning to wonder what the gloves were going to taste like when she jammed them down his throat.

Maybe he should stop worrying about his grandfather's mind and start worrying about his own. There had to be something misfiring in his brain for him to keep wanting a woman who had clearly and repeatedly turned down every one of his overtures.

Hans sat in the booth at McDonald's in Sullivan and silently ate his second Egg McMuffin. Erik, his grandson, had already polished off his second and was working his way through a hash brown and an apple cinnamon danish. Erik had been acting strange all morning.

Getting the blood work hadn't been bad. Hadn't even hurt. He just wished he could remember why he had needed to get it. He wished he could remember a lot of stuff lately. What had happened to the days when he was sharp as a tack and could remember the name of his third-grade teacher? Lately Erik and Gunnar had been staring at him funny. The boys had worry in their eyes, and that scared him.

They were the only family he had left. What would he do if they left him?

For a man who had had three beautiful daughters, money, and such dreams of the future, he had ended up with none of it. Yet God had been merciful. He had sent his grandsons across the ocean to be with him. His two daughters out in Minnesota had abandoned him when they had learned his money had run out. It hadn't mattered to them that he had spent it all on them and their families. He had paid for everything, and had been left with nothing.

Gunnar and Erik didn't care about money, but he couldn't think of one reason they wouldn't abandon him once they learned his mind was going. They were both young, strong boys with their whole lives ahead of them. Why would they want some old man who had difficulty remembering which day of the week it was or where he had put the remote? Why would they want an old man who had disowned their mother and not been a part of their lives for the first twenty-four years?

"I need to stop at a few places after we load up at the Marine Supply," Erik said.

"No problem," Hans replied after swallowing the last of the Egg McMuffin. "I didn't have anything to do anyway." *Or at least anything I remember having to do.*

"Have you ever noticed how many different coins there are?" Erik asked.

"Coins? What kind of coins?" What in the world was Erik blabbering on about now? Earlier, on their way in to Sullivan, Erik had been jabbering on and on about stamps. Simple postage stamps. As far as he knew, the only good stamp was the one you licked and stuck on a envelope so the electric company didn't turn off the juice. Why anyone wanted to collect the sticky pieces of paper was beyond him.

"All kinds of coins, *Bestefar.*"

Erik was up to something. His grandsons only called him grandfather in Norwegian when they wanted something. He was being buttered up for something he was probably not going to like. "Coins are only good for buying things."

"Some people collect coins. They consider them little

miniature works of art." Erik finished off his orange juice and gave him a brilliant smile. "Most collectors collect coins from all over the world."

"What's with you, Erik? You thought stamps were miniature works of art, too." He crumbled up his wrappings and put them on the tray. "Is there something you aren't telling me?"

"Like what?"

"I don't know." He finished off the rest of his orange juice. "Maybe you have taken an interest in art. Do you want to go to school and become an artist instead of a fisherman?" He wiped his mouth with the paper napkin and studied the shocked look on Erik's face. "It's nothing to be embarrassed about, Erik. Lots of men draw."

"I'm not embarrassed, and I don't want to go to school or even to a museum. I just thought you might enjoy taking up a hobby. Stamp or coin collecting are very good hobbies."

"Why would I want a hobby?" *God, the next thing I know, they'll have me making peanut-butter-and-pine-cone bird feeders and putting me into a home!*

"I don't know. I thought maybe you get lonely or bored while Gunnar and I work all day."

"Hell no, I'm not bored." He slid out of the booth and picked up the tray. "Can't a man enjoy his well-earned retirement?" He stomped across the restaurant, dumped the garbage, and prayed that Erik couldn't see him too well. A cold sweat had broken out across his brow, and his fingers were trembling.

His grandsons knew something was wrong with him. It was only a matter of time now before they abandoned him, too.

Maggie was furiously mad, and deep down inside she was excited. She refused to even think about the warm, wonderful feeling that Gunnar had caused, by not only fixing her car, but by buying her three pairs of gloves, as she drove to the docks, instead of home. She was sticking to being mad. It was safer. Gunnar had had no right to show up at her parents' house and replace the fuel line in her car yesterday. Her mother was giving her sly looks, and her father had praised Gunnar's mechanical abilities all through breakfast. Her father should have saved his breath; everyone in Misty Harbor knew that Gunnar Olsen was a true genius when it came to engines.

Yesterday she hadn't had the time between school and going to her part-time job at the restaurant, where she waited tables, to confront Gunnar. Those remaining few precious hours of the day were her quality time to spend with Katie. Tonight she wasn't working, so she had a few extra minutes to confront Gunnar. How long could it take to thank him and then tell him to butt out of her life?

She parked the car and refused to dwell on how smooth it had run. That still didn't excuse Gunnar for giving her mother, or Katie, the wrong idea. Her two precious hours yesterday with Katie had consisted of her daughter telling her everything Gunnar had said and done. Including the fact that Katie had told Gunnar she wanted a baby brother for Christmas.

She stared out the windshield at the long dock where Gunnar moored his boat. It was there, riding next to the pier on the gray, churning sea. It was late afternoon, and already the light was beginning to fade from the sky. By the amount of clouds building in the south, she wouldn't be surprised if they had snow again tonight. She shivered at the thought and got out of the car. She wanted to be home, tucked safely and warmly inside the house, before that first flake fell.

Maggie waved or called a greeting to just about every fisherman on the docks. She knew them all, and they all knew her. Misty Harbor was a tight-knit community that had a musketeer mentality. All for one, one for all. When she had hurt one of the town's residents five years ago, they had banded together around him and shunned her. It was nothing more than what she had deserved, and she didn't hold it against the townspeople. When Daniel Creighton, the man she had hurt, had forgiven her earlier this year, the people had once again opened their arms and hearts to her.

She was finally back home and at peace. She had her priorities straight and not only a short-term goal, but also a long-term goal. None of those goals or priorities included a man. It didn't matter that Gunnar's deep, rumbling voice turned her knees weak or that she became in danger of hyperventilating whenever she saw him. It was lust, plain and simple. That was all the attraction could be. She had done the "lust" thing before, and all she had gotten out of it was heartache, pain, and the greatest gift she had ever received, her daughter, Katie. She wasn't going that route again. Single parenthood wasn't all that it was cracked up to be.

The wind whipped around her, plastering her long coat against her legs and tugging the hood off her head. In the summer months she envied the fishermen and their freedom to ride the waves and make their living from the bountiful sea. During the winter months she felt sorry for the men who fought the weather and the freezing cold for whatever the sea would part with. Her father and brother were both fishermen. She had lived with their glory in the summer and their misery in the winter. It was a hard life.

She approached Gunnar's gleaming white-and-green boat named *Norsk Drøm.* The Olsen twins were known for the cleanest boats in the harbor. She could see Gunnar in the wheelhouse; but his back was turned to her, so he hadn't spotted her yet. She took a moment to study him as she carefully stepped on board. Today he wore a thick coat, making his shoulders appear wider, and a green knit cap. The bobbing of the boat gave her a sense of comfort. She could now blame her weak knees on the churning water.

Gunnar turned before her second foot landed. His welcoming smile nearly stole her breath. She forced herself to glare back at him as he stepped out of the wheelhouse. "Maggie, what brings you here?"

"You know darn well what brings me here." She wrapped her arms around herself as a sudden gust of wind kicked up.

"You can thank me someplace warmer." Gunnar grabbed her elbow and gently ushered her into the glass-enclosed wheelhouse and closed the door behind them. A portable heater warmed the interior somewhat.

"Who said I was going to thank you?" Maggie snatched off her gloves and tossed them onto the cushioned bench.

"You will, you know." Gunnar leaned against the door frame and smiled at her.

"How do you know I will?" She didn't like him being so smug about it. Of course she was going to thank him, and then she was going to tell him to butt out of her life. She knew Misty Harbor was short on females, but she was officially out of the running. For goodness sake, she was a mother. Gunnar should go cast his beguiling net elsewhere.

"Because your mother raised you with manners." Gunnar's smile turned into a grin. "If Connie ever found out you didn't personally thank me for fixing your car, she would be mortified."

"Leave my mother out of this." She unbuttoned her coat. "I didn't ask you to look at my car." Why in the blazes did Gunnar have it so warm in here?

"Think of me as a Good Samaritan." Gunnar pushed away from the wall and took a step closer.

"It was a low blow promising Katie a ride on your boat." She impatiently brushed her windblown hair behind her shoulders and away from her face. "Katie will do just about anything to get on a boat. She's either going to end up being a lobster fisherman or marrying some guy named Noah."

"We made a deal." Gunnar glanced at the gloves she had tossed onto the bench and took another step closer. There was barely a foot between them. "I see she held up her end of the deal, so I'll hold up mine."

She could feel the heat of his body, and her treacherous body reacted immediately. Her mouth went dry, and her stomach dropped to the vicinity of her knees. Lust was a horrible emotion. She was a grown woman with a four-year-old child who depended on her. She should be able to control such a reaction. Only Gunnar made her lose that control. His identical twin brother, Erik, never so much as struck a spark. Gunnar caused an inferno.

Furious and scared by her reaction to his nearness and the desire she saw burning in Gunnar's light blue eyes, she raised her voice and demanded, "What gives you the right to butt into my life?"

Gunnar closed the remaining distance between them, tilted her head back, and growled, "This does." His mouth covered hers before she could offer up a protest.

The moment Gunnar's mouth touched hers, she lost the battle with her control. Lusting after Gunnar without touching him was one thing. Being in his arms was an entirely different story. Heat branded her, and his mouth consumed her every thought. Her arms encircled his neck, and she stretched up on her toes to get closer.

Gunnar groaned when she bit his lower lip. Strong arms hauled her closer as his tongue thrust into her mouth. Heavy winter coats and layers of clothes made it impossible to get as close as she wanted. Her fingers yanked off his knit cap and threaded their way through his long golden hair.

Gunnar's chest rumbled with his pleasure as he deepened the kiss further. His hands swept inside her coat to cup her jean-clad bottom and press her hips upward against the front of his jeans and his obvious desire.

She could feel how much he wanted her, and she trembled with anticipation. Gunnar was a big man, and she hadn't been with a man in a very long time. She couldn't remember ever wanting her ex-husband, Jeremy, this badly. Not even the night Katie had been conceived. Her hips thrust upward in a silent plea, and Gunnar groaned.

The wooden door frame touched her shoulders as Gunnar broke the kiss, raised her higher, and trailed his hot mouth down her throat. She gasped and arched her head back as his lips moved against her throat. "*Jeg vil ha De.*"

She had no idea what he had just said, but it sounded like poetry to her. Her hands were busy trying to push his coat off his shoulders. Too many clothes were between them. She needed to touch him. Her breathing sounded harsh and loud to her own ears. "English," she begged.

Gunnar fought the haze of desire, raised his head, and gazed at Maggie's flushed face. Passion had put color into her cheeks, and her mouth was moist and swollen from his kiss. Her green eyes darkened with fire. Emerald fire. His fingers squeezed her lusciously curved bottom, and he could feel himself about to explode. He had to swallow the groan lodged in his throat before he could say, "I said, 'I want you.' " Never had he wanted a woman the way he wanted this flame-haired spitfire. With one kiss he was about to embarrass himself.

He took a deep breath and tried to regain control over his body.

Maggie's eyes darkened further as her gaze darted to the cushioned bench in the wheelhouse. Slowly she nodded.

Temptation reared its ugly head, and for one wild moment he thought that maybe his control would shatter. He closed his eyes and prayed for strength. They couldn't do this. His fingers trembled as he slowly lowered her back to the deck. What they needed was space between them. Lots of space. He needed to think. There was no way he was making love to Maggie for the first time on his boat.

Maggie frowned as he stepped away from her and shook his head. "What's wrong?" Her voice held a deep, seductive note and confusion.

"We can't do this, Maggie." He inhaled deeply and tried to control his breathing. It wasn't helping. Nothing seemed to be helping. All he wanted to do was lay Maggie down and bury himself so deep inside her she would never want to be anywhere else but in his arms.

A red tide of embarrassment started to sweep up Maggie's face as she pulled her coat closed. Maggie's gaze lowered to the wooden deck. "Okay," she whispered.

His fingers plowed through his hair at her timid reaction. Where had the spitfire disappeared to? The last thing in the world he wanted to do was embarrass Maggie or make her uncomfortable. "There is no way you can know how much I want you right this minute." He jammed his hands onto his hips and proudly stood in front of her. The evidence of his rock-hard desire was plain to see. It was going to take him a long time before he would be able to walk the dock to the parking lot.

Maggie's gaze shot to the front of his jeans before dropping back down to the deck. If possible, her blush intensified.

In frustration, he snapped, "There is no way I'm making love to my future wife in the wheelhouse of my boat!"

Maggie's head snapped up at that announcement. The fire of desire that had been burning in her eyes turned into a different kind of fire. *"Future wife?"*

That didn't come out like he had hoped. It was a little too soon to be talking about the future or marriage, but he wanted her to know he wasn't interested in a quick roll on the high seas. He respected Maggie too much for that. "Yeah, future wife."

"Who in the hell said anything about marriage?" The

flush that had been staining her cheeks had drastically faded. Maggie looked pale and shaken.

"I guess I am." The more he tried to get his foot out of his mouth, the farther it seemed to go in. This wasn't going at all like he had hoped.

"It's lust, Gunnar, not love." Maggie straightened to her full height of five-foot-six. "There is no way I'm allowing lust to lead to marriage again."

"Is that all you think that was about, Maggie? Lust?" He couldn't keep the hurt out of his voice. Had he been wrong all along?

"What else could it be? You don't know me, Gunnar, and I don't know you."

"Whose fault is that? Every time I've asked you out, you said no. You are the one who won't give us a chance."

The fire in her eyes dimmed. "Four times."

"Four times what?"

"You've asked me out on four different occasions." Maggie rebuttoned her coat, but wouldn't meet his gaze. She looked forlorn.

He slowly nodded. Maggie had remembered exactly how many times he had asked her out. Did that mean anything, or was he being the eternal optimist his brother always accused him of being? "And you politely turned me down each and every time."

Maggie slowly nodded. "It was the smart thing to do. I'm sorry, but there's no room in my life for a relationship, Gunnar."

"So we could have made love a moment ago and it wouldn't have meant anything to you?"

Tears seemed to fill her eyes. "It would have meant more than you would have ever known." Maggie opened the door and hurried across the deck.

He watched as she gracefully stepped on the dock and hurried toward the parking lot. He wanted to go after her, but knew it wouldn't have done any good.

"Dumb, dumb, dumb!" He wanted to bang his head

against the wall, and probably would have if he could have found a solid wall. Calling himself stupid wasn't going to solve anything. He never should have mentioned marriage. He never should have called a halt to their lovemaking.

He should have loved Maggie the way she deserved to be loved, and maybe, just maybe, she wouldn't have hated him come tomorrow.

Chapter Six

Sydney absently flipped through the channels on the television and wondered why there never seemed to be anything good on. She was in the mood for some mind candy, and her usual reading material didn't fit that requirement. Tonight the channels were filled with depressing news, game shows, and the inside scoop on Pierce Brosnan's love life. She thought Pierce was a great actor and incredibly good looking. But the last thing she wanted tonight was to listen to how he, or anyone else, was getting "some" while she spent her thirtieth birthday alone and wallowing in self-pity.

She was having a pity party, and she had purposely invited no one. It wasn't a pretty sight to see a thirty-year-old single woman look back upon her life and examine all her mistakes.

It was her own fault she was alone. Gwen had invited her to dinner at the restaurant, but she didn't feel like watching Gwen hustle between eating her dinner and checking constantly on things in the kitchen. Daniel, Gwen's husband, would have kept her company, but all he would want to talk about would be Gwen. Daniel had a one-track mind, and it ran straight to Gwen. It would have been cute if it didn't pound home the fact that Gwen wasn't supposed to be the one to get married first. She was. Being the oldest daughter, she should have been the one Daddy walked down the aisle first.

In the make-believe world of Barbie dolls from her youth, she had been the one to wear the white lace gown with its pearl-seeded bodice to walk down the aisle and marry the perfect man, Dr. Ken. Barbie's kid sister, Stacey, had been the flower girl, never the bride.

She wasn't really mad at Gwen, and deep down inside she was truly happy for her sister and Daniel. She was only disappointed in herself. Her younger sister had shown her what true happiness could be. Gwen had reached for her dream of owning her own restaurant. Not only had she achieved that dream, but she had managed to find love along the way. It hadn't taken her four years to do it either. More like four months.

Four years of living with Richard should have given her a pretty good idea as to what kind of man he was. It hadn't. For some perverse reason she had yet to examine, she had had blinders on where Richard had been concerned. Even both of her sisters had known he was a jerk. A tight-fisted, needle-ass jerk. She wasn't sure which sister had originated Richard's nickname of Needle Ass, but she could now see how it had fit. Richard was so tight with his money, hence the reasoning that a needle wouldn't fit up it.

When she had first met Richard, she had fallen instantly in love. What wasn't to love about a tall, dark, and gorgeous man who shared the same dream she had. He wanted to become a doctor. They had met in med school and were living together by the end of the year. They had had so much in common that it seemed to be inevitable that they would end up together forever. They had been perfect for each other. Or so she had thought.

Over the years she had learned their differences. To

her, becoming a doctor meant achieving her goal, helping other people, and loving to do it. To Richard, becoming a doctor meant playing at God, expecting everyone to bow down before him, and becoming rich. The money meant more to Richard than the act of healing someone.

To her, achieving her career goal meant she could move on to the next goal of marriage and starting a family. She had visualized a well-balanced life consisting of a husband, two or three children, and her career. Her parents had balanced their careers with a family. She had wanted the same. After Richard had achieved his career goal of becoming a doctor, all he wanted to do was reap whatever rewards he could get out of it. Fancy vacations, a high-powered sports car, and an expensive condominium. To top it all off, Richard had expected her to pay for half of it. Like a fool, she had.

Sydney clicked off the infomerical on the television and sighed as blessed silence filled the cottage. If she had to listen to that annoying woman's voice spouting on about the cleaning power of Wonder-Klean for one more minute, she would have screamed. Tonight was definitely not a television night. She was allowing herself this one night to feel sorry for herself and the loss of a dream. Then she was putting it all behind her and moving on with her life.

So what if she wasn't married yet and the possibility of children seemed farther into the distance. Did she really want to be married to a man like Richard? Not in this, or any other, lifetime. What kind of father would he have made anyway? Not a very good one, that was for sure.

She should be counting her blessings instead of feeling sorry for herself. Walking in on Richard and the big-breasted ER nurse was probably one of the best things to happen to her in a long time. It had awakened her to the fact there wasn't going to be a future with

Richard. She would have preferred a much gentler way of waking up to that fact, but it had served the purpose.

Walking out on Richard had been easier than she had thought it would be. Her heart had been broken, not because of Richard, but because she had had to release the dream of a family she had been clinging to for so long. She could live with that. What she couldn't live with was a man who had cheated on her.

Richard was pond scum, and logically she knew the entire episode had been his fault. But deep down inside, there was an emotional little voice that questioned why he had done it. Was there something wrong with her? Should she have been more passionate in bed? Had she been too clinical? Too cold? Her love life with Richard had been okay, but nothing to write a book about. She should have been home more, and spent less time at the office and hospital. She should have been more understanding and supportive of Richard's career. She should have been *more.*

She knew she was a good doctor and had confidence in herself and her growing practice in Misty Harbor. Her confidence in herself as a "desirable" woman had been shattered by her first and only lover. If she couldn't hold a man who had so much in common with her professionally, how was she ever to find, and hold, a husband and then start a family together?

Depressed by that thought, she got up from the couch and headed for the refrigerator. Gwen had surprised her when she had gotten home from work and found dinner waiting in the refrigerator with directions on how to microwave it taped to the Styrofoam container. There was also a bottle of white wine chilling and a brightly wrapped present sitting on the counter. Gwen's present had been a pair of white flannel pajamas with puffins printed all over them and a pair of fluffy black slippers with big puffin heads. Tonight she would be sleeping in style.

Her youngest sister, Jocelyn, had had a bouquet of

balloons delivered to the office. All of the balloons had been black with such endearing sayings as, *Over The Hill, The Big 30!,* and *Trust No One Over 30!* printed all over them. To soften the blow, the balloons had been tied to a jewelry box containing a gold bracelet made out of sea creatures and starfish. She had called her sister earlier to thank her and to deliver a promise of a payback when she turned thirty.

She had also talked to both of her parents and her grandfather about an hour ago. They were all saving her birthday presents for when they came up next week for Thanksgiving. This year Thanksgiving was being held at Gwen and Daniel's place. It would be nice to see the whole family again, but she wasn't looking forward to the concerned, "knowing" looks. Her family had been very supportive of her move to Maine, but they all seemed to be treading very carefully around her. It was as if they thought she would fall apart if someone slipped and mentioned Richard's name.

Richard, the obnoxious jerk who obviously didn't understand the meaning of "get lost," had sent her a huge, expensive bouquet of flowers with birthday wishes and a "missing you" message. She had taken the beautiful arrangement out to the local nursing home with her this morning and had given it to one of the residents who never received visitors or flowers. Richard's money had been well spent when she saw Maude smile for the first time.

Her heart lightened at the memory of the soft, hesitant smile that had curved Maude's lips. She carefully arranged the food on the plate, placed it in the microwave, and pressed the appropriate buttons. The pity party was now officially over. She had nothing to feel sorry about. She had her health and the love of her family. She had a wonderfully rewarding career, a hot meal warming in the oven, and a bottle of fine wine chilling in the refrigerator. Being thirty wasn't too bad so far. She slipped on her new puffin slippers, jiggled her new bracelet, and dug through the drawer looking for the cork screw.

The sound of the doorbell chiming and the beep from the microwave echoed simultaneously. She went to answer the door.

Her heart skipped a beat and then picked up an extra one or two when she saw who was standing on her door stoop. "Erik?" For one wild moment she prayed that Erik moonlighted as a male stripper and that one of her sisters had indeed sent her a birthday present to remember.

"How do you do that?" Erik shook his head and glanced over at his brother's Jeep parked in the driveway. "Did Gunnar call you to warn you I was stopping over?"

"No, Gunnar hasn't called." The phone had rung twice; both times Richard's number had flashed on the caller I.D. She hadn't bothered to answer either time. She had nothing to say to the jerk, and she had no idea why he was being so darn nice all of a sudden. "Is Hans okay?" She stood back and allowed Erik to step into her cottage. Disappointment tugged at her gut when she noticed he wasn't carrying a boom box. Strippers always brought their own music, didn't they? So much for really celebrating the big 3-0.

"He's fine, but stubborn." Erik glanced at the blazing fire and smiled. "I see you got the hang of it now."

"Thanks to you and the kindling you chopped the other night." She felt a little self-conscious about not having the fire going the right way the last time Erik had stopped by. Erik probably thought she was a total moron, but at least he had been nice enough not to laugh.

"You still have plenty of it left? If you're running low, I could split some more for you."

"No, there seems to be plenty." She hadn't gotten around to splitting some of the logs herself yet, but she was planning on it. How hard could it be? Being a self-sufficient woman meant doing it herself or at least paying someone to do it for her. She didn't think Erik would accept money from her. "What brings you by?"

"Hans won't go to see that specialist you told us about." Erik stared at the dozen black balloons tied to the banister. "The big 3-0?"

She knew from his chart that Erik was twenty-seven. He was three years younger than she was. It didn't matter that in January he would be twenty-eight and only two years younger. Tonight he was three years younger, and she should be ashamed of her indecent thoughts, all concerning his hot, incredible body. "My sister's idea of a joke."

"Gwen?"

"No, Jocelyn." Erik knew Jocelyn. He had danced with her three times at Gwen's wedding. She remembered that vividly, because not once had Erik asked her to dance. She had danced with every single man invited to the reception, and most of the married ones. Everyone, that is, but Erik. She hated to admit it, but Jocelyn was the perfect age for Erik. "She's coming up next weekend for Thanksgiving."

Erik gave her a funny look she couldn't interpret. "That's good. I guess you are missing her by now."

"Not really. I talk more to her now than I did while living in the same city." Jocelyn had been busy with her new career as an assistant district attorney while she and Richard had concentrated on their careers. When she had left Richard, she hadn't gone home to her parents; she had headed straight for Jocelyn's. Her sister had welcomed her with open arms, a pull-out couch, and unlimited access to her wardrobe. Which was a good thing considering Sydney had shown up on her doorstep without any shoes on.

"Sisters should be close." Erik glanced toward the kitchen when the microwave beeped again. "Am I interrupting your dinner?"

"Not really." She headed for the kitchen. "Gwen

took pity on me and brought me over dinner. There's enough here for two if you want to join me."

"Thank you, but I just finished dinner at home."

"How about a bowl of Gwen's chili and a glass of wine? I don't want to eat in front of you." She reached into the refrigerator and pulled out a container of chili from yesterday. "I even have some French bread to go along with it."

"You talked me into it." Erik took off his coat and hung it on the back of one of the dining room chairs. "What can I do to help?"

"Open the wine." She nodded toward a drawer that was still pulled out as she poured the chili into a bowl. "There's a cork screw in there someplace."

Erik rummaged through the tangled mess of metal utensils. "Is it really your birthday?"

"Afraid so." She removed her dinner from the microwave and put in the bowl of chili. She glanced at the mess piled on the dining room table and decided the counter would have to do. She moved the box holding her puffin pajamas onto the pile and tossed the wrapping paper. "Glasses are in the cabinet above the dishwasher."

Erik poured them each a glass of wine as she set out the silverware and the bread. They worked in harmony as she finished getting their dinner ready, and he straightened the pile of newspapers and magazines that were threatening to cause an avalanche off the counter.

A moment later she joined Erik at the counter and placed a bowl of steaming chili in front of him. "Sorry for the mess; I wasn't expecting company." At least tonight she wasn't already dressed in her Tigger pajamas. She had changed out of her office clothes and pantyhose as soon as she had gotten home from work. Her pity party attire consisted of worn jeans, thick socks, and a baggy Baltimore Ravens gray sweatshirt. The puffin slippers added a nice elderly touch. No one could ever accuse her of being Mrs. Robinson and trying to seduce the younger man.

"No problem."

She studied the rough planes and angles of Erik's chiseled face. Some time tonight he had taken the time to shave. His jaw was smooth bronze. His long golden hair, which brushed the top of his shoulders, looked clean and silky. It was the clear honesty in his light blue eyes that drew and held her attention. Erik didn't mind that the dining room table had been too cluttered for them to use. Richard would have hit the ceiling and demanded to know what she had been doing all day long. It wouldn't have mattered to Richard that she had just spent ten hours at the office. Or that she had to make do with coffee and crackers for lunch because she had been too busy talking to a high school senior who had just found out she was pregnant and was in a panic as to how to break it to her parents.

Erik picked up his wineglass and held it up until she repeated his action. "Happy birthday, Sydney." Erik's glass lightly tapped against hers.

"Thank you." She took a sip of wine and was suddenly glad for the company. No one should celebrate his or her birthday alone, even when that person didn't want to celebrate it. "How's the arm?" Tomorrow Erik was scheduled to come in and get the stitches out.

"Fine." Erik picked up a slice of bread. "It itches like the devil, though."

"It's healing."

"That's what my grandfather says." Erik chewed a bite of bread. "Last night he talked only in Norwegian."

"Was he making sense?" Norwegian was Hans's native tongue. She wasn't surprised, even though she had learned that Hans had been fluent in English even before coming to America.

"Yes. I'm trying to come up with a hobby that would catch his interest and hopefully give him something to do during the days while Gunnar and I have to work. I already struck out with coins and stamps."

"Hans doesn't seem like the type to lick stamps into books, Erik."

"I know, but it's hard finding a *safe* hobby, one where he doesn't have to use power tools and saws. Tonight Gunnar brought home some football and baseball cards."

"Any luck?" The flounder Gwen had prepared melted in her mouth.

"None. My grandfather doesn't care for either sport. He prefers ice hockey." Erik scraped the bottom of the bowl. "He can't understand why anyone would want to collect pictures of the players when they could be watching the game."

She grinned. "I have to agree with him there, Erik. I never saw the sense in card collecting."

"So what do you suggest?"

"Well, let's see, my grandfather plays golf."

"Taking up golf in Maine, in the middle of winter? Why didn't I think of that one?" Erik's eyes sparkled with laughter.

"I didn't say for Hans to take up golf. I was just thinking out loud. What about tying flies? Doesn't Hans like to fish?"

"He fishes all right, but not with flies. As my grandfather would say, real men use real bait." Erik finished his light meal.

"Yuck." She refused to think about how the flounder on her plate had been caught. "Did you and Gunnar try to talk to your grandfather again about going to the specialist up in Bangor?"

"For two hours straight, and he won't budge an inch. He refuses to go. Says there is nothing wrong with him that a good night's sleep wouldn't cure."

"I was afraid of that." This afternoon she had sat with Hans in her office and gone over the blood test results. His cholesterol was only a couple of points over two hundred. A modification in his diet should handle that. Blood sugar was fine and within range. His thyroid was working just fine, and everything else appeared to be normal. Hans had sat there, smiling and nodding his head the whole time, muttering, "I told you so." Hans didn't want to hear about the next step.

Erik and Gunnar, who had both come with their grandfather to the appointment, couldn't get him to see reason. Hans's grandsons were big enough to drag the man to the specialist, but it wouldn't do any good. If Hans wouldn't cooperate with the doctor, there was no sense in going. "Somehow we have to convince Hans it's in his best interest to go. If it is Alzheimer's, there are some promising medicines out there that might help him."

"How?" Erik got up and started to load the dishwasher. "He won't listen to us. Can't you just prescribe the medicine for him?"

"I can't do that, Erik. I can't diagnose him with Alzheimer's on the basis of a simple blood test. He needs psychiatric and neurological examinations. Memory loss is a symptom of the aging process. Hans isn't getting any younger."

"None of us are." Erik ran his fingers through his hair and looked around in frustration. "So what are we supposed to do now? Nothing?"

She knew her hands were about as tied as Erik's and Gunnar's. There were a couple more tests she could perform, but in reality they weren't what Hans needed. She wasn't even sure she could convince Hans to do the tests, let alone come back and see her again. As Erik had stated, Hans was being stubborn. "You and your brother can keep a closer eye on him and document everything."

"How will writing down everything help my grandfather?"

"You bring it with you when you finally convince him

to see a specialist." It was the best advice she could give, and she felt so inadequate offering it.

"What if we can't convince him to go?"

"He needs to see the doctor, Erik."

"He already has a doctor, Sydney." Erik's gaze bore into hers. "You."

She glanced away from the anxiety gleaming in Erik's eyes. Being a pediatrician had been a lot easier in one regard. The patient could be as stubborn as he wanted to be about going to the doctor, but the parents always won out in the end. "You heard him today. Hans doesn't feel there is anything wrong with him, so he isn't coming back to see me, Erik."

"Fine, then you come to him."

"You want me to do a house call?"

"Not exactly."

"What exactly do you want me to do? I can't just stop by and take his blood pressure and temperature and ask him what he has forgotten lately."

"You could come around more and watch him."

"I can't just stop by your house and monitor your grandfather, Erik." She shook her head and wondered at the insanity of it. "I think Hans will catch on pretty quickly as to what is happening and would resent us both for it." She took a sip of wine.

"Not if you're there as my girlfriend."

As his words sunk in, the wine went down the wrong way, and she ended up choking. Erik was on his feet immediately and hurried around to the back of her stool. He looked ready to start pounding on her back as she got her breath back, shook her head, and croaked out, "I'm fine." Her hand came up to ward off any helpful blow.

Erik reached for a clean glass, filled it with cold water, and handed it to her. "Here, drink this."

She took the glass and slowly sipped. She wasn't too positive her throat would work, but was thankful she hadn't embarrassed herself by spitting the wine out of her nose or something equally as gross. The second sip went down smoother, and she managed a small smile. "Thanks."

"I didn't say that right, did I?" Erik sat back down, and for some reason, he was the one who looked embarrassed.

"It depends on what you were trying to say." She didn't think she had anything wrong with her hearing, but she couldn't imagine why she had heard the word "girlfriend."

"Hear me out on this, Sydney." Erik played with the stem of his empty wineglass. "You're right about you not being able to just stop in and check up on Hans. He would see through that in a minute and be mighty upset. The last thing we want to do is get Hans upset or to cause him more aggravation."

"That's true." She wanted to be perfectly honest with Erik. "Especially if he is already noticing his confusion and the memory glitches."

"Since he won't go to another doctor, or even go back to see you, I've decided to bring the doctor to him." Erik glanced up at her. "If you will act as my girlfriend, you can be at the house to watch him, without causing him to be suspicious. Hans already has gotten the impression that we like each other from the other night when you brought him home. He won't be surprised if you show up for dinner."

"I only stopped in and stayed for dinner because of Hans." She could feel a blush sweep up her cheeks. "I couldn't just leave him in the driveway."

"I know that, and you know that, but Hans doesn't see it that way." Erik's cheeks had a rosy glow to them. "I'm sorry to put you in such an awkward position, but I can't think of anything else to do. I will understand if you'd rather not play the part."

Erik's heartfelt plea tore at her heart. How could she refuse such a simple request? She was worried about

Hans, and this would give her plenty of opportunities to try and talk some sense into the older man.

"I know it's a lot to ask. I will pay you for your time."

"If I do it, I couldn't possibly take your money!" Being paid to spend time with a man smacked of prostitution or at least an escort service. She glared at Erik and for the first time realized she really didn't know the man at all. "What exactly will the acting entail?"

Erik's face turned a dull red. "Not what you are thinking." His gaze stayed on her face. "You only have to act like you like me in front of my grandfather, no one else. What would you be comfortable doing in front of your boyfriend's grandfather?"

"Not very much, that's for sure." There was a big ick factor involved in public displays. Heck, she never had given Richard more than a quick peck in front of his parents, and they had been living together for years.

"Then, that's all you have to do." Erik went back to studying the wineglass. "Since this will be taking a chunk of your time, I figured I'd invite you to dinner when it's my night to cook. You get a free home-cooked meal while you are observing Hans. My grandfather usually goes to bed soon after dinner, so you won't have to stick around too long."

"I'm not worried about my time." Eating dinner with Erik and his family didn't sound too bad. She had enjoyed herself the other night. Hans had kept her entertained with stories of Norway, and Erik was a wonderful cook. What else did she have to do with her evening besides flip through television channels and listen to the marvels of Wonder-Klean? "What about the rumors? Do you think you can handle them?"

"What rumors?" Erik seemed to perk up at the prospect of being in the center of a rumor.

"That you're dating an older woman." She couldn't help it. Their age difference had been playing on her mind all night long.

Erik's warm and hardy laughter filled her small

kitchen. He had a big, deep laugh that was full of heart. "That's the last thing the town would be gossiping about." Erik rubbed at the moisture gathering in his eyes.

"What would they be talking about?"

Erik's laughter faded, but the warmth stayed in his eyes. "Everyone will be talking about how lucky I am."

She felt the bottom drop out of her stomach. Erik was serious. He thought he would be lucky to be romantically linked with her! A fiery blush swept up her cheeks, and for some absurd reason, she felt sixteen all over again. It was one of the nicest and worst birthday presents she had ever received. Who in the hell wanted to be sixteen all over again? Not Sydney. When she had been sixteen, she had a mouth full of braces, was flat chested, and was considered one of the biggest nerds to ever attend Francis Scott Key High School. Striving to become a doctor had consumed all her time and energy. At sixteen she wouldn't have known what to do with a man like Erik. Heck, at thirty she still wasn't entirely sure.

She could feel her face grow hotter and reached for her wineglass. "Thank you."

"One other thing I should mention."

"What's that?"

"We single men of Misty Harbor have this code between us. Once a woman is romantically linked with someone else, all the men back off and leave her alone. I'm afraid once the rumors start, linking us together, you won't be receiving any more flowers or candy."

"What about cod?" She could definitely do without opening any more Styrofoam containers filled with beady-eyed fish and ice chips.

Erik frowned. "Who sent you cod?"

She chuckled at the look on Erik's face. Flowers and candy didn't seem to upset him, but mention a slimy fish and he got all huffy. "It's not important." She grinned. "So far I haven't heard a downside to our little playacting."

"What I'm trying to say is if there's someone special in town, I will understand why you won't want to do this."

She shook her head. "There's no one special, Erik." She got up and loaded her dishes into the dishwasher. "In fact, this will help me halt the constant line of suitors who show up either on my doorstep or at the office." She took the dirty breakfast dishes out of the sink and placed them into the dishwasher. "If it will stop Wendell Kirby from calling me every other day, it will be worth it."

"Wendell bothering you?" Erik handed her an empty coffee cup that had been buried under a magazine on the dining room table.

"Not really. He's just the kind of man who thinks perseverance will get him somewhere." Wendell Kirby, the owner of the Misty Harbor Motor Inn, had sent her flowers, candy, and dinner invitations as though she was, indeed, the last female on the face of the earth.

"Want me to talk to him?" asked Erik a little too eagerly.

"No thanks. I believe he understood my last no." She had delivered it standing in the middle of her reception area with a screaming toddler in her arms and Abraham Martin, a local lobster fisherman, bleeding all over the rug.

Erik slowly nodded. "So what do you say?"

How could she possibly say no? "Okay." She knew all the reasons she was saying yes to Erik's strange proposal, but there was one explanation she refused to examine too closely. She found the big Norwegian hunk irresistible.

Chapter Seven

Sydney's sister Jocelyn tossed her suitcase on the guest room's bed and pinned her with a knowing look. "So, tell me, how does it feel to be dating a Viking god?" Jocelyn's gray eyes sparkled with mischief and curiosity. "Is he as good as he looks?"

Sydney frowned at her sister as she opened the closet door and reached for a hanger. "You've been in Maine, for what, three hours?" She had been afraid of this. The rumors about her and Erik had been circulating around town for the last week, but she had been the one to make the fatal mistake that had obviously sealed their fate. She had invited Erik, his brother Gunnar, and Hans to her family's Thanksgiving dinner at Gwen's. Hans's excitement over a "real" American Thanksgiving dinner had been too hard to resist. The invitation had slipped out of her mouth before she had thought the repercussions through.

"Yeah"—Jocelyn grinned—"and an hour of that was fighting with the car rental place, and another hour was spent driving from the airport to Gwen's."

"So who told you I was dating Erik?" If Jocelyn knew,

so did her parents, who had arrived yesterday at Gwen and Daniel's, and her grandfather, who had flown in with Jocelyn this morning. There had to be a way to do some damage control.

"Well, I asked Daniel about the Norwegian hunks, and he told me one was already spoken for. Imagine my surprise, and Daddy's, when Daniel said it had been my older sister who captured the heart of the Viking."

"I didn't capture his heart," she muttered in disgust. This holiday dinner was definitely starting to go downhill fast, and it wasn't even scheduled to start for another three hours. Plenty of time to drive over there and choke the life out of her brother-in-law.

Jocelyn gave her a wicked grin as she opened the suitcase. "What body part did you capture?"

"Get your mind out of the gutter, Joc." She shook her head as she hung up a pair of her sister's slacks. "Erik and I are just friends."

Jocelyn snorted in disbelief as she placed a small pile of underwear and bras into a drawer. "Tell me another one, dear sister. No woman with a beating heart would want to be 'just friends' with Erik."

"Why not? He's a very nice, intelligent man." Erik was also hard working, caring, gorgeous, and an excellent cook, but she wasn't going to stand here and spout all his good qualities to her sister. Her obviously sex starved, gorgeous sister. "When was the last time you had a date?"

Sweaters landed in the next drawer. "Let me think, it's been so long." Jocelyn tossed back her long golden hair and glanced around the room. "Gwen was still living in Philadelphia and had came to Baltimore to visit us. She prepared a wonderful beef Stroganoff, which I tried to pass off as my own cooking to my date. He had caught on to the small white lie when I screwed up dessert. He then had the nerve to ask me for Gwen's phone number."

"What was his name?" She had heard this story a

couple of times, and never once did her sister mention her date's name.

"Warren, or was it Wade? Something like that, why?" Jocelyn tossed the shoes that she had packed onto the closet floor.

"Don't you find it interesting that you remember what Gwen prepared, but not your date's name?"

"Nah, Gwen's cooking is out of this world, while No-Taste Wayne hasn't left an endearing impression. Besides, he was more interested in the fact if I could cook or not." Jocelyn closed the empty suitcase and set it against the wall. "What's my dating have to do with you and Mister Hot Chest? Are you trying to change the subject?"

"Would it be possible?"

"Nope." Jocelyn bounced onto the neatly made bed and patted a spot. "Park your butt here and tell me all the juicy details. After living with Needle Ass for four years, dating Erik must be like dying and going to Valhalla."

She sighed and slowly sat down onto the bed. "I'm not dating Erik."

"Sure you are. Daniel told me you were."

"I'm pretending to date Erik." It was about time someone, besides herself and Erik, knew the truth. She hadn't even told Gwen the truth, because her other sister hadn't asked. Gwen, as usual, was minding her own business. Jocelyn, the lawyer in the family, had to know everyone's business. One day Jocelyn's curiosity was going to get her into a world of trouble. "Erik's grandfather, Hans, is getting confused and sometimes forgetful. I had him into the office for a physical and some blood work, but I can't diagnose a particular illness. Hans is refusing to see a specialist or even come back into my office. I'm concerned, and Erik and Gunnar are troubled by their grandfather's behavior. Since Hans refuses to go to the doctor, Erik thought up the idea of bringing the doctor to him."

"Why Erik?" Jocelyn fluffed a pillow and placed it between her back and the headboard.

"Why Erik what?" She didn't like the fact that Jocelyn appeared to be settling in for a long gossip session. Her sister didn't engage in girl talk. Her sister went on fact-finding missions.

"Why are you Erik's girlfriend and not Gunnar's?"

"Maybe Erik drew the short straw." Sydney flopped back onto the mattress and stared up at the ceiling. That particular question had popped into her mind more than once over the past week. It would have been so much easier being Gunnar's girlfriend. She could have pretended and teased with Gunnar. With Erik, everything felt too intimate. Too real. "It was probably Erik's idea, so he got to act like the sacrificial lamb."

"Erik doesn't strike me as the sacrificial lamb type."

"Does Gunnar?"

"They're identical twins, Syd." Jocelyn rolled her eyes. "There isn't any difference between them."

"That's where you are wrong. There are plenty of differences."

Her sister looked at her curiously. "Name them."

"Erik is a great cook, while Gunnar's cooking is edible, but not very tasty. Gunnar can fix any engine around, while Erik is better at working with wood." *Erik's voice is deeper, sexier, and can cause an avalanche of shivers to slide down my spine. Erik's crystal blue eyes darken to the color of worn denim when he stares at my mouth. Erik can steal my breath with only a look.* Sydney didn't think her sister needed to know all that.

"So all this dating business is just pretend? You don't get anything out of it? No fancy dinners? No movies? No tonsil hockey in the front seat of his pickup truck?"

"Well, I get dinner cooked for me, and all I have to do is help with the dishes."

"Don't they have a dishwasher?" Jocelyn sounded so incredulous, that one would think Sydney had just told her they had no indoor plumbing in the entire state of Maine.

"Afraid not. Drying's not too bad, plus I get to keep my eye on Hans." She laced her fingers together behind her head and wondered when the ceiling fixture had been dusted last. "Some nights Hans seems perfectly fine. Others, he's a little confused and forgetful. At least he hasn't taken any more evening strolls."

"So you are doing all of this for one of your patients?"

"All of what? Having someone cook my dinner isn't a hardship, believe me."

"I've tasted your cooking, Syd. The hardship would be eating your own meals." Jocelyn threw the other pillow at her.

She caught the pillow with one hand, tucked it behind her head, and grinned. "I'm not the one who tried passing Gwen's cooking off as her own."

"No, but you and Needle Ass used Gwen's cooking skills at all your parties."

"I paid for the food, and Gwen wanted an excuse to test some of her own recipes. It was a mutual benefit to us both."

"Now who's sounding like a lawyer?" Jocelyn started to toy with the ends of her hair. "So what you are telling me is that Erik is unspoken for?"

She turned her head and stared at her sister. "If you're planning on developing an international relationship, do it with Gunnar."

"You're awfully possessive of a man you claim not to be dating." Jocelyn innocently continued to braid the last six inches of her hair.

Sydney knew there wasn't an innocent bone in Jocelyn's body. She was leading the witness, and the witness was gullible enough to fall for it. "Hans thinks Erik and I are sweet on each other. He wouldn't understand you flirting with Erik."

"Or Erik flirting back." Jocelyn was now inspecting her fingernails.

Jealousy spiked hot and cruel. "Who said Erik would flirt back?"

Her sister took one look at her face and burst out laughing. Jocelyn's finger pointed right at her. "You should see your face, Syd."

She had felt the fiery flush that had swept up her face, but she had been praying that in the weak afternoon light, Jocelyn wouldn't be able to notice. "What's wrong with it?"

"I haven't seen you blush since you were sixteen and nerdy Ralph Whineman, from up the street, kissed you under the mistletoe in our living room."

She watched as Jocelyn collapsed into a fit of laughter, either from the memory of Sydney's first embarrassing kiss, which had been witnessed by her entire family, or the blush. She wasn't sure which. Between clenched teeth, she managed to mutter, "I'm not blushing." She wasn't embarrassed. She was mortified that for a split moment in time she had been jealous of her own sister. The Fletcher sisters had never allowed a boyfriend or a man to come between them. Jocelyn wouldn't dare flirt with Erik.

Jocelyn pulled herself together and leaned on her elbow. Tears of laughter were still wet on her cheeks. "You like him!"

"Who?"

"Erik, who else?"

"Well, he's a very nice man. Of course I like him." She hurriedly stood up and retucked her silk blouse into the waistband of her slacks. "We better get going to Gwen's. I promised her we'd help with dinner."

"I'm sure our sister would rather we didn't step foot into her kitchen while she's cooking. Cleaning up, definitely; but the last time I tried to help her cook, I scorched her cream sauce, and she hasn't forgiven me yet."

"Then, we can set the table." She nodded in the direction of the bathroom. "There are clean towels in the bathroom if you want to freshen up before we head for Gwen's." Why had she ended up with Jocelyn staying with her for the holiday? It would have been a lot easier having Grandpop Michaels, or even her parents, use her guest room.

"Syd?"

She turned at the sound of concern in her sister's voice. "Yes?"

"It's all right to like him, you know." Joc stood up and gave her a quick hug. "Don't let your experience with Richard ruin your life."

She returned her sister's hug and managed a wide, innocent smile. "Richard who?"

Jocelyn's eyes were filled with concern. "Does he still look at you the way he did at Gwen's wedding?"

"Who?" Richard hadn't been at Gwen's wedding.

"Erik." The concern in Jocelyn's gaze turned to amusement. "He couldn't take his eyes off of you during the whole reception."

"Funny, I remember Erik dancing with you three different times." She refused to even think about Erik staring at her during Gwen's wedding. Richard hadn't bothered to accompany her to her sister's wedding last June. He had stayed home in Baltimore pretending to be hurt and neglected because he had to work while she had been out having fun. Later she had learned that he had been entertaining one of the dietitians from the hospital for the entire weekend. In their bed.

"He's a wonderful dancer." Jocelyn grinned. "But I always wondered why he had never bothered to ask you to dance."

"Maybe because he didn't want to."

Jocelyn countered right back, "Maybe because he had been too scared."

"Erik, afraid? What in the world would scare a six-foot, two-inch Viking? Last time I heard, Godzilla was still in the Far East and fire-breathing dragons were extinct."

Jocelyn chuckled as she picked up her cosmetic bag and turned toward the bathroom. "Maybe he's afraid of some five-foot, five-inch doctor with auburn hair and green eyes."

"If he's so afraid of me, why does he want me to be his pretend girlfriend?"

"Well, if you won't be his real girlfriend, I guess he's making do with at least having you as a pretend one."

"Joc, you got it all wrong. My hair's not auburn; it's brown. And Erik has never asked me out on a real date. Every other man in this town has sent me flowers, candy, tickets to the local high school rendition of *Midsummer-Night's Dream,* and coolers full of gutted cod."

Jocelyn wrinkled her nose in disgust. "Maybe they do things different in Maine than in Maryland."

"And maybe my sister was dropped on her head when she was a baby." She shook her head at her baby sister. Could their five-year separation in age really make this much of a difference? How did Jocelyn see attraction while she saw avoidance?

Jocelyn laughed as she stepped into the bathroom. "We'll see tonight, big bad doctor. I plan on keeping an eye on you two." Jocelyn closed the door and shouted, "We'll see tonight."

Erik took the bowl of candied yams from Sydney and put only one spoonful on his plate. There was barely any room left on his large, dark green dinner plate, and there seemed to be a half dozen bowls of food that hadn't made it around the table yet. Gwen had truly outdone herself with this feast. Everything looked so delicious that he wanted to make sure he got to try it all. He just wished Sydney wasn't sitting so darn close. The enticing fragrance she wore was driving him nuts and heating his blood. The same exotic scent of flowers had permeated his dreams for the past week, making it impossible to get a good night's sleep. Every morning he woke more frustrated than the morning before.

He knew the closeness couldn't be helped, and she wasn't driving him crazy on purpose. With eighteen people sitting down for dinner at one time, he was amazed he didn't feel like a sardine in a very small can. Daniel Creighton, a carpenter by trade, had added temporary extensions to their dining room table. With the flowing white linen tablecloth and three beautiful evergreen-and-candle arrangements acting as centerpieces, he couldn't tell where the table ended and the plywood began. Sixteen adults and two children filled the dining room with plenty of talk and laughter. He knew everyone there and was amazed that the table actually held four separate families.

Sydney's invitation to join her family for Thanksgiving had come as a shock to him. He hadn't been expecting her to carry their charade that far, but his grandfather's reaction to the offer had made it impossible to refuse. Gunnar had thought the whole thing funny and wasn't about to be left home alone. His brother wanted to see how he acted the part of being Sydney's boyfriend in front of her parents. So far he had been doing a really terrible job at it. He had barely spoken a dozen sentences to Sydney since they arrived. Sydney seemed just as anxious to avoid him, too.

He had met Sydney's family before, but today they definitely seemed more curious about him. Her mother, Gloria, kept giving him funny looks, while her father, Stan, glared. Sydney's grandfather had cornered him earlier by the fireplace and told him if he hurt his granddaughter, he would answer to Grandpop Michaels. The older man had then mumbled something about breaking kneecaps. Erik had been so stunned by the comment that he had managed only to nod weakly and say something stupid like "Yes, sir."

Jocelyn, Sydney's youngest sister, seemed amused by the situation and grinned like an idiot every time he looked at her. Jocelyn was also flirting shamelessly with Gunnar. For some reason his brother, while being polite, wasn't flirting back. Gunnar hadn't been acting like himself lately. Maybe there was something wrong with the heating system back at their house. Maybe they were all suffering from a form of carbon monoxide poisoning. Since Sydney had sewn up his arm, he hadn't been feeling like himself either.

Daniel's family represented the majority of the people gulping down the turkey and stuffing. Daniel's parents were sitting down at the far end of the table, along with their daughter, Rebecca, and her husband, John. Rebecca and John's daughters, Kaitlyn and Abby, were holding court and had all the adults hopping to their every desire. They seemed to love being the center of attention. Daniel's grandfather, Jonah, had escorted the town's matriarch, Millicent Wyndham, into the house. But he wasn't sure if they came as a couple or if he had just picked up Millicent for Gwen.

Everyone in town knew Gwen and Millicent were great friends. It had been Millicent who had gotten Gwen to move to Maine to open her restaurant. Millicent had also had a heavy hand in persuading Sydney to take over for Dr. Jeffreys when he wanted to retire. Millicent was alone in the world. Her husband had passed away before Erik and his brother had come to Maine, and she didn't have any children. He thought it was awfully nice of Gwen to invite her to dinner so she wouldn't be alone. Hans seemed to be enjoying her company, so was Sydney's grandfather. Jonah appeared to be taking all the attention Millicent was receiving in stride.

"Erik?" Sydney's voice finally penetrated through his thoughts.

"I'm sorry, what did you say?" He automatically reached for the bowl of cranberries she was holding out.

"I didn't say anything." Sydney glanced down to the

other end of the table where he had been staring. "Aren't Kaitlyn and Abby cute?"

"They're cute as buttons." He could see that the little blond-haired girls were dressed in their prettiest dresses and had on matching black shiny shoes. Kaitlyn, who was six, had on tiny blue earrings, while Abby, who was four, wore a glittery necklace. Abby was currently making a funny face at the corn her mother just put on her plate. "I wasn't looking at them, though." He leaned closer and whispered, "I was watching our grandfathers flirt with Millicent. She seems to have her hands full with three different men vying for her attention."

Sydney took the gravy boat from Daniel and chuckled as she poured some over her mashed potatoes. "My money's on Millicent. She can handle those three with her hands tied behind her back."

"I don't know. I've seen my grandfather be charming when he sets his mind to it." His hand covered Sydney's as he reached for the gravy boat. He felt the trembling of her fingers and glanced up at her face.

Sydney was staring back at him. Her voice was a soft, seductive whisper. "Must run in the family."

He felt the whisper skim his tightly leashed control. Sydney's green eyes were darkening, and a breath seemed to hitch in her throat. He watched entranced as her soft, moist lips parted. His fingers tightened over hers, and he wanted to kiss every trace of lipstick off her provocative mouth. Hell, he wanted to devour that mouth and then slowly work his way down that luscious body that had been tormenting his every thought and dream. When he reached her toes, he was going to work his way back up and not stop until she was shuddering with her third climax.

Sydney's gaze dropped to his mouth, and the room seemed to disappear around them. Conversations faded away, and the only sound he could hear was the small catch in Sydney's throat that happened with every breath she took. He could see the desire swimming in the depths of her eyes. There was no denying the truth. Dr. Sydney Fletcher wanted to kiss him, as much as he wanted to kiss her in return.

Driven by need, and without thought, he started to lower his head toward her waiting mouth.

A sharp kick to his right shin stopped his descent and caused a grunt of pain to escape his lips. He whipped his head around and glared across the table at his brother.

Gunnar rolled his eyes and very slightly tilted his head toward the head of the table.

Erik slowly turned and looked in that direction. Sydney's mother was eyeing her daughter with a great deal of interest. Her father's glare had turned into a full-blown scowl. Gwen was trying to nonchalantly pass the peas to her husband; but Daniel's head was lowered, and he seemed to find something on his plate very amusing. Jocelyn gave a bark of laughter before jamming a roll into her mouth and turning her gaze upward to study the ceiling.

He closed his eyes and wondered what Norse god he would have to pray to, to have the floor open up and swallow him whole. He had known this meal wasn't a good idea. With a deep breath, he opened his eyes and looked at Sydney. As blushes went, hers was a nice shade of fire engine red. His probably matched hers.

Miraculously, they were both still holding the gravy boat, and none of it had spilled. He carefully took the boat from her trembling fingers and politely said, "Thanks."

Sydney nodded, but wouldn't look at him. She turned her head away and took the bowl of peas Daniel was patiently holding out for her.

Erik poured gravy across his potatoes and turkey and passed the boat on to his grandfather. Thankfully, the bottom half of the table hadn't caught what he considered a very private moment between Sydney and himself. Heat still throbbed throughout his body, and the dark green napkin lying across his lap was covering more than his Dockers. His fingers were barely shaking as he reached for his water glass and downed half the contents in one gulp. If he didn't look at Sydney and tried not to breathe the scent of her perfume in too deeply, he just might make it through the remainder of the meal without embarrassing himself further.

It was a long shot, but if he concentrated on icebergs and Sydney's father's scowl, he just might make it home tonight without getting his kneecaps broken by Sydney's eighty-year-old grandfather.

Sydney hung up the damp tea towel she had been using to dry the pots and pans Gwen had used to make dinner. Most of the dishes had fit into the dishwasher, but there hadn't been any room for the pots. Jocelyn had started to scrub the pots while the rest of the women cleared off the table and straightened everything up. The men, as usual, were gathered in front of Daniel's big-screen television watching a football game.

She glanced at Jocelyn, who was running water into the sink and watching the last of the bubbles float down the drain. Amazingly, Jocelyn hadn't teased her about that stupid moment of insanity during dinner when she almost allowed Erik to kiss her. *Allow! Hell, you practically threw yourself at the man.* Her mother had given her a few looks, as if she wanted to say something, but so far she hadn't said anything. Gwen kept giving her sly, knowing smiles.

"It doesn't seem fair, does it?" Jocelyn turned off the water.

"What doesn't seem fair?" Gwen joined them as she filled the coffeepot with water. The other women were in the dining room getting it ready to serve dessert, leaving the three sisters alone in the kitchen. Millicent had brought along two pumpkin pies. Rebecca had contributed a Jell–o and marshmallow salad mold, while Daniel's mom, Mary, had brought an apple pie and a plate of cookies. Gwen had baked a cake and decorated it for Sydney's birthday.

Jocelyn nodded toward the living room. The couch was packed with boisterous men; so were the two chairs. Daniel had carried in two chairs from his den. One held a Viking. The other Grandpop Michaels had commandeered and then promptly fallen asleep. A few chairs Gwen had borrowed from her restaurant completed the odd assembly of furniture. A few beer cans littered the coffee table, and the bowl of peanuts was being devoured. All eyes were glued to the set as Tampa Bay scored a touchdown. "How come the men get to crash in front of the television while the women get to clean up?"

"You want to watch the football game?" Sydney looked at her youngest sister. Jocelyn had never shown an interest in the game before, only the muscle-bound players.

"No, but it doesn't seem fair. Gwen busted her butt all day long making the meal, and now she's in here cleaning up."

Gwen measured out the coffee grounds and smiled. "I'm not cleaning up, you are." Gwen fit the filter basket into the coffee machine and hit the switch. "I enjoy cooking, Joc. To me it's not work, and I'd rather peel potatoes than watch a bunch of sweaty men pound each other into the ground."

Jocelyn grinned. "Speak for yourself, you've got Daniel."

Gwen grinned right back and went to join her husband, who was shouting something about "not up the middle!"

Sydney watched Daniel's arm wrap around Gwen's waist and then pull her down onto his lap. A sharp little pang of jealousy stabbed her in the gut, but she quickly brushed it away. Gwen deserved her happiness and the love she had found with Daniel. Her gaze slid to Erik, and she was surprised to discover he wasn't paying a bit of attention to the game. Erik was staring at her.

Jocelyn elbowed her in the side. "He's staring again, Doc. Think he's got something wrong with his eyes?"

She turned to her grinning sister and frowned. "Knock it off, Joc."

"Hey, I wasn't the one who nearly set the tablecloth on fire during dinner. If you and Erik had gotten any closer, the candied yams would have been scorched."

From the corner of her eye, she saw Erik say something to Hans and then stand up. Erik opened one of the patio doors and walked out onto the darkened deck. She knew the deck, which practically surrounded Daniel and Gwen's house, had a breathtaking view of the Atlantic Ocean during the daylight. She also knew it was freezing cold outside and that Erik hadn't bothered with a coat. "Erik was just playing his part, that's all."

Jocelyn gave a choking laugh. "Maybe you were the one who was dropped on her head as a baby, Syd. I saw the look on his face. That man wanted to do a whole lot more than just kiss you." Jocelyn shook her head. "I also had a clear view of your face, big sis. You would have let him, too, if Gunnar hadn't spoiled the moment by kicking Erik under the table."

"Thank God for Gunnar." She couldn't very well argue against the truth with Jocelyn. When she had looked into the molten depths of Erik's gaze, she had forgotten everyone else in the room even existed. She would have done a lot more than just kiss Erik. She would have done anything he wanted, and probably begged for more. She was shameless and wanton. It was an interesting fact to learn about oneself at the ripe old age of thirty.

"Syd?" Jocelyn's voice was low, so it wouldn't carry.

"Yeah?"

"I would give anything to have a man look at me the way Erik was looking at you. Don't throw it away." Jocelyn gave the faucet one last swipe of the dishcloth and then walked out of the room.

Sydney stood there staring at the door Erik had disappeared through a moment ago. If Jocelyn noticed the way he had been looking at her, then she couldn't have imagined it. Could she? Erik really had wanted to kiss her, and it hadn't been an act put on for Hans's benefit. Hans hadn't been paying them any attention. He had been too busy charming Millicent.

"Sydney, where's Erik?" Her mother came into the kitchen and was looking at the men watching the game. Gwen got off Daniel's lap and started to usher the men away from the television.

"He stepped outside for some air." Hans joined them by the sink and answered her mother's question. Hans reached for and unwrapped a piece of candy that Gwen had set out in a fancy dish on the counter. The chocolate piece of candy disappeared behind Hans's smile.

"Could you go get him, Sydney? It's time for the dessert and for you to cut your birthday cake." Her mother reached into a cabinet and started to take down coffee cups and their matching saucers.

The last thing she wanted was to be reminded, yet again, she had turned thirty. She also didn't want to join Erik out on that dark deck, but she couldn't very well refuse. Hans would think something was wrong. "Sure." She walked across the room and out the patio door.

The light pouring from the living room and kitchen reached only part way across the wooden deck. The thin slice of the moon was hidden behind thick clouds. Thankfully, it wasn't snowing. It took a moment for her eyes to adjust to the darkness. The deck appeared empty. She hoped Erik hadn't gone wandering toward the cliff. Daniel had a split-rail fence up along the dangerous drop, but in the darkness anything could happen. The constant pounding of the sea against the rocks filled the sea-scented air, and the wind whipped at her hair and clothes. She wrapped her arms around herself and moved toward the steps that lead to the walkway to the cliff.

"Syd?" Erik's deep voice came from the corner of the house.

She instantly turned in that direction. "What are you doing over there?" Erik was standing on the side of the house that faced the garage and driveway. The front porch light was too far away to offer any kind of illumination.

"There's no wind on this side. The house blocks it."

"If you're cold, why didn't you come back in?" She hurried around the corner and out of the wind. It was still cold outside, but at least now it wasn't biting through her clothes.

Erik moved closer and, as naturally as if he had done it a hundred times before, wrapped his arms around her to offer her his warmth. "Why did you come out here?"

"To get you." She swayed deeper into his arms. Into his warmth. "Dessert's ready." Her silk blouse felt like ice, while the dark blue sweater Erik had on felt like her electric blanket on high. She instinctively moved closer.

Erik groaned. "This isn't a good idea." His hands rubbed up and down her back.

"What?" She lifted her face to see his eyes. She could make out the outline of his rugged jaw and the sweep of his hair pulled back into its usual ponytail, but none of the details of his face. "Dessert?" What could possibly be wrong with dessert?

"No," growled Erik as he lowered his mouth toward hers. "This."

Erik's mouth took possession of hers, and the world seemed to tilt on its axis. He wasn't slow, cautious, or hesitant. Erik, true to his Norwegian bloodline, conquered. She stretched up on her toes and went wherever he was leading willingly. With a bold sweep of his tongue, he parted her lips and invaded her mouth.

One of them moaned, or maybe they both did. It didn't matter. All that mattered to her was to get closer to Erik. Closer to his heat. His desire. She could feel the long, hard length of him pressing against her stomach. No, she hadn't imagined the desire that had burnt in his gaze earlier. Erik really did want her.

She raised her arms and wrapped them around his neck as she opened her mouth wider and met his thrusting tongue with a boldness that not only surprised her. It aroused her.

Strong fingers cupped her bottom and brought the junction of her thighs against his straining arousal. Right where she wanted to be. Right where he wanted her to be. Every thought fled her mind, but one. She wanted Erik like she had never wanted a man before. Her breasts felt heavy and full, and liquid heat was moist between her thighs.

A startled, high-pitched gasp broke the silence. Erik froze as Sydney's eyes flew open. She tried to take a quick step back, but Erik's grip on her hips was firm. That gasp hadn't come from her or him.

Tiny running footsteps could be heard crossing the back deck, and then the sound of a patio door being flung open. "Guess what, everyone?" shouted Kaitlyn. "Dr. Sydney is kissing Erik! Dr. Sydney is kissing Erik!"

Chapter Eight

Sydney sat next to Hans on the couch and carefully studied the photographs in the book spread across both of their laps. It was a thick, large book that appeared to contain Hans's entire life. Erik and Gunnar had been concerned about Hans reliving the past, but she had reassured them it would be good for their grandfather. From her research over the Internet, she had learned that many health professionals tried to encourage patients with Alzheimer's to reminisce about past memories as a way to reduce depression without the use of drugs. She still wasn't sure Hans had Alzheimer's, but all the signs were pointing in that direction.

What harm could a little reminiscing do?

"These are my daughters, Hilde, Berta, and little Merete." Hans lovingly caressed the side of the black-and-white photo with a trembling finger.

"They look like a handful." The three little girls, ranging in ages from about six to two, all had light blond hair and sparkling, laughing eyes. Their adorable faces were smeared with the ice cream they were eating, but their grins were contagious.

"Ja." Hans softly smiled at the distant memories. "They wrapped their *pappa* around their fingers."

"I imagine they did." She looked closely at the youngest girl, Erik's mother. She didn't see a lot of resemblance in the face, but Erik's blond hair could have come from his mother. All three girls also appeared to have light-color eyes. So maybe Erik got his crystal blue eyes from her, too.

"Jegødela dem." Hans's voice was low, loving, and just a bit too sad.

She glanced at Erik, who was sitting on the other side of Hans, and raised an eyebrow.

"He said he spoiled them," Erik translated for her. *"Bestefar,* you must speak in English or Sydney won't understand."

"Ya, I spoiled my little princesses too much. Way too much." Hans turned the page, and he seemed to go pale.

She studied the eight-by-ten portrait of a young smiling woman. It was a black-and-white photograph that a studio had touched up with hand-painted color. The blond hair was a bit too brassy, her cheekbones glowed with a tad too much rouge, and her lips were berry red. Even with the off coloring, Sydney could tell that the woman was beautiful. Very beautiful. "Who is she?" She was intrigued by the love, yet sadness in the woman's blue eyes.

"My Inga." Hans's gaze got misty, and his voice seemed husky with tears.

She once again looked at Erik for the answer.

"My grandmother, and Hans's wife."

"She had this picture taken in Oslo for me." Hans's fingers trembled, but he didn't touch the photograph. "She wanted me to have something to remind me of her when she was gone." Hans glanced at the mantel where a framed picture of the same woman sat. In the black-and-white picture on the mantel, the woman was younger and had a smile that was breathtaking. She was also wearing a white bridal dress and veil, and there definitely wasn't a hint of sadness in her eyes. "We went to Oslo to see a specialist. To see if there was any hope of stopping the cancer the local doctors had discovered." Tears clogged Hans's throat. "There wasn't any hope."

She reached over and gently squeezed Hans's hand. "I'm sorry." Maybe Erik and Gunnar were right. Talking about the past was too painful.

Hans turned his hand over and tightened his grip around her fingers. "Don't be sorry. We had seventeen years together. Seventeen good years. Most people don't even get one." He nodded back down at the picture. "She died about six months after this picture was taken."

She now understood why that particular portrait was in the book and not on the mantel. "Your daughters and you must have missed her terribly."

"Ja." Hans looked at the assorted small snapshots on the other page. "I took them on a holiday that year. We went to London."

She recognized a blurry Big Ben in the background of one of the pictures. "So I see." The little princesses, ranging in ages from fourteen down to ten, appeared to be having a good time and smiling. She could see that the older two took after Hans's side of the family, while Merete looked like her mother. It must have been rough on the girls losing their mother at such a young age.

Hans's fingers traced the edge of a picture of Merete standing in front of a statue grinning. "She was always such a happy girl. Merete had a laugh that just touched your heart and made you glad you were alive. And sing! Oh, could my little angel sing. Merete had a voice that even the angels would be jealous of."

Erik raised his brow at that statement, but didn't offer up a comment.

Hans turned the page. "This is our trip to Stockholm." The next several pictures were of the girls either in ballet costumes, on ice skates, or a few shots where they were on a fishing boat. A couple shots had the girls posing very prettily in front of sparkling fjords or skiing high in the mountains in brightly colored coats and hats. "This is when we went to Denmark." Hans turned another page. "Hilde loved to travel. She insisted we go everywhere. Berta was crazy for the boys, while Merete wanted everything she saw."

She noticed the girls were growing older and more sophisticated in each photo. Hilde, the oldest, appeared to be seventeen or eighteen and was very well built and beautiful for such a young age. Hans's hands hadn't just been full; they had been overflowing. She wasn't up on style from about forty years ago, but the Bergesen girls appeared to be dressed in the finest money could buy. By some of the pouting going on in some of the snapshots, she would guess that Hans had been right. The princesses had been overindulged.

Merete was looking more and more like her mother with each passing page. The beautiful stone house that sat on top of a hill that overlooked the sea, where they had lived in Norway, attested to the fact there had been money at one time. A lot of money. "Your home was beautiful, Hans."

Hans glanced away from the book and studied the small, comfortable living room where he now sat. The roaring fire crackled, and the smell of dinner still hung in the air. Hans smiled. "I like this place better."

The next several pages were filled with pictures of Hilde's wedding. Hilde looked to be nineteen at the most and extremely proud of herself. The young man, whose arm she clung to, appeared bewildered as if wondering how he had ended up in this particular photograph book.

"Hilde married an American. He came over the summer he graduated from college to visit with his grandparents. By July Hilde had him to the altar; by August she had left to go back to America with him."

She noticed there were a lot more photos of Merete in the book than of her sisters. It could have been because she was the "baby" of the family. More than likely it was because the resemblance to Inga was remarkable. No one had to ask who Hans's favorite had been. At fifteen, the tall and willowy Merete had the promise of super model written all over her. By seventeen, Hans must have been beating the high school boys away from his front door with a stick.

Hans turned the page, and there was Berta in her wedding finery. "Berta wanted to visit Hilde in America. For her eighteenth birthday I drove her to Oslo and put her on an airplane. A month later she returned with this American and demanded to get married." Hans shook his head at the photos and the memories. "I told her she was too young. Hilde had married too young, and now here was Berta demanding to do the same."

When Hans didn't say anything else, she asked, "What did she say to that?" Whatever it was must have been good because Sydney was looking at the wedding pictures. By the superior, smug look on Berta's face, no one would doubt that she had gotten her way.

Hans snorted. "Told me it better be a quick wedding because there was a good chance she was carrying my first grandchild."

She shuddered and snuck a glance at Erik. Somehow she didn't think Erik appreciated having all the family dirty laundry hung out in front of a stranger. And she was a stranger. What did it matter if they had shared the most mind-blowing kiss she had ever experienced? Erik obviously didn't want a repeat, because he had been avoiding her since they had stepped back into Daniel and Gwen's house on Thanksgiving night to face the music. There hadn't been any music. Only a whole bunch of knowing looks and her grandfather muttering something about knees.

"So was there a grandchild?" asked Erik.

"Not for many years." Hans turned the page, and Merete stared back up at him. "She was beautiful, was she not?"

"Yes," she said as she looked to Erik for his confirmation.

Erik was staring at the colored eight-by-ten of his mother as if he had never seen her before. He didn't answer his grandfather.

"She was the prettiest girl in the county. The mayor of Egersund tried to win her hand, but she chose me." Hans skimmed his fingers over the portrait. "She could have had anyone, but Inga chose me."

"Bestefar, that's Merete, not Inga," said Erik gently.

Hans shook his head as if coming out of a daze. "I know that, son." Hans tapped the small picture on the opposite page. "I gave your mother that necklace on her seventeenth birthday. It was this huge sapphire surrounded by diamonds. I thought it was too old and sophisticated for her, but she saw it in some store window and pleaded and pleaded until I gave in." Hans glanced at Erik and smiled. "Does she still wear it all the time?"

Erik glanced helplessly at her. She could feel the distress just rolling off of Erik. How many times must he break his grandfather's heart by telling him his beloved daughter was gone?

Sydney reached for the older man's hand. Tonight she would do it for Erik. "Hans, Merete passed away over three years ago." She watched Hans's eyes and could see his heart breaking all over again. "Don't you remember, Hans? It was an auto accident. Erik and Gunnar came to America to find you after the accident." She blinked back the swell of tears forming and plastered a big smile onto her face. "They liked you so much they decided to stay with you."

Hans nodded. *"Ja."* He glanced at Erik. "Boys stay with me now."

Erik threw his arm around his grandfather's shoulder

and squeezed. "Can't get rid of us now if you wanted to."

Hans beamed, and the heartache was momentarily forgotten. "I've got pictures of Erik in his diapers. Want to see, Doktor Sydney?"

Erik groaned while she grinned and bobbed her head. "Please."

Hans turned the next page. The last photograph was of Merete sitting in a sun-drenched meadow filled with flowers. There were no pictures of Merete's wedding to Erik's father. Erik had told her that Hans had disowned Merete for marrying his father. She found it hard to believe, but it obviously was true.

Hans turned several empty pages before coming to an old assortment of pictures lovingly pasted into the book.

The first two were side by side, and they were pictures of Erik and Gunnar when they were only days old. Both babies were pink and chunky with a few stray blond hairs on the fat round heads. Their eyes were closed, but their lips were puckered as if waiting to be fed or kissed. Both babies were wearing long-sleeve blue T-shirts. Someone had taken the time to embroider an *E* on one of the shirts and a *G* on the other.

She leaned in closer for a better look. "My God, you were cute, Erik." She tilted her head to smile innocently at the big, strapping Viking. "What happened?"

Hans chuckled as he pointed to the next snapshot. This one was an old black-and-white shot of the twins when they were about a year old. They were both standing on a dirt-covered path, and the only thing they had on were diapers. Droopy diapers and huge, drooling smiles. Both boys had about four teeth in their mouths, but they were now sporting heads full of blond curls.

"Which one is which?" They were the kind of babies that if you saw them on the street, you would want to pick them up and pinch their fat little cheeks. Heck, they even had dimples on their little knees.

"Don't know. Old Nils never wrote it on the back."

"Who's Nils?"

"Nils was an old villager I wrote to after I came to America." Hans smoothed an old crease in the photo. "I came to live by Hilde and Berta after Merete married her fisherman." The tip of his finger ran over the crease again. "I didn't know Merete had the boys until they were about five years old. Nils wrote me then and sent me as many pictures as he could find."

It looked as if Nils had searched the town's dump to find them for Hans. None of the photos appeared to be in great shape. Nearly every picture had old crease marks and torn edges. Some of the snapshots were out of focus and blurry. Some appeared to be old school pictures that had been passed between friends and left in someone's gym bag for the year.

One photo captured and held her attention. The twin boys, who looked to be about four at the time, were sitting on the shoulders of a huge smiling man. A dozen boats were in the background. She leaned in closer to study the man. "Is that your father, Erik?" There was no mistaking the family resemblance. Erik's father was a huge mountain of a man with long golden hair and shoulders as wide as a house. He was also drop-dead gorgeous, in a rough, sea-faring way. Erik and Gunnar looked just like him. Both grinning boys looked extremely comfortable on their father's shoulders and were mugging it up for the camera.

Erik looked at the picture, and a small smile tilted up the corner of his mouth. "Yes, that's my father." His finger tapped one of the boats in the background. "That's his boat."

"Rolf Olsen was a hardworking, good-hearted man, wasn't he, boy?" Hans looked at Erik and seemed to hold his breath, waiting for an answer.

Erik nodded. "Yes, *Bestefar,* he was. No one worked harder or longer than my father." Erik tapped the next snapshot. This one had seven-year-old Erik and Gunnar with their arms around each other and grinning. One boy had a black-and-blue eye, the other a fat lip. "He loved us no matter how much trouble we managed to get in."

Sydney looked at the picture and shook her head. "I would hate to see what the other guy looked like."

"We were the other guy." Erik's finger tapped the boy with the black-and-blue eye. "That's me. Gunnar got in the first blow, but I finished it."

"What were you fighting about?"

"Can't remember now, but I do remember that it happened quite a bit as we were growing up. We were always scrabbling over something back then."

Hans chuckled. "Boys will be boys."

"Boys shouldn't be pounding on each other." She sighed. "Someone could have gotten seriously hurt."

Hans looked ready to argue when Erik cut in. "She's right, Grandfather. Even though those punches weren't really thrown in anger or hatred, someone could have gotten hurt." Erik gave her a quick flash of a smile. "I hardly ever wallop Gunnar now."

"It would be like the clash of the Titans." She shook her head as she tried to imagine the two Vikings going at it. She couldn't. Erik and Gunnar seemed to get along very well for two brothers who were still living with each other. "No fair picking on Gunnar while he's not here." Gunnar had gone to do the food shopping right after dinner.

Hans shook his head and chuckled. "Raising boys sure would have been easier than raising girls. All those fancy dresses, stockings, unmentionables, and makeup. Boys would have been happy with pants, shirts, and hockey sticks. They wouldn't have needed eighteen pairs of shoes in their closets or hair dresser appointments every other week." Hans gave another humph as the memories came flooding back. "Girls cry all the time, too."

Sydney lightly bumped her knee against Hans's.

"Speak for your own daughters, Hans. I didn't cry all the time."

"Well, you're a doktor. You better not cry all the time." Hans shook his head as he turned the page. "No one would trust you to fix their aches and pains if you cried all the time."

She grinned. "There is that." She glanced down at the last two pictures. One photo was of the boys fishing with their father. Rolf Olsen's smile didn't look as bright, but he was still a handsome man. She could see the height and the weight on the twins now. Erik and Gunnar didn't appear to be older than nine or ten, and already they reached their father's shoulders. There was no way Rolf Olsen would be strutting around with his boys on his shoulders now. The other picture was of the twins proudly displaying their catch in front of their father's boat. Both boys wore dirty clothes and wide grins. "I don't know, Hans. I bet boys were harder to keep clean."

"Ah, what's a little soap?" Hans closed the book with a sigh.

She realized that was all the pictures Hans had of Merete's boys. Those, and what was on the mantel. She got up and walked to the fireplace to study the framed pictures. Hans had framed the two best pictures of his twin grandsons. Both photos showed the boys either fishing or displaying their catch. It was quite obvious that fishing was in their blood. There weren't any pictures of Hans's other daughters or their families on the mantel. She had to wonder why.

Hans got up and carefully placed the book back on the shelf. "I think I'll turn in now. It's getting late, and I'm sure you two would like to spend some time alone."

Sydney wanted to protest, but Hans did look tired. Ever since last week, at Thanksgiving, Hans had been pushing Erik and her closer together. What did he expect them to do in the living room while he was only two rooms away and Gunnar was due to walk in the door at any moment? "Good night, Hans."

"Good night, *Bestefar,*" Erik said.

"Good night, you two." Hans smiled at her and then turned to Erik and said, *"Vakkere kuinner ikke vokser påtrær."* Hans left the room humming softly to himself.

Sydney watched him go. With a smile she asked, "What did he say to you?"

"He said that 'Beautiful women don't grow on trees.' " Erik started to clean up the empty coffee cups and carry them into the kitchen. "I agree with him." Erik didn't even look at her as he placed the cups into the sink and turned off the coffeepot.

Any other woman would probably take that as a compliment. She didn't because Erik hadn't bothered to look at her once. When a man tells a woman she's beautiful, he should at least look at her when he says it. Erik seemed to have a hard time looking at her since their kiss. It was a depressing thought. With that one kiss she had felt not only desire and excitement, but she had felt her self-confidence climb just a couple of notches. Erik, a strong, gorgeous, and younger man had wanted her. She knew they were only pretending to be a couple for Hans's sake, but there was no way Erik had faked that response to their kiss. Either Erik had been very happy to kiss her, or he had been smuggling yule logs out of Daniel's house.

For the first time in five months, since she walked out on Richard, she had felt like a desirable woman. Erik had given her that, and a week's worth of frustrating lack of sleep.

"I guess I should be going." She glanced at Hans's closed bedroom door and knew he wouldn't be making any more appearances tonight. There was no reason to stay. "Thanks for dinner; it was delicious as always." Erik had made a mouth-watering pot roast, complete with potatoes and buttermilk biscuits.

"I'll walk you out." Erik turned off the water and dried his hands.

She didn't argue that she was quite capable of walking the fifteen feet to her car out front. Erik always walked her out, no matter how cold it was. She zipped up her heavy coat and tugged on a knitted hat and thick mittens. She knew she looked about as appealing as a snowman, but she didn't care. It had been darn cold outside when she had driven over earlier.

Erik zipped his coat and then opened the door for her. The December wind whipped at the hair that hung out of her hat. She hunched her shoulders and hurried to her car. If it was this cold during the first week of December, what was it going to feel like come February? She shivered and shuddered just to think about it. She opened the door to her S.U.V. and slid in behind the wheel.

Surprisingly, Erik went around to the other side of the car and climbed into the passenger seat. He briskly rubbed his hands together and said, "Start the car and get the heat going before you turn into a popsicle."

She closed the door and started the engine. It would take a couple of minutes before there would be any heat. "I'm taking it that you need to talk to me?" Erik could have followed her back to her cottage, but then Hans would be alone. Erik wouldn't do that. It was bad enough Gunnar and he worried about Hans all day long while they had to work. She was working on a solution to that problem, and hopefully by tomorrow morning she would have the answer.

"Hans thinks I'm moving too slow."

"About?" She couldn't read Erik's face in the darkness of the car. The porch lights didn't reach this far, and she didn't want to flip on the interior light. Being in the dark with Erik reminded her of the other night. It was a naughty, sexy feeling, one she wasn't willing to give up, even if all he wanted to talk about was Hans.

"Us." Erik leaned back in the seat. "He thinks someone else from town will cut in and steal you away from me."

"Why would he think that?"

"Because we really don't spend that much time together. You come over every other night for dinner, and as soon as he goes to bed you leave. Hans knows you leave as soon as he leaves us alone."

"Should I stay longer?"

"That won't help. Hans can't understand why we only get together at our house, when you have a whole cottage to yourself where we can be alone. We aren't teenagers, and at our age we surely don't need a chaperon."

"I see." She didn't know if spending a lot of time alone with Erik was such a good idea. She would probably do something really stupid, like rip his shirt open and draw figure eights on his chest with her tongue.

"He's afraid that if I'm not making any moves on you, someone else will." Erik ran his fingers through his hair and stared straight ahead.

"No one has made any 'moves' on me since the rumors about us being a couple started to circulate through the town."

"That's good." Erik turned his head to look at her. "Maybe we should be seen going out more. I could take you to dinner at Gwen's restaurant."

"You don't have to date me, Erik."

With a heavy sigh, he said, "Yeah, maybe I do." Erik reached over and lightly caressed her cheek with his fingertip.

"Why?" The salesman that sold her this car had promised her that there was more than enough room in the front seats. She wanted her money back because all of a sudden she not only felt crowded by her passenger, but she could barely breathe.

"Because I want to kiss you again." Erik's finger traced her lower lip. "I'm afraid, though."

"Of what?" Erik's finger moved with her lips, and for

one wild moment, she wanted to suck the digit into her mouth and lathe it with her tongue.

"I'm afraid that once I start kissing you I might not stop." Erik's work-roughened palm gently cupped her jaw. "You make me want things I have no right wanting."

"If you kiss me like you did the other night, I might not want you to stop."

Erik's fingers tightened slightly, and his eyes closed. "Don't say things like that, Sydney."

She could hear the catch in his voice and feel the trembling in his fingers. Heat poured off his body, and the windows started to fog up inside. "Don't say the truth?" She reached for his face only to frown when her mittened hands touched his cheek. To hell with the mittens, she tugged his face toward hers.

"Syd, do you know what you are doing?"

"I'm about to kiss you, Erik, that's all. Just a kiss." She brushed her lips against his chin. "I need to know if I imagined that kiss from the other night." Her lips skimmed his lower lip, but she pulled back before he claimed her mouth. She smiled at the groan that rumbled in the back of his throat. Kissing was some powerful stuff.

"If you imagined it, so did I." Erik's mouth caressed the line of her jaw.

She tilted her head as his mouth nipped at her chin. "Mass hallucination?"

Erik's chuckle tickled her ear as he tried to move his body into a better position. "Your car is too small."

"Your body is too big." She reached up and tried to wrap her arms around his neck.

Erik froze. "Does my size bother you?"

She blinked. The concern in Erik's voice penetrated the sensual haze that had surrounded her. She thought about Erik's body a lot lately. In fact, some would say she was becoming obsessed with it. Not once in all those fantasies would she say he was too big. "I was teasing, Erik. Your size doesn't bother me; it's perfect."

"Perfect for what?" Erik's breath was released against her lower lip as he playfully nipped.

"Kissing." She nipped him right back and then swiped her tongue over the mark she left behind. "It's definitely perfect for a lot of things, Erik, but kissing is all we'll be doing tonight." She needed to set some ground rules. She told herself they were for him, but she was afraid they were mainly for herself. She wanted to do a lot more than just kissing.

Erik shifted his weight so that his chest was rubbing against hers. The nylon of her coat swished against his. "You make the rules, Sydney. I'll obey them." His mouth then captured hers in a kiss that imitated their last kiss. Right down to the fact that if they weren't jammed into the front seat of her car, and if it wasn't seventeen degrees outside, she would have given him everything he wanted. Everything she wanted.

No sudden gasps or little girl voices announcing to all the world that they were kissing forced them apart. Erik slowly pulled away when things were just getting interesting. She was happy to note that his breathing didn't sound any better than her own.

Erik slowly sank back into his own seat. "Well, that answered that question."

"What question?" Did someone ask a question? She sure as hell didn't remember any question. Heck, she could barely remember her own name.

"I didn't imagine that kiss the other night." Erik turned his head and looked at her.

In the dim light she saw the flash of his teeth and smiled back. "Neither did I."

"How about I take you out on a real date tomorrow night? We can do a movie or dinner, whatever you want."

She tried to ignore the stupid fluttering in her stomach. Erik was finally asking her out. "The office is open till eight tomorrow night, Erik. How about you meet me at my place at about eight-thirty and I fix us something to eat."

"You trust me to be alone with you after that kiss?" Erik sounded amused, but curious.

"It's not you that I don't trust, Erik. It's me."

He leaned over and softly kissed her mouth. "Never tell a man you can't resist him, Syd."

"Why?" Erik already knew she was having a hard time resisting him.

"Because I have to go into that house"—Erik jerked his thumb toward the front windshield—"and after a very cold shower try to get some sleep. How do I do that, knowing you want me and are sleeping alone in some nice, warm bed across town?" Erik opened the door and got out of the car.

"Erik?"

He bent over and looked at her. With the help of the dome light, she could see the heat burning in his gaze. "What?"

"Frustration works both ways, you know."

Erik studied her for a long minute before slowly smiling and shaking his head. "Didn't they teach you self-preservation in that fancy medical school you went to?"

"Obviously not." She chuckled at his amazed expression. What had he been expecting? That she would deny the attraction between them? "I'll see you around eight-thirty tomorrow night."

"I'll be there." Erik closed the door and stood in the driveway to watch her drive away.

Chapter Nine

Gunnar looked at the next item on the shopping list and frowned. What in the world was marjoram? Erik had finally either gone out of his mind or was in love. Gunner's money would be on the latter. Only a man in love would make a food shopping list two pages long. Ever since Sydney had been joining them for dinner, not only had the lists grown longer, but they had gotten a lot more complicated. First there had been olive oil, then virgin olive oil, and now tonight he was supposed to pick up extra virgin olive oil. How could something be an extra virgin? Either you were a virgin or you weren't. It was like the old joke, "Not to worry, she's only a little bit pregnant."

One good thing had come from Erik trying to impress the cool, beautiful doctor with his culinary skills. They were sure eating good in the Olsen-Bergesen household lately. Most nights there was more than enough leftovers that he didn't have to do anything but reheat them for his turn in the kitchen the following evening. Tonight's pot roast would definitely stretch for another meal and a lunch or two. On the downside, the food shopping sure did take a lot longer.

Barley's Food Store was doing a booming business for a Tuesday night. The prediction of a storm hitting late tomorrow night probably had something to do with the brisk business. He could have waited until tomorrow night to do the shopping, but he had wanted to give Erik a chance to be alone with Sydney. Hans had probably stayed up and talked, maybe for an hour or so, but then he would head off for bed to give the young couple some privacy.

Not that it would do any good. Erik seemed to be moving slower than syrup in January when it came to the beautiful doctor. If his brother wasn't careful, someone was going to steal Sydney right in front of his eyes. He knew Erik's and Sydney's relationship was all a sham; well, at least it was supposed to be. He had begun doubting their pretend romance before Thanksgiving. No woman that he knew of would have entered into such a situation without feeling something toward her "boyfriend." Sydney felt something for his brother; he could see it in her eyes whenever she looked at Erik and he wasn't looking back.

He would give everything he owned to have a certain pair of green eyes look at him the way Sydney looked at his brother. With a heavy sigh he pushed the shopping cart over to the shelves of tomato sauces and picked up his gourmet staple. Heat one jar of sauce, boil the noodles, and voilà, spaghetti. For those who wished for something more savory, he usually placed a can of Parmesan cheese on the table and opened up a can of Hawaiian Punch. Gwen Fletcher Creighton, owner of The Catch of the Day restaurant, would never have to worry about competition from his direction.

The basil and garlic tomato sauce went into the cart. His list was only half done, and the cart was looking worse than an oil heating bill in January. He had to wonder if Erik had taken the time to figure out how much having a pretend girlfriend was costing him. Gunnar chuckled at that thought and pushed the cart around the end of the shelves and into the cereal aisle.

He stopped when he came face-to-face with the woman of his dreams, Maggie Franklin Pierce, and her daughter. They were having a discussion about sugar content and misleading advertising about the toy that was supposed to be inside the sparkling box of cereal. At least Maggie was discussing; Katie wasn't buying it for a moment.

"But, Mom, it has a penguin inside."

"I know it's a penguin, sweetie, but it's not in the box." Maggie flipped the box over and quickly scanned the back. "You have to send in twenty box tops and six dollars and ninety-five cents for postage and handling."

"I have three dollars that Uncle Gary gave me yesterday." Katie Pierce was bouncing up and down and smiling so sweetly at her mother. The pom-pom bear on top of her hat was flopping from side to side.

Gunnar stood there and watched. If Katie would have smiled up at him like that, he would have bought all twenty boxes of the sugar-coated cereal on the spot. He switched his gaze to Maggie and felt heat uncoil low in his gut. Bundled up in more clothes than a nun entering a strip poker competition, Maggie still had the power to make him want. To make him burn.

"It's not the money, sweetie. It's the twenty boxes of cereal you would have to eat."

"Polar Crispies are good, Mom. I like them, and so does Grandpop." Katie hugged the box closer to her chest. "Please, Mom, please."

He knew the moment Maggie gave in to her daughter. It was written across her face in love. "Okay, I'll buy one box tonight, but I'm not promising anything. The offer is only good to March, but I have a feeling you and Grandpop both will be sick of Polar Crispies by then."

Katie flashed a smile so bright, it touched his heart.

Maggie would smile like that. He was going to make it his life's mission to make Maggie smile like that as often as possible. Katie turned to put the cereal box in their cart and spotted him. "Gunnar!"

He smiled at the excitement in Katie's voice. No one had ever greeted him so enthusiastically before. "How do you know it's me and not my brother, Erik?"

Katie stopped her approach in midstep and studied him curiously for a minute. Her gaze skimmed him from the tips of his work boots to his wind-tossed hair. Finally, Katie said, "Your smile."

"My smile?" He quickly glanced at Maggie, but she seemed just as amused and impressed as he felt. Katie knew his smile.

"Yeah, you have a better smile than your brother." Katie closed the distance between them and showed him the cereal box. "See what I'm going to get." Katie pointed to a stuffed penguin that was on the front of the box.

Maggie rolled her eyes and muttered something about getting a tummy ache.

He chuckled and took in the sight of beautiful Maggie doing the weekly food shopping. It had been over a week since he kissed her in the wheel house of his boat. One very long and frustrating week, where sleep was impossible and cold showers the norm. Their nuclear meltdown kiss didn't seem to be having any ill effect at all on Maggie. She looked more beautiful, if that was possible. The winter wind had put color into her cheeks, and her mouth was moist with a shimmering lip gloss. "Hello, Maggie." Just because she appeared so unruffled and kissable, he said teasingly, "You're just the woman I need."

Maggie blushed a becoming red that made every one of her freckles stand out more. "Gunnar, I really don't think this is the appropriate time to discuss this."

He tried to hide his grin, but was pretty sure he had failed. So the lass, who surely had ancestors that hailed from the Emerald Isle, did remember their kiss. By the hue of her blush, he would say she hadn't been as unaffected as she would like him to believe. "Not appropriate?" He gave a small chuckle and held out the shopping list. "Where else do you suggest I bring up the subject of marjoram?"

"Marjoram?"

"Yes, marjoram." He looked down at the list, still in his hand. "My brother wants me to pick up marjoram, but for the life of me, I don't know what it is."

"It's a spice." Maggie looked at her cart, her daughter, and the wall of cereal boxes to her right. She looked everywhere but at him. "It's mint."

"Wonder why he just didn't write down mint?" Gunnar shook his head and quickly scanned the rest of the list to make sure there was nothing else he didn't recognize. There wasn't, but what his brother wanted with three kiwis was beyond him.

"You'll find marjoram in the spice aisle."

"Thank you." He felt a tugging on his jacket and glanced down.

Katie was smiling up at him. "I gave her the gloves, just like you asked me to."

He smiled back. "I know. Thank you." Maggie had already lost one pair. She had left them in the wheelhouse of his boat. He had them in the glove compartment of his Jeep, waiting for the perfect opportunity to return them. He glanced at Maggie's big pocketbook sitting in the basket of the cart. The fat, fluffy mittens with the knitted-in snowflakes that he had bought her were sticking out of the top. "Did your mommy tell you how much I loved your cookies?"

"She said you ate them all up."

"Well, almost. I had to share a couple with Erik and my grandfather." He squatted down so that he was on Katie's level. "They begged so pitifully I had to give them a couple." His smile grew. "It was truly pitiful.

They were whining"—he raised his voice to a high squeal—" '*Please, please, please.*' "

Katie giggled, and if he wasn't mistaken, so did Maggie. His heart lightened at the sound. It wasn't a full-blown laugh, but it was a beginning. He slowly stood to his full height and decided he was tired of waiting for Maggie to get used to him. He knew the way to Maggie's body was through hot, deep kisses, but the way to her heart was through her daughter, Katie. He didn't want to go through Katie; he wanted to include her. Maggie was a package deal, and he was more than willing to pay whatever price it took to get them both into his life.

"Hey." He plastered on his most polite smile and prayed that Maggie didn't see how badly he was sweating under his winter coat and flannel shirt. "How would you two like to go up to The Christmas Village? I heard it opened up last week." The Christmas Village was a small farm up the coast a piece and inland about thirty miles. It was decorated with thousands upon thousands of lights and hundreds of decorated Christmas trees. There were shops, choirs, sleigh rides, and little men dressed like elves. It was beautiful and peaceful during the day, but it was spectacular when night fell and the lights were turned on. It was a typical tourist trap in its truest form, and he had never been there.

He wasn't playing fair, and he knew it. Playing fair hadn't gotten him anywhere.

Katie's eyes got round, and she started to bounce on her toes. "Can we, Mom? Can we?" Katie turned to her mother and said the magic word, "Pleeeeease."

He cringed. Maggie was going to rip into him any second now, and he couldn't blame her. He never should have asked in front of Katie.

Maggie glanced at her daughter and then up at him. Amazingly, there wasn't any anger in her eyes, only wariness. "That would be nice, Gunnar." Maggie took hold of Katie's little hand. "I have Friday night off if that's convenient for you."

It took him a moment to realize Maggie was accepting his offer. He had a date with Maggie Pierce! Okay, it wasn't going to be candle light and soft music, more like hot cocoa and "Rudolph the Red Nose Reindeer" sung by little men wearing pointy green shoes and bells. But who cared? Not him. His smile was slow in coming, but it would have taken a plastic surgeon to remove it from his face. "Great. I'll pick you both up around five. We'll get dinner there."

The next evening, there weren't any guests at the Olsen-Bergesen dinner table. "I just wanted both of you boys to know how happy I am that Merete proved me wrong." Hans passed Erik the platter holding the left-over roast beef.

"Proved you wrong about what?" Erik took only one slice because he was meeting Sydney at her cottage in three hours and she was going to make them something. He couldn't wait another three hours to eat, but he didn't want to stuff himself. He passed the platter to Gunnar.

"I've been thinking a lot about Merete lately, and it saddens me how much I misjudged my little girl."

Gunnar shared a concerned look with Erik, and then casually asked, "What exactly did you misjudge about her?"

"I underestimated her and the love she felt for your father." Hans passed the bowl of reheated potatoes and carrots. "It just goes to prove that love can conquer all, and people can change."

Erik glanced at his brother, and Gunnar looked just as confused as he felt. "*Bestefar,* we don't know what you are talking about."

"Merete. We are talking about your mother." Hans chewed on his biscuit for a moment before continuing. "Merete was so sweet and special as a young girl. She was always happy, singing and laughing. I tell you, the sun rose with that child."

Erik could feel his jaw lock against the retort he wanted to make. The only time he had heard his mother sing was in church, and then it had been stiff and flat. He couldn't recall her laughing or even seeing her happy. His mother had been such a bitter, harping woman that he and Gunnar had moved out the first chance they had gotten. Visits to their old home had been short and seldom, but they had stopped by their father's boat every chance they had gotten.

"The only time Merete fussed or pouted was when she didn't get her way," Hans said.

Amen to that! Erik took a small bite from the biscuit and wondered if Hans's version of the past was correct or if he was getting confused again. He wished Sydney was there; she would know. "Last night you said you tended to spoil all your daughters."

"Yes, to my shame, I did. Spoiled them rotten, and especially Merete. Your mother looked so much like my Inga that I would have given her the world if I could have. With Hilde and Berta married and living in America, Merete was all I had left. She had been the light in my life."

"Until she decided she was going to marry Rolf Olsen," Gunnar said as he piled potatoes and carrots onto his plate.

Hans slowly lowered his fork and stared at them. "I want both of you boys to know I didn't have anything against Rolf. From what I knew about him, he was a hardworking young man. Big as a mountain, fair, kind, and handsome as sin." Hans smiled. "You two look like him."

Gunnar flashed a quick grin. "Thanks."

"I was against their marriage for a couple of reasons. Merete was only eighteen and far too young."

"But our aunts, Hilde and Berta, both were allowed to marry young." Erik remembered the photographs from last night. Both of his aunts had not only married before their twentieth birthdays, but they had had big, splashy weddings with all the trimmings. No photos had been taken at his parents' wedding, at least none that he or Gunnar ever saw.

"My fault," whispered Hans. "I never should have allowed it. I didn't know how to say no to my girls then. I learned, but it was far too late; the damage had been done. When Merete said she was marrying Rolf, I finally said no and put my foot down. It was a horrible scene with words shouted in anger that never should have been uttered. We fought for two weeks, me and my Merete." Hans pushed a potato around his plate for a moment and then looked up. "I don't want to speak ill of my baby, especially to her boys, but I have to tell you two, your mother used to be so spoiled. She demanded the best of everything, and I got it for her. I spent a fortune on fancy designer clothes, jewelry, and even a brand-new car for her eighteenth birthday. I indulged her, so the blame must be laid at my door."

"I don't remember her as being spoiled." Erik could see the distress in Hans's expression and wanted to relieve some of it. His mother hadn't been spoiled. There hadn't been any money to spoil her with. Merete Olsen had been bitter and mean. There had never been any joy in the Olsen household. Joy had been found out on the sea, with the sky above them, the waves beneath them, and if it was a very good day, a net full of fish.

"Merete was used to the finer things in life. I did that to her, and I honestly thought I was saving her from a horrible mistake. I thought she would never be content to live on a fisherman's wages. She proved me wrong."

Erik and Gunnar just stared at their grandfather. As far as they knew, their mother had never been content a day in her life.

"I even accused Rolf of marrying Merete to get his hands on my money." Tears pooled in Hans's eyes. "I'm sorry about that most of all, boys. Your father was a good man and never once asked me for a krone." Hans took a moment to compose himself. "When Merete disobeyed me and married Rolf in some secret ceremony, I allowed pride to form hateful words. I publicly disowned my own flesh and blood. Within two months I sold everything I had and moved to America to be close to your aunts."

Erik saw the opening and jumped. "How come you only stayed in Minnesota a couple of years?" One of the questions that had always bothered him was why his grandfather had only stayed near his two other daughters for about four years. What had happened to sever that relationship? And why hadn't he come back to Norway?

"Pride's a horrible quality in a man." Hans shook his head. "You both deserve the truth, but I'm afraid neither of you will think very highly of your grandfather once I'm done. The greatest joy and responsibility a man can have is fatherhood. I'm afraid I failed at it. I'm afraid I have a lot to answer for when I am finally reunited with Inga in heaven."

Erik reached over and covered Hans's trembling hand. "*Bestefar,* we love you. Our feelings for you won't change because of the past." He was torn inside. His grandfather had been right all along about Merete, but he had been wrong about his father. Rolf Olsen was a proud man and would have never asked Hans for a dollar.

"Erik's right, *Bestefar,*" added Gunnar while laying a hand across Hans's other arm. "We do love you, and the past will stay in the past if that is what you wish."

Hans smiled with gratitude. "No, you need to know the whole truth, so I might as well spit it out now. I arrived in Minnesota with a heavy heart and heavier pockets. Hilde and Berta appeared to be so happy to see me, and I went back to my spoiling ways. I helped Hilde and her husband buy a bigger, fancier house.

Berta wanted a vacation home on a lake. Hilde's husband's business was experiencing some hard times, and I helped him with what I thought was a loan." Hans sadly shook his head. "I didn't think there should be paperwork between family. Everyone was happy; but I felt I was becoming a burden living in their home, so I started to look for a place of my own. Berta wanted a new car, and Hilde said she needed a vacation. Before I knew it, the money was almost all gone. I finally had to tell them no more and that I needed some of my loan back."

"Let me guess," Gunnar said. "Hilde's husband claimed it wasn't a loan; it was a gift."

Hans nodded. "When they learned the money was gone, they didn't want me any longer. Said they couldn't support an old man. They were just starting their own families and had no room for me. So I left."

"Why didn't you come back home? Back to Norway?" Erik asked. Maybe with her father back in their village, Merete wouldn't have been so bitter. So miserable.

"As I said, pride is a horrible quality in a man. My pride wouldn't allow me to go home. I couldn't face Merete or her husband, especially after I had accused Rolf of marrying her for my money."

"Why Maine?" Gunnar popped a piece of potato into his mouth.

"I went to what I was familiar with. I went to the sea. I traveled eastward and stopped when my boots hit the ocean. Misty Harbor seemed like a peaceful little village twenty-three years ago. I liked what I saw. Unknown to my daughters, I had a few dollars left. It was enough to get me this land and to put a down payment on a lobster boat. I became what I ridiculed the most in your father. I became a fisherman. If a fisherman was good enough for my Merete, it would be good enough for me."

Erik smiled. "And you contacted Nils back in our village, and he told you you were a grandfather."

"He sent me letters telling me how happy Merete

was, and how she was the envy of the entire village. He told me about how Merete was a wonderful, loving mother and that Rolf was an excellent provider. He said that my grandsons and daughter wanted for nothing. Nils also wrote everything he could think of about you both. Occasionally, a snapshot would come with the letter. He never did manage to find a picture of Merete for me."

Erik knew why. Hans would have been appalled at the changes in his youngest daughter. One look at Merete's face and Hans would have known it was all a lie. Last night Erik had looked at those pictures of his mother at seventeen and had been shocked himself at the difference. The beautiful, vibrant woman in Hans's book had never been his mother.

Erik glanced up to meet Gunnar's gaze. Most people thought that identical twins could somehow magically read each other's minds or that they had some type of secret language between them. It was a bunch of bull. He couldn't read Gunnar's mind, and Gunnar couldn't read his. He didn't feel his brother's pain, and Gunnar never knew when something bad was going to happen to him. They were close, but no closer than what he would consider average brothers to be.

Tonight he didn't need to be a mind reader to know what Gunnar was thinking. Nils had lied to Hans, but neither one of them wanted to be the one to tell their grandfather the truth. What harm could there be in allowing Hans his illusions of a happy Merete?

Sydney pulled away from the office and tried not to step down on the gas too hard. She was running late, and worse, she hadn't had time to do some food shopping during lunch. Erik had been due at her cottage ten minutes ago, and she had promised him dinner. What in the world was she going to feed him? Misty Harbor had picked a terrible time for the flu to sweep through the schools and cram her appointment book. She had to double up on appointments, and in one instance, triple up.

When all three of her one o'clock appointments showed up, and she still hadn't had a chance to eat the chicken salad sandwich Gwen had sent over, she had made an executive decision. She needed to hire a receptionist. Maybe not full-time, but definitely someone part-time to answer the phone, make appointments, and file. She hated filing, and today she had lost three charts and had wasted precious minutes trying to locate them.

She mentally went through an inventory of her freezer as she turned down her street. Conrad Street was quiet, and a couple of her more ambitious neighbors already had Christmas lights up and blazing. There was even a lit Christmas tree in the Burtons' living room window. Great, she now had one more thing to add to her already overcrowded To Do List. Decorate for Christmas and let's not forget the shopping that would entail. She didn't so much as own one twinkle light or plastic candy cane.

Erik's truck was parked in front of the cute white picket fence that surrounded her yard. She pulled into the driveway, glanced at his empty truck, and then at her dark cottage. She had no idea where Erik had gone, but hopefully he was visiting a neighbor so that she had some extra time to change and to start thinking about dinner.

What she needed was quantity first, quality second. She had seen first hand the amount of food Erik could put away in one sitting. Gunnar had matched him serving for serving. Hans hadn't been a slouch himself. Between the three Norwegians, Barley's Food Store would never go out of business. The other night, Hans had complained that she ate like a bird, a small, skinny bird at that. If she ate like Erik or even Hans, she would split the seams of every one of her jeans and would have to be fork-lifted into her car. The amazing part was,

Erik didn't seem to have an ounce of extra fat on him. The high-calorie intake converted straight to muscle. Incredible muscle.

The last thing she needed to think about before spending the evening alone with the Incredible Hunk was his muscles. Or his crystal blue eyes. Or his rich, deep laugh. Or his sinfully hot kisses. She shouldn't be thinking about Erik at all. She needed to concentrate on food. Lots of food.

Sydney hurried into the cottage, kicked off her shoes and hung up her coat. Her purse, a tightly tied plastic bag, and an overstuffed tote bag landed on the couch as she hurried into the kitchen. A soft *thack* and a glowing light in her backyard told her where Erik was. She flipped on the porch light and opened the back door. Erik was out at the old stump being used as a chopping block, and he was splitting kindling. A high-powered, battery-operated lantern was nearby and giving him plenty of light to work by. "Hi, sorry I'm late, and you don't have to do that, Erik."

"Hi yourself, no problem, and you're running low." Erik gave her a quick flash of a smile before swinging the axe downward. The piece of wood that had been standing on its end split in two.

"You can stop now, Erik." The man was impossible. The kindling box in the living room was full, and there were still a couple more tiny pieces by the back door. "Come inside where it's warm."

"I'm not cold. I'll be in in a minute or two."

"Fine." If the man wanted to chop her firewood, who was she to argue. "I need to get changed, and then I'll start on dinner." She closed the door, made sure it was unlocked, and then hurried upstairs for a quick shower. Six-year-old Jennifer Wallace hadn't made it to the bathroom at the office when the stomach virus hit with its usual results. Jennifer's mom had been mortified, Jennifer had cried, and Sydney had politely excused herself to change into the extra set of clothes she kept at the office for such emergencies.

Fifteen minutes later Erik was starting a fire in the living room while she stood in front of the open freezer door, frowning. It was worse than what she had expected. The good news was she had a container of frozen vegetable soup Gwen had made. She could defrost it in a saucepan for the appetizer, and it would be delicious. Gwen didn't know how to make awful soup. The bad news was, Erik had a choice between frozen pizza or fish sticks for the entree. On the more good news front, she had a frozen Sara Lee pecan coffee cake. She grabbed the soup, fish sticks, and the cake. To round out the meal and to increase the quantity, she tossed a bag of frozen french fries onto the pile and dumped everything onto the counter. She now understood why Richard had constantly harped at her about her culinary skills and why they had eaten out nearly five nights a week. Julia Child, she wasn't.

While the frozen cylinder of soup melted into the saucepan, and the fish sticks and french fries baked in the oven, she cleaned off the dining room table. The mess in the dining room wasn't too bad or deep. When Jocelyn had stayed the three nights during Thanksgiving weekend, she had started to organize the books for Sydney. The two floor-to-ceiling bookshelves in the living room were now crammed with books and magazines. Most of the cardboard boxes had been unpacked and thrown out, and she now had lots of counter and table top space because the men of Misty Harbor had stopped sending her flowers. She had liked the scent of roses, but she missed the candy more. Now she was the proud owner of eight different vases, all of which were empty and on the top shelf of the coat closet.

Erik joined her in the kitchen and started to wash his hands in the sink. "What can I do to help?"

"Stir the soup, while I set the table." She reached around his massive shoulders for two dinner plates and matching bowls. The dishes were Gwen's old ones, but they were still pretty. "Sorry, this dinner isn't exactly what I had in mind when I invited you."

Erik chuckled as he turned the heat down beneath the pot. "What did you have in mind?" Erik's gaze caressed her face. "Something more intimate? Candle light? Soft music?"

She forced herself to look away from the heat burning in his eyes and cracked the oven door and gave the sizzling french fries and fish sticks a quick glance. "No, something more substantial."

Erik's booming laughter filled the small kitchen. "I happen to like fish sticks."

She glanced at him curiously, trying to figure out if he was lying or not. If he was fibbing, he was doing a very good job at it. "The other choice was frozen pizza, and that just didn't seem to go with the soup."

"Fish sticks are fine." He rooted through a drawer and came up with a wooden spoon. "What did you have in mind for dinner, if not this?"

"On my lunch hour I was going to pick up some meat and potatoes and throw it into the Crock-Pot. Make a stew or something."

Erik stirred the soup. "What happened on your lunch hour?"

"A little girl lost her lunch on me." She shrugged off one of the not so pleasant aspects of being a doctor. "The flu is going through the schools."

"After a day like that, it sounds like I should be the one cooking you dinner."

She stared at Erik in wonder. Richard would have snapped something about her coddling her patients and that she should have known better than to stand that close to a sick child. Richard had been "christened" only once while he had been doing his residency. From that day on, Richard had avoided children as though they carried the plague. Richard also had never once offered to cook her dinner, no matter what kind of day she had had. "You cooked last night, and two nights before that, and two nights before that."

"So." Erik took a step closer and tenderly brushed an untidy hair off her cheek and tucked it behind her ear. The ends of her hair were still damp from her hurried shower. "I didn't realize in America you keep score of that kind of stuff."

She had to moisten her lips before she could answer him. "We usually don't."

Erik's gaze had followed the sweep of her tongue. Blue flames flared in his eyes as he stepped closer and backed her up against the counter. "Do American men tell their women when they are going to kiss them?"

"Sometimes." She lost herself in the desire burning in his eyes as Erik gently cupped her chin and tilted her mouth upward. Her arms reached for his shoulders as she raised herself up on her toes to get closer to his mouth.

"This time I will tell you." Erik's teeth nipped at her lower lip. "Next time I won't." His mouth captured hers as his arms wrapped around her and pulled her closer.

Her world exploded into an inferno of heat and desire. There was nothing tentative about Erik's possession of her mouth. He kissed as though he knew her every secret, her every desire. Her breasts were tender and achy as they pressed against his rock-hard chest. She wanted his touch. She craved his touch.

Erik's large hands cupped her bottom as he pressed himself against the junction of her thighs. She was left in no doubt of his response. Erik wanted her as much as she wanted him. One of the glories of mankind was that men couldn't fake or hide their response to women. She wove her fingers into his long hair and tugged the rubber band free.

Erik groaned her name and, with a slight rippling of muscles, lifted her completely off her feet. Her butt landed on the counter, and Erik's hands slid under her sweatshirt and up her bare back. She pressed herself against his warm, rough hands and tangled her tongue around his.

A loud, annoying sound started to penetrate the sexual haze surrounding them. She tried to ignore the noise. It was Erik who broke the kiss with a muttered curse. "Damn."

She gulped in a quick breath. "What?"

Erik leaned his forehead against hers. His ragged breathing matched hers. "The fish sticks are done."

Chapter Ten

Sydney slid the pecan coffee cake into the oven and then looked over at Erik, who was busy wiping down the dining room table. She wasn't sure if he was an oddity among men or the norm. Richard never would have helped load the dishwasher or wipe down the table after a meal. Occasionally, he had managed to bring his dirty plate to the kitchen sink, but that was about it. She knew she shouldn't be comparing Erik to Richard all the time, but she didn't have a whole lot of other men to draw from.

When she was a little girl, her parents had employed a full-time housekeeper to help with the housework and the three girls. After she and her sisters grew into teenagers, the housekeeper had come in only twice a week, and they had been the ones to pick up the slack. Gwen excelled in the cooking arena, so she and Jocelyn usually had clean-up duty and laundry. Her parents were strong believers in self-reliance. She could scrub a bathroom with the best of them, but for some reason cooking had never clicked. She knew her father pitched in around the kitchen and could barbecue just about anything on the grill. Come to think of it, she had seen Gwen's husband, Daniel, scrubbing pots and even running a vacuum.

Erik wasn't the oddity. He was the norm. Richard couldn't have been the norm, because if he was, there would be a whole lot more homicides taking place in kitchens across America.

"Would you like some coffee with the cake?"

"Sounds great," Erik said as he tossed the dishcloth into the sink.

"We can have it out in the living room. The fire is going nicely out there, and I need to talk to you."

"About?" Erik leaned against the counter and seemed to watch every move she made.

She filled the coffee machine with water. "Hans." She put in a paper filter and measured out the coffee. "I believe I solved your problem of leaving him home all day while you and Gunnar work."

"You have?"

"It wasn't really me. Millicent found the solution."

"Millicent Wyndham, the town's matriarch?"

"The one and only." She led the way into the living room. She frowned at the tightly tied plastic bag sitting on the couch, picked it up, and put it in the closet off the kitchen where the washer and dryer were. She would take care of that mess later. Her purse she moved to the coffee table as she sat and started to dig through the canvas tote bag. "I stopped by her house this morning on the way into work, and she had it all figured out."

Erik tossed another log onto the fire and replaced the fire screen before joining her on the couch. "Okay, let's hear it."

"You and Gunnar pay some of the women in town to stay with Hans during the day."

"You want us to hire baby-sitters?"

"No, you'll be hiring adult companions for your grandfather. Someone to check up on him and give him a couple of hours' worth of company during the day. I don't think he needs someone with him constantly. Maybe they could stop in around nine or ten in the morning and then leave about two or three in the afternoon. Five, maybe six hours a day, that's all."

Erik seemed to think about it for a moment. "True. He hasn't wandered off lately, but he is still getting confused and forgetful. I think he forgot to eat lunch today. I made him a nice sandwich and wrapped it up on a plate and put it in the refrigerator for him. It was still there when I got home."

"Did you ask him about it?"

"Yes, but he said he ate it for lunch." Erik shook his head. "There weren't any extra dishes in the sink, so I don't think he ate anything."

She found what she was looking for and pulled it out of the bag. "Millicent made up a list of women who said they would be interested in keeping Hans company maybe just for one day a week. The Women's Guild has offered to handle every Tuesday. They would take turns, so that each member would only have to do it about once a month or less. The money will go to the Guild and not the women. It would be like a fund-raiser for them."

Erik chuckled at the thought. "Hans will become a fund-raising project."

"Sorta, yeah." She looked down at the list. "Evelyn Ruffles, who lives next door to me, says she could do it Mondays or Thursdays. Priscilla Patterson would do one day a week even though she's a member of the Guild. Sadie Hopkins will do it a couple days a week or as much as you need her."

Erik appeared stunned. "All those ladies would help Hans?"

"You would be paying them. Maybe minimum wage for about four, five, or even six hours a day. Will you and Gunnar be able to swing the financial end?"

"Of course, he's our grandfather. Money isn't a problem, it's time." Erik relaxed into the couch and breathed a big sigh of relief. "I didn't think it could be solved that quickly or easily."

"There are still some hurdles, Erik. Hans might resent having the ladies of the village constantly checking up on him."

"He might, but I know he would definitely resent being put into one of those assisted-living homes." Erik shook off that depressing thought.

"You and Gunnar still have to keep trying to get him to go see that specialist, Erik. He needs to be tested."

"I know."

"If it is Alzheimer's, it will only get progressively worse. But in the early stages there are some medicines that could help him, maybe even slow the process down. The medical field is starting to make some progress with the disease. Hans needs to be diagnosed as quickly as possible."

"The other day I stopped in the library over in Sullivan." Erik leaned back and closed his eyes. "Alzheimer's is one nasty disease."

"Yes, it is." What else could she possibly tell him? She couldn't lie to him about it. "But we don't know if that is what Hans has, Erik."

"I know. He could have a tumor." Erik leaned his head back and closed his eyes. "Hell of a choice, Doc."

Friday morning Hans stood in his doorway and stared at the woman on his doorstep. He had known Sadie Hopkins for over twenty years, and never once had she shown up at his door. "You want me to what?"

"Come to art class with me." Sadie tossed her white boa scarf over her shoulder and beamed. A stray white feather floated on the breeze and slowly descended to the ground. "Today we start on oils, and it's a 'Bring a friend for free' class. That means I get to bring a guest."

Lately, Hans had secretly thought and feared he was

losing his mind. With Sadie, he knew she had. The woman was a menace to fashion and to the streets of Misty Harbor. Sadie was at least ten years younger than he and matched his five-foot, ten-inch height, inch for inch. They stood eyeball-to-eyeball, and Sadie could probably pin him in wrestling. He didn't ever remember seeing her in anything but overalls. Today's overalls were an obnoxious shade of dull green, and they were tucked into laced-up combat boots. General Eisenhower would have been proud to have her on the beaches at Normandy. "Why me?"

He couldn't say Sadie had a beautiful face, not even in her younger days. But it was definitely interesting. No one would ever be bored in Sadie's company. The woman apparently didn't know the meaning of the word.

"What? You aren't my friend?" Sadie's shocking pink lipstick matched the fake fur jacket she had on over the overalls and the hair curlers in her hair. Her sunglasses had zebra-print frames, and they matched the hair net she wore over those curlers. She looked as if she was going on a feminist safari adventure.

Hans had never once seen Sadie without those curlers in her hair. He was bored enough with his own company to take her invitation seriously. "I can't draw for spit."

Sadie's pink mouth stretched into a grin. "Neither can I."

"So why do you go?"

"It's a great place to pick up men." Sadie put her hands on her ample hips. "So, are you coming or not? There's plenty of lonely women there, Hans. A man like you could have his pick of the old birds."

He shook his head in denial, even though he could feel his own chest puff out an extra inch or two. "I don't have any supplies. The only brush I own I used to paint the bathroom last spring."

"Not a problem, I told you, my treat today. If you

like it, you can get your own supplies, and I can swing by on Fridays and pick you up."

He glanced at the pink Cadillac sitting in his driveway. He knew it was old and considered a classic, but that wasn't what impressed him the most about it. What caught his eye every time he saw Sadie maneuvering the old boat through the narrow streets of Misty Harbor was the fact that she never had the top up. Sadie with the wind whistling through her curlers and the trail of her feather boa whipping in the breeze behind her was a sight to see. Today was no exception. The top was down, and it was barely forty degrees in December. Thankfully, it was sunny. Sadie was a woman after his own heart. "I get to ride in your car?"

"Sure do." Sadie pulled out a pair of lime green driving gloves. "The *Bruce* is very particular about passengers. So feel privileged."

The entire town knew the reason behind the pink Cadillac's name. Bruce Springsteen had recorded a song about a pink Cadillac, and Sadie was in the habit of blaring Bruce's songs whenever she was driving. How could he refuse such an invitation. "I'll go on one condition."

"What's that?"

"I get to take you to lunch after class. You get to pick where you would like to eat."

"McDonald's in Sullivan is my favorite place." Sadie rubbed her hands together in glee and actually patted her stomach. "I love those Big Macs."

He chuckled at her enthusiasm. "Let me get my coat."

"Well, hurry up, old man, time's a wasting and I'm not getting any younger." Sadie turned and hurried back to her pink boat of a car.

Hans thought the car with its big fins and fluffy dice hanging from the rearview mirror and Sadie matched pretty well. Once you considered there weren't any tanks in Misty Harbor for her to drive.

* * *

Gunnar stared out of the living room window in amazement. On one hand, he was totally relieved that Hans was finally home, and apparently in good health if the smile on his face was any indication. On the other hand, he didn't know what to make of the situation. When Erik told him about Sydney's and Millicent's idea, it had sounded like the answer to their prayers. Now he wasn't too sure.

He hadn't figured Sadie Hopkins and her big pink Cadillac into the equation.

He watched as his grandfather got out of the convertible and waved Sadie on her way. Hans, who had a spring in his step, was wearing his normal dark brown jacket. For some strange reason, he was also wearing a pair of leopard-print earmuffs. Hans was carrying a painter's canvas and smiling like a fool.

The slamming of the front door announced that his grandfather had made it inside. For some insane reason he wanted to rush out into the foyer, confront his grandfather, and demand to know where he had been. Gunnar forced himself to sit on the couch, pick up the closest magazine, and begin to leaf through it as though he hadn't been pacing in front of the window.

"Gunnar, the most amazing thing happened today," Hans said as he hurried into the room. The coat and earmuffs were gone.

"What?"

"I discovered I can paint!" Hans proudly held up the canvas for his inspection.

Gunnar dropped the magazine back onto the end table and stood up so he could get a closer look at his grandfather's painting. He managed not to cringe. "It's the West Quoddy Head Light." He knew that for two reasons. One, even a six-year-old could manage to draw a recognizable lighthouse. Two, the West Quoddy Head Light was the only red-and-white-striped lighthouse in

Maine. His second guess would have been a deformed candy cane surrounded by big brown things and blue. Lots of blue.

"See, you knew what it was, and it's not done yet." Hans propped the unframed canvas on the mantel. "Sadie said I had a true gift, and even the teacher admitted I had an unusual style."

"You went to an art class?" Erik and he had been racking their brains trying to come up with a hobby that fitted Hans. Neither one of them had thought of art classes for their grandfather.

"Sadie stopped by and invited me. She's been going for six months now, and today was a bring a guest for free class." Hans stood back and admired the painting. "I signed up for the rest of the oil painting classes. In February we're starting on pottery. Sadie says that's the class that separates the men from the boys."

Gunnar just stared at his grandfather in dumbfounded shock. "Pottery?"

"Yep." Hans moved the canvas an inch to the right. "I need one of you boys to drive me into Sullivan sometime this weekend."

"Sure, what do you need?" He was going to The Christmas Village with Maggie and Katie tonight, but that still left him free most of Saturday and all day Sunday. Just thinking about Maggie made his palms sweat. For the past two nights he had been waiting for the phone to ring and for Maggie to back out of tonight. The phone had rung a couple of times, but it never had been Maggie.

"I need to stop in at that video rental place." Hans moved the canvas back to where it had been originally. "Sadie says if we get good at making pottery, we'd be like them people in the movie *Ghost.* She wants to be that Demi person, and I get to be some guy named Swayback."

Gunnar felt his mouth drop open wide enough that Sadie could have parallel parked her Cadillac into it.

He couldn't seem to close it. His grandfather had finally gone around the bend, and Sadie had been the one driving.

Hans frowned, shook his head, and removed the canvas from the mantel. "The smoke from the fire might ruin it." He placed the picture on the bookshelf and propped it up in front of a set of leather-bound classics, all written in Norwegian and worth a small fortune. "I need to watch that movie so I know what she's yakking about."

Gunnar felt the pain in his jaw and slowly closed his mouth. He had to leave in three minutes or he was going to be late picking up Maggie. He didn't have time to handle this right now. Sadie Hopkins playing the role of Demi Moore was just too ludicrous to contemplate. As for his grandfather, he didn't know what to make of him. Let Erik try to figure it all out. After all, this was his "girlfriend's" idea. "I'll take you Saturday afternoon, okay?"

"Thanks." Hans went over to the fireplace and tossed another log onto the fire. "What are you all dressed up for? Got a hot date?"

Only Hans would consider jeans, with more blue than white in them, and a sweater dressed up. "I'm taking Maggie Pierce and her daughter to The Christmas Village." He tried to keep his expression neutral. "Remember, I told you last night." *And the night before that, and again over breakfast this morning.*

"Must have slipped my mind." Hans dusted off his hands. "I'd be careful with that one, son."

Gunnar felt his whole body stiffen in outrage. He knew all about Maggie's past and the hurt she had caused Daniel Creighton. Maggie had paid dearly for that one mistake, and if Daniel could forgive her, who was he not to? The busybodies in town should mind their own damn business and leave Maggie alone. "What do you mean by that, *Bestefar*?" He had never known his grandfather to cast stones.

"She's a redhead, a true redhead." Hans gave him a knowing grin. "You know what they say about redheads."

There were quite a few jokes and rumors about redheads. Most were in such poor taste that he hoped his grandfather had never heard them. "No, what do they say about redheads?"

"They have a fiery temper to match that fiery hair."

He flashed his grandfather a quick smile. "I'm counting on that one, *Bestefar.* I'm counting on it." A hot temper he didn't mind at all. Because a temper was a sure sign of passion.

Hans's laughter filled the living room as Gunnar headed for the foyer and the coatrack. He put on his coat and grabbed his best hat and gloves. It was going down below freezing tonight, and he wanted to be prepared. He hoped Maggie and Katie dressed for the weather. "I don't know when I'll be home. Shouldn't be too late. Don't worry about dinner, Erik said something about Sydney coming over again. So I'm sure he has something planned."

"I'm not really hungry yet anyway. Sadie and I had a late lunch at McDonald's in Sullivan." Hans shook his head and chuckled. "Never saw a woman put away that many Big Macs before."

Oh, yeah, definitely Demi Moore material. "Well, Erik should be home in a little while. I'll see you either late tonight or in the morning." He headed for the door.

"Drive carefully."

"Will do." He stepped outside and into the approaching darkness. The last of the light was fading from the sky. By the time he picked up Maggie and Katie, it would be dark. The perfect time to visit a tourist attraction famous for its "Over two hundred thousand lights extravaganza."

Forty minutes later he found himself following the glow sticks of the parking lot attendants. Only high school kids would think it was fun to dress up as green elves and park cars. Maggie had been surprisingly quiet during the thirty-minute drive. Katie, if given a choice between breathing or talking, would have given up breathing.

He parked the car and then turned in his seat to look at Katie. Her mouth formed a perfect *O* as her gaze took in the sight before them. The Christmas Village was lit up in all its glory. It was indeed a remarkable sight. So was the absolute childish wonder on Katie's face. "Are you ready to go be dazzled, Katie?"

"Yes!" Katie reached for the seat belt release, but couldn't undo it. Her fat golden mittens were getting in the way. "It's so pretty."

Gunnar released his seat belt and angled his shoulders through the space between the two front seats. He undid Katie's belt for her. "Don't open your door, Katie. Let your mom or me get it for you. There are too many cars in the parking lot." Lord, she was adorable with her bear hat, red-and-gold-striped scarf, and matching bear mittens. While the daughter might be adorable, the mother was delectable.

Maggie Pierce with her quiet, almost shy, answers and nervous hands had been driving him crazy for the past thirty minutes. What happened to the feisty, spitting-mad woman who had confronted him in the wheelhouse of his boat? Being in a closed space with Maggie was like a contest of self-control. He could smell the light floral scent of her perfume, and it had distracted him more than once during the drive. What was that scent?

He started to pull himself back into the driver's seat and glanced at Maggie. She was watching him with soft, warm green eyes that held the same kind of wonder that her daughter's had. Except Maggie wasn't looking at the colorful display of lights, and there was nothing childish about the look. She was watching him. He quietly asked, "Are you ready to be dazzled, Maggie?"

Maggie's smile held a hint of shyness as she quickly glanced away from him. "I believe I already am." Maggie opened her door and stepped out into the cold, clear night before he could answer.

It took him more than a moment to clear the haze of desire from his mind. Had Maggie been referring to him? Impossible, he hadn't done anything to dazzle her. Hell, he didn't think he had what it took to dazzle a woman like Maggie. He was a simple, hardworking lobster fisherman. The same as her father and brother. There wasn't one thing dazzling about him.

After several deep breaths and a futile search for his gloves, he exited the Jeep. He joined Maggie and her daughter in front of the vehicle only to discover his gloves had been in his coat pocket all along. A steady stream of tourists were walking through the plowed parking lot and were heading for the main gate. The storm that had hit late Wednesday night and early Thursday morning had left behind a good eight inches of fresh snow here. Back in Misty Harbor, and along the coast, they had gotten mostly frozen rain mixed with snow. The lawns still held a couple of inches of snow, but the streets had been cleared long before noon on Thursday.

"Make sure you hang on to your mom's hand, *Liten.*" Gunnar reached down and playfully swatted the pom-pom bear on Katie's hat. "We don't want to lose you in this crowd."

"What did you call me?" Katie reached for her mom's hand and grinned up at him.

"*Liten,* it means little one." They started following the crowd. "What do you want to do first? Do you want to see some of the displays or grab something to eat? I'm not sure what all they have here to do."

"Sometimes you talk funny." Katie pulled at her mom's hand and tried to hurry them along.

He chuckled, but Maggie looked horrified. "Katherine Leigh Pierce!" Maggie stopped walking, forcing them all to halt. "That wasn't a very nice thing to say. You apologize to Mr. Olsen immediately."

Katie looked ready to cry. The tears filling her eyes tore at his heart, but he knew instinctively not to interfere between the mother and daughter. He hadn't earned that right yet.

"I'm sorry, Mr. Olsen." Katie's voice was thick with tears.

He hunched down until he was just about on her level. He would have to be sitting on the ground to get any lower. "Apology accepted, but I thought we were past that Mr. Olsen stuff. You called me Gunnar all the way here."

Katie glanced up at her mother, who nodded. "I like how you talk, Gunnar."

"Thank you, and I like how you talk, too, *Liten.*" Katie's smile grew with his every word. "But your mother is right." Katie's smile slipped. "You can't go around telling people they talk funny. It could hurt someone's feelings. I know I have an accent here, but in Norway it would be you and your mommy that would talk funny. You wouldn't like it if they said you talked funny, would you?"

Katie shook her head. "I would cry." Katie took a step closer to him and lightly patted his cheek. "You no cry."

Gunnar laughed and gave the little girl a quick hug. "No, I won't cry." He stood back up and glanced at Maggie. She looked thoughtful about something. "Come on, ladies, I think I smell hamburgers cooking."

Katie, holding on to her mother's hand, took two steps and then stopped. He glanced down to see what was wrong now. Without saying a word, Katie slid her mitten-covered hand in his much larger one. Between his leather glove and her golden bear mitten, he couldn't feel the warmth or the softness of her tiny hand, but he could have sworn he grew another inch or two to accommodate the swelling in his heart.

It took Maggie another thirty minutes or so to relax and start to enjoy herself. Katie and he had made the appropriate *ohs* and *ahs* over the fantastic light displays. Katie liked how an old barn was completely outlined in red and white lights. He thought someone had been out of his mind to wrap green or white lights around every branch of every tree within in the place. There were hundreds of trees. Pathways were shoveled, and plastic candy canes, with lights strung between them, outlined every walkway. Cute little cottages aglow with thousands of lights were each a different type of store. There was a toy shop, a candle emporium, a candy shop, and a decorating shop called Deck The Halls. The old farmhouse had been converted into a fast-food type restaurant.

Amazingly, it was Maggie, not Katie, who was drawn to the barn, where Santa's reindeer were on display. They entered the barn that smelled of fresh hay and animals. On either side of the aisle were neatly painted stalls. Each stall held a live reindeer.

"Which one is this, Mommy?" cried Katie as she ran up to the first stall and looked inside.

Maggie read the fancy painted sign above the stall's door. "This one is Donner." Maggie smiled at Katie. "The one next to this is Prancer."

"Wow, look at his ears."

"Those are antlers, Katie. Their ears are behind the antlers, see?" Gunner reached his hand in through the thin slats of the door. "In the far north of Norway, the Lapp people raise and train reindeer. They can pull sleighs, supply meat, and even give milk." Donner wasn't too interested in sniffing his hand, so he pulled it back out.

"These pull Santa's sleigh." Katie ran to the next stall and stared in at Prancer. "They fly, too."

"They sure do." Gunnar chuckled as he joined Katie.

"They aren't as big as I thought they would be." Maggie frowned at Prancer.

Without the impressive rack of antlers, the reindeer weren't very big. Maybe three and half feet at the shoulders. Add the neck and head and then the huge antlers and Prancer was topping his six-foot-two height. "You're probably thinking about the wild reindeer of North America, the caribou. They are bigger than the European and Asian reindeer."

"A caribou named Dancer just doesn't have the same ring to it, does it?" Maggie pulled her mitten off and stuck her hand in between the slats. Prancer glanced up from his trough of grass, gave a loud sniff through his hairy muzzle, and then went back to eating his dinner. "I guess he doesn't like the way I smell."

Gunnar leaned his forehead against the stall and prayed he had enough willpower not to grab Maggie and show her exactly what her scent did to him. "Prancer either can't smell or he's a girl." He turned his head and looked at her standing so close. "It's lavender."

"What's lavender?"

"Your perfume. I've been trying to place the scent all night."

"I'm not wearing any perfume, Gunnar." Maggie looked confused for a moment, before the corners of her mouth tilted upward. "It's the soap I use that you're smelling."

"Are you telling me you smell like that all over?" The erotic images flooding his mind made it nearly impossible to breathe.

Maggie gave him a quick nod before hurrying after Katie. "Slow down, Katie. What are you looking for?"

"Rudolph, I can't find Rudolph."

He watched Maggie scurry away and wondered if anyone would miss him if he went rolling around in the snow for a while. He knew it was impossible, standing this close to Prancer's pen, but he would swear he could still smell a faint whiff of lavender. He closed his eyes and took a deep breath, and immediately started to cough up the dust mites and hay seeds he had dragged into his lungs.

With a bemused shake of his head, he followed after his dates for the evening. They were both standing at the other end of the barn, reading a sign above one of the stalls. Of course Rudolph had to be in the stall where about eight people were already there jostling and pushing to get the best view. Maggie slowly walked Katie over, but neither mother nor child could see into the stall.

He hunched down and patted his shoulders. "Ready to see Rudolph, *Liten?*"

Katie nodded, but glanced at her mother for permission. Maggie bit her lower lip for a moment. "Okay, but don't drop her, Gunnar."

He gave her a hard look of disbelief. Like he would drop the child. "Come on, princess, up you go." In one smooth move, he put Katie on his shoulders, held both of her tiny hands, and stood.

Katie gave a squeal of delight as she was raised into the air and then carried over to the side of the stall. The nearly six-foot-tall sides blocked most people's view of the animal within. All Gunnar had to do was stand on his toes, and he could see the star of the show, Rudolph. Katie wiggled wildly on his shoulders. For one horrible moment he did envision dropping her, straight on her head and into Rudolph's stall. He tightened his hold on her hands and silently cursed her mittens. He should have made her take them off before climbing onto his shoulders. "Stop wiggling, Katie, or your mother is going to kill me."

"I can't see his nose," Katie whispered into his ear.

Rudolph had his nose buried into the trough and was pigging out on grass and what appeared to be imported lichens. "I guess he's hungry." He surveyed the rest of the stall. For being the star, they hadn't given Rudolph any special treatment. His stall was the same as the other reindeer's. "If you've seen one reindeer nose, Katie, you've seen them all."

"Rudolph's is red."

"Ah, that's right." He had forgotten about that. He wouldn't put it past the owners of this place to dye or paint the reindeer's nose red, but he would be darned if he could figure out how they would make it glow. An electric cord running to Rudolph's nose would be a tad noticeable. He shifted his weight as the reindeer raised his head, gave the curious onlookers a bored glance, and then went back to his dinner.

He backed away from the stall and lowered Katie back to her own feet. Katie appeared to be pouting. Maggie glanced between them and asked, "What's wrong?"

"Rudolph's nose isn't red," snapped Katie. "It's supposed to be red."

He could tell Maggie was trying real hard not to laugh. She wasn't succeeding very well.

"Maybe it only turns red when he's flying." It was a horrible excuse, but it was the only one he could come up with on such short notice.

Some father, who had been standing close by, latched on to his lame excuse for his own child. Gunnar, Maggie, and Katie stood there and listened to the long-winded explanation about aerodynamics and wind velocity. By the end of the man's speech to his six-year-old son, Gunnar was beginning to believe that Rudolph's nose would light up once he was airborne.

Maggie's eyes seemed a bit glazed over, but Katie was nodding along with the other little boy. As the other family made its way out of the barn, Katie grabbed his hand and asked, "Can we get dinner now? I'm hungry."

Rudolph's nose was history.

Chapter Eleven

It was close to ten o'clock when Gunnar finally pulled his Jeep into Maggie's parents' driveway. Katie had fallen asleep in the backseat, clutching the giant polar bear he had bought her in one of the shops. Maggie had protested the gift, but it had been an unfair argument from the beginning. He had already handed Katie the bear, and the child had already named him. Paul the Polar Bear seemed like a strange name to him, but what did he know about little girls and stuffed animals. "I'll carry Katie in for you."

"I can manage." Maggie undid her seat belt.

"I didn't say you couldn't manage. I just don't see why you should have to struggle with her when I'm right here. She might not have weighed much when she left home. But, after putting away a Pig in a Sleigh, a sack of fries, a large frosty soda and two orders of Penguin Gummies, I bet she weighs a ton now." He had been astounded by the amount of food one little-bitty girl had managed to put away.

"Any man who could tuck away three Santa burgers, a sack of fries, a Blitzen chocolate milk shake, a pack of Mrs. Claus cookies and a box of Comet's Chocolate Stars shouldn't talk." Maggie chuckled softly and shook her head.

"You forgot the Choo Choo Cocoa and the roasted chestnuts we had after the sleigh ride." He loved Maggie's soft laughter. She didn't do it much; maybe that was what made it so special.

"I didn't forget." Maggie looked shy again. It was an interesting contradiction to the woman he thought he knew. "I enjoyed myself tonight, Gunnar. Thank you."

"You're welcome." He glanced in the backseat. Katie appeared to be out for the night. Short of Paul the Polar Bear coming to life and tap dancing on her stomach, he didn't think she would open her eyes till morning. "I think *Liten* enjoyed it, too."

"I don't have to think about that one. I know she did." Maggie's gaze followed his. Her expression softened more as she looked at Katie. "It was very sweet of you, but you still shouldn't have bought her the bear, Gunnar."

"Why?" He looked away from the child and studied the mother.

"She already has a lot of stuffed animals."

"So, now she has another one." He reached over and turned the heat up more. It would be more comfortable and warmer talking to Maggie inside, but by the number of lights still lit in her parents' house, he would have to guess they were still up. He couldn't talk to her privately in there, and he surely couldn't do more than talk to her now, with Katie in the backseat. He couldn't take her back to his house, because not only would Erik be there, but his grandfather as well. It was a sad state of affairs. He was twenty-seven years old, with the woman of his dreams, and all he could do was have a hushed conversation with her in the front seat of his Jeep.

It was long past the time for him to look for a place of his own. Except, with Hans's current mental state, he couldn't. It wouldn't be fair to Erik if he bailed out of the house now. His grandfather needed him now.

"So tell me the real reason you didn't want me buying her the bear?" He knew there was more to it than Katie having another animal cluttering up her room.

Maggie seemed to be studying her fingers. "Katie already likes you too much."

"Too much?" He couldn't read Maggie's expression in the murky darkness of the Jeep. "How do you like someone too much?"

"In Katie's case, she's looking for someone to replace her father. She misses him terribly. She has her grandpop and her Uncle Gary, but they just aren't the same as a real daddy."

"I see." Or at least he thought he was beginning to. "Do I look like him?" That could explain Maggie's turnaround in the grocery store when she accepted his invitation for tonight. Maybe Katie wasn't the only one missing the man.

Maggie gave an unladylike snort. "He'd wish."

Gunnar clamped down on his initial joyous response. His roar would have wakened Katie. Score one for the Norwegian. "When was the last time Katie saw her dad?"

"Jeremy actually took her for what he considered a whole weekend this summer. Picked her up Saturday afternoon and had her back by lunch on Sunday." Maggie's voice held bitterness and resentment.

"That was months ago!" What kind of man had Maggie married?

Maggie quickly glanced in the backseat at her daughter. "Shhhh . . . Keep your voice down." When she seemed satisfied that his outburst hadn't disturbed the sleeping child, she turned back around. "Jeremy has seen her only twice since we moved to Misty Harbor in March."

"The man has seen his daughter twice in nine months?" Jeremy wasn't a man; he was an unfeeling monster. "The man has visitation rights, doesn't he?"

"Oh, yeah, he can have her every other weekend, two weeks in the summer, and we get to split the holidays."

"So he can see her if he wishes." It was still unbelievable that the man wouldn't want to see his own daughter. Especially *Liten.* Katie was the most precious child he had ever spent an evening with, not that he had spent a lot of his nights with kids. He knew more about raising mountain lions than he did about raising kids, and he had never even seen a mountain lion.

"He doesn't wish, Gunnar." Maggie quickly glanced at her daughter. "As Jeremy put it, he's ready to move on with his life."

"Without his daughter?"

Maggie snorted again. "Without his daughter and without his wife. Not to worry, though, he took a lot in the move. He got his master's degree, the brand new S.U.V., the large-screen television, and a live-in girlfriend with a set of thirty-eight Ds, and she pulls in an income of about seventy thousand a year."

So the stories were true. Maggie's husband had left her and Katie for another woman. The man was a complete idiot. "What did you get out of the divorce?"

"The only thing I wanted. The most important thing." She tilted her head to the backseat. "I got Katie."

He chuckled. "I do believe you got the better end of the deal."

Maggie's smile flashed in the dimness. "I do believe you're right."

He settled more comfortably into the seat and flashed his own smile. "So when are you going to kiss me again?"

"Shhhh . . ." Maggie glanced at her daughter.

"Okay, we take it slower and quieter if that's what you want. When can I see you again?" He wanted to reach over, haul her into his lap, and show her how sweetly slow he was willing to go.

"Gunnar, I don't know." She went back to studying

her wringing hands. "I don't have a lot of time for dating and such."

His smile grew wider. "I might like the 'such' part." His smile faded when he saw she was serious. Serious about not seeing him again. "I thought you said you had a good time tonight?"

"I did. It's just that my schedule is kind of full right now between going to school full time, working at the restaurant, and then trying to spend some time with my daughter. It doesn't leave much room for a social life."

"I'm not asking you to give up any of that, Maggie. My life's kind of full right now, too, with work and worrying about my grandfather."

"My mom told me that Hans has been experiencing some problems lately. I'm sorry, Gunnar. Is there anything I can do?"

"No, but thanks for asking. Hans is going to be just fine. Even with both our busy schedules, I think we can make time for us."

"Us?"

"You, me, and Katie." He jerked his thumb toward the backseat. "It's obvious that you come as a package deal." He leaned in closer and brushed a silken strand of her hair behind her ear and under her hat. "It's like a two for the price of one sale."

"You shouldn't have to settle on sale merchandise, Gunnar. You deserve better."

"Settle!" He immediately lowered his voice. "You think I'm settling on you, Maggie?" What had that bastard of an ex-husband done to her?

Maggie shrugged and tried to appear nonchalant about the whole conversation. "I'm not a very nice person."

He could see the tears pooling in her eyes. "Bull shit."

"You weren't living here five years ago. You don't know."

He gave a weary sigh. "This is about you and Daniel

Creighton, isn't it?" He knew if they were ever going to have any kind of relationship, Daniel and the past would have to be settled. He just hadn't been expecting to do it in the front seat of his Jeep in the middle of December.

"He was my fiancé then, and I not only cheated on him, I got pregnant by another man while being engaged to him." Maggie swiped at a tear rolling down her cheek, but she kept her chin up.

He willed the spike of jealousy to disappear. It didn't. Not only did he have to deal with Maggie being married to some stupid bastard, but he had to contend with the knowledge that at one time Maggie and Daniel had been together. It was a lot for him to handle, but he had known the facts before tonight. No use complaining about them now.

"So I heard." He had heard the story long before Maggie and Katie had moved back to Misty Harbor. Long before he had taken one look at Margaret Franklin Pierce and fallen head over heels in love. Apparently, Maggie's past had been a huge scandal back then and made for great retelling to all new arrivals. No one was retelling the story now.

"Let me see if I've got the story right." He kept his voice flat and unemotional. "The town's most beautiful princess, Maggie, hooked herself to the most handsome and prosperous prince in town, Daniel. The princess had been attending college away from home, and the royal wedding was being planned upon her graduation. The summer between her junior and senior year, the princess ends up pregnant. The prince thinks the child is his, when in truth the baby belongs to a fellow student back at college. One day a horrible boating accident happens in the harbor. The prince saves a small child and becomes the town's hero. The princess tells the hero the baby isn't his and flees back to the real father and gets married. The prince goes into denial, until blood work proves he couldn't be the father. The town gathers around their poor betrayed prince and shuns the evil princess."

Maggie's eyes narrowed as she glared at him. "Don't make fun of Daniel like that. He was the completely innocent one in the whole mess."

"And what were you? Twenty? Twenty-one?" He was amazed at how fast she had jumped to Daniel's defense, but not her own.

"Old enough to know better." Maggie brushed at her cheeks. "Old enough not to have drunk three cans of beer at some dorm room party and confused a spark of sexual attraction with lust. Old enough to have said no to Jeremy Pierce when he took me back to his dorm room that night."

"One night, and you got pregnant?" The way the townspeople had talked, he thought she had been having a long-term affair with Jeremy Pierce while still being engaged to Daniel.

"That's all it takes, one time." Maggie shifted in her seat. "One mistake and everyone ends up hurt."

"But Prince Daniel ended up with his very own fairytale princess, Gwen. He seems quite happy with how everything has worked out." Lord, one night. One mistake at a young age, and Maggie had paid the price. A very heavy price at that.

"Daniel deserves Gwen. They make a wonderful couple, and I consider both of them my friends."

"So you and Daniel have kissed and made up. The town no longer shuns the princess."

"There was no kissing involved." Maggie glanced out the windshield to the front of the house. "Daniel has forgiven me and moved on with his life."

"Ah." He reached over and captured her chin. He forced her to look at him, even though it was too dark to see clearly. "But when are you going to forgive yourself, Maggie? When are you going to stop punishing yourself?"

Maggie opened her mouth to protest, and he leaned

forward and lightly kissed her words away. "I think we said enough for one night. I'll carry in Katie for you."

He released her chin and got out of the Jeep. He beat Maggie to Katie's door by a mere second and brushed aside her protests as he reached in and picked up the sleeping child.

Maggie conceded defeat, picked up Paul the Polar Bear, and led the way into the house. Bob and Connie Franklin had been watching the evening news when they entered the house, but they both joined them in the foyer. With a quiet greeting, Bob took his sleeping granddaughter and headed upstairs. Connie, looking flustered and excited at having her daughter's date in her home, said there was fresh coffee and cake in the kitchen, grabbed the polar bear, and followed her husband upstairs.

A becoming blush stained Maggie's cheeks. "Sorry about that."

"About what?"

"My mom. I believe she's suffering under the delusion that I'm sixteen again and have just gotten home from the high school dance."

He chuckled. "Your mom must like me; she's always trying to feed me." When he had picked up Maggie and Katie earlier, Mrs. Franklin had whipped out a plate of cookies so fast that the gingerbread men on the platter had gotten nauseous.

"Would you care for coffee and cake?" Maggie took off her coat and hat and hung them on the coatrack. Her long auburn hair crackled with electricity, and a few strands flew around her head. She raised her hands and tried to smooth them back down.

His hungry gaze took in her thick forest green turtleneck sweater and tight jeans. His mind remembered the way she came to the docks to visit her father or brother during the summer months. No one filled out a pair of shorts or one of those skimpy tank tops like Maggie. For only coming up to his chin, Maggie had the most incredibly long legs. "I think I better be going." If Bob Franklin came back downstairs now, he would escort him off the property with the business end of a shotgun and a bucket of cold water. Daughters were still daughters, no matter how old they had become.

Maggie worried her lower lip. "Okay, and thanks again for a wonderful time."

A deep groan rumbled in his chest as he leaned forward and used his thumb to lightly pull her lower lip out from beneath her teeth. "Don't do that, Maggie." His lips brushed across hers. "It drives me nuts."

Maggie's lips seemed to cling to his. "Sorry."

"I'll call you tomorrow."

"Gunnar, didn't you hear me . . ."

His mouth sealed hers, and her words died into a gentle groan. He kept the kiss light, but full of promise. "Get it through that beautiful head of yours, I don't give a rat's ass about your past. I knew it all before you even moved back to town. Even before I first laid eyes on you and knew you would be mine." He brushed his lips across her mouth once more. "The only one it seems to matter to is you, Maggie."

His mouth was a little more insistent with the next kiss. His tongue made a quick and thorough study of the inside of Maggie's mouth before he called a sudden halt and took a step back. He studied her face. Maggie's cheeks were flushed with desire, and her eyes appeared unfocused and dazed. Her harsh breathing matched his.

He nodded in satisfaction. "I'll call you tomorrow." He left her standing in the middle of the entryway. While he still could walk away.

"And I'm telling you it won't be any trouble at all." Erik turned the flounder in the pan and looked at Sydney, who was cutting up a cucumber for their salad. "You gave me and my family a traditional American

Thanksgiving; the least I could do is give you a *Norsk Jul.*"

"What's that? It sounds kind of kinky." Sydney wiggled her brows playfully as she dumped the sliced cucumbers into the bowl of cut-up lettuce and reached for the tomato.

"It means Norwegian Christmas." Erik chuckled and checked on the red potatoes boiling on the back burner. The more he thought about it, the better he liked the idea of showing Sydney some Norwegian traditions.

"Gwen gave you Thanksgiving." Sydney sliced the tomato in half. "Believe me, you wouldn't have wanted to eat any turkey I had cooked."

"You can cook, Syd. I've eaten over here plenty of times." They had been alternating between his house and her cottage nearly every other night. While he liked having Sydney at his house keeping him and his grandfather company, he loved her place more. It was more intimate here, with just the two of them. The downside of spending so much time alone with the beautiful doctor was the constant temptation she represented. He had been purposely keeping their relationship on the "friendship" end of the scale. A few kisses was all they had shared. Mind-blowing, volcanic, and totally tempting kisses.

"If I can cook, how come you're the one frying the fish and doing the potatoes while I chop up the salad and set the table?"

Erik looked down into the frying pan and grinned. Sydney was right; she was a horrible cook, and he was hungry. "I like doing it, and you don't." Erik turned off the potatoes. "Stop changing the subject. Just two minutes ago you were complaining that you didn't know where you were going to find the time to decorate."

"It's not just finding time to decorate. It's finding the time to shop for all those decorations. I don't even own a ladder. How am I to hang those lighted icicles everyone seems to like? Or put the star on top of the tree?"

"Typically, in Norway, people stay away from the colorful outdoor lights. Maybe they would wrap only one or two pine trees in white lights, but that's about it."

"Do you have Christmas trees?"

"Of course we have Christmas trees." Erik chuckled. "What do you take us for, a bunch of barbarians?"

"No, just your average pillaging and plundering Vikings." Sydney laughed and ducked as he threw a potholder at her. "What else do Norwegians do for Christmas?"

"Christmas Day is the quiet day spent with family and friends. It's Christmas Eve when we celebrate with a big feast, plenty of beer, and Julenisse, himself, delivers the presents to the children."

"Julenisse is Santa?"

"Our Santa, yes, but he's disappearing from my homeland. The Americanized Santa is taking over."

"What does your Julenisse look like?"

"Tall, gaunt, and a long white beard. He wears a floor-length gray coat, red stocking cap, and carries a huge sack of toys." Erik quickly quartered the potatoes and garnished them with butter and parsley. He passed the bowl to Sydney. "We also have to make the Christmas porridge for the *nisse.*"

"What's the *nisse?*" Sydney finished setting the table just as Erik carried over two plates with perfectly fried flounder on each.

"A *nisse* is an elf. A bowl of festive porridge is expected by him for his faithful service throughout the year. Dire consequences are suffered by those who fail to provide it. It's sort of like milk and cookies for your Santa."

Sydney snorted as she sat down. "Santa doesn't threaten dire consequences to little kids if they don't leave him a chocolate chip cookie."

Erik laughed as he took his seat and passed her the potatoes. "In folklore, Christmas wasn't a very nice, cheery time. Christmas was a time for remembering the dead. There's a famous folktale called 'The Midnight Mass of the Dead'. It takes place on Christmas Eve."

Sydney chewed a mouthful of fish and muttered, "Charming."

"Then there's the *lussi,* a fearsome witch who roared through the skies on the winter solstice. She wreaked havoc on anyone who didn't have his Christmas chores done." He normally wouldn't tell such stories over a meal with a beautiful woman, but he could see the interest sparkling in Sydney's green eyes. Who could have refused such temptation. "In other regions of Norway, they believed in *julegeit* or *julebukk,* a half-human, half-goat creature that came out of hiding at Christmastime expecting to sample the Christmas feast and beer."

"Were there dire consequences for those who didn't let them?" Sydney passed him the salt.

"Undoubtedly." He chuckled at this vengeful side of the doctor. "The most frightening, though, were the *oskorei.* They were bands of nasty spirits who rode the Christmas skies on black, fire-eyed steeds. They were too bad for heaven, and not horrible enough for hell, so they were doomed to roam for eternity. They made themselves known during strong winds and winter storms, which sounds and effects they imitated."

"Do you leave porridge out for them, too?"

"No, you didn't want them to dismount at your farm. Legend has it that murder, foul play, or natural death soon visited any farm where the *oskorei* dismounted. Farmers warded them off with painted crosses on stable doors, and it was widely believed that sharp instruments, like sickles, knives, and blades, would ward off the marauding riders' fury. Peasants put axes, knives, or scissors over the doors of their dwellings or drove sharp implements into the walls, where they remained until Christmastime had passed.

"Christmastime isn't just Christmas Eve and Christmas Day, like in America. Here everyone seems to be in a hurry to get the tree down and the decorations boxed back up as soon as the New Year is rung in. In Norway, we celebrate till January sixth, the thirteenth day of Christmas. We spend the days visiting friends, relatives, and enjoying the company and delicious food."

"What kind of food do you serve at this Christmas Eve feast? Ham and turkey?"

"No, *lutefisk* is a must."

"What's that?"

"Cod soaked in lye."

"Gross." Sydney stuck out her tongue. "People honestly eat that?"

"There is no middle ground with *lutefisk*. You either love it or hate it. Most people have either a roast rib of pork or steamed ribs of lamb. Turkey is becoming more popular, too. There's pork sausage, potatoes, flat bread, of course the Christmas porridge, and you must have seven different kinds of cookies."

"Seven?"

"Seven's the norm. Some make nine or eleven, but it always has to be an uneven number." Erik cleared his plate and helped himself to some of the salad. "Why so interested in what we eat?"

"I was thinking about having an open house, possibly on Christmas Eve. You know, invite some neighbors and a couple people from town that have been so nice to me since moving here. You and your family, and maybe some of the ladies who are keeping their eye on Hans. I think my family's coming back up from Baltimore. Then there's Gwen and Daniel, and Daniel's family."

"And you were going to feed them what?"

"Not *lutefisk*, that's for sure." He watched entranced as Sydney nibbled on a cucumber slice. "I was thinking more on the line of a sliced ham, a couple different salads, and a cake."

He shook his head at such pitiful fare on Christmas Eve. "Let me help."

"With what?"

"Everything. The decorating, the cooking, the seven different kinds of cookies, and not one of them is chocolate chip." He slid his chair around to the side of the table, closer to her. "You will get your open house without doing all of the work, and I get to show some of the residents of Misty Harbor, and you, what Christmas in Norway is like."

"I don't know, Erik. Seems like a lot of work." She toyed with the lone piece of lettuce left on her plate. "It also sounds wonderful, exciting, and something different. We could do it between eight and eleven. I heard most of the churches are having midnight services, so people can drop by before heading there."

He knew by the gleam in her eye that he had her hooked on the idea. "Hans can help with some of the baking; he's a darn fine cook when he sets his mind to it. I think he'll enjoy showing off to your family. Even Gunnar can manage a batch or two of those cookies we'll need."

"Once Gwen hears about this, she is going to want to help with some of the cooking and preparations."

"I'll teach her how to make *lutefisk.*" He couldn't help but smile. This was the first thing Sydney wanted to do to strengthen her ties to the town. His heart practically soared with possibilities. Were her roots sinking deeper into Misty Harbor?

"Yuck, I don't have to try it, do I?"

"Just a tiny piece." He chuckled at the way her nose crinkled up. "So, what do you say?"

Sydney raised her glass of soda in a salute. "Here's to a merry *Norsk Jul!*"

He tapped his glass to hers and held her gaze. "Here's to the first of many."

Anyone looking at Sydney could tell she came from money. She had "class" stamped all over her from her luxury S.U.V. parked in the driveway to the ridiculously expensive leather boots he had caught her in the other day shoveling snow. She had more education than half the male population of Misty Harbor combined. She was smart, sexy, and rich. So what in the hell was she doing in Misty Harbor? She belonged in some big flashy city or high-end suburb having dinner at the local country club and going to the theater.

Sydney was a horrible housekeeper, and calling her a mediocre cook would be giving her a compliment. There were usually books, magazines, and papers spread throughout the downstairs. Boots and shoes were piled by the doors, and two days ago he had to remove a stack of kindling off the kitchen counter. She wasn't lazy, just extremely busy. Sydney had her priorities, and she stuck to them. She put in some very long hours at the office. Most nights her phone rang or her pager beeped with someone from town wanting her opinion on this or that. Sydney never seemed to mind and usually went out of her way to put the person on the other end of the line at ease.

It was one of the things he loved most about Sydney. The genuine caring she felt for the residents of Misty Harbor. A perfect example of that was all she was doing, and giving up, just to keep an eye on Hans.

He hadn't been upstairs in her cottage, but he assumed it was probably in the same condition as the downstairs. Sydney might sleep on satin sheets, but she was probably surrounded by tomes on forensic pathology, murder, and mayhem. The woman was a bloodthirsty wench, he would give her that. Hell, she would probably make a better Viking than he would.

The other night when her mother had called, he had picked up a book she had been in the middle of reading. While Sydney had spent twenty minutes catching up with her mom, he had started to read where she had left off. By the time she had rejoined him in the living room, he had been pasty white and wondering if he would be able to hold his dinner down.

He couldn't say Sydney was spoiled, though. Hans had said his mother had been spoiled and never would have been happy living on a fisherman's wage. Hans had been right. His mother never had been happy, and she had hated living in their tiny fishing village. He remembered overhearing one of his parents' many arguments when he was still a small boy. His mother had referred to the townfolk as peasants. His father had thundered back that she better get off her high horse, because she had married one of those peasants. Rolf Olsen had then stormed out of their cottage, only to return hours later drunk enough to make it in the front door, but not bed. Erik had been the one to sneak out of bed and to place a blanket over his father's sleeping form on the cold, wooden floor.

There were many similarities between his mother and Sydney, but there were just as many differences.

Would Sydney get tired of living in a small fishing village? The nearest mall was almost an hour away. There wasn't a country club within three counties, and you had to travel to Bangor to get decent theater seats.

Was she here only to lick her wounds from a failed relationship? He knew she had been living with some young, successful doctor back in Baltimore. Gwen had told him they had lived together for over four years. Sydney never mentioned the man. Was she still in love with the doctor? Or was there now room in her heart for a hardworking fisherman?

Tonight Sydney had done something his mother never had tried. Sydney, with the planning of an open house on Christmas Eve, was trying to fit in to the tiny fishing village.

There wasn't a doubt in his mind that Sydney could fit in to Misty Harbor if she wanted to. The question was, would she want to stay?

Chapter Twelve

Erik carried the four-by-eight sheet of plywood into the living room and asked Gunnar, "Where do you want me to put this?"

"On the horses in front of the window." Gunnar grabbed an end of the plywood and helped him position it on the saw horses he had made earlier.

Erik released the wood and backed up. He muttered a curse as he almost tripped over his grandfather, who was sitting in the middle of the room surrounded by train parts. Lots of train parts. Hans had on his reading glasses and was muttering derogatory remarks in Norwegian at the instructions. Tonight Erik had come home from work all excited about telling his grandfather and brother of the Norwegian Christmas Eve Sydney and he were planning. He had been feeling so good about it, he had been willing to beg for both of their help.

Instead, he had stepped into the house and straight into a preschooler's nightmare. Gunnar had lost his mind, and he was taking dear old Grandpop with him. Boxes, bags, and power tools were everywhere. The four-by-eight sheet of plywood had been blocking the stairs, and one of the end tables was in the foyer. The coffee table was in the kitchen, and dinner hadn't been started. It was Gunnar's night to cook and Erik's turn to do the laundry. Sydney's office was open until eight, and she would be stopping by on her way home with the notion they would be discussing the open house. Fat chance that was

He glanced around the room and shook his head "How many train sets did you buy?'

Gunnar actually looked sheepish. "Three."

"And some extra track," said Hans as he inspected a tiny caboose.

"Do you honestly expect to fit all three trains sets on that one piece of plywood?" The darn thing took up the entire space in front of the huge picture window. All the furniture had been shoved to one side of the room, and he would have to breathe in deeply to make it to the patio doors on the far side of the room to haul in the firewood. What in the world had Gunnar been thinking?

"Don't forget the Christmas tree," said Hans as he slid open the doors to a freight car and peered inside.

He looked at his brother and wondered when his brains had leaked out of his ears. They were identical twins, which meant they had identical-size brains. So that made their intelligence the same. Gunnar was exactly eight minutes older than he. So, logic told him that in eight minutes he would do something incredibly stupid, like go into Krup's General Store and buy out their entire inventory of trains. Or he could do something worse. Like commit himself to a Norwegian Christmas Eve open house for about fifty guests. When he had left Sydney's last night, the number was up to forty-eight, but he figured on double that amount showing up.

Whatever insanity was running through the family, it was either genetics or highly contagious. Maybe their heater was leaking carbon monoxide.

Gunnar slid the board a couple inches to the left, to center it. "I figured it out in Krup's. All three sets will fit. The first one will be the standard oval track that comes with the set. The second one, we add a couple extra lengths of track, and we run them one inside of the other."

Erik picked up one of the sets of trains that had caught his eye. It was a circus train with clowns painted on the freight cars. One car had giraffes' heads sticking out of it. Another was a flat car, with two tiger cages on top. He had to admit that the darn thing was adorable. "What about the third set?"

"We do a figure eight with the tracks inside the oval tracks. In the center of one of the loops we put up the Christmas tree." Gunnar drew an imaginary figure eight on the board and pointed to the spot where the tree would go. "I'm figuring no higher than a four or five footer."

He was afraid to ask, but curiosity was a horrible thing. "What goes in the other circle?"

Hans pointed to a big paper bag with handles that was sitting on the couch. "The town." Hans stood up and headed for the bag. "Wait until you see some of these buildings, Erik. They have lights that really work and miniature people, too."

He looked at his brother and shook his head. "I'm gathering all this has to do with Maggie somehow?" He had known his brother had it bad for the pretty divorcee this summer. No one had been happier for Gunnar than he when Maggie finally consented to go out with him. Ever since that trip to The Christmas Village, Gunnar was impossible to live with. One minute he was singing while vacuuming, and the next he would be snapping your head off over nothing.

"Her daughter, Katie." Gunnar grinned. "They are coming for dinner Friday night, and I wanted to surprise her. She loved the trains at The Christmas Village. You should have seen her eyes light up when the whistle sounded. She would have spent the entire night in the Choo Choo Barn if we would have let her."

"You expect all of this done by Friday night?"

"Not the tree, of course." Gunnar frowned at their grandfather, who was pulling every box from the bag. "And maybe not the entire town."

"He would let me buy only twelve of them. So I picked the best ones." Hans handed him a small white box with a picture of a grand Victorian house on the front.

He looked at the box in horror. "It's a model!" There were probably a couple hundred tiny, tiny pieces inside the box. Pieces intricate enough to cause blinding headaches and a new vocabulary of curse words. Enough pieces that it would take days to put one of the models together. They would be lucky to have all twelve of the buildings done by Easter.

"Of course it's a model, boy. What did you expect? Cardboard cutouts?" Hans showed him a model of a miniature freight platform, complete with workable loading dock and a crane. "We bought every tiny tree in the place." Hans hurried across the room toward another bag.

"What's that?" He pointed to a hunk of Styrofoam sitting on one of the chairs. It was painted in different shades of green.

"It's a mountain tunnel." Gunnar held it up and grinned like a little boy in a candy shop with a dollar clutched in his hand.

Erik shook his head. It was worse than what he had first suspected. Both Gunnar and his grandfather had that gleam in their eye. "Who's going to put all the models together?" Between trying to make a living, getting ready for the Festival of Lights, and Sydney's open house, his schedule was so jammed that he didn't know where he was going to find all the hours in the day he needed.

Gunnar gave him a knowing look, winked, and said, "*Bestefar* told me in the store that he used to build models all the time. He can build them during the day while we are at work."

Erik understood his brother's message. Gunnar had found a hobby for their grandfather. Trains were a perfectly safe hobby. He silently applauded his brother's fast thinking. "That's a wonderful idea. Grandfather, you can start on that freight platform tomorrow." Little tubes of plastic cement were scattered across the end table.

"Love to, boys," Hans said. "But I can't tomorrow."

"Why not?" Gunnar asked.

"Sadie called earlier. She's picking me up tomorrow morning, and we're going someplace special." Hans was rummaging through what appeared to be about fifty packages of little miniature trees and shrubs. "Dang woman won't tell me where we're going, only that it's a surprise."

Erik didn't know what worried him more. Hans driving around town in Sadie's pink Cadillac with the top down or the thought of what Sadie would consider a surprise. Hans had remembered that he used to put models together. Hans had even remembered Sadie's phone call earlier today. What his grandfather hadn't remembered was to make breakfast this morning. For the first time in over three years, Hans hadn't started the coffee or the meal. That had worried him. So had the fact that they had two boxes of Polar Crispies in the cabinet. Cereal in the house was an oddity. Hans had always insisted that they start their day with a big, hot meal.

This morning he had downed two bowls of sugar-coated flakes, with miniature marshmallow polar bears floating in between the flakes. He had had a sugar high till around nine o'clock.

"You be careful with Sadie," he said. He was searching for a nice way to say that he had his doubts about the old gal having all her oars in the water. "The woman seems a little 'wild.' "

Hans chuckled. "You gotta admire a woman who isn't afraid to be herself."

Gunnar rolled his eyes while he managed to keep a straight face. Sadie was herself, all right. "Well, there's always Thursday and Friday to build some of the models."

"Thursday, sure, but Friday's out." Hans started to line the trees up by size on top of the television. "I've got art class on Fridays."

Erik glared at his brother and then at the stack of models to be built. Gunnar should have considered their grandfather's new art classes before buying a dozen models that needed to be put together. All Hans had been talking about was Sadie and his painting class. And the fact that Evelyn Ruffles had stopped by on Monday with a chocolate cake and that Priscilla Patterson had dropped in on Tuesday and finished it.

Their grandfather hadn't figured out yet that they were paying the ladies to drop in and keep him company. It was worse than that. Hans thought he was turning into a ladies' man, and he was loving every minute of it. The Norwegian Casanova was determined to leave his mark throughout Misty Harbor.

The thought of Mrs. Ruffles' delicious cake made his stomach rumble. He was hungry and in need of a shower. Gunnar obviously had better things to do than worry about dinner, but they still had to eat. He walked into the kitchen and slammed his shin into the coffee table and invented a new curse word. Amazing. He hadn't even opened one of those model boxes, and already his vocabulary was improving.

Erik picked up the coffee table and moved it into his grandfather's bedroom, where there was plenty of room for it at the foot of the bed. He then walked back into the kitchen, pulled out the phone book, and dialed the phone.

"Catch of the Day, Gwen speaking." Gwen's voice sounded cool and calm.

"Gwen, it's me, Erik, and I need a big, big favor."

"What's wrong?"

Erik could hear a masculine voice rumbling in the background. It was either Hunter, Gwen's assistant, or Daniel was paying a visit to his working wife. "Nothing's wrong, Gwen." He rubbed his aching shin. "I know you don't do takeouts, but I would pay dearly for three takeouts of any meal you have."

"I don't know, Erik, this sounds desperate." It was Daniel's amused voice that spoke into the receiver. Daniel must have taken the phone from his wife.

"It is, Daniel." He leaned against the counter. "What are you doing there?"

"I say I'm visiting my hardworking wife. Gwen says I'm begging for food and bugging her." Daniel's voice held laughter and a teasing note.

He thought about how hard it must be for Daniel to have a wife who worked quite a few nights a week. "If you're bored, we could use your help." Daniel was a professional carpenter. There wasn't anything the man couldn't build. Setting up the train platform should be a snap for him.

"With what?" Daniel sounded interested.

"Know anything about trains? Gunnar just bought out Krup's General Store's complete inventory of miniature trains, and he expects to have them up and running by Friday night. His heart seems to be set on impressing a certain four-year-old girl and her momma."

"Hot damn!" Daniel sounded excited now. "I'll be there as soon as Gwen has time to throw together four take-out dinners. Do you need me to bring anything else?"

"No, we've got plenty of beer and enough power tools to make even you ecstatic."

Sydney opened the front door, before the doorbell even rang, and allowed Gwen to enter the total chaos.

She took the bag her sister held as Gwen hung up her coat. "I'm afraid you're too late."

"For what?" Gwen glanced around curiously. The sound of arguing men and hammering was coming from the right.

Sydney shook her head. "They have already taught Daniel at least three Norwegian curses, and I'm pretty sure he can now conjugate a certain verb in Norwegian that should get his mouth washed out with soap."

Gwen laughed. "That bad?" She hurried to the opening of the living room and stared inside at the total mess. Daniel's jean-clad legs were sticking out from underneath the train platform. No one had noticed Gwen's arrival.

Sydney looked over her sister's shoulder at what once had been a very charming living room and shook her head sadly. "That bad."

Train boxes seemed to be everywhere. A bright orange electrical cord was now draped over the couch, a chair, and a table lamp. It ran straight to the drill lying at Erik's feet. Someone had hung a droplight from the curtain rod, and the sports channel was blaring a hockey game on the television. "That's why I called you. Thanks for coming, and bringing dessert." Sydney jiggled the bag in her arms. She could feel half a dozen Styrofoam containers.

"No problem, I was curious what was up when Daniel rushed me around the kitchen getting four meals ready to go. There had been a certain boyish gleam in his eye when he told me they would be setting up trains. For the first time in our married life, he seemed anxious to leave me."

"I haven't had the guts to step into the room yet." When she had first arrived, Erik had greeted her and quickly ushered her into the kitchen, away from the mayhem. They hadn't had two minutes alone when an argument broke out between Gunnar and his grandfather. It seemed Hans had the electric drill and was wanting to make Swiss cheese out of the platform. Erik had stepped back into the disorder, and she hadn't had a moment alone with him since.

She had called her sister, who had been just closing up the restaurant for the night. Gwen had been the one to insist on bringing dessert and coming to see what she referred to as "this feat of engineering." Sydney was happy for the company, but she hadn't seen any great feat of engineering yet. Only a bunch of arguing, mumbling, and a few invented swear words when one of the men whacked his fingers while trying to nail in those little-bitty nails that held the track in place.

"All this for a four-year-old girl?" Gwen chuckled softly. "I'm gathering all of this is for Katie Pierce. Rumor has it that Gunnar is seeing Maggie."

Sydney glanced between Daniel's legs and Gunnar's profile. Neither man seemed upset to be in the same room with the other. "So Erik tells me." She knew Daniel wouldn't be troubled by Gunnar dating Maggie. Her sister's husband had put his past behind him before he married Gwen. It was Gunnar's reaction to Daniel that she had been watching. Amazingly, Gunnar had treated Daniel as a friend. The only argument that had broken out between the two men had been about where the bridge and trestle work should go. Gunnar had won that argument, but Daniel had won the one about the placement of the water tower.

Katie Pierce was one very lucky little girl. Then again, the way the men were obsessing over the trains, she doubted if the little girl would get to work the switches at all.

"The coffee's ready." She had put on a fresh pot as soon as she had hung up with Gwen. "Should we call them now?"

"I don't know." Gwen watched in dread as Gunnar, or was it Erik, nearly stapled his finger to the platform with the staple gun. Both men had their hair tied back. "How do you tell them apart?"

Sydney shrugged. "I'm not sure. I just know."

Gwen looked at her for a long moment. "You like him, don't you? This isn't some pretend relationship just to keep on eye on Hans any longer, is it?"

Sydney slowly shook her head as she watched the play of muscles ripple across Erik's back. Her sister was right. What she was beginning to feel for Erik had nothing to do with Hans, or anyone else for that matter. No one had ever made her feel the way Erik did. All warm and wonderful inside one moment, and then all hot and needy the next. She was confused, anxious, and frustrated. She wanted him in her bed and in her life. It was a frightening and sober thought. One she thought never to have for years to come. She hadn't moved to Maine to fall in love, but she was afraid that was exactly what she had gone and done.

She was falling in love with the big Viking, and it was scaring her to death. Erik had kissed her many times in the past weeks. Some of those kisses had been hot and demanding. Others were soft, light, and incredibly tender. None had led to the bedroom, and it was always Erik who had halted their progress. She wasn't sure how to take that. Either Erik was the most patient man to ever draw a breath, or he wasn't interested in taking their relationship any farther.

What if she couldn't please Erik in bed? She obviously hadn't pleased Richard. If she had, he wouldn't have gone looking for it elsewhere. Richard had not only looked, he had touched. Repeatedly. The last thing she wanted to do was to disappoint Erik.

Erik must have felt her gaze, because he turned around and looked directly at her. He raised a brow in a silent question.

She gave him a small smile and prayed her thoughts weren't written across her face for all the world to see. "Hey, you guys," she called into the room, trying to ignore the blush sweeping up her cheeks. "Gwen's here, and you should see the goodies she brought."

Daniel's head popped out from under the platform. He grinned lecherously at his wife as his body followed his head out from under the wood. "No one sees my wife's goodies but me."

Hans chuckled, and Gunnar sadly shook his head.

Erik continued to stare at her with a questioning look.

She quickly turned away, before he saw too much, and headed for the kitchen.

Maggie picked up the wet plate from the rack and slowly ran the towel around its surface. She slid a quick glance at the man beside her washing the dishes. Gunnar Olsen was the most impressive man she had ever seen, let alone kissed. And talk about gorgeous! "Thank you for dinner. It was delicious." It was Friday night, the only night of the week she didn't have to work or worry about homework. When Gunnar had called and invited her and Katie to dinner, she knew she shouldn't accept, but it was beyond her to refuse. She wanted to see Gunnar again.

"You should thank Erik and Sydney; they did the cooking." Gunnar slid another plate into the rack.

"Yeah, but you are the one who invited us." She nodded her head in the direction of the living room, where all the noise was coming from. She could hear Katie's laughter and squeals of delight mixing with the occasional train whistle. "You went through a lot of trouble to set the trains up for Katie." When they had first entered the house, Hans had been as giddy as a schoolboy with a new toy. Sadie, Hans's date for the evening, had dragged Maggie's daughter into the living room before she even had her coat off.

"It was a joint effort." Gunnar rinsed another plate. "Erik, Hans, and Daniel helped. It's still under construction, but we did manage to get all the trains running about eleven o'clock last night." Gunnar reached for a stack of pots and dunked them into the soapy water. "How did school go today?"

"Good, I guess." She placed the dried plate into the cabinet and reached for another one.

"Don't you know?"

"Ask me in January when I get my mid-term grades." She picked up another wet plate. "School seemed to be easier six years ago. Maybe I was smarter back then. One thing I do know is that I had more energy back then."

Gunnar chuckled. "Yeah, I can see that you're old and decrepit now." Gunnar's gaze traveled the length of her body.

She felt the heat of his gaze and froze as desire softened and melted her body. She turned and put another plate onto the shelf. Lust was a horrible and troublesome emotion. One she wished never to experience again. She liked Gunnar, honestly liked him. She didn't want to cloud her feelings with lust.

What wasn't to like about the man? He always asked about her schooling and took an interest in what she wanted to do come May when she got her degree. On the drive home from The Christmas Village, he had listened to her aim of making a better life for herself and Katie, and had applauded her goal of owning her own business one day. He was attentive and sweet. He seemed to adore Katie, and both of her parents thought he walked on water.

The most amazing part was, he didn't seem to care about her past.

Physically, Gunnar was perfection come to life, and he kissed like a man who knew what he wanted and wasn't afraid to go after it. This evening he was acting like the perfect gentleman, and it was driving her nuts. Even now, being alone in the kitchen with him, he hadn't done or said anything that could be taken the wrong way. She was disappointed.

What did that say about her? Gunnar was being polite

and discussing her schoolwork, and she was thinking about what his chest had looked like when she had spotted him this past summer washing down his boat. Gunnar was scrubbing pots with a Brillo pad, and she was thinking about that kiss they had shared in the wheelhouse of his boat the other week. She wanted that kiss again, and the conclusion that kiss had promised. She wanted the heat and the lust. She wanted to lie beneath him and taste the passion.

Her fingers trembled as she picked up the next plate to be dried. She could feel Gunnar's gaze still on her face, but she refused to look at him. Lord, what if the entire town of Misty Harbor had been right five years ago? What if she was a slut?

"Hey, you two," called Erik from the doorway of the kitchen. He didn't want to interrupt Gunnar and Maggie, but he figured someone should know where he was. Hans, Sadie, and Katie were having such a good time with the trains that they hadn't paid him any attention. "Sydney and I are going for a walk around the cove. We'll be back later."

He stepped outside and joined Sydney, who was pulling on her gloves and waiting for him. "Ready?" The temperature wasn't too bad for a walk. It was in the low thirties, but there wasn't any wind. The snow had melted, and the stars were shining beautifully in the night sky. It was the perfect evening for a romantic walk.

"As I'll ever be." Sydney pulled her hat down over her ears and grinned. "Are you sure it's safe?"

He held up the high-powered flashlight he had grabbed from the closet on the way out. "The path runs along the water's edge mostly. It's not hard to follow in the moonlight." He slipped the flashlight into his coat pocket. He had walked the path enough times over the past three years to be able to walk it in the pitch dark, blindfolded. He reached for Sydney's hand and gently tugged her around the side of the house toward the water and the path.

"I see Hans and Sadie are getting along nicely." Sydney moved closer to him as the path narrowed. "How did his art class go today? I saw he added to his painting of the lighthouse."

He shortened his steps to match hers. "He's very proud of that painting." He gave a soft chuckle. "Sadie claims he has a gift. Grandfather has a gift, all right, and it isn't painting."

Sydney laughed, and her shoulder brushed against his arm. "If he's enjoying it, Erik, let him go. Sadie will be good for him. The art classes will be good for him."

"Sadie's going to get him in trouble." He shook his head and remembered his shock when Sadie had joined them for dinner. He had known she was invited; he just hadn't expected her to show up wearing a John Deere safari outfit and curlers. "I didn't know that they made leopard-print overalls."

"Neither did I, until tonight." Sydney's voice held laughter. "You've got to admit, Sadie's one of a kind. You also have to admit there's a certain spring in Hans's walk lately."

"Probably because he's drinking too many beers since Sadie started keeping an eye on him."

"Hans is drinking?"

"No, I was kidding. Hans hasn't touched a beer in weeks." He hated to admit it, but Sydney was right. There was a certain bounce in Hans's step lately. "Let's agree that Sadie is having an affect on my grandfather. I'm just not sure if it's a good one or a bad one yet."

"Well, I for one think it's a good one."

"Yeah, well, you weren't there Wednesday night when he dropped his latest bombshell on Gunnar and me. Sadie took him with her to her organ lessons Wednesday morning."

"Let me guess, he wants organ lessons, too."

"Worse." Last night they had spent the evening at his place getting the trains up and running. Sydney had sat at his kitchen table glueing a plastic Feed Store together while he had been constructing the overpass on track number three. Daniel had been there, and Gwen had joined them after the restaurant had closed for the night, once again bringing dessert. They hadn't had time to discuss Hans, which was pretty telling now that he thought about it. Wasn't Hans the main and only reason for Sydney and he to be together all the time?

"What could be worse than organ lessons?"

"Accordion lessons. My grandfather wants accordion lessons."

Sydney's sweet laughter joined his low, rumbling chuckles. His entire life was being turned upside down, yet he could still find the joy in it. Sydney was showing him the way. "Laugh all you want, Doc, but I'm making sure you'll be the first one he invites to his initial recital."

"Wouldn't miss it for the world."

They continued along their walk, and he had to wonder if she would even be in Misty Harbor by the time Hans was ready for his first recital. Sydney had been acting, he didn't want to say strange, maybe leery was a better word for it, since Tuesday night. The first night they had been setting up the trains. He could even remember the moment it started. He had his back to the room when he felt her gaze. There was some internal radar that always went off whenever Sydney looked at him. He had turned around to face her and to possibly make some comment. The expression on her face had stopped his words. Sydney had looked stunned, as though someone had just told her something really shocking. Later on, when he had walked her to her car, he had asked if anything was wrong or if something had happened that he didn't know about. She couldn't meet his gaze when she said nothing happened. He had known right then and there that she had lied. Sydney had lied to him, and he hadn't figured out why.

Sydney kept a hold of his hand and walked beside him. "It's beautiful here."

"You mean the cove or Maine in general?"

"Both." Sydney was quiet for a moment, then she said, "I wasn't sure how I was going to like Maine when I first moved here."

"There's a big difference between Maryland and Maine." He tried to keep his tone casual. "There's also a big difference between a big city like Baltimore and Misty Harbor."

Sydney laughed and seemed to study the calm surface of the water. "There is that."

"So which do you prefer? Big city lights, museums, and up-to-the-minute hospitals or nosey neighbors, no red lights, and your office in a renovated old house on Main Street?"

"Let's see, the blaring sound of a traffic jam or the gentle cry of a seagull?" Sydney gave him a strange look, but continued walking. "The anonymity of living in a big city or the warm feeling you get when your neighbors actually know your first name? The smell of exhaust and pollution or the reflection of moonlight rippling across the water?" She stopped walking and waved her hand in the direction of the cove. "I don't know, Erik, what do you think?"

"I think you're beautiful." He stepped closer and tenderly cupped her chilled cheeks. "You do like Misty Harbor, don't you?" His mouth brushed across hers once and then lifted.

"If I didn't," Sydney whispered against his lips, "I wouldn't be here."

"But for how long, Syd? How long?" With a groan of surrender, he captured her mouth and kissed her like he had been dying to. There was nothing sweet or hesitant about the kiss. He took possession of her mouth and molded her body against his.

He didn't give her a chance to answer his question. His heart was afraid of what she might say. He was falling in love with a woman who might not be around come next year, or even next month, and he didn't know how to stop the fall. Hell, he didn't even know if he wanted to. All he knew was that he wanted Sydney like no other woman before her. Sure he wanted her body, no breathing man wouldn't. But he also wanted to hear her sweet laughter and to be the one who kept her warm. Keeping Sydney warm during the cold winter months would be a full-time job.

The swish of their nylon coats rubbing against each other filled his ears. Metal zipper clashed against metal zipper. Soft down cushioned softer breasts. Sydney's arms encircled his neck as he cupped her rounded bottom and yanked her closer. He wanted her to feel what she could do to him with just a kiss. He deepened the kiss and wrapped his tongue around hers.

Sweet moans and harsh breathing filled the air. Puffs of frozen breaths were released into the night sky.

Sydney felt something for him. He could taste the desire in her kiss and feel the way her body responded to his. No woman could react to a man in the way Sydney was responding to him without wanting him. At least physically.

Being wanted physically wasn't enough. He wanted more. So much more. It took every ounce of strength to slowly and gently break the kiss. "Syd, we have to stop." *While I still can.*

Sydney's mouth reached for his again, and he took a step back. He was teetering on the edge of desire, and it would be so simple to go over. He would give up his fishing boat to lay her down in front of the fireplace back at her cottage and make love to her until she was content to live out the rest of her days in Misty Harbor with him. Making love to Sydney might satisfy her, but it wouldn't guarantee her contentment to live in Misty Harbor for the rest of her life.

He didn't think he could survive having Sydney in his bed only to watch her walk away later. His heart might get a little dented now if she went back to Maryland. But once he knew what it was like to love her totally, it would be shattered if she walked away.

He wanted a wife and children. He wanted a home. He wanted Sydney.

Chapter Thirteen

"Are you sure you know what you are doing?" Sydney moved closer to Erik on her couch. It was early Sunday evening, and dinner was already cooked, eaten, and cleaned up. Erik had shown up at her house earlier carrying a bag of art supplies and two boxes of Polar Crispies, minus their box tops. The cereal she understood after Erik explained how Katie wanted to send away for the penguin. Gunnar was buying the sugar-coated cereal every time he drove by Barley's Food Store. The construction paper, scissors, and glue she didn't understand.

"Of course I know what I'm doing. Every child in Norway knows how to make a *julekurv.*" Erik used a ruler to get the lines straight and even on a piece of folded red construction paper. The white paper was folded inside the red one, so when he cut through one, the cut went through the other.

The scissors looked small in Erik's large hands as he carefully rounded one end of the paper and cut two long slits at the other end. The two pieces of paper matched perfectly. "What does *julekurv* mean? Christmas what?"

Erik flashed her a smile as his large, callused fingers delicately wove the slit ends of two papers together. "You're getting very good at that."

"At what?" She watched amazed as the two pieces of paper formed a heart. A basket-weave heart that opened up and could actually hold something light inside.

Erik took a piece of paper and glued it on as the handle. "Speaking Norwegian." He held the basket up for her to see. "It means Christmas basket. In the old days, these were hung on the Christmas tree and filled with raisins or small pieces of candy for the children. Now they are left mostly empty, but they are used for decorations on the trees. This is a *julehjerte,* which means heart-shaped Christmas basket. It's believed that Hans Christian Andersen made the first one. American children do colorful paper chains; we did Christmas hearts."

She took the heart from him, being careful not to touch the handle yet. "It's beautiful. Can I do one?"

"Sure, but I thought you were going to be working on the invitations." He glanced at her laptop sitting on the coffee table.

"I already wrote it out. When we go shopping tomorrow night, I'll stop at the office supply store and pick up some Christmas computer paper and some envelopes. Writing out the addresses will take the most time." She slid closer and selected two different color pieces of paper. "So you get my help tonight."

Erik cut out another piece of paper and passed it to her to use as a pattern. "Hans said he'll make *hjortetakk* and the *sandkaker* cookies. He's also going to do the pork sausage because he says he owes you for building the Feed Mill for his town."

"He doesn't owe me anything." She concentrated on making each cut precise. She didn't want to be shown up by a bunch of Norwegian school children.

"I noticed that he wrote down what he told me he would do, and then he taped it to the refrigerator door."

"I saw there were quite a few messages taped to the door on Friday night." She made sure the pieces of paper matched perfectly and then started to weave the strips through each other. It wasn't as easy as Erik made it seem. "Is that his idea or yours and Gunnar's?"

"His." Erik was watching her fingers. "He knows he's forgetting a lot of stuff lately, so he's doing what he can to stop it."

"That's a good sign."

"How?" Erik started to cut out another heart. This one he made smaller.

"If he's admitting his memory glitches to himself, he'll eventually admit them to you. He'll accept our help easier, and hopefully he'll go for the tests sooner."

"Hopefully." Erik passed her the two pieces he had just cut out. "Gunnar wants to help with the cookies, too."

She chuckled and started to weave the next heart. "Let me guess who he's trying to impress."

"You don't need to guess." Erik shook his head and picked up another two pieces of paper. "I placed some orders today for the special imprinted irons I'll need for the cookies. Hans had one or two, but that was about it."

"Let me know how much I owe you." Her brow wrinkled in concentration. The weaving was definitely getting harder the smaller Erik cut the hearts.

Erik stiffened. "I don't want your money."

She glanced up when she heard the offended tone in his voice. "What?"

"I said I don't want your money." Erik was staring at the paper in his hands.

"But you're ordering these imprint irons for my open house. Why shouldn't I pay for them?" She had always paid her own share for everything. Sometimes it seemed as though she had paid more than her fair share.

The condominium she and Richard had shared had been in Richard's name. But she had paid half the mortgage and half the utilities every month. When they had gone out to dinner, she usually was the one to pick up the check. Last spring Richard had surprised her with a four-day trip down to Hilton Head. He had also surprised her when he told her she had to pay for half the trip. A trip where he either played golf or tennis all day long with a bunch of other doctors. She had amused herself with lying on the beach reading or shopping. It had been that particular trip that had finally shown her exactly how different they were. If she had been smart, she would have ended the relationship then, instead of thinking things would change. Thinking Richard would change.

People didn't change. They were what they were. And Dr. Richard Wainbright was not only a philanderer, but he was cheap. Her sisters had been absolutely right by giving him the nickname Needle Ass.

Erik, on the other hand, appeared angry that she wanted to pay for something she needed for her own open house. It was an interesting twist. One that said a lot about Erik's character.

Erik turned his head and glared at her. He appeared indignant. "I ordered them, I pay for them." Erik's voice made it clear he wasn't going to change his mind on the subject.

She smiled, leaned in closer, and kissed him. Right on his surprised mouth. It was the first kiss she had ever given him. Usually, it was Erik who kissed her. She pulled back and whispered, "Thank you."

"For what?"

"For being you." There were so many things she wanted to tell him, but she was afraid she would sound like some lovesick fool. She bent her head and went back to weaving her heart basket together. It seemed like forever before Erik went back to cutting out the hearts.

Today she had taken extra time with her appearance, knowing Erik would be stopping by. Usually when he came by, she was either in nice slacks and a blouse that she had worn to work, or she had changed into comfortable jeans and a baggy sweatshirt. Tonight she had worn dark blue stretch pants that felt and looked like velvet and a light blue sweater that had over a dozen tiny pearl buttons down the center. The sweater was low-cut by her standards, but was probably classed as modest by anyone else. She had left her hair unbound and flowing down her back and had even put on perfume. All for Erik's benefit.

So far his reaction wasn't what she had been hoping for. When he had first arrived, her appearance seemed to have taken him by surprise for a moment. His gaze had zeroed right in on the low-cut sweater and the skin-tight pants. He had muttered something in Norwegian and then gone out back to chop firewood. Without a coat.

She now had enough firewood and kindling to last till spring. But she had been hoping Erik could come up with a better way to keep her warm. All week long she had been thinking about Erik and the next step in their relationship. The kiss in the moonlight out by the cove had been the last straw. Erik had been the one to call a halt to that wonderfully hot, dreamy kiss. Tonight she wasn't going to allow him to put the brakes on.

Tonight she wanted what those kisses had promised. She wanted Erik enough to open herself up to the possibility of being humiliated if she turned out to be terrible in bed. She was a doctor and knew the human body, both male and female. She had lived with a man for over four years; she wasn't some blushing virgin. She was thirty years old. An adult. There was absolutely nothing wrong with her inviting Erik into her bed. It didn't matter that he was three years younger than she. Erik didn't kiss her as if he thought she was some old lady.

Erik kissed her as if he wanted to invite her into his bed and never let her out of it.

Tonight she was going to seduce Erik.

She didn't know how to go about that exactly, so she eased into a conversation. "I met Simon O'Connell today."

"Simon? Where did you run into him?" Erik handed her another cut-out heart and tried to put a couple of inches between them.

She wiggled closer and noticed his other thigh was pressed up against the arm of the couch. "He was walking his dog, Goliath." She concentrated on the paper heart in her hands. "I knew Simon worked for you, but I didn't realize he lived down the street from me."

"Yeah, it's his parents' old house. They moved to Florida last year and left him the house."

"Simon seems very nice, and so does Goliath, once you get over the sheer size of the animal."

"He's a Newfoundland, and he's gentle as a lamb, despite weighing close to one hundred and fifty pounds. We take him out on the boat with us sometimes." Erik studied her face. "Some people call Simon names, like Crazy Simon, but he's not crazy. He's one of the best fishermen I've ever worked with. Hell, half the time I don't need the underwater radar to spot a school of fish. Simon knows where they are instinctively."

"Sounds like he's an asset to you." She had liked the thirty-something man when he had politely introduced himself to her this morning and then helped her carry in the rest of her groceries. When she had tried to thank him, he had brushed her thanks aside and told her he would do anything for Erik's girlfriend. Since she hadn't had any dog bones in the house, she had given Goliath a big carrot and made a friend for life.

"He's more than an asset. I'd be lost without him. Simon gets called names because he talks to everything."

"You mean everyone."

"No, everything. Simon talks to fish, rocks, and even telephone poles. He claims the seagulls tell him where the large schools of fish are, and I usually would be the first one to scoff at that notion. Except, I've seen seagulls land on my boat and start squawking and carrying on. Simon listens, tells me which direction to head in, and the next thing I know, we're catching fish faster than the lines can handle." Erik shook his head. "If I hadn't seen it with my own eyes, I would never have believed it."

"Aren't you afraid he'll get his own boat and catch all those fish without you?"

"Simon is one of the few men in town who doesn't want to own his own boat. He seems happy working for me and getting a percentage of our catch."

"Aren't you afraid other fishermen will try and steal him away from you?"

"They've tried, many times." Erik grinned. "Simon won't go. Not even for a larger percentage."

"You must be a very good boss." It said a lot about a man who had such a faithful employee.

Erik shrugged. "I treat Simon no differently than any other man I know."

"Ah, that explains it." She had noticed that Simon had a childlike quality to him. He hadn't acted mentally challenged, only sweetly boyish to be in a full-grown man's body. Simon must have suffered quite a few hateful remarks while growing up. To be treated like a man, like an equal, meant more to him than a higher percentage of the catch.

There were two more cut-out hearts sitting on the table, waiting for her. Erik was faster at cutting than she was at weaving. "Tell me about your boat."

Erik's blue gaze seemed to burn into hers. "Why do you want to know about my boat?"

Thirty was much too old to be playing coy. "It's important to you." He always asked about her day and then listened when she told him about it. Many nights she had listened enthralled as he shared his day or stories about the fish he had caught. Erik never dominated the conversation or belittled her when she had handled nothing deadlier than a case of bronchitis or had come home with nothing worse than a paper cut. She knew from the rough calluses on his palms and his reddened, wind-burned cheeks that Erik's job wasn't as easy as he made it sound. The gleam of contentment and pride that glowed in his eyes when he told her about his day spoke of the love and enjoyment he felt for his job and the open sea. Erik was not only a fisherman in body. He was a fisherman in his heart. She didn't know of too many men who were that content in their jobs.

"Why did you name her *The Maelstrom?* Isn't that a whirlpool?" She put the heart she was working on onto the table, turned to face Erik, and tucked her legs up under her. If she got any closer, she would be in Erik's lap. "Seems like a strange name for a boat."

"I wanted something Norwegian. Yes and no." Erik tried to shift away, but there wasn't an inch of free space left on the couch. "And I've heard stranger."

She grinned. Something was making Erik extremely nervous, and she hoped it was she. "Do you miss Norway?"

"At times, but I've learned to love it here. I would miss Maine more if I went back."

Her knees pressed into Erik's jean-clad thighs. "What did you mean by yes and no? Either it's a whirlpool or it isn't."

"The maelstrom's a swift and very dangerous current in the Arctic Ocean that flows back and forth between two islands off the northwestern coast of Norway. It's been a hazard to sailors for hundreds of years. Between high and low tide, when the wind blows against this current, it becomes extremely dangerous. Immense whirlpools form then, and they destroy small ships."

"And you named your boat after that?"

"Most stories about the maelstrom have been greatly

exaggerated. Only the foolish go against its power. Only the foolish die. Most people think of a maelstrom as a whirlpool, when in reality it's only a current."

"A very dangerous and swift current."

"A current, just the same."

With the tip of her finger she lightly drew a small circle on his thigh. She could feel the muscle clench beneath her finger. "So when are you going to take me out on your boat fishing?" Round and round her finger went. Just like a whirlpool.

Erik's hand captured her hand and held it still against his thigh. "Maybe in the late spring." His voice sounded rougher and deeper. "Once it warms up some." His fingers lightly squeezed. "But if you're real good, maybe I'll have you ride along with me on Christmas Eve for the Festival of Lights."

"Christmas Eve?" Her open house was on Christmas Eve.

"Not to worry, it won't interfere with your open house. Every Christmas Eve all the boats string up lights and head out to sea. Once it gets dark, we all sail into the harbor. The whole town and the surrounding community come out and line the shore and docks. They sing Christmas carols and drink hot chocolate. We are always done by around seven."

"It sounds lovely. I bet it's a beautiful sight."

"I don't know what it looks like from shore. I've always been out on the boat, but it's a glorious sight from there."

"And you'll take me out with you this year?" She leaned forward, and her breasts pressed against his arm.

Erik groaned. "I told you I'll take you if you're good. Real good." Erik looked as if he didn't know if he should bolt out her front door or kiss her senseless.

She took it as a good sign. A very good sign. She raised up and practically climbed into his lap. With one hand she reached up and traced the enticing curve of his lower lip. "What do I have to do to be 'real good'?"

She tried to give her voice a seductive tone and prayed she didn't come off sounding like Donald Duck.

Erik captured her wandering hand and trapped it on his other thigh, forcing her breasts forward. Her cleavage was even with Erik's chest. "You're playing with fire, Syd." His gaze didn't meet hers. It was too busy devouring her chest.

She could feel him thick and hard beneath her hip. Erik wanted her as much as she wanted him. Yet he was still fighting it. Why? "I'm not very good at this, Erik."

"At what?" Erik's jaw was clenched so tight that the words seemed to hiss out from between his teeth. Something hot and dangerous had flared in his eyes.

"Seduction." What did he think she was doing? Checking the thread count in his shirt?

Erik seemed surprised by her answer. "If you got any better at it, I'd be a dead man." His gaze dropped down to where the front of her sweater was gapping, giving him a clear view of her cleavage. Erik groaned and closed his eyes. "You're wearing the lacy blue bra, aren't you?"

Her confidence was soaring. Erik looked as though he was going to toss her onto the floor and ravish her at any moment. "You've been peeking into my lingerie drawer?" She never had been ravished in her life, and it was getting more and more tempting by the minute.

Erik's grin was pure devilment. "You bought it the night you found Hans and brought him home. When I walked you out to your car, all your packages were spilled all over the back, remember?"

"They all tipped over when I slammed on the brakes."

"That lacy scrap was poured out of the Victoria's Secret bag like some erotic dream. I've been thinking about what it would look like on you since that night." Erik leaned forward and placed an openmouth kiss at the base of her throat. "Hell, I've been dreaming about what you would look like once I've taken it off you."

She arched her neck as her breath shuddered out.

Erik's mouth was hot against her skin. She could feel her nipples harden against the lace of her bra. She could feel the trembling in Erik's fingers as he released her hands. One big, rough, incredibly tender palm flattened on her back. Drawing her closer. His other hand reached for the buttons on her sweater. She shifted her weight and straddled Erik's lap.

Erik groaned as the junction of her thighs cupped his arousal. "Syd?"

Lord, she loved how he growled her name. It almost sounded like a plea. "Erik"—her fingers caressed his chest, his shoulders, up his neck, and then buried themselves into his hair—"make love to me." She tugged the rubber band out of his hair.

Erik raised his head to gaze into her eyes. Whatever he saw there must have convinced him she was serious. *"De er slik vakker."*

"I hope that's a yes." His hair felt like silk between her fingers. Warm, golden silk.

"I said you are so beautiful." Erik's hand twisted into her hair, and he brought her mouth to his. "You smell like island flowers"—he kissed her long and deep—"and taste like sin."

She was breathing hard when he broke the kiss. A soft smile tugged at the corner of her mouth. "Do you like sin, Erik?" Seduction was a powerful aphrodisiac.

"On you, I believe, it could be quite addictive." Erik took her mouth and proceeded to taste every inch. This time when he raised his head, he was the one gasping for his next breath. "You've got two choices, Syd."

"I vote for naked, and now." Her fingers started to undo the row of buttons down the front of his shirt.

Erik chuckled and tried to capture her hands. "The couch is definitely out. It's too short." He raised her hands to his mouth and nipped at her fingers. "So either you're going to get some mighty interesting rug burns on your bottom or we're going upstairs."

She leaned forward and ran her tongue over his jaw.

"Those are my choices? Rug burns or a queen-size bed with satin sheets?"

Erik had her in his arms and halfway across the room before she could catch her breath. "Stop!" she cried as her arms encircled his neck.

"What's wrong?" Erik didn't look like a man who wanted to stop, but he did.

She nodded to the front door. "Lock it and put the chain on. Gwen has a key, and there's no way I want her walking in here tonight." She brushed his jaw with another kiss. "You don't want company, do you?"

Erik growled something in Norwegian, and holding her entire weight with one hand on her butt, he turned the lock and hooked the chain. He hit both the porch light and the living room light switch for good measure. The fire in the fireplace was low, and the screen was securely in place. Erik gave the room a quick glance and then carried her up the flight of stairs.

Sydney didn't consider herself overweight, or even chunky. At thirty her hips were starting to spread, and her stomach, while not exactly hanging over her bikini underwear, would never be as tight as it was when she was eighteen. But at five feet, six inches, she wasn't a lightweight. Erik carried her up the stairs, and his breathing never even hitched once.

The last time she had been carried by a man, she must have been five or six, and it was probably her father or one of her grandfathers. Erik made it appear so damn easy.

Erik carried her into the bedroom and slowly lowered her to her feet. "Are you sure, Syd?" His gaze caressed every inch of her face.

Was she sure? Hell no, she wasn't sure. She might be about to ruin a perfectly good friendship with sex. She had excelled at school and graduated at the top of her class. She had been the youngest pediatrician ever to join the ranks of Peterson, Matthews, and Price. She was a Fletcher, and in the city of Baltimore, that name was pure gold. But could she please a man in bed? The million-dollar question was standing in front of her. The million-dollar answer was a foot behind her draped in midnight blue satin sheets, with the comforter turned down and the pillows fluffed. She had set the scene for seduction earlier this afternoon.

"Sydney?"

She nervously shifted her feet. "I've got to warn you, Erik, that I might not be very good at this."

Erik blinked. "At what?" His gaze went to the bed, to her breasts, which were covered in blue lace and hanging out of her half-unbuttoned sweater, then to her face.

Her arm waved in the direction of the bed. "This."

Erik's gaze blazed in anger for a moment before a slow smile of understanding curved his mouth. He took the step that separated them and tilted up her chin. "All I'm going to say on that subject is, consider the partner."

With those last words, he lowered his head and kissed her. If she thought his other kisses were hot and sinful, they had nothing on this one. Erik kissed her as though he was trying to capture her soul. She melted.

A deep groan vibrated in his chest as his hands tugged her sweater over her head. She reached for the buttons on his shirt and cursed when she couldn't even get one through the hole. Erik brushed her hands aside, undid the buttons, and shrugged out of his shirt. Her hands reached for the hem of his white T-shirt and started to tug.

Erik muttered something she didn't understand as he tried to unlace his boots while she tugged his T-shirt up his chest. Erik straightened his arms, and she ended up flat on her back on the bed, clutching his T-shirt. Erik grinned and pointed a finger at her. "Don't move."

She wiggled her hips and tossed his shirt over her shoulder and onto the floor on the other side of the bed. Her gaze was riveted to his broad chest. Every bulging muscle was clearly outlined. Dark golden curls swirled their way across sun-kissed skin. She tried to swallow, but her mouth was too dry. Lord, he truly was a Viking come to life.

Erik bent and practically ripped his boots and socks off his feet. His hands went to the front clasp of his jeans. His gaze locked in on hers.

She smiled and raised herself up on her elbows to enjoy the show. She might not be any good at this, but she was female enough to appreciate the male body. A perfectly aroused male body.

Erik lowered the zipper of his jeans. With one steady motion, he pushed the denim and cotton underwear over his hips. The material pooled at his ankles. In full masculine glory, he rid himself of the last of his garments.

She took one look at him, slammed her eyes closed, and collapsed onto the bed. Her trembling elbows couldn't support her weight. Lord, he was magnificent. Huge, but beautifully magnificent. She felt her breath speed up and wondered if she was going to hyperventilate. Wouldn't that add a touch of romance to the moment? She could be breathing into a brown paper bag while Erik made love to her.

She jumped when Erik's fingers skimmed her ankles and then removed the dark blue ballet slippers she had on.

"Relax, Sydney." Erik's deep voice rumbled into the room. "You don't have to do anything you're not comfortable with." Strong, sure fingers caressed her calves and the backs of her knees.

She peeked beneath her lashes. Erik was squatting at the side of the bed. She had a perfect view of his chest, arms, and head. She relaxed. Warm palms slid up her thighs and over her hips.

Erik hooked two fingers into the waistband of her pants and slowly pulled them down over her hips and legs. She wasn't relaxing now. The small triangle of powder blue lace, barely covering her womanhood, matched her bra. Erik groaned, "Why didn't you tell me it was a matching set?"

"You didn't ask." If this was his reaction to the set, she was stopping in Victoria's Secret tomorrow night and buying a set in every color they had. Hell, she was buying stock in the company.

Erik gently lifted her and placed her on the bed, with the pillow cushioning her head. The satin comforter slithered to the floor. He lowered himself beside her and shivered as his naked body came in contact with the sheets. "Satin is cool against the skin."

She leaned over and pressed a kiss into the center of his chest. "It's because your skin is so hot." She loved the way he groaned and clenched his fists. He was being so careful and slow with her. She didn't want careful, and she sure as hell didn't want slow. She traced the dark circle of his nipple with the tip of her tongue. "Erik, I'm not afraid to make love. I'm just not sure I will satisfy you." Her next kiss was lower.

A growl escaped Erik's clenched jaw. "Put your mouth a little lower and you'll see how well you satisfy me." His hands slid into her hair, and he started to tug her up his chest.

Her mouth was smiling as it moved up his throat and over his chin. She brush her lips over his. "Touch me, Erik. Love me."

With a mighty groan Erik pulled her down on top of him and kissed her. Really kissed her. There was no light brush or gentle probing. There was heat and hunger and need.

She went wild in his arms. She met his tongue, thrust for thrust. Her hands stroked and caressed the heat of his chest and the wild pounding of his heart. Her back was pressed into cool sheets as Erik deepened the kiss, and his hot, sun-kissed body blanketed her. Somehow Erik had removed her bra. His warm, moist mouth replaced the powder blue lace. With a gentle tug of his lips, she arched off the bed wanting more. Everything she knew, or thought she knew, about sex was a lie.

Where did all this need come from?

Erik's hands were everywhere. Soft and tender one moment, penetrating and wild the next. Words she didn't understand were chanted against her hip as Erik's mouth followed the path of his hands. Her panties were replaced with hot palms and probing fingers. Foreign words sounded like endearments and blatant sex talk. Desire and need thundered through her body. She wanted Erik inside her. She wanted him now.

Erik's mouth skimmed the inside of her thigh, and she dug her fingers into his hair and tugged him back toward her mouth. She cried his name in a prayer as he slowly kissed his way back up to her lips. Erik settled himself between her thighs and caught her lower lip between his teeth. His elbows took most of his weight, but she could feel the tip of his penis nudging her. "Do you want me, Syd?"

She wrapped her thighs around his hips, and he slowly penetrated her. She could feel every inch, thick and hard, ease its way into her body. Her throat arched, and she closed her eyes against the wave of pleasure consuming her. Her "yes" was a soft whisper of need.

Erik grunted and plunged the rest of the way in. Her eyes flew open as the full impact of him penetrated. She gazed at the heat flaming in his blue eyes. Erik was staring back at her, half in concern, half in awe. She slowly smiled and arched her hips.

Erik muttered a word that she knew wouldn't be in any translation dictionary and proceeded to set a pace that was guaranteed to make her scream. To drive her wild.

Scream she did. Sure, quick strokes pushed her right over the edge Erik had taken her to. Her climax took her by surprise. First by its intensity and second by how quickly it had come.

Erik cried her name as he joined her.

She waited until her breathing sounded just fast and deep, instead of desperate, before opening her eyes. She knew Erik was beside her. Most of his weight was off her, but his one arm encircled her waist. One massive thigh and leg was lying across her legs. She turned her head and smiled.

Erik's head was buried into one of the midnight blue satin pillows. His golden hair shielded her view of his face. A light sheen of sweat coated his tan back. Even with his breath bellowing in and out, he appeared magnificent. So that was what she had been missing all those years.

Lord, she could kick herself for being such a fool. She should have been a foreign exchange student. She needed to update her visa. She needed to chain her Viking to the bed and never let him leave.

Erik must have felt her gaze. He brushed his hair away from his face, turned his head, and looked at her. His voice was as rough as sandpaper. "I thought you said you weren't very good at this."

She grinned. "I guess my partner had something to do with that."

Chapter Fourteen

Erik held Sydney against his chest and listened as the sound of her breathing finally returned to normal. The first time he had made love to her, it had been all fire, flash, and hurry. This time it had been slow, sweet, and just as shattering. He tenderly brushed a lock of her hair away from her face. "You okay?" Personally, he didn't think he would ever recover from the experience.

Sydney muttered something into his chest that sounded suspiciously like "I just might live."

He chuckled and hugged her closer. Somewhere there was a blanket for the bed, but he would be darned if he knew where it had gotten to. It probably had joined the pillows which had slipped off the bed earlier. Who would have thought satin could be so slippery?

Erik stared up at the ceiling and lightly stroked Sydney's hip. Who would have thought that a woman could be so incredibly soft? So incredibly responsive? Sydney had stolen not only his breath, but his heart. He was in trouble. Deep trouble. But lying naked in the middle of a queen-size bed with a naked woman sprawled across his chest, he didn't care that he had managed to fall in love with the wrong type of woman.

How could Sydney be wrong, when this felt so right? His palm caressed the sweet curve of her butt, and unbelievably he felt the faint stirring of desire tighten his gut. Loving Sydney for a third time just might kill him. He grinned up at the ceiling as the woman in his arms wiggled her tush. But what a way to go.

"So, want to tell me about it?" How could Sydney believe she wasn't any good at this? No man could have been that much of a moron not to appreciate her warm and giving nature. Hell, Sydney had been hot enough to scorch his chest hair and curl his toenails.

Sydney raised her head and gave him a saucy grin. "Gee, Erik, you were great. Wonderful even."

He lightly smacked her bottom and then proceeded to rub the smooth cheek. "That's not what I was referring to. I don't need you to tell me how great we are together." He toyed with the ends of her dark hair. In the night, her hair appeared dark brown, but when Sydney stepped out into the light, he noticed the intriguing red highlights. "I was curious as to why you thought you weren't any good at this?"

Not to flatter himself, but Sydney had gone up in flames within his arms. Hell, she had screamed her release. Twice.

Sydney lowered her face back down onto his chest. "Oh, that." She was quiet for so long he was afraid she wasn't going to answer. "I lived with a man for over four years before moving here."

"I know. He is some big-shot doctor back in Baltimore." Erik continued to brush his fingertips over her ass and tried to pretend jealousy wasn't snapping at his gut. He didn't want to think about Sydney living with another man, especially one that seemed so perfect for her. Sydney deserved a rich, successful doctor. "What happened?"

Sydney gave an unladylike snort. "I came home when

I wasn't supposed to and found him in our bed with some big-breasted ER nurse playing hide-the-salami."

Erik flinched. He hadn't expected that one. What man, who had Sydney in his bed every night, would even look at another woman? Let alone screw around on her. "I thought doctors were supposed to be smart."

"You mean he was supposed to be smart enough not to get caught?"

"Hell no. The man's obviously a moron. He had you in his life and in his bed, and yet he slept with another woman."

Sydney snorted again. "They weren't sleeping, Erik."

"You know what I mean." The bastard deserved to lose Sydney. Hell, the bastard never deserved to have her in the first place. He stared at her bent head and wondered if her heart had begun to heal from such an experience. She must have loved her doctor very much to live with him for four years. Sydney hadn't seemed too shattered when she moved to Misty Harbor. But then again, some people just hid their emotions and pain better than others. "Were you afraid you wouldn't respond to another man's touch the way you responded to your doctor?"

Sydney's head jerked up. "You got it all wrong, Erik. I never responded to Richard the way I just did with you. Why do you think he had another woman in bed with him? I hadn't satisfied him."

He studied her face. The light at the top of the stairs was lit, and the bedroom door was open, allowing in some of that dim light. Sydney was serious. She honestly thought she was to blame for Richard bringing another woman into their bed. In one quick movement he rolled over, bringing Sydney beneath him. His elbows supported most of his weight, and his hips maneuvered their way in between her sweet thighs. He wanted her to feel exactly what she was doing to him.

"You've satisfied me twice, so far, tonight, Syd." He arched his hips, and the length of him pressed into the tight riot of curls between her thighs. "There is absolutely nothing wrong with you. The fault lies with the man who failed to satisfied you."

Sydney wrapped her thighs around his hips and tried to bring him into her. "But it's different with you." Her hands were greedy as they tugged his mouth down to hers.

He gritted his teeth as the head of his penis slipped into her moist, hot opening. "Damn straight it is." He couldn't control the heat any longer. He had to have her and have her now. He captured her mouth and plunged.

The light from the sun slipping into the bedroom and the smell of something cooking woke Erik from his exhausted, yet totally satisfying sleep. The minute his brain kicked into gear, he knew Sydney was no longer in bed with him and that he was late for work. Simon could ready the boat without him, but Sydney was another story.

The morning after was always a difficult call. Which was why he had always avoided the situation, until last night. Sydney's cottage would have to have been in the process of burning down before he would have left her bed.

He rubbed a hand over his jaw and cringed at the rough stubble. Lord, he hoped he hadn't marked Sydney's soft skin with his whiskers. The first two times they had made love had been mind-blowing and powerful. The third time had been perfection. They had climaxed together, and Sydney had been left in no doubt as to how well he had been satisfied. His roar of satisfaction had probably disturbed the neighbors. He slid out from beneath the satin comforter and reached for his jeans.

Three minutes later, he quietly made his way down the stairs, carrying his boots and shirt. He found Sydney, wearing a thick green, floor-length robe, in the kitchen frowning down into a frying pan. Two tall glasses of orange juice were sitting on a tray, and a fresh pot of coffee had just finished dripping into the glass container. He was starved.

He stepped up behind Sydney, wrapped his arms around her waist, and glanced over her shoulder into the pan. Every ounce of hunger disappeared. Scrambled eggs weren't supposed to be that color. He brushed her hair to one side and kissed her neck. "Morning."

"Morning yourself." Sydney tried to turn around, but his hands held her still. "I was making us breakfast."

"So I see." He reached around her and turned off the stove. He would rather eat live bait than what was in the frying pan. He also would rather stick a fish hook in his most prized appendage than to hurt her feelings after she had gone to all the trouble of making him breakfast. In one quick motion, he swept her up into his arms and headed for the stairs. "I've got another hunger that has to be satisfied first."

Sydney laughed. "Erik, put me down. I've got to be at the office in an hour."

He took the steps two at a time and nearly stumbled on the last step when her robe gapped open and he realized she wasn't wearing a stitch of clothing underneath it. He hitched her higher into his arms and kissed the berry-hard nipple poking so enticingly up at him. "I promise to hurry."

Forty-five minutes later, he was sitting at her counter wolfing down his second bowl of Polar Crispies and drinking orange juice. The scrambled eggs had been scraped into the trash can. He watched as Sydney rushed around getting everything ready for her day. She had eaten only one bowl of the cereal, but had managed a cup of coffee he had brought her as she had showered and dressed. He couldn't tell if she was normally this hyper in the morning or if the sixteen-hundred-calories-per-bowl cereal had anything to do with it.

After last night, he needed all the calories he could

get. "Syd, relax. You are going to give yourself a nervous breakdown." He glanced at the clock. She had plenty of time, barely. "I'll close up here and make sure everything is fine. You get to the office."

"You'll check the fireplace?"

"Yes." He walked toward her and brushed her slightly swollen mouth with a gentle kiss. Sydney's cheeks were flushed, her eyes were sparkling, and her mouth was puffy from his kisses. Sydney looked as though she had been thoroughly ravished this morning. He grinned, and she blushed. "Hans and I will see you tonight around five-thirty. Remember your shopping list and walking shoes."

"You seem awfully happy for a man who's going to go shopping all night."

His next kiss wasn't a gentle brush. It was deep, probing, and intense. He forced himself to take a step back as soon as he felt Sydney melt against him. "It's not the shopping, Syd. It's the company I'll be in."

Sydney turned her car down Conrad Street and grinned. The Whos in Whoville had nothing on some of the residents of Misty Harbor. Christmas was coming, and even the Grinch wouldn't be able to stop it. Every house had electric icicles, plastic Santas, complete with eight reindeer and a sleigh, wired to rooftops, and enough lights to keep the local power plant in business till June. Every window was outlined. Every tree, bush, shrub, and plant was draped with enough lights that if they were strung end to end, they would probably reach Milwaukee and back.

Evelyn Ruffles, her next-door neighbor, had a six-foot Santa, complete with a motion sensor, at the end of her driveway. Every time someone walked past, Santa waved, gave a good belly laugh, and shouted "Ho Ho Ho." Of course, Santa went into action every time a car drove past, too. The first time Santa had waved her down, she had stopped to see what he wanted. It had been dark outside, and she had mistaken the plastic, beer-bellied man for a real person. There was no way she was telling Erik or her sister about that little mistake.

Two doors down from Evelyn's place, a young couple had no trees or shrubs in their front yard at all. It seemed strange to her, but she had learned a long time ago, to each his own. To compensate for the lack of decorating choices, they had purchased a dozen of those spiral metal hoop trees that lit up in multiple heights and colors. Their front yard now looked like something out of the *Jetsons.*

Simon's house was the most interesting of the festive display. Years ago, someone had built an eight-foot lighthouse, complete with revolving light, in the corner of the yard. Surrounding it was a wonderful garden and a fish pond during the warmer months. In the dead of winter, the lighthouse appeared forlorn. Simon, getting into the spirit of the holidays, had replaced the white lightbulb with a red one. Sydney wasn't sure if it looked as if the police were raiding his place or if Simon was running a whorehouse.

The Burtons, directly across the street from her cottage, had some giant, twelve-foot-tall blow-up snowman that actually lit up from the inside. Frosty was anchored into the yard with tent stakes, and thick ropes wrapped around his neck. The darn snowman looked as though he had escaped from the Macys' Thanksgiving Day Parade. Frosty was tall enough and positioned just right to appear to be looking straight across the street and into her upstairs bedroom window. Erik had laughed himself silly when she had stopped at the general store and bought mini blinds for the room. But she had noticed that he had put them up for her the same evening without a fuss. Frosty's shiny black eyes, gleaming in the moonlight, were downright freaky.

Living on Conrad Street at Christmastime was like

living on the Las Vegas strip. All that was missing were the slot machines and the Elvis impersonators.

Sydney slowed her S.U.V. to a halt and admired the simple beauty of her cottage. With all the flash and glitter surrounding her place, it soothed the eyes and quieted the chaos of the season. She had allowed Erik to decorate as he saw fit, and the results were simply enchanting. Just like the man.

White lights were strung only around the largest pine tree in her front yard. A gorgeous wreath, with a silver-and-blue bow, decorated the front door. Erik had set up a spotlight to accent the front entrance of the cottage. The finishing touch was the yards of pine garland draped along the white picket fence. At every post, Erik had tied a silver-and-blue bow.

When she had questioned Erik about the silver-and-blue color theme, he had seemed indignant. He had said men did not do color themes; men used their common sense. Since the trim on her cottage was blue, and blue was used throughout the interior of her home, what other color would he have chosen? He just happened to think that silver went better with blue, than gold.

He had then proceeded to show her what else his common sense was telling him to do. He had shown her so well, that they had to put off buying her Christmas tree until the next night.

In the ten days since they had become lovers, she had fallen completely and utterly in love. It wasn't just the physical side of Erik that she had fallen in love with either. She had never felt the way Erik made her feel when they were in bed together. It had taken her a couple of days, but she had finally realized it hadn't been her fault that her love life with Richard had been boring. Maybe it had been Richard's fault, but she was more inclined to believe that they just hadn't been right for each other.

With Erik, everything was different. Erik was different. For the first time, she felt like an equal partner in a relationship. A very crowded, very full relationship. Erik's career was important to him, yet he always made the time to ask questions about her day. He never complained about the hours she put in at the office or her trips to the nearest hospital to visit some of her patients.

She knew that Erik's workdays were shorter now than when the warmer months started rolling around. Right now he seemed to have more free time than she did, but come April and May, both of their hours would be amazingly long. Erik seemed to enjoy cooking all the time, which was great by her. She didn't particularly care for the job, but she did insist on doing her share by cleaning up after their meals. It was the least she could do, and it was working out nicely.

Erik spent most of his nights in her bed. His loving concern for his grandfather touched her heart. Erik could have easily shoved the responsibility of Hans onto Gunnar's shoulders. His twin brother would have taken care of Hans, and Erik could have had a lot more free hours every day to do what he wanted to do. Neither of the Olsen men was shirking his responsibility to Hans. Both were there for the older man, or at least making sure one or the other was. If Erik missed a night in her bed because Gunnar had plans with Maggie and Katie, that was all right with her. It showed Erik's character.

Erik was a family man.

Everything she had ever wanted in a man was in Erik. She had seen the way he played with Katie when she and her mother came visiting Gunnar. Erik liked children. He would make a wonderful father, assuming he even wanted children. She wasn't going to assume anything about Erik. Everything was too new. Too fragile. Too perfect.

She hadn't even told him that she loved him. Of course, Erik hadn't given her any words of love or promises of tomorrow either. She would love the words, but she didn't need them to know the truth. Erik loved her. She could feel it in his kisses and in his every touch.

No man could make love to a woman the way Erik did and not love her.

Tonight she just might tell Erik how much she did love him.

Sydney thought about Erik and what his reaction might be to her declaration of love and smiled as she parked in her driveway, behind Erik's pickup. Last week she had given him a spare key to her cottage. It was nice coming home in the dark to a house well lit and knowing someone was inside waiting for her.

She hurried to the front door, and her smile grew as she spotted the unadorned Christmas tree framed in the living room's bay window. Tonight they were going to decorate the tree together. Christmas Eve was one week away, and she hadn't been this excited by Christmas since she was five and still believed in Santa Claus.

The first thing she noticed when she opened the front door was the aroma of something delicious cooking. Considering lunch had been seven hours earlier, that wasn't surprising. The second thing she noticed was that Erik had been very busy this evening. The living room was completely decorated, except for the tree.

Erik had wrapped the banister in pine garland and interwoven it with miniature white lights, blue ribbon, and silver beads. Pine bough had been placed across the mantel, and Erik had added fat blue candles sitting on silver bases. Half a dozen silver and blue glass Christmas ornament balls scattered throughout the pine reflected the candles' flames. Sprigs of pine and more glass ornaments were tucked randomly throughout both bookcases. A large woven basket, overflowing with pine cones and sporting a blue-and-silver bow, sat near the fireplace. The house smelled of dinner cooking, the fire burning in the fireplace, and pine.

Sydney closed her eyes and just breathed in the scents of Christmas. When she opened her eyes, Erik was standing in the opening to the kitchen, staring at her with concern. "Are you all right?"

"I'm fine." She kicked off her shoes and hung her coat on the coatrack. "You did a wonderful job in here. It looks like something out of a magazine." She hurried across the room and stepped into Erik's arms. "Martha Stewart would be jealous."

Erik chuckled and brushed her mouth with a slow, sweet kiss. "I doubt that. I saw her on television once. She made some kid's Halloween costume out of a roll of aluminum foil and a couple of pipe cleaners."

"What was he, a TV antenna?"

"Nope, a knight in shining armor." Erik kissed her again, and this time there was nothing slow or sweet about it. When he finally pulled away, they both were breathing hard. "Are you hungry?"

She teasingly ran her fingers down his chest and grinned. "Oh, yeah."

Erik captured her fingers in his hand and pulled her into the kitchen. "I hope you like stew."

"Spoil sport." She stepped into the kitchen, and her heart melted into a puddle of love. If she wasn't already in love with the man, she would have fallen for him the very instant she spotted her little dining room table set for two. A candle was burning in the center of the table, and a small salad was sitting on each plate. "Where did you find the time to do all of this?"

"I didn't take the boat out today. The weather was too rough, and the catch wouldn't have been worth the fuel." Erik ladled stew into two bowls. "I didn't make the stew; it's your sister's. I stopped by the restaurant and picked up a container of it about an hour ago." Erik carried the bowls over to the table. "Gwen also gave me the salad and the bread."

"My sister must really like you." She took her seat and started in on the salad. "How is Gwen? I haven't seen her in days."

"Busy. She held two Christmas parties at the restaurant on the nights she should have been closed, and she's really getting into Norwegian cooking. She's doing the *lutefisk, surkål,* and *rømmegrøt.*"

"What's that?"

"You already know what *lutefisk* is. *Surkål* is sauerkraut with caraway seeds, and *rømmegrøt* is a sour cream porridge." Erik ate some salad. "Gwen said to tell you that you are working too much."

"Hmmm . . ." She sipped the wine Erik had poured into her glass. "Someone should tell the people of Misty Harbor to stop breathing on each other and getting each other sick. It always seems to be worse around the holidays, when the malls are so crowded and everyone is jammed together at the registers."

"Doesn't mean that you have to put in a twelve-hour day."

"True, I'll just tell anyone who wants an appointment to call the other doctor in town."

"There isn't another doctor in town." Erik chuckled, but didn't seemed concerned by the fact.

"True." Sydney tasted the stew. It was delicious. "I guess that means you won't be pulling twelve-hour days come summertime."

"Nope." Erik grinned. "More like fourteen- and fifteen-hour days." He tapped his wineglass. "So don't get too used to this."

"I won't." She felt her heart soar. It was the first time Erik had mentioned the future. A future that obviously included her.

Forty minutes later, she was muttering dire threats to the manufacturer of her Christmas tree lights. What in the world would possess some factory to pack a string of a hundred little bulbs into eight pounds of super-strength plastic? Erik had unpacked three strands of lights, and she had barely managed to yank half of hers out of the protective insert. What did they do, glue them in?

"Need any help?" Erik's face was expressionless, but she could see the laughter in his eyes.

"You think it's funny, don't you?" She was sitting on the floor, in front of the tree, and she was surrounded by yards of green electrical wire and miniature lightbulbs. Behind her were three stacks of boxes, all containing glass ornaments. Two boxes of silver tinsel were on the chair. Blue bows and the Christmas hearts Erik and she had made were scattered by the couch. A brown box that a friend of Erik's had mailed from Norway was on the other chair. The box was filled with delicate handmade straw ornaments, bent and sewn into different configurations, and tiny Norwegian flags.

Erik gently put down the star that was to go on top of the tree, leaned over, and kissed her. "No, I think you're beautiful."

She smiled against his mouth. "Sweet talker." She pushed the lights off her lap. "Do you know what is missing?"

"What?"

"Mistletoe." She wrapped her arms around his neck and nibbled on his lower lip. "I think we should get some."

"I think you're dangerous enough without it." Erik tenderly unwrapped her arms from his neck and stood up. "Come on, Doc, let's finish the tree."

She wanted to pout, but knew she couldn't stay mad at Erik. His breath had hitched when she had toyed with his lip with her teeth. He wanted her, just as much as she wanted him. "Okay, you finish getting these lights out of the box, while I go pour us another glass of wine."

As she refilled their glasses, she listened to the messages on her answering machine. One was a hang up, and two were from Richard.

Erik gave her a disconcerting look when she came back into the living room, but continued to wrap the tree in lights as she opened boxes and started to put the bows on the tree. By the time the star was shining brightly at the top, she had everything else ready to go on and the trash neatly bagged. They worked side by side until every last ornament, flag, and strand of tinsel was hung. She neatly arranged the white lace skirt around the base of the tree as Erik took out the trash. On his way back into the room, he shut off the lights in the kitchen and living room. Only the tree, banister, and fire lit the room.

Sydney scooted out from underneath the tree, sat in the middle of the floor, and admired their work. The tree was gorgeous. She glanced up at Erik and held out her hand. "Sit."

Erik lowered himself to the floor next to her.

"It's beautiful." She could see Erik's reflection in one of the silver balls hanging on the tree.

"She sure is." Erik's gaze never left her face.

Amazingly, after everything they had done with each other, the man still had the power to make her blush. "Thank you." She leaned back on the soft blue carpeting and watched as the firelight played across Erik's strong face. "Have you ever made love under a Christmas tree?" Her fingers started to unbutton her blouse.

Erik's gaze was riveted to the streak of skin she was revealing. "No." His voice sounded harsh and on the edge of control. "But I'm about to." Erik yanked his sweater over his head and tossed it behind him. His T-shirt quickly joined it.

Sydney watched the golden glow of the fire play and dance across his chest. "Do you have any idea what you do to me?"

"No." Erik's fingers stilled on the snap of his jeans. "Tell me."

Her stomach clenched at the heat rumbling in Erik's voice. "I'll do better than that." She shrugged the gold silk blouse off her shoulders and reached for the front clasp of her bra. "I'll show you."

She wasn't sure which one of them moved first. In the end, it hadn't mattered. Jeans were tugged from Erik's legs, and her dark brown wool pants lost a button and would have to be dry cleaned; but it didn't concern her one bit. The only thing she was interested in was Erik.

Her golden-hair Viking made love to her with a mixture of tenderness and possession. He stole her heart and soul as he took her higher with each thrust of his hips. She felt her climax start and cried his name along with the words that she had been holding in for so long. "Erik, I love you."

Erik's rhythm increased, and he cried, *"Jeg elsker De,"* as he followed her over the edge.

Moments later Sydney was using Erik's chest as a pillow. The sound of his thundering heart was loud beneath her ear. Tiny white lights and golden flames gave the room and their damp bodies a romantic, yet satisfying sheen.

She thought she knew what Erik had said in the heat of passion, but she wanted to be sure. She wanted to hear the words. In English. For the past week every time Erik said something in Norwegian, she pretended to misunderstand him, so he would have to tell her what he had said. She tried to control her rapid breathing as she lightly toyed with a patch of silky golden chest hair. "I do not have the nose of a pig."

Erik chuckled as he rolled them over so once again he was on top. His legs and elbows took his weight as he stared down into her flushed face. "You have an adorable nose." He leaned down and kissed the end of it.

She wrinkled her nose and pouted. "That's not what you just said."

Erik's fingers brushed her hair away from her face. "That's not what I said." There was a gleam of mischief in his light blue eyes. Viking devilment.

"Well, if you think my ass is fat, why do you keep caressing it?" She smacked his hand when he stroked over her hip and headed right for the offending part.

Erik chuckled and playfully squeezed her cheek. "If your nose is adorable, your ass is perfection."

Sydney slowly shook her head at such nonsense. "Do all Vikings have such wicked tongues?"

"You should see what I can do with my tongue, Syd." Erik actually leered at her.

She tried not to blush. "I think I saw what you can do with it the other night in bed." She could still remember her scream of ecstasy when he had done that little trick that had to be illegal in twenty-six states.

Erik's hands threaded their way into her hair, and his palms cupped her cheeks. Blue eyes stared down into hers. She saw his heart and her reflection gazing back at her. "I said I love you." Erik brushed a tender kiss across her mouth. "I, Erik Olsen, love you, Sydney Fletcher."

Chapter Fifteen

Sydney couldn't have gotten any happier. If she did, she would actually be skipping down the aisles of Barley's Food Store, instead of walking sedately behind her cart. Erik loved her! Last night he had said the words, both in English and in Norwegian. Then he had carried her up the stairs to her bed and showed her exactly how much he loved her.

She wasn't sure if it was the *lutefisk* or the Polar Crispies in Erik's diet, but whatever it was, it should be bottled and sold in health stores as stamina tablets. The man had been incredible. Fantastic even.

Rows of neatly labeled canned vegetables had no appeal to her. Not when her mind was stuck on a certain blue-eyed Viking. She stopped her cart and studied the cans. Erik had asked her to pick something up today, but for the life of her, she couldn't remember what. Next time she would know to write it down. Was it corn or peas?

Shoppers passed her, and the occasional one even said hello; but she wasn't really paying any attention. All day long she had paid complete attention to her patients and their problems and complaints. She had been the concerned and caring doctor. She just wanted a couple of minutes to revel in this newly found love. If she wanted to do it in the middle of the vegetable aisle, who cared? She didn't. Noise and conversations floated around her as she stared dreamily at the succotash. It was hearing Erik's name that finally pulled her from her daydreams of happily-ever-after and little knee-high Vikings that had their father's blue eyes.

"It just isn't fair," groused a man's voice that Sydney recognized as Abraham Martin, a local lobster fisherman. He was standing directly around the corner of the aisle, and she could overhear the conversation without even trying. They couldn't see her, but their voices were raised loud enough that the people three aisles over could have heard them.

"Erik's not even a U.S. citizen!" snapped the whining Wendell Kirby. She would have known Kirby's voice anywhere. The man had left countless messages on her answering machine before he had taken the hint that she wasn't interested. Wendell was the president of Misty Harbor's Chamber of Commerce and had been one of the first residents to welcome her to town. Wendell also had hit on her before she had even unpacked all her worldly possessions from her S.U.V.

She didn't know Erik wasn't an American citizen, but now that she thought about it, Kirby was probably right. Erik and Gunnar had come to this country only three years ago. How long did it take to become a U.S. citizen?

"I heard they are pretty serious," Abraham said. "Some folks are even speculating about a spring wedding."

Sydney grinned, absently picked up a can of succotash, and placed it into her cart. So she wasn't the only one thinking about wedding bells and white lace.

"That's what is so unfair," cried Wendell in disgust. "Not only does Erik get a beautiful woman, a doctor no less, but if he gets her to marry him, he becomes a U.S. citizen automatically."

Sydney felt the first shiver of dread quiver in her gut as Wendell continued in his rant. "If he needed to get married to become a citizen, why couldn't he have picked someone a little less perfect than our town's doctor? Sydney's beautiful and *rich!* Why did she have to pick some foreigner who's only using her to get his citizenship papers? Sydney could have the pick of the town."

All of a sudden the air in the food store seemed a little thicker. Sydney was starting to have a difficult time breathing. Wendell couldn't be right, could he? What did a motel owner know about Immigration and Naturalization Law? What did she know about it? Absolutely nothing, besides what she had seen in the movies. Wasn't there a movie called *Green Card* where an American woman married a foreign man so he could stay in the country?

Impossible! Erik wouldn't do that to her. Erik wouldn't use her like that. A little voice in the back of her mind added, *the way Richard used you for your last name and all the connections your family has in Baltimore.*

Erik believed in family. If he was being threatened with deportation, and Hans needed him here, how far would Erik go to stay in this country? She didn't want to think about that question, or Erik's answer. She wasn't going to second guess Erik or give in to her doubts and insecurities. She loved Erik, but she was past the point in her life where she lay down and played doormat. Erik was due at her house in an hour. She would act like a rational adult and ask him. Simple, calm, and in control.

By the time Sydney heard Erik pull up out front, she was a complete nervous wreck. Abraham Martin and Wendell Kirby's conversation kept playing over and over in her mind. Like some broken, twisted record. Deep down inside she knew Erik loved her, but that nagging little voice kept pounding at her skull. Erik hadn't shown any interest in her at all until his grandfather's symptoms became noticeable. Their whole relationship had started because of Hans.

Every single, able-bodied—and some not so able-bodied—man had tried asking her out, sending flowers, candies, and dead fish to court her. Erik and Gunnar, the magnificent Viking twins, had been the exception. Gunnar she understood, because he had been hung up on Maggie for months. Erik, she could never figure out why he had avoided her. Hell, at her sister Gwen's wedding reception, Erik hadn't even asked her to dance. He had danced with her younger sister, Jocelyn, three different times, but never her. At the time she had chalked it up to Erik knowing she was living with someone back in Baltimore, even though that hadn't stopped the other men in town from dancing and flirting with her.

Now she wasn't so sure. Doubts were a horrible, breathing monster devouring her common sense.

Erik walked in the front door and called her name, "Syd?"

"In here." She was standing in the kitchen, still unpacking the food she had bought. A can of succotash was in her hand, and she had no idea why she had purchased it. She hated lima beans.

"How come you didn't turn on the Christmas lights?" Erik must have flipped the switches, because the living room lit up, and then he walked into the kitchen. "Hi, babe." He went to pull her into his arms, but stopped in midmotion. "What's wrong?"

She held out the can. "I hate succotash."

Erik's gaze went from her face, to the can, back to her face. "Okay." He took the can and placed it on the counter. "You don't have to eat it if you don't want to."

Her gaze took in the assorted groceries lining her

countertops and the confused look on Erik's face. He knew something was wrong.

"What's wrong, Syd?"

There was no getting around it. She couldn't think of any clever way of asking without letting Erik know how important his answers were to her. In frustration, she blurted out, "Are you a U.S. citizen?" She had the right to know if the man she was practically living with was a citizen or not.

Erik blinked, but it appeared to be a confused blink, instead of an "Oh shit, I'm in trouble now" blink. "No, I'm not a citizen, yet. I have a Permanent Residency status. Why?"

"What does Permanent Residency status mean?"

"It means that in two more years I can apply to become a naturalized citizen of the USA." Erik leaned back against the counter and frowned. "Why are you so upset, Sydney? You knew I wasn't born in America." Erik's voice had a hard, anxious edge to it. "You knew I came here from Norway. Why all the questions all of a sudden?"

She started to bristle under Erik's growing confusion and anger. Why was he the one acting all upset? She was the one people were talking about in the middle of the grocery store. "Then, you could still be deported, right? They could send you back to Norway, couldn't they?"

Erik pushed away from the counter and towered over her. A spark of fear leaped into his blue eyes, and he demanded, "What are you talking about? No one is going to deport me." Rough, weather-redden hands tunneled through his hair, causing the rubber band to snap. "Who in the hell have you been talking to?"

At the look of fear in Erik's eyes, all her self doubts and past pain reared their ugly heads. "Abraham and Wendell said that if we got married, you would automatically become a citizen. Then you couldn't be deported." She crossed her arms against her chest and stated her worst fear. "I'm not marrying you so you can stay near Hans."

Erik forced himself to keep breathing. For one wild minute there he thought Sydney had known something he hadn't, like someone was trying to get his Permanent Residency status revoked and him deported. He would have been forced to leave Gunnar and Hans behind, but more importantly, Sydney.

The truth was much worse. Sydney actually thought he wanted to marry her so that he could stay in this country. How could she even think such a thing? Didn't she know him at all? Didn't his love mean anything to her?

He had never mentioned marriage to her. Dreamed it, yes. Broached the subject, no. Last night, when they had made love under the Christmas tree, he had almost asked her to become his wife. It hadn't mattered then that he was a fisherman and that she came from a well-to-do family, just like his parents. It hadn't mattered that she was the total opposite of what he thought he wanted in a wife. The only thing that had mattered last night was the fact that Sydney loved him. Thankfully, he hadn't voiced his proposal, because there was no way Sydney could possibly love him and think he would do something as deplorable as marry a woman so he could get his citizenship papers.

"I don't need to marry you, Sydney, to become a citizen. I'm doing that all on my own. No one is going to deport me, and in two more years I will be naturalized. If I married you and tried to get my citizenship based on that marriage, it would take three years." He could see the doubts swirling in her gaze. The need to hurt her, as much as she had just hurt him, ruled his tongue. "Why would you assume I want to marry you when I haven't even asked?"

Erik turned on his heel and marched out of the kitchen and her cottage without another word.

* * *

Four hours later, Sydney was still curled up on the couch with a mug of hot tea cradled between the palms of her hands and an afghan wrapped around her shoulders. The tears had finally stopped, but not the heartache. How could she have been so wrong? How could she have been so stupid?

In her heart she had known Erik would never do such a thing. So why had she allowed her fears, instead of her heart, to overrun her tongue? How could she have accused Erik of such an atrocious act? To top it all off, she had just assumed he was going to ask her to marry him. Talk about a relationship faux pas!

She gave another sniffle and took a sip of tea. Her mother always swore that a good cup of tea could help any problem or calm any worry. It wasn't working tonight. Maybe she needed something stronger than chamomile. A nice Kentucky bourbon might do the trick, but the strongest drink she had in the house was white wine and a few bottles of Erik's beer. What she really needed was to turn back the clock about five hours so she could deck Wendell and Abraham for making such asinine assumptions about Erik and her relationship.

Sydney leaned forward and placed the mug on the coffee table next to the mound of damp, tear-soaked tissues. The Christmas tree was still lit, but she hadn't even bothered with the fireplace tonight. She had cranked the thermostat up a few degrees, changed into her warmest flannel pajamas, and reached for the afghans.

It wasn't Wendell's and Abraham's fault that she was so insecure when it came to men. It wasn't even Richard's fault. She wrapped the afghan tighter and pulled her knees up to her chin. It was all her doing. She had been the one to allow Richard to walk all over her like some doormat. She had known all along that Richard had been using her parents' and grandfather's connections. She had just refused to admit it, that was all. Richard hadn't been attracted to her. He had been attracted to her last name and the fact that her wallet seemed healthy.

Gwen and Jocelyn had seen Richard for what he was worth and tried to warn her. She hadn't listened to her sisters. She had figured they were too young to understand the idiosyncrasies of a serious relationship. For a relationship to work, there had to be a lot of give and take. A lot of compromises. She had given Richard everything she had. In return, Richard had given her the illusion of a future together. She had been a fool once. She wasn't about to play that part again.

She owed Erik an apology and an explanation.

Tears once again overflowed, and the Christmas tree blurred. Hundreds of miniature white lights fractured into thousands as she reached for another tissue. Erik would or would not accept her apology. But that still didn't answer the question that was burning in her heart. What kind of a woman was she that men would live with her and never want to marry her?

Gunnar parked his Jeep in the parking lot adjoining the docks and glanced around. Maggie's car wasn't there. Maybe she had walked to the restaurant or had gotten a ride with someone. Or maybe she was just running late. This date had been her idea, yet she didn't want him to pick her up at her parents' house. It had seemed strange at first, but then he figured if Katie saw them leaving together, without her, she might become upset. He wasn't used to children, so he was better off leaving those kinds of calls to Maggie. He got out of the Jeep, straightened his tie, and headed for the best restaurant in town, Catch of the Day. Their reservation was for six o'clock.

It was Friday night, four nights before Christmas Eve,

and Maggie's night off at the restaurant. It would have seemed unusual that she chose to eat dinner at the place she worked part-time, but Misty Harbor and the surrounding towns didn't have a very large selection of restaurants. Catch of the Day was the best place to eat within forty, maybe fifty miles. A person would have to drive into Bangor or even Bar Harbor to get its equal.

Maggie and he had spent the last two Friday nights with Katie. One night had been spent at his home; the other he had taken them both into Franklin for pizza and the latest Disney movie. A couple nights during the week he had had them both over for dinner and for Katie to play with the trains. Much to his amusement, Katie now wanted to be a conductor or an engineer when she grew up.

This was his and Maggie's first official date without Katie as a buffer, and if he was honest with himself, he was somewhat nervous. What were they going to talk about, without Katie putting in her two cents' worth every other sentence? He was a fisherman, and Maggie was almost a college graduate. They should have nothing in common. Yet when he pulled her into his arms and kissed her, they went together like melted butter and lobster.

Last night on the phone with Maggie, he had suggested moving up their dinner reservation so that they would have time to catch the seven-thirty movie in Franklin. Maggie had vetoed the idea, claiming to have a surprise for him. He hated surprises. He detested them when they happened, and he absolutely loathed knowing one was about to happen. One of these days he would have to tell Maggie that, but not tonight. Tonight he would allow her her surprise and pray it wasn't too bad. His birthday wasn't until February, so he wasn't worried about any surprise parties.

Hopefully, Maggie's surprise had something to do with being in his arms. He wondered if he could convince her to go parking at Sunset Cove after dinner.

They surely couldn't go back to her house, with her parents and Katie there. They couldn't go to his place. When he had left, Hans and Sadie had been putting together a jigsaw puzzle on the kitchen table, and Erik had been sulking in front of the television. Erik and Sydney must have had a fight. At least when his brother wanted to spend some time alone with the lovely doctor, he could go to her place.

He was a healthy twenty-seven-year-old male who was reduced to necking at teenage hangouts or sneaking quick, frustrating kisses. It was time he started looking for a place of his own. Way past time. But what about his grandfather? He couldn't leave Hans alone, and Erik had been spending just about every night at Sydney's. He was between a rock and a hard place. Just thinking about Maggie waiting for him in the restaurant had caused the hard place in his pants to stir to life.

Gunnar tugged down his jacket and straightened his tie, once again. The wind had played havoc on it and his hair. He ran his fingers through his hair and expertly wrapped the rubber band back around it. He opened the door and stepped into the restaurant.

Tess Dunbar, the receptionist for the sheriff and part-time hostess at the restaurant, came hurrying toward him. "Hi, Gunnar." She glanced at her watch. "You're right on time."

"Hi, Tess." He gave her an absent smile as he glanced around the room. No beautiful redheads sitting alone at any of the tables. "Maggie must be running late." The whole town knew that he and Maggie were dating, so there was no use in pretending otherwise.

Tess pulled an envelope out of her pocket. "Maggie asked me to give you this."

He looked at the pink envelope as if it were a poisonous snake. This couldn't be good.

The envelope waved back and forth. "Take it, Gunnar." Tess was smiling as if she knew a secret. A delightful secret.

He took the envelope. Maybe this was part of Maggie's surprise. He took a step back and opened the sealed envelope. A small piece of pink paper was tucked neatly inside. He pulled it out and quickly read the six words. *Misty Harbor Motor Inn, Room #216.* The second time he read the message, the words finally penetrated his desire-fogged brain. He was out the restaurant door before anyone could notice he forgot how to breathe.

The cold night air didn't help his breathing or the rapid pounding of his heart. It was a joke. What else could it be? Maggie wasn't the type to go around renting motel rooms by the night. It had to be a joke, and Maggie was in on it. He would get to room 216, and his brother and a bunch of other fishermen would all be there laughing their heads off. Abraham Martin had to be the one coordinating this hoax. It would be something he would do.

He got back into his Jeep and pulled the note out of his suit pocket. It looked real. Abraham wouldn't have thought to use pretty pink paper and an envelope. He could almost imagine the faint scent of lavender. The old relic of a fisherman would have used the back of a fueling slip or a label off a beer bottle. Gunnar started the Jeep and headed for the motor inn. If Abraham's old Ford pickup was in the parking lot, he was going to accidently tap it with the bumper of the Jeep and send it over the cliff and into the sea. Misty Harbor Motor Inn sat on top of the bluff, overlooking the town and the harbor. Abraham's truck was going to make one hell of a splash.

Gunnar slowly pulled into the parking lot and glanced around. Four cars were in the lot. One was in front of the office. Two others were parked in front of different rooms. The fourth car was parked directly in front of room 216. Maggie's old green Chevy. He eased the Jeep into the spot next to it.

He studied the tightly closed drapes on the room's only window. He could tell the light was lit in the room, but that was about it. His gaze went from those dark drapes, to the room number, to Maggie's car, to the note clutched in his hand. The pounding of his heart thundered in his chest.

What in the hell was Maggie thinking? Whatever it was, it couldn't be what he was thinking. Because if it was, he was going to die a very happy man tonight.

Gunnar slowly got out of the Jeep and slipped the pink note into his pocket. He refused to even think about what was on the other side of the door. He wanted Maggie willing and waiting. What he was probably going to get was Abraham Martin in some sleazy, extra-large mermaid outfit and a roomful of drunken fishermen.

Wintertime in Maine could get downright boring. Practical jokes played an important part down at the docks in relieving that boredom. This one was going to be a winner. Abraham was finally going to get back at him for planting fake Spanish doubloons in some of his lobster pots back in October. Abraham had been so sure he had found a sunken pirate ship off the coast of Maine that he had called the papers and an oceanographical unit out of Woods Hole in Massachusetts.

No matter how disappointed he was going to be when Maggie didn't answer the door, he would allow Abraham the win and act surprised. No one could say he wasn't a good sport. He raised his hand and knocked.

Half a minute later, Maggie opened the door. A soft, hesitant smile curved her mouth. "You came." Maggie opened the door wider, and he stepped inside.

He heard the door closing behind him, but he didn't pay it any attention. He was too busy checking out the room for the punch line that was sure to be a joke on him. No hairy-legged, drunken mermaid. No washtub full of beer and ice. Nothing but sweet Maggie and a picnic basket.

The Big Bad Wolf never had it this easy.

"You look very nice in a suit, Gunnar." Maggie was

leaning against the door. Both of her hands were behind her back holding onto the doorknob.

He wasn't sure if she was trying to keep him in or if she was planning a fast escape. "Thank you." She looked all sweet and cuddly in a pair of skin-tight jeans, a gold sweater, and bare feet. Maggie's toenails were painted a deep burgundy. She also appeared nervous as all hell. Before he said another word, he walked to the bathroom and peered inside. It was empty. Totally empty. No one was hiding behind the door or in the tub.

"Who are you looking for?" Maggie asked as she followed him across the room.

It was awfully warm in the room. He wondered what Wendell Kirby had the temperature set at. He tugged his tie loose and chuckled. "Believe it or not, I was looking for Abraham Martin dressed up in some mermaid outfit."

"That's one image I don't want to imagine." Maggie wrinkled her nose. "Want to tell me why you thought Abraham would be here?"

He took off his suit jacket and hung it over the back of a chair. "I thought this was all a joke."

Maggie's teeth nibbled on her lower lip. "A joke?"

A groan vibrated in the back of his throat as he watched her lip get puffy and moist. He wished to hell she wouldn't do that. He wasn't sure how much longer his control was going to last. "Abraham owes me one."

"For the sunken pirate ship number you pulled on him." She smiled. "That was brilliant, by the way. My father and brother are still laughing about that one." Maggie walked over to the round table in front of the window and started to unload the picnic basket. "I'm still not sure why you thought my message had anything to do with Abraham."

He could see Gwen Creighton's hands all over that basket. "When did Catch of the Day get into the picnic basket business?" The bottle of wine and two tall stemmed glasses added a nice touch. There wasn't a paper plate or plastic fork in sight.

"They haven't. Gwen pulled this together for us as a favor to me." Maggie's hands were trembling slightly as she handed him the chilled wine bottle and a cork screw.

"Can I ask a question?" He undid the top two buttons on his shirt, rolled up his tie, and slipped it into the pocket of his jacket. The king-size bed behind him was making him extremely anxious.

"Sure." Maggie refolded the linen napkins and set them beside the plates. Not once did she look at him.

"What's this about?" When Maggie glanced up, he swept his hand in the direction of the food. He wanted to point to the bed with its dark blue spread and demand to know if she was trying to seduce him or just drive him insane?

"It's dinner."

"We had reservations for six o'clock." He twisted the corkscrew into the cork and slowly worked it out of the bottle.

"I canceled them." Maggie continued to unpack the basket, setting assorted dishes in the middle of the table. When the basket was empty, she placed it on the bureau, next to the tourist information booklet.

"Why?" He poured the wine, but didn't offer her the glass yet.

"I thought you might want some privacy."

He raised a brow at that one. "To eat?" He was rock-hard and ready to howl at the moon. The seductive scent of her lavender perfume was driving him nuts. If Maggie would honestly look at him, instead of casting a few quick glances his way, she couldn't help but see how close to the edge he really was. Maggie Pierce was about to be ravished, but he wanted to make sure he wasn't reading any signals wrong. No woman got a motel room just to eat dinner.

"I thought about having you over for dinner at my

parents', but since they live there, I couldn't very well ask them to leave. I could have cooked dinner for you at your place, but Hans and Erik live there, too." Maggie toyed with the silverware and stared at the plate. "Catch of the Day is a great restaurant, with terrific food and all, but there wouldn't be any privacy. Anything we said to each other would be overheard and spread around town before the dessert course. And then there's Katie. She doesn't understand . . ."

Gunnar smiled and sat on the edge of the bed. He had never heard Maggie string that many sentences together at one time. She was rattling on about Katie, the weather, and something about Santa Claus. He tried not to chuckle. He tried not to crow with satisfaction. Maggie was as nervous as he was about the next step in their relationship. "Maggie, come here."

Maggie's voice trailed off in the middle of a sentence. She gave him a blushing look, but took a step toward him. Their knees bumped.

He opened his thighs and whispered, "Closer." *Said the Big Bad Wolf to Little Red Riding Hood.*

Maggie stepped between his legs.

His hands reached out and lightly grasped her waist. Her sweater was soft beneath his fingers. But not as soft as her skin would be. *"Kjœreste,* I love your surprise." He fell back onto the bed, bringing her with him.

Maggie wiggled into a more comfortable position on his chest. "What did you call me?"

He reached up and tenderly tugged at her lower lip with his teeth. "In English it means sweetheart."

"I like the way you say it better." Maggie's mouth captured his in a kiss that was all heat and flames. Small, delicate fingers wove their way into his hair as she nibbled her way to his earlobe. "I like the way you taste, too."

Wasn't that supposed to be my line? Gunnar felt as if he was going to explode by the time she released his ear. Two could play her game. He pressed his lips against the thundering pulse in her neck. "I haven't even begun to taste you, *kjæreste.*"

Maggie shivered and raised her head. The smile that had been straining Maggie's mouth earlier was now soft and seductive. "You don't mind being seduced by a pushy woman?"

He spread his arms out wide across the bed and grinned. He was living every man's fantasy. "I'm Jell–o in your hands."

She rocked her hips against his straining arousal and grinned as she shook her head. "Jell–o? I don't think so." She reached back into the back pocket of her jeans and pulled out a trio of foil-wrapped condoms. She tossed them onto the bed. "Saddle up, cowboy, I think we are about to ride."

Chapter Sixteen

Maggie sat on the park bench and tilted her face up toward the sun. What a glorious morning. Fifty-four degrees and sunny was so unusual for Maine at the end of December that it seemed the entire town was out and about. Katie and she were no exception. After breakfast, a quick bout of cleaning, and doing some laundry, they headed for the park in the center of town. By the looks of things, so did just about every other kid. A cold front was due to come through tomorrow night, and they were predicting snow on Christmas Day.

She closed her eyes and smiled as Katie's laughter reached her ears. A bunch of kids were playing on the monkey bars, and Katie was right smack in the middle of it all. Katie's best friend, Elizabeth, was right beside her either cheering or egging her on. Sometimes it was hard to tell with those two. Elizabeth Burton with her big brown eyes and Katie with her fiery hair and a face full of freckles were going to be a pair of heartbreakers in another fourteen or so years. She wasn't looking forward to those angst-ridden teenage years. She wanted Katie to be her little girl forever.

Impossible wishes, on a heavenly day. Her daughter had the laugh of an angel. A beautiful, feisty, intelligent angel. But then again, she was prejudiced. Extremely prejudiced. Nothing and no one was more important to her than Katie. At least that had been true until last night.

Gunnar Olsen had changed everything with his hot kisses, tender hands, and sweet words. She had known she was attracted to the hulking Norwegian. She had even known there was a good probability she was falling for Gunnar in a big way. What she hadn't counted on was the absolute rightness when they had made love. What they had shared hadn't been just sex or scratching each other's itch. They both were adults. They both had needs, but what they had experienced last night hadn't been about those needs. It might have started that way, but it had ended up being about love.

She still couldn't believe she actually had the guts to go through with that big seduction scene last night. It just went to prove how desperate she had been. It had all been Gunnar's fault. The man had been driving her crazy with his gentlemanly manners. Gunnar never would have rented a motel room for the night. The big Norwegian had been treating her like Katie's precious and fragile mother. He had bought her gloves and mittens. He had tuned up her car and spent a fortune on trains to keep Katie happy. Gunnar said the right things and did all the proper gestures, such as opening car doors and helping her with her coat. Gunnar Olsen treated her like a lady.

The truth was, she didn't want to be treated like a lady. She wanted Gunnar to treat her like a woman. A desirable woman. Last night he had, and she had fallen completely in love with the man. The hardest thing she had ever done was to slip out of his arms, while he slept, and drive away from the Misty Harbor Motor Inn. She had to go home to her daughter and to her parents. Her mother and father had suffered enough from her past mistakes. She wasn't about to cause them any more heartache or shame.

Gunnar would understand. At least she hoped he would. She would have left him a note if she could have figured out what to write. *Thanks* seemed like he had done her a favor. *Call me* sounded too high schoolish, and *I'll call you* had the ring of a brush-off. She had actually taken a piece of paper from her purse and written *I love you* on it, but she hadn't had the guts to leave it behind. She had used up her quota of guts on the big seduction scene.

Gunnar had told her he loved her last night when he had made love to her for the second time. She had believed him then, and even poured out her heart to him in return. After they had polished off most of the food, Gunnar had used the last of the trio of condoms and showed her what love meant between a man and a woman.

When she had eased out of his arms and had gotten dressed, things started to look different. She knew she loved him, that hadn't changed. But what if Gunnar was mixing up lust with love? What if she screwed up this relationship just like she had screwed up every other romance in her life?

She would be the first to admit that her track record sucked when it came to men.

Maggie squinched up her face, but refused to open her eyes. She was not going to mess up with Gunnar. For the first time in her life, she was honestly and truly in love. Nothing possibly could go wrong. The warmth of the sun and the pleasant soreness in her body made her drowsy and content. Sleep had been near impossible once she had returned to her parents' house. She had missed Gunnar. She had lain in her childhood, twin-size bed and pictured Gunnar as she had left him back in the motel. He had reminded her of a bear. A big golden bear spread facedown across that king-size bed with a white sheet wrapped and twisted around his waist.

A dreamy smile curved her lips as she thought about how soon could she get him back into that same position.

Katie's shout pulled her from her erotic daydream. "Gunnar! Gunnar! I'm over here."

Maggie sat up to look across the playground toward her daughter. A massive chest blocked her view. Her gaze hungrily caressed that chest. She liked it better without the flannel shirt or the jacket covering it. She softly smiled as her gaze met Gunnar's. "Morning."

In a quick movement, Gunnar leaned down and brushed a fleeting kiss across her mouth. "We need to talk."

Gunnar turned and grinned as Katie flew across the playground and straight into his arms. He twirled Katie around twice, high in the air, and then slowly lowered her back to her feet. "Hello, *Liten,* you're out and about early."

"I'm playing with my best friend, Elizabeth. Remember, she's the one that already has the baby brother."

Maggie groaned silently. Leave it to Katie to bring up baby brothers now. That child was starting to obsess about becoming a big sister.

Gunnar looked over at a little girl standing by the monkey bars looking at him. "So I see." He gave Katie's ponytail a playful tug. "Why don't you go play with your friend. I'm going to sit right here and talk to your mommy."

"Bye." Katie took off running.

Gunnar sat down next to her. His big hands were clasped together between his knees, and his head was bent. "Want to tell me why you left without even bothering to wake me?"

"I had to get home to Katie." The last thing she wanted to do was to hurt Gunnar. She could feel the glances the other mothers were giving her and Gunnar. "I couldn't stay till morning, I'm sorry."

"I understand why you couldn't stay. I'm asking why you didn't wake me." Gunnar's gaze was probing.

She turned to face him fully. Gunnar was a proud man. A gorgeous man with his Norwegian roots and his golden mane. This morning there appeared to be a touch of vulnerability about him. Had her leaving done that? She softened her voice, allowing it to caress him when her fingers couldn't. "You sleep like a bear."

One golden brow arched. "I snore?"

"Not that I heard." She chuckled and swung her legs up onto the bench. Her knees pressed into his thighs. "You were sleeping so peacefully, and I didn't have the heart to wake you."

Gunnar's hands covered her knees. "Do you know what I thought when I woke up at dawn to find you gone? Why didn't you leave a note?"

"I wrote you a note." She reached into her pocket where she had placed the missive in the early morning hours. "I just didn't have the guts to leave it." She held it out to him.

Gunnar took the piece of paper and read the three words: *I love you.* He looked at her, smiled, and visibly relaxed. "Then, I didn't dream that part last night?"

She shook her head and melted at the look of hunger burning in his eyes.

"I need your opinion on something," Gunnar said. One of his fingertips was drawing a circle on her knee.

"Okay, shoot." She had to work tonight or she would be thinking about giving him more than just her opinion.

"What kind of house do you like? Any particular style?"

She blinked. "Excuse me?"

"Houses, Maggie. Think houses."

"Why do I need to be thinking houses?"

"Because we are getting married, and you, me, and Katie will need someplace to live." Gunnar's fingertip drew a little higher. "My vote would be for a place where we can be close to the water."

Maggie heard Gunnar's voice, but it seemed to be coming from a great distance away. "Married?" She brushed his hand away from her thigh. "Who said anything about marriage?"

"After last night, *kjæreste,* I don't think we have any choice."

She shook her head in denial. "We used protection, Gunnar. All three times. There is no way that I am pregnant. You don't have to marry me." She would not repeat the same mistake twice.

"I love children, Maggie. I love Katie as if she was my own daughter." Gunnar gently caught her chin and prevented her from shaking her head again. "But, I sincerely hope you aren't pregnant from last night. There are too many things that you have to do before the babies start coming." Gunnar glanced around the park, shrugged, and then leaned forward to kiss her anyway. "First thing you have to do is graduate from college, and then you have to start that business you have been talking about. Marriage wouldn't interfere with those goals, Maggie." His gaze dropped to her stomach. "Being fat with my child might. And make no mistake about it, Maggie, love, you will be fat with my child one of these days."

Maggie felt her heart pound in her chest. Gunnar was serious. The man she loved wanted to marry her, now. He supported her education and her future business goals, loved Katie, and wanted more children. It was all her wishes rolled up into one nice, neat package. So why was she so scared?

"There are some other problems to work out, though," Gunnar said.

"Like what?" She wasn't agreeing to anything, but she wanted to hear what else Gunnar considered a problem. She could think of a dozen right off the bat.

"Gwen's going to be awfully upset to lose her best

waitress. I would prefer you not work part-time while you finish up your schooling. Being a full-time wife, mother, and college student is enough to keep you busy. I'm selfish. I would want you home as much as possible."

She almost agreed to marry Gunnar tomorrow on that condition alone. No more aching feet. No more sore back and arms from lifting heavy trays. Time with Katie, and Gunnar in her bed every night. "What else?"

"My grandfather."

"Hans?"

"He needs me, Maggie. I can't just leave him."

"I know." She reached out and gently caressed his cheek. Sometime this morning Gunnar had taken the time to shave. "I like Hans, and I would never want or expect you to just abandon him." It was one of the things she loved most about Gunnar, his concern and love for his family.

"I need to talk to Erik, but we'll figure something out, okay?"

She slowly nodded. "There's no rush, Gunnar."

"Yes, there is." Gunnar's jaw tightened. "I want us to get married right away. I've waited a long time for you; I'm not waiting any longer."

"I rushed into a marriage once, Gunnar. I won't do it again. Let's leave things the way they are for now. If you still feel the same way in June, after I graduate, we'll get married." She knew she wasn't confusing lust with love, but what if Gunnar was? Would he still want her once the hot edge of desire was appeased?

"I will not wake up in some strange motel room alone and aching for you again, Maggie." Gunnar brushed another kiss across her lips. "You will have your June wedding if that is what you want. But there will be no more lovemaking until the wedding night. Once you are back in my arms, I won't be letting you go."

She looked at Gunnar as if he had just lost his mind. Maybe he had. Maybe she had. They were getting married in June, and there wasn't going to be any more midnight romping in room 216 of the Misty Harbor Motel Inn! Gunnar looked determined enough to stick to his word. She, on the other hand, had melted the second she spotted him in the park. She wanted him now. How was she ever going to hold out till June?

Hans looked in wonder at the woman sitting across the booth from him. Who would have thought Sadie Hopkins would turn out to be such an interesting woman? Not him, that was for sure. In the weeks that he had gotten to know Sadie, he would say she had become a friend. A dear friend.

Today, she was going to become his confidant.

He was an old fool, but he had finally figured out what his grandsons were up to. "So, Sadie, how much are they paying you?"

Sadie continued to munch on her Big Mac and then took a sip of her milkshake. "Not a cent, why? Are you finally figuring out you aren't such a ladies' man after all?" Sadie chuckled and swiped her french fry through a mound of ketchup she had poured onto her wrapper.

He tried to hide his bristle, but he was pretty sure Sadie had seen it. Sadie noticed everything. It was one of the things he liked best about her. He might be some poor old four cylinder puttering up a hill and misfiring through life, but Sadie was still running on all eight cylinders.

"They had me going there for a while." He still couldn't believe he had been gullible enough to think that all those nice ladies from town showing up on his doorstep every morning had been interested in him.

"What gave it away?" Sadie unwrapped her second Big Mac and went to town.

"Grace Winslow showed up Thursday with an apple pie and her knitting."

"The minister's wife?" Sadie chuckled. "Yeah, I bet that gave you food for thought."

"She made me real nervous; that's what she did." He toyed with his french fries. His appetite was off today. "I kept expecting to have the hand of God smite me."

Sadie seemed to be enjoying herself immensely. "I told them it wouldn't work for long, but those boys of yours just wouldn't listen."

He nodded. "So, how much are they paying you to watch me during the day?" His voice broke in frustration, but his face reddened with humiliation.

"Like I told you, not a cent." Sadie wiped her mouth on a paper napkin. "I like your company, Hans. You don't whine and complain like most men. Now, the Women's Guild is a different story. They are taking turns, and last I heard they were arguing about what to do with the money Erik and Gunnar are paying them. So far it's a toss-up between new curtains for the social hall or a dishwasher for the church kitchen."

He snorted. "I don't need no baby-sitters! What were those boys thinking?"

"I reckon they were thinking how much they love you." Sadie took another sip of her milkshake and pinned him with a glare. "Never saw two boys so crazy about their grandpop before. Most men Erik and Gunnar's age want to get on with their own lives and don't have much time to think about, let alone worry about, their grandfathers. At the first sign of trouble, old people are shipped off to retirement homes or nursing homes. Same thing if you ask me." Sadie reached over and swiped one of his fries. "Seems to me you should be counting your blessings, instead of sitting here crying into your Coke."

"It's root beer, and I'm not crying." He knew he had been whining, but hell, he was scared to death. "What did they tell you was wrong with me?"

Sadie shrugged. "That you were having a hard time remembering things and that you had already wandered off on them one night. Heard Dr. Sydney brought you home."

He felt his heart sink. "What else?"

"They are thinking it's Alzheimer's." Sadie nodded to his fries. "Are you going to finish those?"

"No, you can have them." He pushed them across the table. "Alzheimer's bad?"

"I've seen worse stuff."

"You have?" What did he really know about Sadie? She had some children and grandchildren around. Her husband died years ago, and she took over their blueberry farm.

"Nursed my husband for the last year of his life. Lung cancer took him. It wasn't a pretty sight." Sadie glanced out the window and studied the flow of traffic down Main Street in Sullivan. "Know anything about Alzheimer's?"

"Yeah, you lose your mind."

Sadie laughed. "Hell, Hans, people already think I've lost my mind, and I don't even have it." Sadie worked her way through the fries. "I looked up some information on it the other day."

"Why?"

"Curious."

"Doctor wants me to get some tests. Sydney says they can't test for Alzheimer's. They test to eliminate everything else. When there's nothing left, you got Alzheimer's."

"So when are these tests scheduled? Need a ride?"

"I haven't agreed to them."

Sadie finished off her shake with a loud, slurping sound as she moved the straw across the bottom of her cup. "Let me get this straight. Your grandsons are worrying themselves sick over you, and you won't even go for tests?"

"What if I have it, Sadie? What then?" He voiced his greatest fear. "Why would my grandsons want an old man around whose mind is slowly disintegrating?"

"Maybe because they love you." Sadie reached across the table and reached for his hand. "You can live with this disease for years, Hans. They have new medicine out there right now for people like you in the beginning stages. It's showing promise of slowing the disease in some patients. Maybe you will be one of the lucky ones." She shook her head, and he could see the concern in her eyes. "All I know is that if you don't get some medical attention, you already are a loser. Might as well curl up your toes now and stop causing all the worries at home."

"They will probably stick me with needles and make me drink horrible-tasting stuff."

"Probably."

"They will ask me hours and hours of questions and make me relive my childhood."

"Probably."

"They will strap me onto some board and shove me into one of those big machines so they can look at the inside of my brain."

Sadie smiled. "Stop your whining, Hans. It's not dignified."

"Will you drive me to Bangor so I can take those tests without my grandsons missing any more work?" Erik and Gunnar had done enough for him already. Lord, they were paying for baby-sitters for him while he was sitting on a pretty good nest egg in the bank. He would pay for his own keepers from now on.

"Only if Erik and Gunnar want me to, Hans. I have a feeling those boys are going to be with you every step of the way."

"They are stubborn like that." He felt a smile tug at his own mouth.

Sadie raised one dark eyebrow, and the curlers in her hair jiggled. "Wonder where they get that from?"

Hans chuckled and balled up the wrappings and tossed everything onto the plastic tray. "Are you ready to roll? There aren't going to be very many days like this left to go hot-rodding through town with the top down." Joyriding in Sadie's convertible with the cold wind blowing in his face reminded him of being out on the sea. Sadie was the captain of her pink boat. He preferred to just sit back and pretend to be the first mate.

An hour later, Sadie and Hans were driving down White Pine Street on their way to Hans's house. Abraham Martin's old, rusty pickup truck took a turn too tight in front of them. Two ancient lobster pots covered in dried seaweed fell off the back, directly in the path of Sadie's pink Cadillac. Hans gave Sadie credit for a quick response and a wicked swerve around the broken wood. It would have been a perfect save and a near miss if it hadn't been for the telephone pole.

The impact jarred his dentures.

Hans felt his seat belt tighten across his chest, but his hands still flew out in front of him. His left wrist whacked the dash with a resounding crack. Sadie appeared unharmed, and if her language was anything to go by, she was mad as hell.

Abraham Martin's truck disappeared down the road in a cloud of exhaust. A lone hubcap rolled off Sadie's Cadillac and followed in its wake.

"That no good son of a bit . . ." Sadie's voice trailed off as she turned and looked at him. "Oh, my God, you're hurt!"

He cradled his arm against his chest. "It's nothing. I just hit my hand against the glove compartment, that's all."

Sadie gave him a concerned look and then rammed the gear shifter into reverse. "Hang on, Hans, I'll get you to the doc."

"You aren't supposed to leave the scene of an accident, Sadie." The front grill of her car was indented, and the hood was all crinkled. Steam was rising from the radiator, but Sadie didn't seem to care. His wrist hurt, but he didn't think it was broken. He had suffered worse in his years. "You could get in trouble with the law."

Sadie snorted. "They have to catch me first." The

big pink Cadillac backed into the street with a hiss and a groan, but the engine was running as smooth as silk. Sadie glanced in the rearview mirror and tugged her zebra-print hair netting more securely around her curlers. With a steely look of determination, she rammed a Springsteen tape into the player, cranked up the volume, and dropped the car into drive.

Hans glanced at the telephone pole as they whizzed by. Pink paint was smeared across the dark wood, but it appeared to be sound and not in any immediate danger of falling down. He held his wrist and grinned as Sadie barreled down the street and headed for Sydney's office as if his life depended on it. Nothing impressed him more than a woman who knew how to take charge in an emergency. There was no screaming and tears coming from his Sadie.

Fifteen minutes later, Sydney had just finished wrapping Hans's wrist. "I'm pretty sure it's just a sprain, but you need to go into Camden and have it x-rayed to make sure."

"I'll take him," Sadie said as she walked back into the exam room. "My son's bringing me my pickup, since Bruce appears to be out of commission."

Sydney raised her brow and looked at Hans. She hadn't gotten too many details of the accident, only that it apparently had been Abraham Martin's fault and that Hans had the only injury. Thank goodness it appeared to be merely a sprain. When Sadie first came running into the office shouting something about Hans being injured, she had nearly panicked. Before her heart could pick up a couple extra beats, Hans had followed Sadie in, and she could see for herself he wasn't too bad off.

"Don't you think you should tell Erik or Gunnar before you go heading off to the Camden Medical Center? You know they are going to hear about the accident, probably sooner than later, Hans. I think you should be the one to tell them and to reassure them you aren't hurt too badly."

Hans looked abashed. "We'll stop at the docks on the way out of town."

A loud commotion could be heard coming from the reception area. She wondered what was going on now as the sound of someone blowing a horn filled the air.

"That's my truck," Sadie said as she hoisted her purse over her shoulder and reached for her coat.

Sydney handed Hans her order for the x-ray. "They'll take care of you there and fax me the results of the x-ray. Sadie, you drive carefully, and try not to hit any more telephone poles."

Sadie snorted, "Wasn't my fault," as she helped Hans get into his coat.

Sydney's laugh died in her throat as Erik barged into the small exam room.

Erik's gaze went directly to his grandfather, and he seemed to study every inch of the older man. *"Bestefar?"*

"I'm fine, Erik." Hans wiggled his fingers and zipped his coat with his other hand. "It's only a sprain."

Erik's shoulders relaxed slightly when he turned to Sydney. "Only a sprain?"

"Probably." She jammed her hands into the pockets of her white lab coat. She wanted to comfort Erik and assure him everything was going to be fine. Hans was going to be fine. "Sadie's taking him into Camden for an x-ray of the wrist, just to make sure I'm right. He'll be as good as new in a couple of weeks, Erik."

"I'll take him." Erik looked at his grandfather. "Are you ready?"

Hans shook his head at Erik. "I'm not a child, Erik, and Sadie is perfectly capable of driving me. It's idiots like Abraham that shouldn't be allowed on the road."

"I didn't say Sadie wasn't capable." Erik sighed and ran his hands through his wind-tossed hair. He looked as if he had just run to Sydney's office from the docks. "I just want to make sure you're all right."

"Is that why you hired baby-sitters for me?" Hans turned on his heel and walked out the door.

Sadie shrugged. "I told you he'd figure it out, Erik. He wasn't too happy with you or Gunnar, but I think it's all going to work out, though." Sadie squeezed Erik's arm. "I'll take good care of him and bring him home later this afternoon."

Erik sadly watched as Sadie left the room. "I screwed that up, too, didn't I?"

"No. Give Hans some time. I'm sure he'll see that you and Gunnar were only doing what you thought was best." More than anything, she wanted to walk into Erik's arms and hold him. Have him hold her in return. She had missed him these past two days. "Sadie will take good care of him, Erik. You should have seen her charging in here like some mother hen with a wounded chick." She chuckled softly. "I think Hans was lapping up all the attention."

Erik leaned against the counter.

Her heart melted. He looked as bad as she felt. Erik obviously wasn't sleeping any better than she was. Her queen-size bed was awfully empty without her Viking. Why in the hell had she ever listened to Wendell Kirby and Abraham Martin?

"Syd, about the other night . . ."

She stepped closer to Erik and lightly placed a finger against his mouth. "Shhhh . . . I get to go first." She stroked his lower lip lightly and then lowered her hand. "I owe you an apology, Erik. A very big apology. I allowed past insecurities to ruin my judgment. I never honestly thought you were using me to get your citizenship papers."

"Syd, I . . ."

"Please let me finish, Erik. I also owe you another apology." The hardest one. The one where all her doubts and insecurities had blossomed into a nightmare. A nightmare where Erik didn't love her enough to make her his wife.

"What for?"

"For assuming our relationship was going to end in

marriage." She shrugged and studied the cabinets behind him. She couldn't meet his gaze. "You hadn't made any promises, and it was wrong of me to assume something like that."

Erik took a step closer to her, but stopped when someone else stepped into the exam room. "Quinn?"

She looked away from Erik, toward Sheriff Larson. "Sheriff?"

"Sorry to interrupt, but do you know where Sadie Hopkins is?"

"She took Hans into Camden for an x-ray," Erik said.

"I hope nothing serious."

"No, just a sprained wrist, but Sydney wanted to make sure." Erik took a step closer to her.

"Why do you need Sadie?" She didn't know if Erik's movement toward her was a protective gesture or one of a male claiming his territory.

"I need to fill out an accident report." A small smile teased the corners of Quinn's mouth as he looked at Erik's close proximity to her. "If you happen to see Sadie before I do, tell her to get in contact with me." Quinn stepped out of the room before adding, "Oh, your next patient is in the reception area waiting for you, Doc." The sheriff walked away chuckling.

Sydney studied the toes on her shoes. She wasn't sure how Erik had taken her apology. "My last patient is due in at four. Would you like to come over for dinner?"

Erik gave a frustrated groan as a child's cry filled the reception area. "Syd, you're only half right, and you're half wrong."

"About?"

Erik's smile was devastating as he tilted up her chin and brushed a kiss across her startled mouth. "I'll be by around six to tell you."

She was left alone in the exam room, wondering what she had been right about and what it was that she had gotten wrong.

Chapter Seventeen

Sydney opened her front door to Erik before he had even made it up the walkway. She had been waiting for him. The ends of her hair were still damp from the shower, but she had managed enough time for some makeup and perfume. Tonight she had chosen the low-cut, blue, button-down-the-front sweater that Erik loved. She also was wearing the blue lace panty set from Victoria's Secret just in case she got lucky.

She was planning on getting lucky. Real lucky.

"Hi, come on in." She opened the door wider, and the spotlight focused on the entryway nearly blinded her. The tree out front was lit, and so was the one in her living room. She had started a fire and lit the candles. Last night, after she had decorated the dining room, she had wrapped all the presents she had bought. The pile of silver-and-blue-wrapped presents under the tree was impressive.

Erik stepped into the house, and she closed the door behind him. "Hi yourself," Erik said as he unzipped his coat. He glanced at the presents under the tree. "I see *Julenisse* has come already."

"Not quite," she chuckled. "Come see the dining room and tell me if you think it will be enough table space for the buffet." Her brother-in-law, Daniel, had stopped by last night with saw horses and plywood. With the magic of a linen tablecloth, she had turned it into a buffet table. She had spent a good portion of her evening swagging garland around the bay window and arranging pine branches and candles on the table. She had copied Erik's decorating technique and added blue and silver Christmas balls. It looked perfect to her, but she wanted Erik's opinion. She grabbed his hand and dragged him through the living room.

Erik stopped before the dining room and smiled. "I see you've been busy." He eyed the table pushed against the far wall, leaving most of the room empty. "I like. Plenty of room for mingling."

She relaxed. Everything was going to be all right. She hadn't been worried about what she was going to be serving everyone come Christmas Eve if Erik had bailed out on her. Between Gwen and her own limited cooking abilities, they would have managed. Even if it had been tuna fish sandwiches and Oreo cookies. She had been worried about not sharing the night with Erik. She not only wanted Erik beside her Christmas Eve, but she wanted him there permanently.

Before she could ask his opinion of placing some chairs around the room, the doorbell rang. "I'll be right back." Whoever it was, she was getting rid of them fast.

Sydney opened the front door and stared at the man standing on her stoop. "Richard?"

"Aren't you going to invite me in, Sydney?" Richard took her stunned silence as permission because he walked right on in as if he owned the place. "Whose old pickup truck is in your driveway? I had to park my rental out in the street." Richard glanced around the Christmas tree and out the living room's bay window. "It will be all right out there, won't it? I had to go through a lot of trouble to get that car. You might have thought they never heard of the name Lexus way up here." Richard glanced at the tree branch poking his arm. "Why are there flags on your tree?"

She stared at Richard and wondered when she was going to wake up from this latest nightmare. She answered his last question first. "It's a Norwegian tradition."

"The pickup would be mine." Erik stepped into the living room. His intense blue gaze seemed to take in everything at once. He held out his hand. "Erik Olsen."

Richard nodded, but didn't shake Erik's hand. "Wainbright, Dr. Richard Wainbright."

Sydney frowned. "I was just asking Richard what has brought him all the way to Maine."

"Now, darling, you know I couldn't possibly stay away from you during the holidays." Richard flashed her a brilliant smile and then turned to Erik. "My fiancée is very partial to Christmas."

"Fiancée?" Sydney stared at Richard and wondered if he was drunk. He never used to hit the bottle, but she figured there was a first time for everything. "I'm not your fiancée, Richard." She never had been his fiancée, which had been part of their problem from the beginning. That and a naked D cup ER nurse.

Richard patted his coat pocket as though there was something special buried in its depths. "You will be come Christmas morning."

Erik cleared his throat and pulled his jacket back on. "I think I better be going."

"No!" Sydney couldn't help the note of panic in her voice. She didn't want Erik to leave.

"Darling, I think if the man wants to leave, we should let him." Richard started to unbutton his designer leather jacket. "After all, we have a lot of catching up to do. We haven't seen each other for a long while."

She rolled her eyes and wondered what game Richard was trying to play. "Not nearly long enough." She took a step toward Erik. "Please don't go, Erik. I really do want you to stay."

Erik slowly shook his head. "I think I better go. I'm sure you have a lot to discuss with Dr. Wainbright." Erik opened the front door, stepped out into the night, and softly closed the door behind him.

Sydney frowned at the closed door and counted to ten. When that didn't seem to work, she counted to twenty. She was going to kill Erik. What did he think he was doing leaving her here with Richard? Didn't the man possess a jealous bone in his whole body? She would go skinny-dipping in the harbor on New Year's Day before she would leave Erik alone with some lover from his past.

Erik knew what Richard had done to her. Why in the hell would he think she would want to discuss anything with the cheating idiot?

She would deal with Erik later; first she had to get the riffraff out of her cottage.

She slowly turned and faced Richard. Objectively thinking, Richard was tall, dark, and *GQ* gorgeous. Richard could have been a model if he had chosen to go that route in life. His smile was dazzling and his clothes were all expensive and boasting designer labels. Richard was picture perfect until you looked into his eyes. There seemed to always be a calculating and assessing look in those brown eyes.

What in the world had she ever seen in him? With a weary sigh, she asked, "What are you doing here, Richard?"

"I came to see you, Sydney." Richard gave her his most charming and practiced smile. One that never reached his eyes.

"You wasted your time. You should have called first."

"I must have left two dozen messages on your answering machine this month alone. You never bothered to return the calls." Richard tossed his coat onto a chair and started to pace the room.

"There was a reason I never called you back, Richard. I had nothing further to say to you." She could tell by his stride that he was furious and trying to hide it. A year ago she would have been doing everything possible to calm him down and make him comfortable. Not any longer. She refused to even offer him a seat.

Richard ran his fingers through his hair and stared at her. "I can't believe you're still mad about Jennifer. It's over between us, Sydney. I realized you're the one I want."

"To be mad, Richard, I would still have to care about you. I don't." It was the absolute truth. She didn't care one way or the other. She just wanted him gone.

"You'll care when I slip this onto your finger Christmas morning." Richard pulled a black velvet jeweler's box from his coat pocket and flipped it open. There, nestled against more black velvet, was a diamond ring. A huge, two-carat, princess-cut diamond ring. It flashed in brilliance as it picked up the lights from the Christmas tree.

She sadly shook her head. Leave it to Richard to think she could be bought with a ring. As if money could solve their problems. "You won't be here Christmas morning, or any other morning for that matter."

"I'm asking you to marry me, Sydney." Richard took a step closer and tried to pull her into his arms. "We'll get married in June, just like you always wanted."

A quick step to her right had avoided his hand. "I'm not marrying you, Richard." She had a sick feeling this was going to get embarrassing. Maybe Erik had made the right decision by leaving. She now wished she had left with him.

"What about children, Sydney? You want babies, don't you?"

Sydney stopped her retreat and stared at Richard. "You want children now?"

"I'm willing to discuss the possibilities." Richard's smile held nothing but satisfaction. His eyes held that calculating gleam, as though he had just played his trump card.

Everything she had thought she wanted in life was standing right in front of her. Richard, with diamond in hand, was proposing marriage and the possibility of babies in the near future. All her desires were within her reach, and all she could think about was getting Richard out of her cottage and her life. She laughed at the freedom of it all. She would take Erik, without any promises, over Richard any day of the week.

"You don't love me, Richard. You wanted me for the connections my last name could offer you back in Baltimore. What happened? Those connections drying up now that I'm no longer in the picture?" It felt so damn good standing up to Richard and telling him exactly what she thought. "You wasted your time and mine." She walked over to the front door and pulled it open. "I want you to leave, now."

Richard stood there and stared at her as if she had just sprouted a second head. "I'm offering you everything you said you always wanted. Marriage, commitment, children, the works!"

"You forgot about the most important thing, Richard. You forgot about love." She shook her head. She was afraid Richard would never understand that emotion.

"You're in love with him, aren't you?" Richard jammed his arms into the sleeves of his coat.

"Who?"

"That man who was just here. The pirate." Richard stood in the threshold, waiting for her answer.

"Yes, I'm in love with him. And Erik's not a pirate; he's a Viking." With that, she closed the door in Richard's face.

Hans pointed a finger at both of his grandsons and snapped out a command, "Sit."

Erik glanced at Gunnar, who shrugged. They both sat

at the kitchen table. It was barely seven o'clock Sunday morning, and Hans looked raring for a fight. "What's up? How's your arm this morning?" Erik noticed that the coffee was made, but his grandfather hadn't bothered with breakfast. Hans could have forgotten to cook again or he was too upset to make waffles or eggs.

Hans's arm was wrapped in an ace bandage and tucked neatly into a sling. Sydney had been right in her diagnosis of a sprain. "My wrist is fine. It's my grandsons who aren't too well in the head. Must be contagious."

Gunnar leaned back in the chair and grabbed the coffeepot. He refilled Erik's and his cup, but Hans shook his head. Another long stretch and the pot was back on the warming plate. "What's up, *Bestefar?*"

He and Gunnar both knew what was up. Their grandfather had found out they were paying the women of the town to keep an eye on him during the day. His brother and he had agreed late last night to allow Hans to play out this scene. They weren't going to change their minds. Hans needed someone to check on him during the day, if only for their own peace of mind.

"It seems my grandsons think I need a baby-sitter." Hans glared at both of them, but neither said a word in his own defense. "It also seems my grandsons are right."

Erik nearly choked on his coffee. "What happened?" Something must have happened for his grandfather to change his mind like that. He wondered if it had anything to do with his and Sadie's car mishap yesterday.

"Nothing happened. Even I've been noticing that I'm more forgetful lately." Hans seemed to study the wood grain of the kitchen table. "Sadie and I had a long talk over lunch yesterday. I'm calling the hospital Monday morning and scheduling all those tests Sydney wants me to take."

His brother echoed his own sigh of relief. If Sadie was here, Erik would not only kiss her, but he would dance around the kitchen with her. "What did Sadie tell you that we didn't?"

"She told me that you two did it because you were worried about me and that you love me."

"Of course we were worried," Gunnar said.

"Of course we love you," Erik added in confusion. "Didn't you think we love you? You're our *bestefar.*"

"My own daughters didn't want me when my money ran out." Hans shrugged. "I figured once my mind started to go, you two wouldn't want me either."

Gunnar muttered a word Erik felt like echoing. "Where in the hell would you get such an idea?" He could understand some of Hans's fear, but neither Gunnar nor he had ever done anything to cause their grandfather that concern. How could his grandfather think such a thing?

"I wasn't there for you for your first twenty-four years. Why should you be here for me now? I not only disowned your mother, I misjudged Merete horribly." Hans blinked his eyes rapidly to keep the tears at bay. "You two should hate me for that."

Erik looked at Gunnar. The other week they had decided to keep the truth about their mother from Hans. There was no way to change the past, and Hans seemed proud of the fact that Merete Bergesen Olsen had been happy in her married life. Gunnar slowly nodded, and he had to agree with his brother. It was time to tell their grandfather the truth. "We don't hate you, Grandfather."

"You were right about our mother all along," Gunnar said. "She wasn't happy being married to a fisherman. Old Nils lied to you in all his letters. I'm guessing he didn't want to upset his old friend, so he told you how happy and contented Merete was with her life in the village."

"Truth was, *Bestefar,* our parents fought constantly about money, or to be more accurate, the lack of money." He reached over and covered his grandfather's trembling hand.

"Then, you both should hate me more." Hans's voice broke. "I could have helped her out. Given you all a better life."

"We had a good life, *Bestefar.*" Gunnar smiled. "The only one not happy was our mother. We lacked nothing that we needed. Our father put a roof over our heads and food in our bellies."

"He taught us to love the sea and to rely on no one for a handout in life," Erik said. "Rolf Olsen was a fine man, husband, and father. You would have liked him if you would have gotten to know him better."

"Rolf was all that, and she had you two to love, and yet my daughter still wasn't happy?"

Gunnar and Erik's silence answered the question. They hadn't told their grandfather the truth to upset him.

"Why did you two come to America looking for me?"

"Because you are our *bestefar,*" Gunnar said.

"Because you're our family. You are all we had left, besides our aunts in Minnesota." Erik squeezed Hans's fingers. "Families stick together."

"But I didn't stick with Merete. I let her make a youthful mistake, and then I abandoned her."

Gunnar looked thoughtful for a moment. "Did she ever write you? She knew you were with her sisters in Minnesota. She could have written or called."

"She never wrote," answered Hans.

"Then, I say she abandoned you, too." Erik hated to see the distress on his grandfather's face. "We aren't going to abandon you. No matter what."

"Amen to that," added Gunnar. "We'll deal with your test results when we get them back. Sydney says there are some promising drugs out there."

"We don't want you worrying about cost either." Erik could see the concern in Hans's gaze. "We both have been living here for over three years now, rent free. We can afford the tests, medicine, doctor visits, and to pay the ladies of the town to keep you company during the day while we are at work."

Gunnar shoved his empty coffee cup to the side. "We need to know that you are safe, Grandfather. The ladies stay."

Hans shook his head. "I can pay for my own medical care and the cost of my daytime keepers."

Erik knew the tests Sydney wanted done were going to be outrageously expensive. He also knew that an Alzheimer's patient was going to need extensive care for many years. "We'll deal with it when the time comes." The costs were going to be mind-boggling, but there wasn't any other alternative. Hans was family.

Hans leaned back in his chair and chuckled. "I have money, boys. It's a nice-size nest egg."

Gunnar and he shared a doubtful look. "You said your money ran out in Minnesota; that was why Aunt Hilde and Berta didn't want you anymore."

"True," chuckled Hans. "My money was just about gone, but not Inga's. When your grandmother died, I became beneficiary to all her trust funds. Inga's family was loaded. I never touched the money, figuring I would leave it to Inga's daughters when I go. Every year the bank sends me this check for all the interest those trust funds have made. I've been socking it away for thirty-seven years now. I don't think Inga would mind if I used some of it, instead of being a financial burden to our grandsons."

Erik and Gunnar shared a bemused look. What in the world were they supposed to say to that?

Christmas Eve day was bright, sunny, and extremely cold. They were predicting snow by tomorrow night. Erik glanced down at the tray of cookies sitting next to him on the seat as he headed across town for Sydney's cottage. Everything was right on schedule for tonight's open house. He had just left Hans back at the house. With Sadie's help, he was making the pork sausage. Seven different kinds of cookies were made and ready to be devoured. Gwen was allowing him to use her ovens at the restaurant for the pork roast. He was heading there as soon as he delivered the batch of cookies that Gunnar had made last night.

The beer and soda were out on Sydney's back porch keeping cold. The fancy paper plates and cups Sydney had ordered for the occasion had arrived. He had picked up some more candles while he was at the mall last night finishing up his own shopping, just in case Sydney ran low. Sydney hadn't been able to go shopping with him. She had been helping Gwen get ready for their family visit. Sydney's parents and grandfather were once again staying with Gwen and Daniel. Jocelyn had claimed Syd's guest room for the visit.

Simon had done most of the work stringing lights up on *The Maelstrom.* His first mate didn't want to go out with Sydney and him tonight and be in the Festival of Lights Parade. Simon preferred to watch the procession from the shore with the rest of the town. *The Maelstrom* was ready to go, and Gunnar was currently down at the docks doing the finishing touches to his own boat. Tonight there would be twenty-five boats in the parade, and Lord knew how many people were going to show up at Sydney's.

Everything would be perfect if it wasn't for the thousand and one questions running through his mind. The main one being, What in the hell happened to Dr. Richard? Sydney hadn't said, and he hadn't the guts to ask. Within twenty minutes of leaving Sydney's house the other night, he had regretted that decision. Who in their right mind would leave the woman he loved alone with a man she had lived with for four years? Pitifully, the answer was him. He had to be insane.

The other night, at the time, it had seemed like a good idea. Sydney had deserved her privacy, and as she had reminded him in her office earlier, he hadn't made any promises. Wainbright was going to ask Sydney to marry him. Any fool would have seen that and planted himself so close to Sydney it would have taken a restraining order to separate them. Instead, what had he done? He had walked away and allowed Sydney to answer Wainbright's proposal any way she saw fit.

Yesterday, when he had dropped the beer and soda off at Sydney's, Wainbright and his luxury rental car had been nowhere in sight. There also hadn't been any big flashy ring on Sydney's finger. Sydney had acted as though nothing had happened. How could that be when Wainbright was so perfect for Sydney? They were both doctors, both well off financially, and they both had more class than all the members of the yachting club that met in Camden combined.

For the past two days, he had been thinking how wrong he had been about Sydney. All this time he had been comparing her with his mother. Merete and Sydney were nothing alike. Sydney was the most unspoiled and unselfish woman he had ever met. She was also one of the most loving. Sydney would make a wonderful mother.

He had been looking at their future all wrong. He wasn't his father, and Sydney wasn't Merete. Any relationship between Sydney and he would never turn out like his parents'. His parents' marriage could have turned out so differently if only they had tried. His mother could have gone out and gotten a job to ease the financial burdens, as did a lot of the other fishermen's wives. Merete chose to stay at home, complain, and develop a taste for whiskey. His mother could have reached a hand out toward her father, but she had chosen not to. His father could have eased the way there, but he had chosen not to.

They had each set their own path. His father had chosen to work longer and longer hours to support them all better. Merete had chosen to sit at home and seek solace at the bottom of the bottle. It was the perfect impasse that ended in disaster.

He had been so busy trying to avoid such a disaster in his own life, he had been blinded to what was really important. *Love.* Love, respect, compatibility, and equality were all very important qualities of a marriage. His parents' marriage had had none of those qualities. If they had loved each other in the beginning, it had died a painful death long before he understood that emotion.

A future with Sydney would contain all those qualities and more. So much more. Now all he had to do was convince her of that. Convince her to stay in Misty Harbor, marry him, and have his children. And while he was at it, solve world hunger and develop the cure for the common cold.

Erik slowed his truck and pulled into Sydney's driveway. No luxury rental car was in sight. Hopefully, the doctor was back in Baltimore nursing a broken heart.

He climbed out of the truck and reached for the tray of cookies. It was Jocelyn who answered the door and let him in. "Hi, Jocelyn, where's Syd?"

"Upstairs adding a few festive touches to the bathroom." Jocelyn took the tray, lifted an edge of plastic wrap, and swiped a cookie. "I think I've gained five pounds since this morning." Jocelyn bit into the cookie and moaned in ecstasy. "Want to get married?"

"I didn't bake these." He took the tray away from her before she could grab another cookie. "Gunnar did."

"You mean that gorgeous hunk, who makes my knees go weak, can cook?"

"Not as good as me, but it's edible." He carried the tray over to the buffet table and frowned. There was barely any room left for the main dishes. The cookies seemed to have multiplied.

"What's edible?" Sydney entered the kitchen carrying a nearly bald pine branch and a pair of pruners.

"Gunnar's cooking." Erik turned and smiled at her. Sydney looked very festive in blue jeans and a big green sweatshirt sporting a lobster wearing a Santa hat. Printed in white letters beneath the picture were the words "Santa Claws." He chuckled. Maybe Syd didn't have all the class he had given her credit for earlier. He liked this Syd better. "Jocelyn's eating all the cookies."

"Joc," scolded Sydney, "we just had lunch." Sydney dumped the pine branch onto the counter and reached out and took the tray Erik was still holding. "I think we needed a bigger table."

"You could use the counter," Jocelyn said as she reached around Erik and grabbed a *sirupssnipper,* a diamond-shape cookie that was similar to a gingersnap.

"I was planning on putting the coffee and soda up there." Sydney placed the tray on the table and glanced around the room. "We need another table."

"You put another buffet table in here, there won't be any room to move." Erik leaned forward and kissed Sydney's adorable pout. It had been a week since he had shared Sydney's bed, and the innocent kiss stirred his body and heated his blood. Lord, how he wanted this woman. "We'll bring the end table from the living room in here and use it for the coffee and soda. The cookies can go onto the counter like Jocelyn suggested." His arms reached to pull Sydney close.

"Hey, you two, knock it off." Jocelyn was browsing the baked goods. "You aren't the only ones in the room, and this girl here hasn't got a date for tonight."

"I didn't do anything," he said as he threw his hands up into the air and chuckled. He liked Jocelyn, but right now he would like to see her take a very long walk. He wanted to give Sydney a proper kiss. One that would last until the morning hours. He wanted to usher in Christmas buried deep inside her. All he wanted for Christmas was to love Sydney.

"Well, Leif Ericson, your lips might be saying '*No, no,*' but your eyes are saying '*Yes, yes.*' I see the way you are looking at my sister." Jocelyn selected a cone-shaped cookie with a pretty flower imprint. "I think our dad might have something to say about that." She chuckled. "I know Grandpop Michaels does, and I believe it has something to do with your kneecaps."

Erik's knees started to ache. He remembered Grandpop Michaels and his threats to his kneecaps during Thanksgiving dinner. Maybe it was a family tradition in the Fletcher household to put the fear of a baseball bat shattering a kneecap into any potential suitors for the girls. Threats or no threats, it hadn't slowed down his pursuit of the lovely doctor one bit.

Sydney was blushing to the roots of her hair. "Joc, I think you are reading way too much in this."

"It's okay, Syd." Erik wrapped his arm around her shoulder and pulled her close. "Jocelyn is just feeling like a third wheel right now." He gave Sydney's youngest sister a wide grin. "But wait for tonight. I'll put the word out she's looking for romance."

Sydney's eyes grew wide with concern. "She'll be mobbed!"

He pulled her closer and quickly kissed her surprised mouth. He whispered against her tempting lips, "I think she can handle it." Personally, he didn't think the men of Misty Harbor would know how to handle a woman like Jocelyn Fletcher. Now, Sydney was another story. He knew how he would like to handle the beautiful doctor, and by the soft, warm desire flaring in Sydney's green eyes, she wouldn't be objecting. "Joceyln, don't you have anywhere else to go?"

"Nope." Jocelyn laughed. "Gwen gave me orders to help Sydney get ready for the open house tonight. So I guess you two are stuck with me until that boat parade thing starts."

Chapter Eighteen

Sydney snuggled her back against Erik's chest. "So this is what you do all day. I can live like this." The lights from Misty Harbor were so far into the distance she could barely see them. Erik was allowing her to steer his boat. The clear, star-filled night was calm, but cold. Thankfully, *The Maelstrom's* wheelhouse was glass-enclosed and semiwarm. Erik's body was providing the rest of the heat as his arms bracketed her while he helped her with the helm. "How do you stand to come in at the end of the day? The sunset alone would make me stay out on the sea."

Erik's lips caressed the sensitive area behind her ear. "You should experience the sunrise. It is even more magnificent."

They had left Misty Harbor as the sun was just beginning to set. The ride out to sea had been breathtaking as the churning sea changed to a fiery orange, then red, then to near black as the darkness descended upon them all. Twenty-five boats had bobbed in the darkness, away from the curious eyes of the townspeople. Bob Newman's tuna boat, *Madison*, was the designated leader of the group because the mayor of Misty Harbor, Bob's brother, was on it. Paul Newman was a short, rotund man who was trying his hardest to repopulate the small village on his own. Paul's wife, heavy with their seventh child, had cheerfully waved off the procession from the safety of the docks earlier.

Now, with Paul and Bob's signal, they were starting back into the harbor, but this time all the lights that had been strung along the decks and up the masts and rigging were lit. Erik had trimmed his entire boat in white lights. Some of the other boats were white, too, but most were a colorful array of sparkling, glittering lights. Abraham Martin's lobster boat was all blue, while Gunnar's was all green. Bob Newman's tuna boat was an assortment of colors and actually had white icicle lights strung around the sides.

With the starry night, the beautiful glittering boats, and the shimmering reflections of all those lights wavering off the dark water, it was enchanting. Like something out of a fairy tale. She could imagine the view from the shore must be awesome, but she wouldn't give up this ride with Erik for anything.

This was exactly where she wanted to be. In Erik's arms and starring in her very own romantic fairy tale. She had seen the questioning look Erik had been giving her since Richard had shown up on her doorstep. But the hardheaded man hadn't asked one question, and she hadn't been in the mood to volunteer any information. How she could love such a stubborn man was beyond her, but love him she did.

"This is wonderful, Erik." She gazed at the few houses dotting the bluffs along the coast. Somewhere up there was Daniel and Gwen's house. She turned in his arms, reached up, and kissed him. "Thank you for inviting me."

Erik held the helm with one hand and pulled her closer with the other. "You're welcome, but don't kiss me while we're moving. I might run aground." He then contradicted his own warning to nibble on her lower lip. "I have absolutely no control where you are concerned."

She chuckled against his skin. Her mouth was working its way down the strong, tanned column of his throat. She could feel his thundering pulse beneath her lips. Erik smelled like Old Spice and tasted like a sea breeze. It was a heady combination for a land-loving doctor. "That's dangerous information to give a woman, Erik." Her hands crept under his coat and up his back. She had to wonder just how much control he didn't have.

A groan of desire rumbled in Erik's wide chest, but he grasped her by the waist and physically turned her back around. "I thought you said you wanted to steer."

She laughed softly and took hold of the helm. "Spoil sport."

Four boats away, Gunnar held Maggie in his arms as she piloted his boat along the coast. Maggie didn't need his assistance, since she had grown up around lobster boats and had been driving them since she was no bigger than a puffin, as her daddy liked to tell it. Gunnar didn't have to help her, he just liked having her in his arms. Maggie's delightful tush kept brushing up against the front of his jeans, and he was pretty sure the wretched woman was doing it on purpose.

Maggie hadn't taken the "no more lovemaking until the wedding night" very well. His one hand held her hip still, so she wouldn't do that little twitching thing with her ass that was driving him nuts. He was as hard as a pile and as hot as a four-alarm fire in August. Here he had thought that after loving Maggie three times the other night, the hunger would be appeased. He had been wrong. His hunger for Maggie had only increased. "Stop that, you little witch."

Maggie chuckled softly and glanced over her shoulder to her daughter, Katie, who was kneeling on the back bench and looking out the back window toward the boat behind them. Katie's little arm was waving madly. "Do you think my brother can see her?"

He glanced over his shoulder. Gary Franklin's boat was a safe distance behind them, but he could make out the outline of a man at the helm. The lights inside the wheelhouse were low and shadowy. What pulled his gaze and made it harder to see were the red and white lights strung along Gary's boat. "Probably. He might not be able to make out her features, but I'm sure he can see her waving."

Gary tooted his horn, and Katie shouted with glee. "He sees me. Uncle Gary sees me."

"That answers that question." Maggie turned back around. Keeping her voice to a low whisper, she asked, "So have you been giving any thought to breaking that stupid rule?"

He didn't have to ask which rule she was referring to. There was only one rule. "Do I think about it?" His lips skimmed the back of her neck. He smiled as he felt her shiver. "With every breath I take." His teeth lightly tugged on the delicate curve of her earlobe, and a sigh escaped her lips. "But I'm not going to change my mind."

He glanced over his shoulder and saw that Katie, complete with the bright orange life preserver that her uncle had bought her, was still occupied. The little girl wasn't paying any attention to her mother or him. Katie was too busy waving to her uncle and admiring all the pretty lights.

Gunnar pulled Maggie closer and allowed her to feel the effect she had upon his body. His voice was low and urgent. "This is what you do to me, Maggie. Make no mistake about it. I do want you. Some people might call it lust, and I would have to agree with them." He took a deep breath and a step back. He gently turned Maggie, so she was facing him and not the approaching harbor. "I love you, Maggie, and I want to make you my wife.

A husband who doesn't lust after his own wife wouldn't be a very good husband now, would he?"

Maggie slowly shook her head. "I guess not."

"Lust and love go hand in hand." He glanced ahead to make sure they weren't about to ram anything. The two boats that had been ahead of him were already docked. He could just make out the people lining the docks and the harbor. "The more I love you, the more I want you. The more I have you, the more I love you, Maggie. Neither of those feelings is going to fade away. In fact, I'm pretty sure they feed off of each other." He brushed a tender kiss across her mouth and then gently took over the helm. "Think about that for a while and then tell me again that we have to wait until June to get married."

He had Maggie's Christmas present in his coat pocket. It was a small diamond ring. He was planning on giving it to her after they docked and were watching the other boats coming into the harbor. At Sydney's open house, when they were surrounded by family and friends, he wanted to announce not only their engagement, but the wedding date. June was just too far away. He would never last. He was hoping for January. Early January.

Erik stared at the approaching harbor town. Soon this quiet interlude with Sydney was going to end. He didn't want it to end; he wanted to turn the boat around and head back out to sea and hold Sydney captive. Impossible dream. In less than two hours, Sydney's house would be overflowing with family and friends, hopefully enjoying some traditional Norwegian food. There were still a hundred things to do, and all he could think about was pulling Sydney into his arms and never letting her go.

That, and having Sydney's grandfather whack him in the kneecaps every time he kissed her under the mistletoe tonight. And Sydney had put up a lot of mistletoe throughout her cottage.

"Syd, remember the other day in your office when I told you you were half right and half wrong?"

"Yes, and you said you would explain it later that night, but then we were interrupted by Richard." Sydney didn't turn around in his arms. She seemed to be intensely concentrating on where they were heading.

"You were half right about the apology you gave me for believing Abraham and Wendell and for thinking, even for a moment, I wanted to marry you to become a U.S. citizen." He leaned his chin on top of her head and looked at the approaching town. Misty Harbor was his home. It was where he belonged. It was where Sydney belonged. "I understand why you had those doubts."

"You do?"

"Yes, because I also had doubts." When he felt her stiffen in his arms, he quickly added, "Not about my citizenship, Syd. About us. About our future together. That's why you were only half right."

Sydney glanced over her shoulder at him. In the low light of the wheelhouse, he could see heartbreak brimming in her eyes. "You have doubts?"

"Did, Syd." He brushed a quick kiss across her lips. "I don't any longer."

"What kind of doubts were they?"

"Fool that I was, I had been comparing you to my mother."

"Your mother?" A frown pulled at Sydney's mouth. "You think I'm like your mother?"

"No, but there were a lot of similarities between my parents and us. I didn't want to repeat their mistakes."

"Like what?"

"My father was a fisherman, from a little village. I'm a fisherman, and by no stretch of anyone's imagination could Misty Harbor be classed as an urban area. My mother came from money, just like you do."

"I wouldn't say I came from money, Erik. My family

is well known in the medical field in Baltimore and even in the judicial system there. But money? I know a lot more families that have a lot more money than we ever did."

He had to wonder if his idea of rich was the same as Sydney's. "My mother wasn't happy living on a fisherman's wages. It tore whatever love that had been between my parents to shreds. Having Gunnar and me enter the picture nine months after the wedding night didn't help the situation. It only made it worse. My mother drank to compensate for her unhappiness, and my father, not knowing what else to do, stood back and allowed it."

Sydney snorted. "Well then, your mother should have put down the bottle and gotten herself a job, Erik."

He laughed. He couldn't help it. Sydney had summed up twenty-seven years' worth of guilt in one sentence.

Sydney turned around completely. The spark of anger darkened her eyes and heightened the color on her cheeks. "Do you think I'm the kind of woman who would get drunk just because the man in my life didn't buy me a pretty trinket or a bigger house? If I want something, Erik, I will go out and buy it for myself and not expect any man to foot the bill." Sydney's finger jammed into his chest. "I've worked damn hard to get where I am professionally. I love being a doctor, and I intend to continue being one long after a husband and a house full of babies enter the picture. I have hopes, dreams, and more goals than the Baltimore Ravens. I am not, repeat, not your mother."

He didn't know what to respond to first. The crack about the husband or the house full of babies. He glanced ahead and maneuvered the boat into the inlet where the town and docks were nestled. He took the easy way out. "Tell me one of your goals."

Sydney crossed her arms and seemed to dare him to interrupt. "I'm going to open up a medical center close to Misty Harbor. Residents here, and the surrounding area, have to drive too far to get immediate medical attention. I'm not talking a huge hospital where open-heart surgery or major operations can be performed. We're thinking more along the lines of x-ray equipment, a simple testing facility, and an equipped emergency room that could handle anything. We would be able to stabilize patients until we can assure a safe transfer into Bangor or Portland."

"We?" It appeared that Sydney wasn't planning on leaving Misty Harbor in the near future. She was staying and putting down roots. If her goal was any indication, deep, binding roots.

"I've been in contact with a couple of doctors from the surrounding area. We've been E-mailing back and forth and trying to compile a list of our requirements before we begin the hard work of finding some financial backing and a central location that would benefit the most people."

"You can do this?"

"Me alone, no. Me and eight other doctors, the backing of the medical community in Bangor and Portland, and possibly government help, yes."

"Tell me one of your dreams." My God, she was amazing. His mother never would have thought about patients suffering or even dying because the hospitals were too far away. He had to wonder if his father ever asked his mother what her dreams and goals were. He doubted it.

Sydney looked at him for a long while. "Tell me what I was half wrong about first."

"You apologized for assuming our relationship would end in marriage." He glanced at the people lining the docks and the harbor street. In the distance, there was the faint sound of carolers singing "Jingle Bells." He throttled back and slowed his speed. He wasn't in any hurry to reach the docks and the crowds. Sydney's entire family was out there somewhere. His and Sydney's time alone was coming to a close, and they were just getting to the serious part.

"And I was wrong because?"

"You were right in assuming marriage was in the cards." He pulled the throttle into the idle position and got down on bended knee. "I know this isn't the most romantic place to propose, but it will have to do. Would you make me the happiest man in the world, Syd, and marry me?"

Sydney's mouth opened in surprise, but no words came from those lovely lips.

"I'm only a fisherman who will love you forever."

"I'm only a doctor who will love you forever." Sydney's smile was breathtaking.

He studied her face and fell more deeply in love. "Before you answer, I need for you to consider my grandfather."

"Hans?" Sydney blinked in surprise at the change of subject. "What about Hans?"

"I can't abandon him, Syd. He's part of the deal. You know probably more than I do about all the care he's going to be needing in the future."

"Love's not about abandoning people, Erik." It seemed impossible, but Sydney's smile actually grew. "There will always be room in our life together for Hans."

"Is that a yes?"

"Do you want me to shout it?" At his silence, Sydney shouted, "Yes! I'll marry you."

Erik stood up and swept her into his arms for a kiss that could singe the varnish on his deck.

Hans stood on the wharf and stared out into the harbor at his grandson Erik's boat. "What's he doing? How come he stopped?" Hans's eyes weren't as good as they used to be. He thought there had been two silhouettes in the wheelhouse window a moment ago. Now it looked like only one. What happened to Sydney? He hoped to hell the doctor hadn't slipped overboard.

Sadie chuckled and tossed her head like a Hollywood starlet. Long red curls danced upon the breeze and tangled with the white boa wrapped dramatically around her neck. "I believe he's kissing Sydney." For the special occasion, she had finally taken out the curlers, and if her hair, a delightful shade of auburn without a hint of gray, caused a few eyebrows to raise, tough. It was nobody's business but her own.

Sydney's father glanced away from the assortment of cookies Gwen had set out in front of the restaurant. Leave it to his middle daughter to not only offer free hot coffee and cocoa for the occasion, but to try and fatten up the entire village while doing it. Stan Fletcher stared out into the distance and frowned at the boat his oldest daughter was on. He couldn't see anything. But Hans was right; the boat had stopped.

"Oh, my." Gloria Fletcher chuckled as she tugged on Stan's arm. "Don't look, dear. I don't think you have any vacation time left for another wedding."

"What is with the men up here in Maine?" Stan demanded. "Can't they let my daughters settle in first?"

Daniel moved behind his wife and wrapped his arms around her. He seemed awfully interested in the hanging sign above Gwen's restaurant, Catch of the Day. Smartly, he kept his mouth shut.

Hans was startled when Sydney's grandfather, who had been standing next to him all evening, acting like the perfect gentleman, muttered something about breaking his grandson's kneecaps. Hans nearly spilled the coffee he was holding to keep his fingers warm. He had forgotten his gloves.

Gwen and Jocelyn shared an amused look and then went back to staring at Erik's boat where their older sister was being thoroughly kissed. Gwen sighed and leaned back farther into her husband's embrace.

Jocelyn groaned in disgust and rolled her eyes.

A couple cat calls, cheers, and wolf whistles sounded from the dock. A bunch of fishermen started to clap and egg Erik on. One mother actually put her hands over her son's eyes.

A moment later the couple separated, and to the shock of everyone, Erik turned the boat around and headed back out to sea. The crowd cheered and boat horns blew.

"Now what in the blue blazes is that boy doing?" cried Hans as Erik's boat sped up and cruised out of the harbor.

Gwen and Jocelyn both busted out laughing. "I do believe we are now in charge of getting Sydney's open house ready."

Stan Fletcher pointed a finger at his youngest, and still single daughter, Jocelyn. "You, young lady, are not moving to Maine."

Three hours later, Sydney was still red in the face. She couldn't believe it. She had been late to her own open house. Her sisters had thought it was the funniest thing since they had discovered she had padded her bra in eighth grade. She was never going to live this one down. Not that she wanted to. Erik and she were getting married!

Erik had been underhanded enough to apply pressure, by not kissing her, until she had agreed to get married on Valentine's Day. Her mother had shrieked in dismay at that fast approaching date. Erik had taken her father aside and, after humbly apologizing for the scene at the Festival of Lights, had gotten his approval on the marriage. Grandpop Michaels had muttered something about putting away the baseball bat.

Between Gwen, Hans, Sadie, and the rest of her family, they had everything out and ready by the time the first guest had arrived. When she had tried to apologize to Gwen, her sister had laughed and said she understood perfectly well what a man from Maine could do to a woman's hormones. Daniel had puffed out his chest and then dragged Gwen off to find some mistletoe.

Sydney went in search of Erik, who had left her side

to go find Gunnar, to give him the good news. How she could lose a six-foot, two-inch Viking in such a small cottage was beyond her. How there could be two missing Vikings was even stranger. It wasn't as if they could hide in a crowd. She pressed her way out of the kitchen, accepting congratulations as she went. Her open house party had turned into an impromptu engagement party.

She spotted Jocelyn penned in near the fireplace by Bob Newman. Bob was showing her a picture of his tuna boat. Jocelyn had a glazed look to her eyes, but Sydney wasn't going to rescue her sister yet. Erik had put out the word that Jocelyn, being the only single and free Fletcher girl left, was feeling lonely. To the men of Misty Harbor, that declaration must have sounded like a moose mating call. Jocelyn had been avoiding the mistletoe all night.

"Millicent, have you seen Erik?"

"Lost him already?" Millicent laughed as she picked up some dirty plates and cups from the coffee table and placed them in the trash bag she was holding.

She tried to take the trash bag from Millicent. "Please don't do that, Millicent. You are a guest, and you're supposed to be enjoying yourself, not cleaning up. Go mingle with someone good looking."

Millicent Wyndham, the town matriarch, arched one regal brow. "I am enjoying myself, quite immensely, too, if I might add." Another empty cup went into her bag. "I haven't had this much fun since your sister opened her restaurant. It's good to see this town out socializing and having fun."

Sydney squeezed her way around Maggie Pierce's parents and gathered up half a dozen empty cups. She met Millicent at the foot of her stairs and dumped them into the garbage bag. "You have a strange sense of fun."

Millicent chuckled and nodded toward the other side of the living room, where Jocelyn was now being crowded into the corner by Abraham Martin, who for some reason was wearing plastic reindeer antlers on his head. A candy cane was dangling from one of the antlers. "How soon do you think we can get your sister to move up here?"

She watched Abraham's expression as he flinched and hurriedly took a step back away from her baby sister. Jocelyn must have shown some of her "lawyer" teeth to get Abraham to move that fast. "Joc is a lawyer, Millicent, in Maryland. She can't practice law in Maine."

Millicent thought that one over for a minute. "Nonsense, Sydney, all she has to do is pass the Maine bar exam."

She started to choke. "Are you serious? Do you have any idea what she went through to pass the Maryland exam?" She shook her head. "Joc will never leave Maryland. I sincerely doubt she will ever move out of Baltimore."

Millicent was mulling that one over when the front door burst open and little Katie Pierce came barreling into the living room. "Guess what, everyone!" Katie cried at the top of her little lungs, which were extremely healthy.

The entire cottage immediately fell silent.

Erik lumbered down the stairs and pulled Sydney to his side. Since she was standing the closest to the little girl, and it was her house, Sydney asked for the suddenly quiet crowd, "What?"

"I'm not getting a baby brother for Christmas!"

Connie Franklin, Katie's grandmother, groaned in embarrassment and tried to hide behind Bob, her husband. Bob seemed to be choking on his own laughter.

Erik chuckled in Sydney's ear and tightened his hold. "Miss me?"

She nodded and pointed her finger upward, to where a sprig of mistletoe was dangling. It had been ten minutes since their last kiss. She wanted another one. Erik leaned down and gave her a quick kiss before turning his attention to the child in the middle of the crowded room.

Katie's smile grew brighter, and she danced from foot to foot. The pom-pom bear on top of her hair danced wildly. "I'm getting something better! I'm getting a second daddy on New Year's Day!"

The whole roomful of guests turned as one and stared at the doorway, where a red-faced Maggie and a beaming Gunnar stood.

Katie tugged on her grandmom's dress. "Grandmom, when's New Year's Day?"